FOREVER
this time

FOREVER
this time

Maggie
McGinnis

St. Martin's Paperbacks

This is a work of fiction. All of the characters, organizations, and events portrayed in this work are either products of the author's imagination or are used fictitiously.

FOREVER THIS TIME

Copyright © 2015 by Maggie McGinnis.

All rights reserved.

For information address St. Martin's Press, 175 Fifth Avenue, New York, NY 10010.

ISBN: 978-1-250-06907-8

Printed in the United States of America

St. Martin's Paperbacks edition / November 2015

St. Martin's Paperbacks are published by St. Martin's Press, 175 Fifth Avenue, New York, NY 10010.

10 9 8 7 6 5 4 3 2 1

For Joshua and Adriana,
my tiny angels

Acknowledgments

I have so many people to thank for their help in making this book a reality, and I'm thrilled and excited to do so:

First—and rightly so—huge thanks to my superb agent, Courtney Miller-Callihan. Thank you for your tireless work and undying support. I am a lucky, lucky gal to have found you.

To Holly Ingraham, my fabulous editor—Thank you for falling in love with Echo Lake, and for your superb guidance and keen eye. I pinch myself every day, and I'm *thrilled* to be on Team Holly!

To Lizzie Poteet—Thank you for so graciously stepping in to help when Home-team Holly became an instant foursome! I'm so lucky to get to work with you!

To my funny, generous friend, critique partner, and newly-minted Golden Heart sister, Jennifer Brodie—You are my Xanax and my Prozac and my champagne . . . sometimes all on the same day! Thank you . . . for everything.

To the Bartlett Bunnies—None of this would be as sparkly and fun without you gals to share it with! Thank you for the late nights, the hundreds of *what if*s, and way too much chocolate.

To Caroline Lyon MD, MPH, for her grace and patience in answering way too many medical questions—

Thank you for your help, your friendship, and your support!

To Jennifer Carroll, PT, for *also* answering a gazillion questions regarding stroke and recovery—Huge thanks. Any errors are mine alone.

To my family, who keep me grounded, keep me (usually) sane, and teach me gorgeous lessons of love every single day—Thank you, from the depths of my heart.

Lastly, to the parents of those who got their angel wings too early—Our journeys differ, but our hearts share a hole. I am in awe of all who survive it.

Chapter 1

"Dad?" Josie barely heard her own voice over the beeping machinery dwarfing the ICU bed. "Oh God. Daddy?" The words were strange on her tongue as she stumbled closer. This couldn't be her father, this motionless shape under hospital blankets. This couldn't be the man who ran twenty miles a week and crowed his perfect blood pressure and BMI to anyone who'd listen.

She stared at her father's face. His skin was sallow, slack, dry as rice paper. Droplets collecting in the oxygen cannula gave the only indication that he was even alive. She felt her knees jiggle as her breath hitched, and she reached blindly for the rail beside the bed.

"Ma'am?" A sharp voice startled her from behind. "Only immediate family in here."

Josie nodded slowly, but couldn't rip her eyes from the Dad-shaped creature on the bed. "I'm family," she whispered—that word, too, feeling odd enough in her mouth that she didn't even attempt *immediate*. "He just doesn't know me."

Josie felt a hand on her elbow and turned around slowly to face a rotund nurse whose perky blond ponytail tried hard to belie the age lines around her eyes.

"I'm sorry," she whispered, then jumped as blood

pressure cuffs buzzed awake and made the blanket over Dad's legs rise upward. "I'm . . . I'm his daughter."

"Daughter?" The nurse's eyes were quizzical. "Goodness, I'm sorry. We didn't know."

"You wouldn't have. I'm not really . . . expected." Josie winced as she said the words.

The nurse came around to face her, putting her hand out gently. "I'm Gayle."

"Josie." She shook Gayle's outstretched hand.

"Do you want to sit while I check on him?"

Josie stared at the still face on the pillow, unable to open her mouth and answer. Her feet felt glued to the shiny floor, and the chair right next to her felt twenty feet away. This was the man who spent half his life ho-ho-ho-ing around the family's Christmas theme park in a Santa suit, for God's sake. He was *never* still.

She glanced up at Gayle, who was checking machines and typing information into her laptop. "So it was definitely a stroke?"

Gayle nodded, pointing to the side of her head. "Right cerebral hemorrhage." She closed the laptop and started adjusting some tubing that looked all tangled up at the head of the bed. "I'm almost done here. I can leave you alone if you'd like to stay for a couple of minutes. You can try talking to him. He can probably hear you."

Josie shook her head. No, talking was the last thing she wanted to do.

"You can just tell him about your day. Tell him about the weather. Doesn't matter. Just let him hear your voice."

Josie sighed. "I'm sorry, Gayle, but honestly—if he hears my voice, he might have another stroke."

Ethan sat in his desk chair checking the news, but when he'd read the same headline four times, he clicked the window closed. He tried not to stare at the empty chair across from him, but he couldn't help it. He couldn't believe Andy was in the hospital. Couldn't believe he'd had a stroke.

Couldn't believe Josie was on her way back to town.

He pushed his chair away from the desk and looked back out the window. The sparkle and glitter of Snowflake Village twinkled at him from every tree, every ride, every pathway. *Camp Ho-Ho*, Josie had always called it. *Alternate-reality center of the universe.*

For the millionth time in five years, he thought about what she would say if she saw him sitting in the CFO chair at her family's theme park, his desk parked head-to-head with her own father's. He looked down at his red polo shirt with the official snowflake logo on the breast. It was a far cry from the dress blues and military bars he'd always thought he'd be wearing by now, but a Rutland linebacker had altered that life plan with a bone-crushing tackle during the state finals eleven years ago.

Instead of a military assignment overseas, he had a permanency rating in his right knee and a job running a holiday theme park. Not exactly the life he'd envisioned, but he'd been grateful when Josie's father had offered him the CFO job after it became crystal-clear that Josie wasn't going to come back and take it.

But now she *was* coming back to Echo Lake. It had taken a life-or-death situation to get her here . . . but here she'd be.

He swore softly when he realized he was absently rubbing his left ring finger.

Quick footsteps on the stairway startled him, and his stomach leaped. Was she *here*? He caught a flash of flaming red hair coming around the doorway and let out a relieved breath. Not Josie, thank God. Just her old best friend.

Molly burst dramatically into the office. "You have to

save me!" She flopped into Andy's empty chair, her vivid green eyes sparkling as she peered over her shoulder toward the door. "These blind dates are disasters!"

Ethan looked at her, then at the hallway, then back at her. Even to this day, he found it amusing that she and Josie had been best friends for their entire childhood. She was as vivacious as Josie was reserved, as loud as Josie was quiet.

"You being chased by a serial killer? Or an Italian?"

"B." She fanned herself with a piece of paper. "I think I lost him at the Frosty Freeze."

"Need me to check the security cameras?"

She sat up straighter. "Would you?"

"No, Mols, I will not. Your dating issues are your problem, not mine."

"If you'd just marry me, I wouldn't *have* any dating issues. One more stupid lousy setup date and I'll drag you to City Hall myself, just to get Mama off my back."

He raised his eyebrows. "As cave-girlish as that sounds, I think I'll take a pass."

"Mama's convinced I'm going to wither up and die any day now if I don't find a husband."

"I'm not sure it's quite that desperate yet." Ethan tried not to smile.

"Oh, you have *no* idea. The woman's gone off the ledge."

"What's she done now?"

Molly sighed. "Italian love match dot com." She practically spat out the words.

"An Italian dating site?"

"Kill me now."

He laughed. "Looks like Mama B's already got that job wrapped up."

"I didn't even think she knew how to do more than

order restaurant supplies on that stupid computer. Now she's trying to order me a freakin' husband."

"Well, you can't blame a mom for trying."

"Stop laughing."

"I really can't. I'm so sorry." He rattled his fingers on the keyboard, pretending to type. "Italian. Love. Match. Dot com, you said? Let's see. Molly Bellini."

Her sparkly blue flip-flop hit him in the head before he had time to duck. "Can't we just *pretend* to be married or something?"

"No. Absolutely not. Your family is completely nuts. We'd have terrible children."

"But at least we'd *have* some! I don't honestly think Mama cares if I'm married. She just wants grandbabies."

"Sorry, Mols. You're on your own with this one. It'll take a stronger man than me to marry a Bellini."

"You're no fun." She looked at her watch. "Didn't we make a pact back in junior high that we'd marry each other if we hadn't found anyone else by the time we were thirty?"

"No. And we're not thirty."

Molly got up to peer out the window. "Okay, enough about me. Let's talk about *your* dating issues."

"Let's not."

"Not ready to let me click save on that dating profile yet?" She winked.

"Please tell me you didn't."

"You're right." She sat back down in Andy's chair. "I didn't. So what's up? You have your serious face on suddenly." She chewed her pinky nail just like Josie had done long ago when she was nervous. Funny how they'd mirrored each other's habits without even realizing they were doing it.

"Andy had a stroke last night."

"A—what! Andy? Santa?" She shook her head. "No."

Ethan nodded slowly. "Yeah."

"How bad?"

"I don't think anyone's sure yet."

Molly squeezed her eyes shut, rubbing her index fingers on her forehead. "Do you think Josie knows? I mean, I know she doesn't have anything to do with them, but . . ." She looked up. "Should we try to find her?"

"She knows. Diana apparently spoke to her this morning."

"Is she . . . going to come?"

"Yeah."

"Well." Molly edged her next nail into her mouth, nodding slowly. "Wow. But she'll be at the hospital, right? Not here. She wouldn't come back to the park, would she?"

Ethan took a long, deep breath. "I don't know."

"She wouldn't. She hates it here. Camp Ho-Ho, right?"

"I know."

"But you look worried."

"I'm pretty sure Diana will want her at Mercy. Can't imagine why Josie would even want to set foot near this place."

"Except . . . Josie hates hospitals. And her mother."

Ethan nodded. "That's what scares me."

Molly stood up, pacing the small office. "So what's your plan?"

"Haven't had time to make one. We'll see, I guess."

Molly winced as she got to the window and looked down at the courtyard. "Just a suggestion, but you might want a more concrete plan than 'we'll see' if Josie Kendrew walks through that igloo door down there. It's been ten years since you've seen her."

"I'm well aware of that, Mols."

"Are you going to head up to Mercy to see her?" Ethan

could tell she was trying to keep the hurt out of her voice, but he could hear it anyway.

He shook his head, picturing an unworn tux, a set of shiny new wedding bands in a ten-year-old box.

"I don't know, Molly. I don't know *what* I'm going to do."

Chapter 2

"Have a happy ho-ho day!" chirped a big plastic reindeer head, startling Josie as she ducked through the arched igloo entrance to Snowflake Village two hours after she'd fled the hospital. The jangle of Christmas carols spewing from the ceiling speakers still made her twitch, even after ten years away.

It might be August everywhere else in America, but in this little alternate-reality retreat in Vermont, it was Christmas. Always Christmas. Three hundred sixty-five freakin' days of Christmas.

"Stuff it, Rudolph," she grumbled as she tried to wrangle her way through the little turnstile. She'd been sitting in the parking lot for a full forty minutes, baking in the August heat, trying to convince herself to walk through the stupid igloo. It was shaping up to be one of the worst days of her life, and she didn't need a big fake reindeer-on-Prozac recording to remind her what a good mood everyone *else* was in.

"Uh-oh. Is someone having a cranky day?" The reindeer head bobbed toward her, its glassy eyes freakishly focused on her face as she stopped dead and whirled around.

That fake head had been talking since she was a kid, but it had always been just a recording, not a camera with ears. Fantastic. She hadn't even gotten *into* the park yet, and she was already insulting Rudolph.

"I'm sorry." She grimaced. "You weren't supposed to hear that."

"I'm not supposed to hear a lot of things. You have a happy ho-ho day, now." The mechanical head turned toward the family coming in behind her.

Had the fake eye winked?

She headed through the arched doorway that dumped guests into the central courtyard, and dug for her sunglasses. She told herself it was because it was sunny, not because she was hoping to disguise her presence here for as long as possible while she got her bearings.

She'd driven here from the hospital on autopilot, and she still wasn't even sure why she'd come. The psych major in her recognized some deep-seated need to find a way to reconnect with a dad she didn't know anymore—to return to the place where he was so . . . alive—but the angry teenager still buried deep inside couldn't believe she'd just walked back through that igloo after all this time.

After all, this was the place where reality sat happily stowed in the back seat. It was the place where she'd found hope and love . . . and then lost both in one fell swoop.

She hadn't been back here in ten years—had been happy to put the going-nowhere town of Echo Lake firmly in the rearview mirror and head off to Boston to make a new life.

But now? Now the dad who'd been in a Santa suit last time she'd seen him was lying in a hospital bed with more questions than answers in his medical chart. Now, the mom who'd spent most of Josie's childhood in a fog was waiting for her to come back to that wretched hospital.

And instead of facing either of those things, she was

here, where at any moment she could run smack into a muscular, gorgeous, six-foot-two memory.

Josie took a deep, shaky breath as she looked around. As much as she'd spent the entire drive from Boston trying to prepare herself to be here in Echo Lake again, she wasn't at all sure she could handle it. At all.

Yes, she was an adult now. And yes, she'd left a long time ago. So presumably, she'd had plenty of time to steel herself against the past—especially against the man who'd figured front and center in that past. She'd certainly be able to see him again, talk to him, look into his eyes without regretting the fact that she'd left him practically at the altar.

Wouldn't she?

She shook her head. Maybe that'd be true if the man had been anyone but Ethan, whose secretive smile and smoky blue eyes had threatened to undo half the females at Echo Lake High. Maybe it'd be true if he wasn't the guy whose quarterback pedigree and sharp wit could have chosen any female in town, but instead had filled *her* senior year with flowers and silly notes and hot nights at the lake.

Ethan had been her first . . . and she'd thought he was going to be her forever.

She looked to her left, where the igloo entrance gave way to a row of brightly colored cottages. First was the Pepto-Bismol-colored penny candy store, then a tropical-blue gift shop with a rainbow-painted door, and then a sunny yellow ice cream parlor with tiny patio tables out front. The colors practically screamed, *Isn't this just the most happy-happy place in the universe?*

She sighed and adjusted her sunglasses, trying to mute the buildings.

A breeze picked up the ends of Josie's hair again as she reached the edge of the courtyard. Her eyes caught on the polka-dotted umbrella tables at the ice cream parlor, then skated inadvertently toward the administration building, aka Elf Central, a white Victorian with deep purple shutters on every window.

It actually looked cool and inviting on this already hot morning, set back from the courtyard on a grassy lawn with two huge sugar maples out front, but there was no way she'd walk through its double-sized front door before she had to. Ethan was probably in there, sitting at his desk on the second floor—the desk Dad had always said would be hers.

Josie forced her eyes to the other side of the courtyard, trying to focus on anything but Ethan. A split-rail fence still extended outward from the igloo, running behind a portico full of strollers, a Snow White–style cottage that housed restrooms, and what looked like a new medical building with a bright red cross on the door.

"Afternoon, ma'am. Can I help you find something?" An elderly man in a green costume touched her elbow, making her jump. Oh good Lord. She hadn't seen an elf in ten years, either. "Did you lose your family?"

She shook her head slowly as her chest squeezed in pain, but she tried to cover it with a fake smile.

He pointed at her feet. "Hope you got some more comfortable shoes in that bag of yours. It's a big park."

Josie couldn't resist looking at his feet, and he smiled as he followed her eyes. "I know what you're thinking, but these curly toes aren't so bad after the first few falls. You learn." He winked. "You have a happy ho-ho day now."

Josie managed another tight smile, wondering how many times she'd be able to hear that phrase before her head exploded.

She glanced down, realizing that in her pencil skirt and sleeveless shell, she looked like a health inspector on a surprise visit. Employees were probably already squawking the alert code over the radios, sure she was about to tackle the snack cottages with her state-issued clipboard.

So much for blending in.

Taking another shaky breath, Josie set off to her right. Time to get as far away from Elf Central as possible, since she had absolutely no idea what would happen when she finally met Ethan again. All she knew was that she was *so* not ready to find out.

As she rounded the first curve in the path, the sound of the roller coaster assaulted her ears at the same time she got a whiff of sickeningly sweet cotton candy, and she wrinkled her nose at both. She'd loved that roller coaster right up till her ninth birthday, when one too many bags of pink fluff and one too many coaster rides had resulted in one very sick little birthday girl.

The walkway curved around a monstrous rock left by a long-ago glacier, and she came into a clearing that housed Rudolph's Razzamatazz, a snack cottage, and a toddler ride where the kids rode in swings shaped like Christmas ornaments. The rides were the same as when she'd left, but they looked freshly painted and shiny in the sunlight.

As she came to a fork in the path, her breath caught. To her right was the outside loop of rides, which eventually circled around to Ole Ben's maintenance garage. To her left, up a little rise, was the Ferris wheel. She could see its cars sliding by the tops of the trees, and as she watched, her breaths started coming shorter and faster.

Finally, she ripped her eyes away and struggled to swallow the softball that seemed to have lodged itself in her throat. How had she thought she'd be able to walk around this park, where memories were bound to pummel her at every turn?

Just then, a short, chubby elf who had to be a hundred

and twenty years old ambled by with a broom and dust-pan. For a moment, Josie expected she should recognize her, but she didn't. She got a funny, sobering feeling low in her gut as she realized she could very well walk around this park she'd grown up in, and ten years later, not know a soul.

The elf deftly swept up a candy wrapper, then smiled at Josie. "Why so serious, honey? Beautiful afternoon, isn't it?"

Josie looked up at the sky, which was an unusually deep blue for this time of year. The tall firs framed a couple of puffy clouds, and the swish of pine needles preceded a playful breeze that wreaked havoc with her carefully straightened hair. The temperature was just pushing eighty, but the humidity was zilch, so it was one of those rare days that made it onto the gift shop post-cards.

"Sure." Her voice was tentative as she breathed in, realizing just how long it'd been since she'd smelled the crisp pine scent that defined Snowflake Village.

Had she ever missed it?

No. Not possible.

"Well, you have a happy ho-ho day, then, dear." The elf-lady tottered on by, scooping a stray leaf into her dust-pan. *So clean they could eat off the paths, honey.* Dad's voice crept into her brain. *That's the Snowflake Village way.*

Josie took a few steps, pausing under a giant pine to pull her blouse away from her sticky skin. Maybe it wasn't humid, but clearly it'd been a while since she'd done the goat-path thing in heels. She felt for her ever-present Evian bottle, but had left it in her Jeep.

As she looked around, she was struck again by the notion that not much had really changed here. The paint on everything still shined bright, and the employees all had crisp red polo shirts and Santa hats on, along with their supersized Snowflake Village smiles. *Have a happy ho-ho day!* they crowed, piercing Josie's eardrums every time she heard the phrase.

But they were only doing what they were paid to do: don the hat, don the smile, and create a universe where it was Christmas every day of the year.

Once again, she'd entered the world where reality was optional—where for eighteen dollars you could cover your problems with cotton candy and sparkles.

Too bad jingle-bell therapy ended when the gates closed at dusk.

Too bad it also ended when you got old enough to know better.

She heard a metallic clanking sound and looked down the hill toward the maintenance shed. Sounded like Ole Ben was working on his endless to-do list, as he always had. What would he say if she showed up on his proverbial doorstep after all this time?

Would Ethan think to look for her down there, if he got word she was wandering the park? She doubted it, so it seemed as good a place as any to hide until she worked up her courage.

She angled off the path and around the back side of the Penguin Plunge ride, which was teeming with screeching teens. Trying not to ruin her heels beyond repair, she hobbled down the hill behind yet another snack cottage and headed toward the open door of the maintenance garage.

"Well, if it isn't my Twinkle-toes!" Ben's back was to her, but his voice boomed out the open door just as she raised her hand to knock on the frame. "You get right in here, girl!"

Josie felt a laugh sputter out, tension slowly draining out of her pores as she stepped onto the cement floor of the garage and right into Ben's huge embrace. "Hey, Ben! How'd you know it was me?"

"Heard those heels clip-clopping down the hill and figured you were about the only one who'd be running around here in city-girl shoes but still know where to find Ole Ben."

Josie smiled. "You're still in the same place. That helped."

The maintenance area looked as it always had, cluttered and dusty, but somehow homey. She breathed in the smell of fresh lumber and Ben's familiar Old Spice, and felt herself relax a little bit more.

"How's your dad?" He took her hand in his huge one and led her over to one of the spinning stools beside his workbench. "Did you just come from the hospital?"

Josie nodded, trying to clear visions of tubes and beeping machines out of her head.

"He's—I don't know."

"Tough thing, this." Ben nodded. "I imagine it scared the bejeebers right out of you to see him like that."

"I couldn't—couldn't stay, Ben." Josie fought to keep a hitch out of her voice. "It's been forever, but I just . . . couldn't."

He put an arm around her shoulder, hugging her close. "You will, Twinkle-toes. You will. One step at a time. And till you're ready, you just hang out with Ole Ben. It'll help break up the quiet around here."

Josie laughed softly as the cacophony of park noise filtered down the hill. Snowflake Village was *never* quiet.

"Hey! Do you want a grape Popsicle?" He popped up from his stool, heading for the ancient fridge in the corner of the garage. "I got a brand-new box!"

Josie's mouth opened in surprise. "You still keep grape Popsicles down here?"

"Yep." He opened the freezer door. "But the boxes last too long now. Nobody to help me eat 'em. Want one?"

"You bet I do!" Josie laughed. "I haven't had one since . . . forever."

He strode back across the floor and handed her the Popsicle. "So I don't s'pose you've seen Ethan yet?"

"Not yet." Again the softball threatened her throat.

"And you're not avoiding him by sitting on my stool and eating up my Popsicles?" His eyebrows curved high on his forehead.

"Definitely not."

"Then I guess you can stay for a bit." He grinned at her, then reached out to tweak her nose like he'd always done. "It's good to see you, Twinkle-toes. I think Ethan might even agree with me, once he gets over the shock of having you here."

Josie crossed her arms carefully. "That's probably a bit of a stretch, Ben."

"You'll be fine. Don't you worry. You're both all grown up now. Things change."

She pushed out a nervous breath, kicking at a pebble on the floor. "Did you—did you ever tell him what happened before I left, Ben?"

Ben was quiet as he fiddled with a wrench. "That been bothering you all these years?"

She nodded slowly, cringing as she shrugged.

"No, Twink. I never told him about that night."

He looked at her, studying her eyes for a long moment. "But he might know more than you think, honey. I think you'd best be prepared for that."

Chapter 3

Later that afternoon, Ethan rubbed his eyes as he pushed back from the computer screen on his desk. He'd tried to prioritize all of the items in his and Andy's to-do piles, but fourteen of them were still vying for first place, and it was already closing time.

When Josie's mom had called earlier with the news about Andy, he'd assured her that he could hold down the fort until they knew more. Now, after only one day, he wasn't so sure. Between the two of them, the Snowflake Village business office ran like a well-oiled machine, but that was because both he and Andy dedicated far more than the standard forty hours a week to the job.

Could Molly fill in for a few days? *No.* He discarded the thought almost as quickly as it came into his head. Between working at her parents' restaurant and holding down the director's desk at Avery's House, she already struggled to find a spare moment. The fact that she'd squeezed in a blind date on a Friday morning was testament to that.

Diana's parting words this morning had hung over his head all day. *Josie's coming home, and you and I both know how she feels about hospitals. Maybe she could help out? Just get us through the weekend, at least?*

Ethan sighed. The only place Josie hated more than

hospitals was the park, so odds were slim that she'd ever agree to it even if he'd said yes.

Which he hadn't.

He glanced out the window and watched as employees ushered lingering guests toward the exit, then shook his head as he realized his eyes were searching for Josie's long, curly hair. But there was no way she was here. No matter what the circumstances, he couldn't imagine her ever stepping through Snowflake Village's igloo entrance by choice.

She'd made a clean cut ten years ago—of the park, of her parents, of Molly . . . of him.

He pulled open the bottom drawer of his desk, sliding out the double-framed picture that had sat in there since he'd taken it off the wall long ago. He and Josie smiled out of the left frame, sunburned and happy, arms linked around each other at the lake. On the right was a photo Josie probably hoped had disappeared a long time ago.

In it, she wore a ridiculously huge princess costume and was sitting in a giant timpani, laughing, having just fallen off the park's stage during her first-ever solo. He'd never forget how the other actors had ad-libbed their way through the rest of the scene while trying to maneuver her back out of the huge drum, like they'd planned for her to actually fall into it.

Ethan smiled as he touched the photo. She'd kill him if she ever found out it still existed, but it reminded him of happier years, happier summers . . . a happier Josie.

He sighed as he pushed his mug into the Keurig machine on the wide windowsill and plucked the darkest possible coffee from the rotating holder beside it. It was going to be a long night.

As it brewed and trickled, he thought he heard the sound of a woman's shoes coming up the stairway.

Ah hell.

Molly didn't wear shoes that sounded like that.

The heels clacked softly down the hallway toward the office, then slowed just outside the open doorway. He looked up just as Josie lifted her hand to knock on the door, and thanked God he hadn't yet picked up his coffee. If he had, it would have scalded his entire bottom half as he dropped the mug.

Though he'd only had hours to do so, he thought he'd steeled himself for this moment. But seeing Josie framed in the doorway, he realized he hadn't. *At all.* The damn woman had occupied his dreams for more than ten years, but now that she was up close, he could see that eighteen-year-old Josie had grown up. A lot.

Where her body had been a collection of sweet new curves covered by innocent pink and peach cotton, her clothes now exuded an urban vibe. She looked like a model, slim and strong, from her high-heeled shoes to her skirt, wide black belt, and dark gray sleeveless blouse. In place of the curls he'd touched a thousand times, her hair was now sleek, shiny . . . straight. She probably thought she looked the height of fashion, but to him, it looked like she could use a few of Mama Bellini's burgers to put some meat on her bones.

Dammit. She still used that apple-y shampoo, though. He could smell it, and immediately he was eighteen again, sitting on a blanket by the lake with her in his arms.

The silence stretched on just long enough to be completely uncomfortable as he stared at Josie. In her face, he could see the same mermaid-green eyes he'd loved, but they looked more vivid now, accented with eyeliner and mascara. Her nose still turned up at the end, and to his chagrin, it still made him want to run his index finger down it so she'd playfully slap his hand away.

"Josie." It was all he could do to force the word out of his mouth.

He saw her swallow hard before she spoke.

"Ethan," she whispered. Her hand was still poised in the air, ready to knock, but it looked like she'd forgotten it was there. He took some comfort in knowing she looked as off-kilter as he was. His innards felt like a Tilt-A-Whirl on high speed, but he'd be damned if he'd let her know that.

He took a slow breath, studying her while he tried to gain control of his voice. What the hell was he supposed to say to her? Every line he'd rehearsed for the past eight hours fled his brain.

Finally she saved him by speaking first. "I—I don't think I know what to say."

"That makes two of us."

"Did Mom tell you she asked me to help out this weekend? Here? At the park?" Her voice was sort of catchy and nervous, which surprised him.

He shook his head. *Diana had already asked her?*

"Oh." Her eyes flitted around the office. "Um . . . well . . . she did. Which is . . . strange. I know. It's all strange." The smile she attempted barely reached her cheeks, let alone her eyes. "But anyway, she did."

"I see." Ethan hated himself for enjoying her discomfort, but there had to be *some* karma in the universe, right?

"So . . ." She waved her fingers vaguely. "I'm sorry. This is sort of *Twilight Zone*-ish. You weren't expecting me. Obviously. But here I am, I guess."

"Here you are." He sat back down in his chair and threaded his fingers together behind his head, trying to give off a relaxed, unconcerned vibe. Yeah, that was it. He'd play it super-casual, unaffected. Definitely *wouldn't* play it like it was. "It's been a while."

Josie dropped her hand slowly. "I, um, I—" She pointed to Andy's chair. "Do you mind if I sit for a second?"

Ethan motioned with his hand. *Sure. Sit down. Waltz into my office ten years after you went all* Runaway Bride *and never looked back. Make yourself right at home.*

He waited while she settled her purse on the floor and adjusted her high-heeled shoes. Though her hair and body had changed, her voice was still the same one that had haunted his dreams for years now. He hated himself for wanting to keep her talking.

"How's your dad doing this afternoon?"

"Not great. Sounds like it could be . . . pretty bad." She took a shaky breath as she smoothed her skirt.

"How does he look?"

"Terrible."

Ethan studied her as she adjusted her skirt again, pulled off a stray piece of dark hair, rubbed her heel. Had she actually gone through those hospital doors? He could hardly believe it.

"I stayed for a while, but wasn't quite ready for the Mom-reunion . . . so I came here, I guess." She gestured at the metal desks faced toward each other like Ethan and Andy were *Law & Order* partners, then vaguely out the windows. "I walked around a little. Things here look pretty much the same."

"That's kind of the way it goes here, but I'm sure you remember."

He swore he was trying to keep the bitterness out of his voice, but it wasn't quite working. For God's sake, all he wanted to do right now was gather her in his arms and make the scared look on her face go away, wanted to kiss her full lips and see if she still wore strawberry lip gloss, wanted to—*ah hell*—wanted to do a whole lot more than kiss.

Her voice broke through his thoughts. "So . . . what can I do to help? Till Dad's . . . better?"

Right. No way was he going the self-imposed-torture route here. No *way* was he going to let her get under his skin by invading his space—or his brain.

He cleared his throat. "We're fine here. You should be at the hospital with your parents."

"Mom said you'd say that."

"She was right. I can handle things for now. You need to be with your family." *Definitely not here, sitting in your dad's chair, looking like an all-grown-up figment of my imagination.*

He sat up straighter, leaning on his desk like he needed to get back to his big, important job. "We've got things covered here."

Maybe she wouldn't notice the piles of work sitting on both desks. Or realize he was fabricating his confident voice in order to get rid of her before the scent of her had his thoughts spinning in a direction he couldn't handle.

She sighed. "There's nothing I can do at the hospital except sit and wait for news."

"Isn't that kind of what families do in these situations? Doesn't make it easier, but it's normal."

She tilted her head, frown lines crowding her forehead. "We both know there's nothing normal about my family, Ethan. Surely that hasn't changed much since I left."

"You might be surprised."

She nodded slowly, but he could tell she didn't believe him. A tiny, sympathetic part of him understood her reticence. However, a huge, *un*sympathetic part of him wanted her out of this office. Now.

"So what can I do to help?" She was rubbing her heels, which were probably just about raw if she'd been walking around the hilly park for more than ten minutes in those stupid shoes. The Josie he remembered wore nothing but flip-flops from April to October. He wondered when she'd traded them in for these nonsensical high-heeled things.

"Nothing. I promise you everything's perfectly under control here. You can assure Diana that Ben and I are handling things."

"You can't run an entire theme park by yourself, can you?"

"Honestly, Josie, it'd take me longer to get you trained back up than it would be to just do it all myself."

He saw her lips tighten as she prepared a response, then saw her chest rise slowly as if she was taking a calming breath. He was surprised to find himself a little disappointed at her control. The old Josie would have bitten back with a retort, but this older, apparently more mature version simply pushed her shoulders back and looked out the window.

"I know that this is terribly awkward, and believe me—I am no happier to be here than you are to see me, but I *am* here, and I would much rather be helpful at the park than sit in a waiting room trying to pray to a god I lost sight of a long time ago, Ethan. Please just let me help."

Ethan sat back in his chair, studying her for a long moment. "Josie, I'm really trying my hardest to be nice because I know Diana sent you, but please don't insult me by pretending you have an ounce of desire to be here. You hate this place, and we both know it."

"I don't—" She drew in another careful breath. "I told Mom I'd help here. She doesn't need the stress of worrying about the park, on top of Dad's situation right now."

Ethan stared at her, and to her credit, she didn't flinch. This was the same woman who'd taken off in the dark of night ten years ago and left him alone. The same woman who'd left a cryptic note for her parents, but had barely had contact with them since she'd left. Yet here she was, trying to sound like they had Sunday dinners every other week and she was concerned about her dad's health and her mom's stress.

Bullshit.

"You can assure your mom that things are perfectly under control here." He moved his hand to the mouse and his eyes to the computer screen in front of him. "Thank you for stopping by, though. It was good to see you. Please tell Diana I'll come by tomorrow to see how Andy's doing."

"Ethan, stop. We can—"

"We can what, Josie?" He braced his hands on the desk. "We can pretend like we're friends? Pretend you're just the boss's daughter? Pretend you didn't—never mind."

She shook her head miserably.

He took a breath, tried to soften his voice. "I don't want to play pretend. I'm really, really sorry about your dad. This has nothing to do with him. But you made it really clear a long time ago that you wanted no part of this life, and since we haven't seen you in ten years, I have no reason to believe that's changed, no matter what's happening with Andy, no matter if it's just for the weekend. I'm the CFO now, and I'm perfectly capable of running the park until your dad's ready to come back and do it himself. I don't need your help."

"I see." She whispered the words as she gathered her purse from the floor.

Ethan slid his hand back onto his mouse, clicking on random windows, trying to fill the silence that enveloped the office. Josie sat for a full minute in Andy's chair, then clicked out the door and down the stairs. Only after he heard the outside door close did he sit back from his computer and let his shoulders drop back to their normal position.

Ten years ago, he'd thought his future was wrapped in a Josie-shaped package. Ten years ago, he'd thought they'd have three kids and a log cabin at the edge of the lake by now. Or be living together in her someday-house on Sugar Maple Drive.

He pulled himself back to the desk and shook his head to clear the thoughts. There was no point going there. The Josie who'd just left the office was an all-grown-up version of the girl he'd known. She might be back in town, but it was a temporary, guilt-induced stopover. She'd left ten years ago without a backward glance, and she'd be in her car again as soon as her dad was better.

If he got better.

Yes, that traitorous piece of his heart that had lurched awake at the very sight of her in the doorway had better just go back to sleep. There was no going back to the past, and there was no way there'd ever be a future with her. The only thing Josie Kendrew was likely to bring to town was more heartache.

And he'd had quite enough of her version of heartache already.

Chapter 4

Josie flicked on her left blinker, muttering curses at the windshield. "Dammit, Ethan. Why couldn't you have been fat and bald and *ugly*?" But no. The man looked like he'd just stepped out of the Raiders yearbook, except for the tiny frown lines on his forehead, and some that fanned out from his eyes.

Ten years later, Ethan was even more unfairly gorgeous than he'd been in high school. She'd adored every inch of his body back then, and seeing him just now had made her practically ache to touch him.

She'd actually had to clench her own hands together to keep from combing her fingers through his slightly mussed hair like she'd always done. It was still the color of dark chocolate, and his smoky blue eyes still had the power to make her feel completely naked even though she was fully clothed.

As she got to the four-way stop sign in the middle of town, she blinked hard and stepped on the brake. Where was she even going? She had no idea—just knew she needed to get far, far away from Ethan.

She shouldn't have been hurt by the frost in his eyes as he'd dismissed her. She was the one who'd left, after all. But realizing that frigid reception was her own fault made the pain even worse.

A beep from the car behind her startled her, and she swiped at her eyes. Dammit. Josie Kendrew didn't do crying. She didn't do regrets. She most *certainly* didn't sit at the one stop sign in a tiny Vermont town, bawling over might-have-beens.

She pressed the gas pedal, going straight through the intersection and into a downtown area where it looked like time had pretty much stood still. There was a brand-new Rite Aid on the corner of Main and Pine, right where the crumbling old creamery had been, but other than that, everything looked the same as it had ten years ago. Still a bunch of brick storefronts backing up to the Abenaki River on the right, and a matching set crowded together on the left.

The brick was still tired, the paint on the windows was still chipped, and the glass storefronts were still dusty. Even the store names hadn't changed. The tourists rolled in at nine o'clock in the morning, and back out at five, since there was only one decent hotel in Echo Lake.

Josie sighed. The town's name suited it well. Even ten years later, it was just the same thing, over and over and over again.

Just as she headed over the Tumblebrook Bridge and up the hill out of downtown, her phone rang. It was Mom, for the second time today.

Mom, for the second time in ten years.

"Josie? It's—it's Mom. Are you—okay?"

Josie looked out the window, feeling a strong case of déjà vu creeping in. "I'm not sure how to answer that, honestly."

"I know." Mom's voice was quiet, clear, and Josie felt her own forehead furrow at the sound of it. "I'm home for a bit, just to gather some things and grab a bite to eat. Are you—hungry? Would you like to come ho—come over here?"

Oh boy. Besides the hospital and Snowflake Village, her childhood home was the last place she wanted to be, but she'd already managed the other two today. Maybe—just maybe—she could handle this, too?

"I'd like to see you, Josie. That's all. And—" There was a long pause. "I know the hotel's full because of Cara McAllister's wedding. You're welcome to stay here . . . if you want to."

Josie took a deep breath and blew it out slowly. Stay at her parents' house? Could she really roll up that weed-choked driveway, open the creaky door, and pretend she was just a normal adult visiting her also-normal parents?

But did she have a choice? The next decent hotel was a good hour's drive away, and once her current adrenaline overload subsided, she was going to collapse. She took another breath and put on her blinker.

"I'll be there in five minutes."

As she hung up, she put her hand to her stomach, trying to quell the dread.

Five minutes later, as she pulled into her parents' driveway, she was struck by the bright pansies around the mailbox and the neatly trimmed hedges under the picture window. The driveway itself looked like it'd just been resealed, and the roof looked almost new.

Gone were the overgrown weeds. Gone was the peeling paint on the shutters. Gone was the chipped wooden front door with the massive lion-head knocker and fake brass knob. In their places were new sunny yellow siding, dark blue shutters, and a classy paneled front door with beveled windows across the top.

It was the kind of house she'd always wished she'd lived in, back when she'd had friends she wished she could invite over.

Josie pulled her suitcase from the back seat and slung her purse over her shoulder, trying not to gape as she walked up the slate pathway to what looked like new brick stairs. Either her mother had hired a handyman and a gardener and a mason, or her dad was finally home for long enough to do more than wolf down a quick sandwich in front of the television.

When she got to the door, she hesitated. Yes, it was her childhood home, but she couldn't just walk in, could she? She pressed the doorbell, blowing out a breath and squaring her shoulders. She could do this. She could handle her mother, whatever state she was really in these days.

She had to.

The door swung open and Mom pushed open the screen. "Josie! Come in! You didn't have to ring the doorbell!" She ducked her head, motioning Josie in, reaching out almost like she was going to hug her, then slowly clamping her arms back at her sides.

Josie stared. Her mother looked like an L.L.Bean model, with jeans and a short-sleeved pink polo on. Leather sandals were on her feet, and her pink-painted toenails peeked out. Josie's eyes traveled upward, noting the freshly washed hair, clear complexion, painted fingernails, lipstick.

Lipstick.

"Here. Let me take that." Mom took the handle of her suitcase and deftly scooted it through the short hallway toward the kitchen. "This place didn't get any bigger while you were gone." Her laugh sounded nervous as Josie followed her.

"Has Dad woken up?"

"Not really, no. No . . ." Mom took a shaky breath.

"How bad was the stroke? Do they know yet?"

"Come sit down." Mom set the suitcase against the pantry door, then turned to Josie. "You've had a long day already, driving all the way up here. Can I get you anything? Coffee? Tea? Soda?"

"No, thanks. I'm fine." Apparently she wasn't ready to talk about Dad yet. Josie scanned the kitchen, trying to figure out what was different about it. The cupboards were the same aged oak they'd always been, but had new nickel-colored knobs. The countertop was the same tan Formica as always, but she couldn't put her finger on what made it all feel different.

As she glanced toward the shiny sink with a dishtowel hung neatly over the faucet, it hit her. The kitchen was not only clean; it was spotless. No cans on the countertop, no dishes in the sink, no trash overflowing its bin.

"It looks great in here." She pulled her light sweater off and hung it on the back of a chair. "Different."

Mom leaned against the shelf beside the sink. "Well, it's all pretty much the same kitchen as when you left. Maybe a little cleaner, though." She gave a rueful chuckle. "My housekeeping skills are better these days than they used to be."

Josie nodded, unsure of what to say. They both heard the unspoken words in Mom's last sentence.

"Okay, well . . ." Mom spun her wedding ring around as she looked everywhere but at Josie. "Are you hungry? Did you have lunch?" She moved toward the refrigerator. "I have some deli meat. I could make you a sandwich. There's turkey. From Zeb's—you know—the kind you like." She started to open the fridge, then turned back around. "Or, I guess, used to like. I'm not sure you do anymore."

Josie braced herself, ready for whatever assault that was bound to be the next thing out of Mom's mouth. She tried to loosen her clenched hands, one finger at a time.

The last thing she wanted was a processed-turkey sandwich from the fifty-year-old deli in town, the one with a questionable steak tips barrel and pigs' feet in glass jars. But Mom was standing at the fridge, obviously having no idea what to do with the daughter she hadn't seen in way too long. Josie didn't need to make this any harder than it already was.

She tried to smile. "I'd actually love a sandwich, thanks. And maybe a Pepsi, if you have one."

Mom looked relieved to have something to do with her hands as she deftly put together two sandwiches, piled on some potato chips and pickles, and brought everything to the little breakfast table in the corner of the kitchen. Josie took in the woven green place mats and baby rose-buds in a crystal vase as she sat down.

Fresh-cut flowers in the kitchen? In a vase?

"Thanks. This looks great." Josie took a bite of the sandwich, planning to choke it down as best she could. After all, if she was chewing, she wouldn't have to talk—a distinct advantage at this point.

She glanced around the kitchen, taking in the white ceramic canisters that had always snugged up against the fridge, the pot of herbs on the sill, the green teapot-shaped clock over the window. It was quiet enough to hear its soft *click-click-click* as the second hand edged around.

Mom picked up her sandwich, then set it back down with a shaky breath, looking at the clock. "Why is it clocks always move slower when you're worried?"

"Because you're worried." Josie wiped her mouth with the paper napkin Mom had set beside her plate. "How is he really doing?"

Mom shook her head. "I don't know. I don't know *how* to know. They're throwing around so many big words— so many possible outcomes. I just—I don't know." She blinked hard, dabbing her napkin at her eyes.

"When are you going back to the hospital?"

"After we eat. I just wanted to be here in case you came home." She waved a shaky hand near her face. "I mean,

I guess it's not home, really. I mean, not to you anymore." She fiddled with her hair. "Wow. Sorry. I don't know *what* I mean anymore."

Just then the phone rang, and Mom leaped to pick it up. After a series of short responses, she pressed the END button and put it back in its holder. "That was Dad's nurse." She sat carefully in her chair. "The docs have just been through. Things look okay, but they're going to keep him in ICU for a while yet, sounds like."

"How do they define *okay*?"

"At this point, I guess I'm taking it to mean he's not getting worse."

"I'm sorry." Josie wasn't sure what to say. Mom twisted her wedding ring again, the same thin band Dad had gotten for her when they were young and poor. *Struggling,* she corrected herself before Dad's voice in her brain could do it for her. But Josie didn't know whether Mom had put it on for her benefit, for the nurses at the hospital, or because the Kendrew marriage was actually intact again.

"Do you—want me to do anything? Get you anything? Do you need stuff at the store or anything?" Josie grasped at ways she could be helpful.

Mom smiled a sad smile. "Ever since I got a Costco membership, your dad jokes that we *never* need anything anymore. You should see the basement."

Mom stared at her over the little table, quietly assessing her, it seemed. "I'm glad you came, Josie."

Josie didn't know how to answer. At eight o'clock this morning she'd been sitting in her office preparing for her first client and looking forward to Friday-night margaritas and a movie with her office partner, Kirsten.

At nine o'clock, she'd been shoving clothes into a suitcase and trying to find her car keys while she called a cab to take her to where she kept it parked.

At ten o'clock, she'd finally cleared Boston traffic and was headed northwest to Echo Lake, biting her pinky nail to the quick as she tried to fathom what might be in store.

She took a deep breath. "Thank you for calling me."

It was the least she could do, right? Thank her mother for giving her a chance to see Dad one last time before he died—if that's what was happening here? Her hands shook as she set down her sandwich and tried to wash the fear down with a slug of Pepsi.

Mom folded her napkin and placed it over her uneaten sandwich. She adjusted it carefully, evening the edges of the napkin with the green piping on the plate. Then she cleared her throat.

"This may not be the time or place, but I have something I need to discuss with you."

Josie braced herself at the familiar words—words she hadn't heard in ten years, but a phrase she'd heard far too often before then.

She'd been here all of twenty minutes, and here it came. Some sort of assault out of nowhere, just like . . . always.

But this time delivered by . . . a stranger—with makeup and a manicure.

Chapter 5

"I'm worried about the park."

Huh? Josie shook her head, confused. Mom had always felt a lot of things about Camp Ho-Ho, but worry hadn't ever been one of them, not as far back as she could remember. Hate, perhaps. Jealousy, definitely. But worry? No.

"It's going to be beautiful for the next couple of days, and it's the first weekend of August, and I'm sure even after ten years away, you can remember what that means for Snowflake Village."

Josie grimaced. "Hordes. Multitudes. Throngs."

"Exactly." Mom laughed quietly, then drew in a catchy little breath. "And your father's not going to be there to watch over his little kingdom. So I was wondering . . ." She fiddled with her napkin. "I know I mentioned this on the phone, but I'm not sure what you think. Is there any chance you could help out? Maybe just for the weekend?"

Josie swallowed hard. *No.* "I wasn't sure you were serious about that."

"I know. It's been a long time." Mom crumpled her napkin, then smoothed it back out. "But Jos, I know how you feel about the hospital. I'm shocked you even got inside the doors today."

"Me, too." Josie's voice was way smaller and more pathetic than she was comfortable with.

"So I can't expect you to sit there in that hideous waiting room, waiting for those random five-minute slots where we can go sit with him."

Ethan's voice crept into Josie's head. "Isn't that what we're *supposed* to do? I mean, what if something . . . happens?"

"He's stable. I don't think there's any reason to think he's going to get worse." Mom blew out a careful breath. "It's just a matter of when he's going to get *better.* And he's going to do that whether you're in the waiting room or not."

She paused, looking steadily at Josie, her eyes as clear as Josie'd ever seen them. "You'd only be ten minutes from the hospital if I called. You know if he had a choice, he'd love to see you at the park, not sitting at Mercy, wishing you were anywhere else. Plus, he'd absolutely flip out if he thought we'd left Snowflake Village understaffed on one of the busiest weekends of the summer, right?" She tried to smile, but it didn't quite work.

"But—"

"I know. Ethan."

Josie nodded. Just the sound of his name did strange things to her innards. "Yeah. Ethan."

"It's been ten years, honey." Mom's voice was soft, and what was with the endearment? Was she trying to put Josie off-kilter?

Bingo. It was working.

Mom reached her hand toward Josie's, like she was going to touch it, but she pulled back before their fingers met. "That's an awful long time. He's a different man now. He *is* a man now."

Oh God. Josie *knew* he was a man now. An hour ago

she'd seen that with her own eyes, and since then, she hadn't been able to get his face out of her head.

Or the rest of him.

Mom stopped fiddling with her napkin and looked squarely at Josie. "I know it's not my place to have any expectations at all, and I don't. I really don't. I just got to thinking as I sat there this afternoon, that maybe, just maybe for the weekend, you could spend a little time at the park. So you don't have to sit at the hospital."

After a few moments of awkward silence, Mom pushed back her chair and gathered their plates. "Well, I think I'm going to head back to Mercy. You're welcome to come if you'd like to, but if you just want to take some time and catch your breath, you should do that. Come whenever. Or—don't. You choose, of course."

She stood awkwardly, like she had something else she wanted to say, but then she turned away, sliding the plates neatly into the dishwasher. "I just put fresh towels on your bed, and everything else is pretty much where it's always been . . . but let me know if you can't find something."

"Okay . . . thanks." Josie felt completely unbalanced as she sat at the kitchen table, unsure of what to say or do in her own childhood home with her own mother.

Mom closed the dishwasher and leaned against the shelf, staring out the window. "I'm glad you're here, honey." She took a deep breath, twisting her ring around her finger, then looked directly at Josie. "I'm hoping you'll find it's a much different place than you left."

Five minutes later, as Mom backed out of the driveway and onto the street, Josie still sat at the table. Who was this calm, measured woman who'd made her a sandwich like she'd been doing it all her life? Who was this non-confrontational, clear-eyed person whose house—and clothes, and hair—were tidy?

Josie got up from the table and pulled open the drawer that held the trash and recycling bins. She held her breath as she looked into the back bin, but all it held were three Diet Pepsi cans.

Hating herself for doing so, she opened the door into the garage and peered into the huge plastic garbage can that had sat on the landing for thirty-plus years. The cap was on, a clear plastic bag neatly tied to its edges, and when she opened it, all she saw were more Diet Pepsi cans.

She put the cap back on slowly, looking around the garage. No beer cans, no twelve-packs under the stairs, no extra fridge in the corner. She stepped quietly back into the kitchen and closed the door softly, like Mom was listening from the other room.

Old habits.

As she turned off the light and returned to the kitchen, Josie hated the glimmer of hope that brightened her chest for a moment. She'd been here before. She'd hoped before. The bottles had disappeared before. The purple circles under Mom's eyes had disappeared before. The redness in her cheeks had paled before.

But it had always come back.

All of it had always come back.

"Morning, Ethan!" Molly's voice startled Ethan as she came through his office door Saturday morning. She stopped short at Andy's desk and glanced down at the empty chair. "How is he?"

"No word this morning yet, but it's still early."

"You doing okay here by yourself?"

"So far, but I swear that pile of stuff on his desk is growing when I'm not looking. You're not looking for a third job, are you?"

Molly sat in the side chair at Ethan's desk, crossing her legs and retrieving a file folder from her enormous purple bag. "Let's not think like that yet. It's Andy. Santa, for God's sake. He'll be fine. He'll definitely be fine."

"Of course he will. I just meant for the weekend." Ethan pushed back from his desk. "So give me some good news. What's the morning report from Avery's House?" He sipped his coffee, but grimaced when he realized it'd gone cool already. "It's going to be blazing the next couple of days. Did the AC get fixed?"

"All fixed. No roasted patients on the menu this weekend."

"Guests."

Molly tipped her head in acknowledgment. "Guests. Sorry." She looked down at her folder. "Okay, let's see. Tabitha and James checked out yesterday afternoon. Many tears, many hugs, much drama. They *really* didn't want to go."

"As it should be." Ethan felt a small smile creep up his cheeks. When he'd created Avery's House as a free getaway for chronically ill kids, his first goal had been that once they arrived, they'd never want to leave. "How was their mom?"

"As good as a mom can be when one twin's headed for another round of chemo and the other's headed for kindergarten, I guess." Molly's face pulled into a frown, then she blew out a breath and shook her head. "But Tabby's doing well. She really is. Hopefully she'll be done after this round."

She tapped her finger down her list. "Emmy is checking in today. Just finished her chemo, so the docs in Boston gave her the go-ahead to leave town and have some fun for a couple of weeks. Of course this is the only place she wanted to come."

"Again, as it should be." Ethan smiled a real smile this time. "What's this? Her fourth time here?" Although he wasn't supposed to have favorites, he had to admit that

Emmy held a special place in his heart. At eight years old, her bright blue eyes and sweet smile felled him every time she stayed in Echo Lake.

His smile faltered as he realized Josie was the only person in the world who'd truly ever understand why.

"Oh, and that reporter from the *Globe* called again. They're doing a feature on unique pediatric care settings. She wants to come up and interview you."

"I don't have time for interviews right now, Mols. Can't you handle her?"

"Nope. She only wants to talk to you." Molly raised her eyebrows. "Exposure is money, Ethan. The *Globe*'s got serious reach and cred. That's a lot of potential donors you could be reaching."

"I know. I know. You're right."

"Ooh! Can you say that again—but wait till I press record." Molly dug in her bag and came out with her phone, pointing it playfully at Ethan.

"I'll talk to the reporter. Just not this week. Let's see how things go with Andy."

Molly dropped her phone back in her bag and closed the manila folder on her lap. "Heard from Josie yet?"

Ethan swallowed hard. "Ye-es. I have."

Molly slid the folder into her bag, her eyes going wide. "Have you actually seen her?"

"She stopped by last night."

"Oh. Wow. Here?"

Ethan nodded. "Here."

"How . . . was it?"

"Strange. Very strange."

"How'd she look?" Molly squinted her eyes and pulled down her cheeks. "Myopic? Droopy? Has she aged terribly?"

"Sorry. None of the above. She just looked like Josie. Just all grown up."

Right.

Molly paused to study his face. "Huh. Well, does all-grown-up Josie plan to come back here today?"

"No." Ethan cleared his throat as he shifted some papers on his desk. "No, she won't be back. It was just a courtesy visit. Diana sent her over."

"I can't even imagine." Molly studied his face. "You okay?"

"Yeah. Fine. Good." He tried to summon up his best fake smile, but this was Molly. She saw through him in a second.

"Be careful." She put up her index finger. "Do *not* be stupid."

"I have no intention of being stupid. And thank you for your support."

"Shut up, Ethan. You know how this could go."

He raised his eyebrows. "Do I?"

Molly tipped her head back on the chair, sighing. "Yes, you do. Princess Josie waltzes in here after fleeing in the dead of night ten years ago, and you're a man, and she's a woman, and way back when, you were in love. Bam."

"Bam?" He couldn't help but chuckle. "That's it?"

She shook her head as she stood up. "Just be careful, okay? Puh-leeze tell me you'll be careful."

"Yes, Mom. I'll be careful."

Ethan bit the inside of his cheek to try to stop from picturing Josie as she'd been yesterday, all flushed and uncomfortable and so damn gorgeous. Yeah, he hated what she'd done ten years ago. And yeah, he hated what he'd become after she'd left.

But damn, he'd never quite gotten around to being able to hate *her*.

Molly's voice broke into his thoughts. "I wonder if she'll come around to see *me* while she's here? Y'know, to mend fences and all that."

"I imagine she has a little more on her mind than mending fences with any of us, Mols." He shook his head. "But maybe she'll pop into Bellinis for a burger before she takes off again. You never know."

Molly laughed, low and brittle. "I'm pretty sure that's the last place she'll choose to hang out while she's here. Well, next to Avery's House, that is."

She looked at him, unblinking. "I mean, *that* is going to be one *hell* of a surprise, don't you think?"

Chapter 6

An hour later, Ethan looked at the check he'd just written, then shook his head and put it through the shredder. Since Molly'd left, he'd had the attention span of a gnat. That was the second check he'd screwed up in the span of as many minutes. A year ago he'd finally gotten Andy to agree to an electronic payroll system, but the boss still insisted on handwritten checks for the older employees. Said it made them feel like they were working for a real person, not a corporation.

Molly's parting jab about Avery's House had him all off-kilter, and he hated that he'd let her get to him. But she was right. Josie was here in town, and it was only a matter of time before she either saw the house herself . . . or someone told her about it.

He wished he'd had time to prepare for this—wished he had a clue *how* to tell her about Avery's House. He'd dreaded it for years—had been sure she'd be furious or hurt or both—but until now, time and circumstances had been on his side.

But now? Both time and circumstances threatened to conspire against him, and he needed a plan. He needed to tell her about the house before somebody else did.

His phone chimed with an incoming text from Molly.

Don't forget about Santa!!!

He sighed as he glanced at the closet door where Andy hung his Santa suit. *Shit.*

When Andy got back, he'd be grateful to Ethan for keeping the office running, but if he found out Santa had been hanging on his door rather than roaming the park, Ethan would never hear the end of it.

What's a Christmas park without a Santa? he'd bellow. *Especially on a Saturday?*

Ethan got up slowly and pulled the suit from the hanger, frowning. It was one thing to pick up the extra payroll and employee scheduling. It was quite another to don a Santa suit and head out into the park with a basket of candy canes and a big, happy ho-ho voice—especially when the last thing he was feeling right now was happy.

He held the suit up to his chest and shook his head as he looked down. He had six inches and twenty pounds on Andy, who ran five miles a day and hadn't let a carb pass through his lips in years. The Santa pants would be halfway up his shins.

He looked out the window toward the igloo entrance, which was spilling a steady stream of people and strollers into the courtyard. It was nine o'clock and already seventy-five degrees, forecast to be ninety by noon. If he was going to put a damn Santa suit on, he'd better do it now before it got so hot he'd have a heat stroke inside the costume. Maybe the boots would cover up the fact that the legs were almost a foot too short.

His desk phone rang, saving him for another couple of seconds. But when he answered, the voice sent familiar chills up his spine.

"Ethan, it's Diana."

He sat down gingerly. The last call from Josie's mom had brought him both the sobering news that Andy was ill and the accompanying announcement that Josie might be coming home. "Morning, Diana." His voice was careful. "How's Andy?"

"Stable, which is an improvement, so that's something. They're moving him out of ICU this morning."

"Well, that's definitely good news. Is there anything I can do? Do you need anything?"

"It's so good of you to offer, thank you. I think I'm all set right now. Better now that Josie's here."

Ethan swallowed hard. "Of course. It was . . . nice of her to stop by the park last night."

"Did she? That's great! I had no idea she'd already been there." Diana paused, apparently gathering her thoughts. "So listen, Ethan. I know you probably think you can run the entire park on your own, and maybe you can. Goodness knows I have no idea what goes on in that office, which is how Andy and I have engineered it so we don't kill each other."

She took an audible breath. "I've asked her to see if she can help you out—just for the weekend. Just, you know, to keep busy and maybe feel needed. If you could find it in yourself to try to make her feel welcome, I'd be so grateful."

Ethan sent his fingers through his hair, probably making it stand on end. *He* was supposed to make her feel welcome?

He gritted his teeth, then tried to loosen them before he answered. Diana didn't need him to remind her that her own daughter had been AWOL for the past ten years, and that everything about this situation was completely awkward.

"She's headed over there now, actually."

"She is?" Ah hell. *Again.*

Apparently his little *Go away* speech last night had

fallen on deaf ears. He clunked all four legs of his chair back to the floor as he scanned the courtyard outside the window. He blew out a quick, frustrated breath. No way were he and Josie going to hole up in this office and work together all weekend. No frigging way.

But what other option did he have? He might be the CFO of Snowflake Village, but Andy was decidedly still in charge. If the poor man was in a hospital bed, then his wife was the de facto CEO, not Ethan. And if his wife wanted her own daughter to work at the park for the weekend, then there was diddly-squat Ethan could do about it.

He tried to level his voice. "All right, Diana. I'll give it my best shot."

"That might sound more reassuring if I hadn't known you for fifteen years, young man."

He laughed bitterly. "Concerned that my best shot still might involve me throwing her in the lake if I get a chance?"

"Or onto the roller coaster, yes." He could hear Diana smiling now. "Just find her something to do to keep her busy. We both know she can't do waiting-room duty without losing her mind. If she can be at the park, she can at least feel useful, and I can get to her if I need to." She paused. "Do you think that could work?"

"Honestly?" *No way in hell.*

He heard shuffling in the background, like she was gathering together papers. "I'm on my way to the hospital. She should be there in a few minutes." She paused again. "Just do your best, Ethan. Maybe you could help her realize that home isn't all bad . . . at least not anymore."

"But no pressure?" He grimaced, craning his neck to look out the window again toward the entrance. What in the world was he going to be able to find Josie to do here?

As Diana hung up, his eyes caught on the Santa suit he'd been trying to figure out how to struggle into before the phone rang.

Then he almost hated himself for the smile he felt creeping up the edges of his mouth.

Josie took a deep breath as she eyed Elf Central from the courtyard on Saturday morning. How could she be so hot already at nine o'clock in the morning? She imagined the employees going through the Horribly Hot, Humid Day lists in the snack shacks and Care Cottage as she watched three teens in red polos wheeling ice bags down the pathways. They'd be trekking those bags all over the park today in a vain attempt to keep the Slush-Bombs pouring fast enough.

Josie felt a stab deep in her gut as she thought of the icy drink and one little girl who'd probably downed five hundred of them in the two short years Josie had known her.

"What's this?" Avery's eyes lit up as Ethan handed her a sparkly pink bag with tissue paper sticking out the top.

"Happy eighth birthday, Aves!" He leaned down to kiss her on the forehead, then sat beside her on the wishing-well bench. His eyes met Josie's questioning ones over Avery's head, but he just winked and shrugged his shoulders.

Avery pulled out the first piece of tissue paper and folded it carefully. She did the same with the second, then reached in and pulled out a purple T-shirt with letters across the front. As she shook it out to read the letters, her little body quaked with laughter. "Oh, Ethan!! I love it!! It's perfect!!"

She stood up and pulled it over her head, then put her hand on her hip in a model-perfect pose so Josie could see. "OFFICIAL SNOWFLAKE VILLAGE SLUSH-BOMB TES-TER?" Josie laughed. "Does my father know about this?"

"Sure does. He said anytime she's wearing it, she can walk up to any snack cottage in the park and ask for a free Slush-Bomb."

Avery started jumping up and down. "I love it! I'm never going to take it off!"

Ethan pointed to the bag. "I was afraid of that. Look inside again."

Avery peered into the bag and pulled out six more shirts, all with the same letters on the front. "You got one for every color of the rainbow!"

"Every day of the week, Aves."

Avery flung herself into Ethan's lap, hugging him hard around the neck. "You are the best boyfriend-of-a-pretend-big-sis in the entire universe, Ethan. Thank you thank you thank you thank you!"

"You're welcome, munchkin. Happy birthday."

"Can I go test it and see if it works?" She jumped off his lap and danced in place.

"Go for it. Have fun!" Off she went in a blaze of purple, leaving Josie alone with Ethan on the bench.

Josie turned to him. "That was really, really nice of you. She's never going to wear anything else, you know."

"I know. Thus the seven colors. At least she can mix it up a little."

"You're going to be responsible for her teeth rotting, however."

"Nope." He grinned mischievously as he reached into the glittery bag. "I knew you'd say that. Ta-da!"

Josie laughed out loud as he produced a shiny red toothbrush and sparkly toothpaste tube. "Omigod, you think like a parent."

"Nah, a parent would never let a kid eat that many Slush-Bombs. My cool-guy status is still intact."

Josie leaned over to kiss him. "Thanks for doing this, Ethan. She'll never forget it."

He sat back, smile fading. "It's the least I could do, Jos. Who knows if anyone at home will even remember it's her birthday?"

Josie shook her head to knock the memory loose. She was not going to walk around this park and see Avery everywhere. She was not going to remember Ethan as the caring, sweet, eighteen-year-old he'd been then.

Everything was different now.

Wasn't it?

Chapter 7

In the distance, Josie could see more young guys in red shirts erecting the portable misters that would keep the walkways cool and give toddlers something to play in while their exhausted parents camped out on the green benches. She knew from experience that the on-call medic was probably on the way to the park, and that Mario would be delivering fifty extra cases of Popsicles within the hour from his massive freezer at the supermarket.

No. Not much had changed. Even on a day where intelligent humans should be in a pool or a lake or an air-conditioned building, hordes of people would fill the park, running the employees through ice, Popsicles, and patience before noon. And through it all, those employees would paste on those fake smiles and chirp *Have a happy ho-ho day!* even though they just wanted to herd everyone to the exits, strip off their polo shirts, and jump into the river behind the maintenance garage.

Josie had woken up determined to go to the hospital, but Mom had quashed that plan quickly and efficiently. *It's Saturday. It's August. Ethan can't run that park by himself, no matter how good he is. I know it's asking a lot, but the best thing you can do this morning is head*

*over there and help. It's what your dad would want,
honey.*

Then she'd almost stepped close enough to give Josie
a quick hug, but had pulled back and bitten her lip instead. *I'll call you if anything changes.*

Once again, Josie had tried to stomp out the spark of
hope Mom's actions had ignited. The woman was acting
almost . . . Mom-ish, and it was unsettling as hell.

Ten, twelve—heck, fifteen—years ago, Josie would
have given anything for a mother who'd hug her.

Check that.

She'd have given anything for a mother who'd hug her
while *sober,* not just when she needed a pair of shoulders to sling her arm over so she could find her way to
bed without falling down the stairs. Again.

Turning toward Elf Central, Josie took a deep breath,
glancing up at the window where she knew Ethan was
probably sitting right now. Even though she'd known the
arrangements before she got here, seeing Ethan sitting in
that chair across from Dad's—hearing him say *I'm the
CFO now*—had spun her for a serious loop.

So Dad might be the CEO of Snowflake Village, but
since he'd always preferred playing Santa to crunching
numbers, Josie would be willing to bet Ethan made more
decisions about the park's operations than Dad did these
days. And that meant he'd certainly be threatened by anyone else stepping into his office, even if it was temporary.

And especially if it was her.

She'd taken the long way around this morning, but still
the drive from her parents' house to the park had lasted
only twelve minutes. Hardly enough time to come up
with a strategy for surviving the day.

What she did know was this: she needed to tread lightly
here. Snowflake Village was his territory now, not hers,

and as strange as the whole situation was, she needed to respect that. Last night he'd sat there with eyes gone icy, telling her he didn't need her help, and she couldn't imagine he'd thawed any overnight.

No, he didn't want her here any more than she wanted to *be* here, but as her parents' employee, his hands were tied.

She cringed. If this wasn't a lesson in how not to break up, nothing was. Who'd have thought ten years later they'd have to sit face-to-face in an office and work together?

Not her, that's who.

The only thing she could do was put on her ultra-cooperative face and wait for whatever tasks he doled out.

Empty the trash bins? *Sure, Ethan.*

Pour Slush-Bombs until my fingers ache? *You bet.*

Muck out reindeer stalls? *Absolutely. No problem.*

She took a deep breath. She could do this. It was only for the weekend. Dad was bound to be on the mend by tomorrow, and she could be on her way back to Boston. Everyone would be happier that way.

Especially Ethan.

She started walking up the pathway to Elf Central. Whatever he had in store for her, she'd nod and smile and do her time.

It would be fine.

"You want me to do *what*?" Two minutes later, she found out *exactly* what he had in store for her. Holding up the hanger Ethan had pointed her toward, Josie felt her mouth gape open.

"You heard me." Ethan's voice was bland and humorless, and he hadn't even looked up from his computer for more than a quick glance when she'd walked in.

"Santa."

"You said you wanted to help, and Diana said to put you to work. This is work."

Josie tried not to stare at the muscled arms leaning on the desk, or at the pecs straining his polo shirt. Dammit, why did he still have to look so . . . good?

Even while resentment and irritation practically vibrated from his body, she hated the unrelenting desire she had to run her hands over his chest, to see if her head still rested in the same spot when they hugged . . . to see if his hand came up to cradle it there like it always had.

She shook her head, holding the costume up in front of her. "It's huge."

"Roll up the cuffs."

"It's, like, ninety degrees out there. Is it air-conditioned?" Josie weighed the distinct advantage of disappearing into a costume and away from Ethan against the very real possibility of heat stroke.

Ethan pointed to the window thermometer, again without looking up from his computer. "Only eighty-three."

"If I die of heat stroke in front of Rudolph's Ridiculous Reindeer Ride, you're going to have that on your conscience."

She waited for a response, but there was nothing except the clicking of his mouse. She fought the urge to growl. Sending her out in a Santa suit was worse than asking her to shovel reindeer poo and he knew it.

Knew it and was probably grinning inside right now, the jerk.

Fine. She'd wear the damn costume. At least then she wouldn't have to sit here in this office. Wouldn't have to try not to stare at Ethan. Wouldn't have to wonder whether his hands were still as good as she remembered. Or his lips.

She shook her head. What was the *matter* with her? She kicked off the sneakers she'd dug out of her suitcase this morning, then held up the big red pants, still not growling. She pulled them over her khaki shorts and hauled the belt buckle to the last hole, but the waistband slid down her thighs.

Ethan pointed at the closet behind Dad's desk. "Stuffing's in the closet. And it's Rudolph's Razzamatazz. I imagine you remember that, though."

"How could I forget?" Josie muttered as she opened the closet door and pulled out three small pillows. She stuffed them into the waistband, then pulled the red and white jacket top on, but it was all discombobulated. In the air-conditioned office she was already hot. Out on the park's pathways, she was going to turn into a poached Santa in ten minutes flat.

She twisted in the costume. "How does this thing work?"

"Zipper goes in back."

She looked down at the front of the costume. "Who makes a costume that zips in the back?" He shrugged. "How in the world do you get this thing zipped, then?"

"You have to put it on backward, zip it from the inside, then spin it around and stick your arms in. That's how Andy does it."

"Well, of course." She fought not to raise her eyebrows or snarl at him. He was already enjoying this just a little bit too much. Once she wrangled the stupid costume around, she adjusted the hat and looked back at Ethan, who was still staring at his computer. "All right. I'm off."

"Don't forget the beard." He pointed at Andy's desk. "Top drawer, left side."

Josie pulled open the metal drawer and found a pile of self-sticking moustache-beard combinations. "Oh, no way. He doesn't have a nonstick version?"

"Dunno."

Right. She'd be willing to bet he knew exactly where the nonstick version was. "I can't glue one of these things on my face."

"Too delicate?" His eyebrows curved upward as he looked up at her for the first time, eyes sparking in challenge.

"Fine. I'll put it on." She faced the little mirror tacked to the inside of the closet door, pressing the moustache and beard to her face. Ouch. She'd be lucky if they didn't melt to her face in today's heat.

Gathering her dad's basket of candy canes, she paused to roll up the pant legs of the costume, then headed for the door. "Maybe you could call 911 if I'm not back in a couple of hours?"

Ethan gave a single wave, still not looking up. "Have a happy ho-ho day, Josie."

"What does Sno-Cone Sally look like, anyway?" Kirsten's tinkly laugh filtered through the phone Sunday morning as Josie sat on a hard-backed chair in the costume closet tying closed the waist of neon-green pants. Yesterday, Santa. Today, Ethan had her on the schedule as the super-round, super-bright character she'd hated the most as a teenager. Anything to keep her out of the office, she assumed. He had to be earning back some serious karma points for the misery he was inducing with these costumes.

She looked down at the bright orange clown sneakers she had to put on next, right before she donned the ten-pound, Sno-Cone-shaped head with two teeny eyeholes. "You really don't want to know what Sally looks like. Could give you nightmares."

"How's your dad?"

"They moved him to a step-down unit, so that's good news. He's not communicating yet, though, so it's hard to tell how . . . how he's going to be." Josie grunted as she stuffed her foot into one of the clown shoes, trying not to picture her dad lying in a bed, unable to talk. "How's everything there?"

"Umm, pretty okay."

Alarm bells rang in Josie's chest. "Not a confidence-inspiring answer, partner."

"Everything's fine. Just normal full-moon stuff."

Josie recognized the evasive answer for what it was, but didn't want to push. The last thing Kirsten needed was to feel like Josie didn't think she could handle things on her own. "You'll let me know if you need me, right?"

"Gotcha on speed-dial."

"So no emergencies? Are you sure? You don't need me to bust out of this costume and come back, like, stat?"

Kirsten laughed. "I've got things handled here for now. You stay up there and be with your family. I can manage for the next few days. If it goes longer, we'll just have to figure something out. Cross that bridge when we come to it."

There was a long pause. "And as your therapist, I highly recommend you spend less time in costume and more time at the hospital with your dad."

"You're awfully blunt for a therapist. And you're *not* my therapist."

"Best friend. Same thing." Another long pause. "Things weren't always awful, right? Maybe being with him could help you remember the good times, too. And understand each other."

Josie gave a short, bitter laugh. "Excellent advice— for someone else. I'm sorry, Kirsten, but I have no desire to go strolling down memory lane here."

"Just think about it. That's all." Kirsten clicked off, leaving Josie sitting on the bench with seven shades of neon and a giant head.

No, she definitely wasn't heading down memory lane here . . . because her version of it was paved with broken glass, broken promises . . . and broken hearts.

Chapter 8

"So I hear Princess is really back at Camp Ho-Ho." Molly delivered Ethan's burger and fries, then set a plate of lasagna down in front of his dad.

"That she is." It was Sunday night, and they were sitting at Bellinis having a pub version of a home-cooked meal. Between his time at Avery's House and extra hours at the park this weekend, Ethan hadn't had time to go grocery shopping, and the cupboards at Chez Miller were getting pretty bare. Mama Bellini's cooking outweighed the risk of the third degree he'd known he'd get from Molly, but he was already wishing he'd come in on her night off instead.

"Who's Princess?" Pops poured ketchup on his lasagna before Ethan had a chance to stop him.

"Josie."

"Oh. The one who ruined your life."

Molly snorted. "That's one way of putting it." She leaned over and pilfered one of Ethan's French fries. "So how's it been? What's she been doing? Is it totally awkward?"

Ethan tapped his father's fork so he'd know which utensil to pick up. He was having one of his good days, but little things like that were starting to fade from his memory bank. It killed Ethan to watch, but so far they were taking it day by day, figuring it out as they went.

"Awkward does not even begin to describe it."

"I can't believe she's been there all weekend."

"Diana insisted she be at the park, not the hospital. Practically begged me to find a way to keep her busy so Josie wouldn't have to sit in the waiting room."

"Well, we wouldn't want Her Highness to be uncomfortable now, would we?"

"Not nice, Mols."

She raised her eyebrows. "I'm not paid to be nice."

"Actually, I pay you quite nicely to be nice."

"Not here you don't. I use up all my *nice* at Avery's House. This pub is *my* territory."

"And besides, you're a Bellini?"

"Exactly. Nice is practically a liability in this family." Molly motioned him farther into the booth so she could perch on the edge. "So really, how's it going?"

"Are you asking as the town gossip? Or as my friend?"

Molly put her hand to her chest in mock insult. "I am *not* the town gossip!"

Pops looked up and grinned. "No, that job's already taken by her mother."

"You be quiet, Pops." Molly pointed a French fry his way.

"It's fine," Ethan finally answered. "Fine, but weird."

"What has she been doing? Is she in the office with you? She's not in the office, right?" She shook her head. "No, that would be beyond awkward."

"She's been . . . out in costume both days."

"In costume? In this heat? Are you trying to kill her?"

"I think it's mutual avoidance at this point."

No need to point out that he'd engineered said avoidance with creative scheduling.

"You planning to use that strategy till she leaves?"

"Maybe. It's working so far."

"So no come-to-Jesus meetings? No confessions? No late-night apologies for dropping you like a hot potato and disappearing in a puff of smoke?"

Ethan raised one eyebrow. "Not that we'll be dramatic."

"I'm just asking." Molly shrugged. "I mean, how do you spend two days with your former fiancée and *not* discuss things? I don't get it."

"She's barely spoken since Friday, Mols." He dipped a fry in his ketchup, trying not to give away how painful it'd been to *not* talk to the woman he'd once envisioned his entire future around. "It's in the past. Talking about it now won't change what happened. There's no point."

Right. Maybe if he said it enough times he could force himself to believe he meant it.

She shook her head. "I still don't buy it. It never made sense. One day things were all roses and sunshine, and then Avery, and then boom! Gone."

"We both know her life was hardly roses and sunshine. She had a lot to handle that summer. Maybe she finally just broke."

"Well, *you* handled it."

"I wasn't dealing with the kind of stuff she was dealing with."

"No." Molly's jaw went tight. "You were just dealing with an injury that changed your entire life plan. And then Avery."

"You know that doesn't begin to compare. But talking about it isn't going to change what happened. It'll just bring up a lot of—stuff that neither of us wants to relive. There's no point."

Molly sighed, shaking her head. "I have been training you for years, and still you are nothing but a hopeless man. Sure you don't want to marry me and show her you haven't been waiting around for her to return?"

"Sorry. I've heard you're off the market. Newest wonder on Italian match dot—ow!" Ethan ducked as Molly whacked his head with her order pad.

She slid out of the booth, stealing one last fry as she did so. "That's *it*. I'm putting your singles profile live as soon as I get out of here tonight."

As she flounced back to the kitchen, Ethan turned back to his dad, who was shoveling the last of his lasagna into his mouth. *Of course* he wanted to sit Josie down and see if he could finally understand what had sent her flying off in the middle of the night. Of course he thought he deserved an explanation after all this time.

But even though it'd been ten years, he knew that no one besides Josie made Josie talk. There was no way he was going to force the issue, no matter how hard he tried. If he tried to push, the only thing he'd accomplish would be to scare her back away.

Not that that would be a bad thing, necessarily.

Pops was sopping the last of his tomato sauce up with a roll, and Ethan enjoyed the mundane ordinariness of the action for a moment before he spoke. "So Pops, what should we do tonight?"

"I don't know. So many choices. Maybe watch TV? Or, hell, we could watch TV. Or wait. I know. How about some TV?"

Ethan looked at his watch, cringing internally as he pictured the work still waiting on his desk at the park. But it was Sunday night, Pops had spent the weekend with only his television for company, and Ethan couldn't stand the thought of bringing him back home for more of the same.

"Want to go night-fishing?"

Pops looked up, eyes brightening. "How about the chimney hole? Wanna head out to Twilight Cove and try our luck?"

"Perfect." Ethan speared his pickle, smiling at Pops. If you didn't know about his illness, it was one of those rare nights that you could barely even tell he was losing his mind, one painful day at a time.

"Better not tell your mother, though. You know how she hates it when we fish at night. Tell her we're gonna go have a beer at Bellinis, got it?"

Ethan pressed his lips together to silence his sigh. Mom had lost her battle with ovarian cancer twenty years ago. "Okay, Pops. We'll tell her we're heading to Bellinis."

An hour later, Ethan baited his hook and arced the line over his head and out into the glistening water, where it plopped a few yards shy of the line Pops had just cast. The sun was setting, giving a firelight glow to the still lake. Gulls were circling a school of fish about half a mile out, but on the rocky shore it was quiet. As he felt a quick tug on his line, he remembered another night, another fishing trip, another world.

"Omigod, Ethan! I got a bite!" Josie's eyes widened as she peered over the canoe's edge. At sixteen, she was all lush curves and peek-a-boo tan lines in her bikini. Ethan had been having trouble keeping his eyes on his fishing line since they'd paddled out into Twilight Cove at dusk.

"Give it a little bounce. Set the hook."

"Set the hook?" She shook her head, looking mortified that she'd single-handedly stabbed a little fish in the jaw. "No! Get it off!" She stood up in the canoe, rocking it dangerously.

"Reel it in." He set down his own rod and moved slowly toward her. "Reel it in slowly and we'll let it go."

She reeled furiously. "You said we'd never catch anything."

"Well, in my defense, I usually don't!"

"I can't believe I just caught an innocent little fish." She frowned at the water, still reeling.

"Um, weren't you the one who wanted to go out fishing at sunset?"

She stopped reeling and looked at him like he was an idiot . . . which he was, being both sixteen and a male, but still. He grabbed her line as the fish surfaced and quickly disengaged the hook, tossing the tiny sunfish back into the lake.

Josie stared at the water. "I didn't really want to go fishing."

"Then why did you ask me to take you out here—fishing?"

"I just wanted to be alone with you, moron. Without Molly, without Ole Ben, without everyone else around."

"Oh." He sat down on the wooden seat. "Well, you could have just told me that instead."

She shook her head, smiling. "I thought maybe you could figure it out." She pointed at her chest. "I even wore your favorite bikini."

"It's not all that suitable for fishing, now that you mention it." His eyes drank in her gorgeous body. "Come here."

He reached out his arms, and she paused, then moved carefully toward his embrace, wobbling the canoe dangerously. He gathered her into a bear hug, then purposely rocked the canoe just enough to topple them both into the lake.

Josie sputtered as she emerged, splashing him soundly. "Ethan Thomas Miller, I hate you!"

"I know you do, sweetheart." He dodged her, then swam around behind her and pulled her close. "But it's impossible to kiss in a canoe." He stood on the sandy bottom and turned her to face him. She flailed, unable to reach bottom, but finally melted against his bare chest. "You do want to kiss me, right?"

"Yes, Ethan. I do." Her hands clasped his shoulders as his tongue found hers, and he lifted her so her legs wrapped around his waist. In the fading sunlight he undid the thin strings of her bikini top, and then the bottom, and it was well dark before they recaptured the boat and dragged it back onshore.

When his truck rolled up her driveway a little while later, he felt Josie's hand tense inside his own as her mother's voice sailed through the open windows. Mariah Carey tonight, and good God, Diana was no Mariah.

Josie jumped out of the truck before he'd even stopped, waving as she jogged to the porch. The crash of a bottle from inside the house had him reaching for the door handle, but Josie called out, "It's fine! Good night!" and had the front door of the house closed before he could figure out whether he should try to go inside with her.

But that was stupid. He already knew the answer. He'd been dating her for almost a year, and he'd never ever been invited further than the driveway. "The house is messy," she'd say. Or, "My parents don't let me have people over when they're not here."

But Diana *was* always there. Half the time she was looking out a window as Josie claimed she wasn't home, but Ethan never let on that he saw her. He knew there must be a damn good reason Josie didn't want him in that house, but he still hated the powerlessness he felt every time he dropped her off.

He'd heard the rumors, of course. Who hadn't? Even Pops had had a few things to say about Diana, and Pops wasn't the type to entertain the rumor mill. But it was a small town, and there was only one grocery store, and

Mrs. Triggs at the front register was only too happy to raise one judgmental eyebrow as Diana trundled her groceries to the car, then turned to ring up Pops and Ethan one evening.

"Four twelve-packs and an apple this time," she'd said.

"Not our business," Pops had answered.

"Still. That poor child." Mrs. Triggs had clucked while Pops bagged, and back in the truck, Pops had turned to Ethan.

"I'm not judging, and I'm not telling you who to hang out with and who not to, but you watch yourself, son. You watch yourself good."

Chapter 9

"Anybody in here who needs some sherbet?" Ethan poked his head around the half-open doorway to Emmy's favorite room on Monday afternoon. Yes, he should be at Snowflake Village, not here at Avery's House, but he hadn't been able to wait to see Emmy. It had nothing to do with avoiding Josie, who was once again at the park.

Nothing.

Emmy had taken off her wig, and in the rocking chair by the window, she looked tinier than her eight years would suggest. There was nothing tiny about her smile, though, as she saw Ethan come through the doorway.

"Uh-oh. Better hurry before Mommy gets back. She says I'm already getting spoiled here."

"That's our job at Avery's House—to spoil you absolutely, positively rotten." He tweaked her nose. "And as one of our five-star guests, you get first dibs on the sherbet cooler this afternoon."

"All of us are your five-star guests, Ethan."

He pretended to be thoughtful. "That's true. But I wouldn't have it any other way. We only let the nicest kids stay here."

"What do you do with the rest?" She giggled, already knowing the answer.

"String them up by their toes in the tower, of course. So I guess you'd better keep behaving, young lady."

"Yes, sir."

He kissed the top of her tiny, bald head. "So about that sherbet. Can I spoil you now?"

"What flavors do you have?" A half-smile cracked the pale veneer of her face.

"Well, let me see. Today I have a fabulous array of choices for discriminating young ladies." Ethan set down the cooler and lifted the top. "Our most popular item this week seems to be the pepperoni and mushroom with white chocolate chips. How about that?"

Emmy grimaced and giggled. "What else do you have?"

"Hmm. I have a new flavor just in. Seaweed and squash special?"

"Yuck. No, thank you. What else?"

"I have a fantastic chili pepper, chimichanga, and cheese combo. But you'll have to move fast. Only one left."

Emmy giggled again. "Save that one for Danny."

Ethan pretended to set one aside. "Pickles and peanut butter? Croutons and cabbage? Mango and mudpie?"

Emmy shook her head to each choice, her grin growing bigger. "Do you have butterscotch and beans?"

"The lady wants butterscotch and beans today." Ethan fished through the cooler, making ample noise with the ice cubes as he did. Finding the mild lemony sherbet that was the only flavor Emmy's stomach could handle, he raised it over his head with a flourish. "Aha! I have it! Still can't stump me! You'll have to do better tomorrow."

"I already have a plan." Emmy reached out for the sherbet cup and plastic spoon, then tucked her legs under her as she pulled off the cap and licked it. "Thank you."

Ethan sat down in the other chair at the window. "You keeping an eye on things for me today?"

"Looks like the Twinkle Fairy's tired." She pointed

down the hill toward Snowflake Village. "But the Ferris wheel is very busy."

"How many rides today?"

"Thirty-six so far. I think."

"Wowza! How about the roller coaster?"

"Too busy. I lost count of that one."

Ethan watched her as she spooned the sherbet to her lips, savoring each drop. Her tiny little scalp caught the afternoon sunlight coming through the windows, and through her nearly translucent skin he could see the blue veins carrying around the poisonous drugs that were waging a desperate war with her cancer.

Winning the war, he prayed. Though Avery's House, the huge old B and B he'd converted to a care facility for kids facing life-threatening illnesses, was a great place to visit, it certainly wasn't a cure for cancer. The building was situated adjacent to Snowflake Village, and all of the kids' rooms looked downhill toward the park, so on days like today when it was too hot for most of them to handle the heat outside, they at least had a fun view. And at ten, the child life specialist would be here to do some indoor activities.

"Is it hot out there, Ethan? Looks hot."

"Very. You're lucky to be in here."

"That's what Mommy said."

"What did Mommy say?" A female voice sounded from behind him.

Ethan looked around to see Emmy's mom coming through the doorway with two green Popsicles. "Hey, Steph."

"Hey, there. You escaped the park?" Stephanie Stevens was probably ten years younger than the worry lines etched into her face would have anyone believe, but she had the same bright smile he conjured from Emmy at every possible opportunity.

"Couldn't resist coming to visit my favorite friend." He winked at Emmy, who rolled her eyes.

"You say that to all the girls."

"Only the specialest ones."

"That's not a word, silly."

Steph leaned down to stick the Popsicles in the tiny fridge by the bathroom, then motioned Ethan out to the hallway.

Ethan got up, lifting the cooler. "Enjoy the butterscotch and beans. That is a *terrible* combination."

"Mmm. Don't tell Ben and Jerry's. This one's *my* invention." She made a show of licking her spoon clean.

He leaned down to kiss her head. "Got it. See you tomorrow. Maybe it'll be cooler. Save me a ride on the Ferris wheel?"

Emmy gave a weak thumbs-up as her head lolled back toward the pillowed back of the chair. Ethan sighed quietly as he watched her for a long moment, then turned toward the hallway, pulling the door almost closed behind him.

Steph waited, smile now gone. "Thanks for the sherbet."

"Welcome. How's she doing?"

"She's spent, but her numbers are looking better."

"Excellent." He looked at Steph's eyes, which were hopeful for the first time in a year. "That is just excellent. We'll get there, right?"

Steph nodded carefully. "We will. But wow, what a trip. I don't know how you do this all the time with these kids."

Ethan shrugged slowly. "I don't know. I really don't. I think my only saving grace is that they're not my own. I don't know how *you* do it."

"One day at a time, that's how." Steph peeked back in at Emmy, watching her for a second as she rocked slowly at the window. "Emmy was asking me this morning who Avery is. I wasn't sure what to tell her."

She searched his eyes. "I know how places like this usually get named."

He sighed as he leaned back against the wall. "Avery was a little girl I knew a long, long time ago." He cleared his throat. "A—uh—friend of mine got involved with one of those Big Sis/Little Sis programs, and Avery was her little sis. She loved the park. Came here every time she could, knew every employee by name, could tell when the snack cottage had put three squirts in her Slush-Bomb instead of four. If we hadn't pulled her off the Ferris wheel at four o'clock each day, she'd have slept there."

As he talked about her, Ethan could see Avery's brown hair and tiny freckles as if she'd hopped up on his shoulders just yesterday. His chest ached as he pictured her skipping along the pathways and grinning in that impish way that had felled every adult in sight.

Though the Ferris wheel had always been her favorite Snowflake Village ride, she'd also loved the little wishing well that used to sit next to the Polar Penguins ride. He'd never forget the first time he'd found her there with a tiny handful of pennies.

"Whatcha doing, munchkin?"

Avery looked up, long brown ponytail looped through the back of her Red Sox hat. "Making wishes." She closed her eyes and flicked a penny into the water, her concentration making her look somehow older than her nine years.

"What are you wishing for?"

"Can't tell or it won't come true." Plonk.

"Even me?"

"Even you, Ethan. You're special, but not that *special."*

He put his fist to his chest. "I'm hurt."

Avery giggled. "No you're not." She scrunched her eyes and tossed another penny in.

"That looked like an important wish."

"Yup."

"Sure you don't want to tell me any?"

"Nope. You'll just tell Josie."

"Will not."

"Will, too. You're in l-o-v-e love." She sang the last word, then ducked as he pretended to swat her. Avery looked pensive, then plonked another penny into the well. "It's a wish for Josie."

"Are you . . . wishing for a car for her so she can drive us to the ocean?"

Avery smiled. "No. That'd be a waste of a wish."

"A trip to Hawaii?"

"Nope."

"A pet giraffe?"

"Ethan."

"What? She loves giraffes!"

"Have you ever smelled a giraffe? They're stinky! And where would she keep it?"

"Good point. So what are you wishing for?"

Avery was quiet for a moment, her eyes years wiser than they should have been at her age. She plonked in another penny. "Can't tell you. You're not supposed to know."

Late Tuesday morning, Josie found an unoccupied bench outside the Slurpy Seal and sat down gratefully. When she'd arrived at the office at eight o'clock this morning, she'd scooped the Santa suit off the closet door while Ethan was elsewhere. It was day five back in Echo Lake, and she didn't need more than a passing glance at the employee schedule to know he'd put her on costume duty again.

Fine. She wasn't ready to deal with *him,* either.

Some counselor she was. She spent her days helping people learn how to better communicate—with their spouses, with their children . . . with themselves—but when it came to her *own* situation, she had no idea what to say to this man she'd once planned to marry.

There was definitely a missing chapter in her textbooks.

After she'd come home from the hospital last night, she'd tried to come up with some openers, but they all fell flat. She'd thought it would be easier to practice in the mirror, where she couldn't be distracted by those eyes, or the dark hair that sprinkled his forearms, or the lips that had—oh God.

See? It wasn't working.

She pulled at the Santa suit to try to peel it away from her skin. Today she'd stripped down to her underclothing before donning the suit, thinking it would keep her cooler.

Wrong.

The combination of hazy humidity, bright red polyester, and itchy fake cotton was sending her internal thermometer soaring. Of course, saying *Have a happy ho-ho day* eight hundred flipping times wasn't helping with that. Ethan had to be sitting up in that nice, cool office feeling pretty proud of himself right now.

Leave me at the altar? Ten points for you. Poach you in a Santa suit? One point for me. And counting.

Thank God she'd at least found Dad's nonstick version of Santa's beard.

She sipped on her fourth cup of ice water, grateful that she was sweating the water right out so she wouldn't have to do the mens'-room-versus-ladies'-room dance later if the family bathroom was occupied. This was the first time she'd sat down all morning, but within a minute, as an elderly elf walked by, she heard the radio on his belt squawk *Code Stork! Repeat! Code Stork!*

The elf straightened up and walked quickly, eyes scanning right to left, left to right. Oh lordy. "Code Stork" was the park's code for a lost child. Suddenly Josie saw employees pour out from all the buildings and rides. She remembered how it worked. Skeleton crews stayed put so the other guests wouldn't know there was a problem, but every other available breathing human had a grid assignment, and they fanned out across the park to search.

She jumped up and tossed her cup in the penguin garbage can next to her, but stopped short as she debated whether to head left or right. She was Santa. She didn't have a grid to search. She didn't even know who they were looking for.

A teenage girl from the snack shack strode out the side door and headed by Josie.

"Excuse me." Josie put a hand out to stop her. "Who are we looking for?"

The girl gave her a surprised once-over, backing up a step. "Uh, four-year-old named Kelsey. Green shirt, jean shorts, pink hat. Black hair. White sandals. Last seen near the Dolphin Dance. Mom's name's Maria."

"Where's the mom?"

"Down there." She pointed down the pathway toward a frightened-looking young woman pacing beside the dolphin ride.

"Thanks. Go." Josie took a moment to figure out where she should look. The train tunnel made a great hiding spot, but since they'd found so many kids there over the years, she knew someone had already checked it by now. Ditto the polar bear cave at the water park. And backstage at the outdoor theater.

She looked back at Maria. Two employees stayed with her, keeping her planted to her spot, as was search protocol. She headed toward her and put out her hand. "Hi there, Maria. I'm Josie. I'm sure these guys have told you all the things we're doing to locate Kelsey."

"She was right here! Right here! I swear I was just talking to my friend for a minute!"

"We know, we know." Josie put her hand on the mother's arm, trying to reassure her. "All the spots where she could get hurt have already been checked, right?" She raised her eyebrows to the elves, who nodded, radios to their ears. She heard Ethan's voice say *Grid 13—clear!* She pictured him in the office, pacing while he manned the radio and the whiteboard where the grids were recorded.

She pointed to the stroller. "Did she take anything with her that you know of?"

Maria shuffled a light blanket and sippy cup, then peered under the stroller before tossing the blanket around again. "Her duck. She took her stuffed duck."

Josie's internal alarm pinged loudly. "She likes ducks?"

"Loves ducks. Why?" Maria's hand went to her mouth. "Oh God. You don't think she went to the ducks?"

"It's one of the first places we check. Don't worry. I'm going to go help look for her, but you stay right here with these gentlemen and we'll have Kelsey back to you in no time."

As Josie headed toward the pond, she heard another employee's radio squawk *Grid 2, 4, 5 clear*. Phew. The little girl wasn't in any of the three train tunnels, but Josie fought a sick feeling in her stomach as she realized the duck pond grid had yet to be cleared. Why not? That one was the highest priority in the whole park. It should have been cleared within the first minute of the alarm.

Protocol.

She hiked up the huge Santa pants and picked up her

pace, walking as quickly as she could without alarming anyone. As she crested the rise that headed down to the stone bridge over the pond, she was struck by how little stroller traffic there was. Like, none. The noon sun had apparently driven everyone to shadier areas.

What struck her next was the lack of any red polo shirts in the area. Who was checking the pond?

Josie double-timed it to the arched bridge, which was about forty feet across and made of round river stones. Split-rail fencing surrounded the pond itself, with colorful beds of summer flowers running amok along the fence line. From the top of the bridge, she leaned out as far as she could on both sides, but saw nothing. She ran to the other side and peered over the fence, but didn't see any sign of the little girl. Phew.

She bent over to duck through the fence, but stopped with an *Oof* as her Santa belly got wedged between the rails. She yanked and swore, and thankfully no one was watching as she finally heaved the fake stomach through the gap. The hill descended fairly steeply to the pond, which sat only about twenty feet below the pathways. Putting her left hand on the stone archway, she leaned to peer under the bridge to see if Kelsey might be under there, but once her eyes adjusted to the dimmer lighting, all she could see was rocks and ferns.

Then a movement on the other side of the pond caught her eye, and she squinted to see. "Santa!" a small voice gasped.

Chapter 10

"Kelsey? Is that you?" Josie stepped down to the water's edge, squatting down to try to see better. In the dimness under the far side of the bridge, she made out a green shirt, jean shorts, and black hair. She automatically reached for a radio on her belt, even though she hadn't worn one for ten years, but her hand came up empty.

"Santa?" The little girl stumbled a couple of steps toward the water. Oh no.

"Stay right there, sweetheart. I'm going to come get you, okay? Don't come any closer to the water."

Josie straightened up and glanced left and right. The pond was deep, cut by a mountain stream that cascaded through the park all summer long and met the river downstream. It was thirty or so feet across, easily swimmable, but Josie had a Santa suit on that weighed twenty-plus pounds. And nothing underneath besides her favorite Victoria's Secret set.

Did she have time to run up the hill and come to Kelsey on the other side? She stepped out from under the bridge, praying another human had come along, but the pathways were still deserted around the pond.

She looked back at Kelsey. "Stay put, honey. I'm going to walk up to the bridge and come see you, okay?" She turned quickly to head up the hill, then heard the unmistakable *wack-wack-wack* of the resident mallards moving toward the little girl.

Oh no! She looked back and saw Kelsey take another step toward the water, then another, delighted that the ducks were coming her way. One more and she'd be in the pond.

Josie leaned down to pry off her heavy boots in case she had to dive in after Kelsey, but just as she did, she heard a splash. Oh God. Kelsey was already up to her knees, wading toward the ducks.

Before she could properly register the fact that the damn Santa suit was likely to drown her, Josie dove sideways into the water and swam toward the little girl. It felt like it took an eternity to get across the pond in the heavy costume, watching Kelsey wade closer and closer to the ducks.

"Stop right there, sweetie. The water's very deep." She huffed out instructions as she pulled herself across the water. Damn Santa stuffing. She tried to pry it out as she swam, but it was stuck fast.

"No more steps, okay? Freeze those feet!" She tried to make her voice sound playful and calm, but her stomach was anything but.

Finally she was close enough to touch the little girl, but fought the urge to scoop her up and give her Santa nightmares. Kelsey didn't know she was only two feet from where the pond floor dropped out, for God's sake. Josie pulled herself onto the shallow sandy ledge, perching on her knees in the water next to Kelsey. Her breaths came short and ragged, but she wasn't sure how much of that was due to fear, and how much was due to forgetting to renew her gym membership. Again.

She pointed toward the shoreline ten feet away. "Hey! I have an idea! How about we race to the rocks! Ready?"

Kelsey grinned, but as she turned around to match

Josie's pose, her feet slipped out from under her and she squawked as she lost her balance. *Great idea, Einstein,* Josie berated herself as she lunged to catch her.

"Oh my God!" Just then a woman's voice squawked from the bridge. Finally, another human. It was about flipping time. "Help! Somebody help!"

The woman pointed down toward Josie and Kelsey, and within seconds, Josie saw a couple of teens in red polos blast out the doors of the photo studio next to the pond. The girl immediately put her radio to her mouth while the guy scrambled through the fence and down toward the pond.

He put out his hands to help haul Kelsey out of the water, and as the little girl struggled to get her balance on the pebbles, she started crying. His eyes flew from Kelsey to Josie. "What *happened?* Are you okay?"

"This is the little girl we're looking for." Josie huffed out the words. "She was visiting the ducks."

"Wha—"

Josie drilled him with a look. "Code Stork? Did you miss the alarm?"

"Uh—" Spots of color rose in his cheeks as he glanced up the hill toward the girl he'd probably been making out with in the photo booth. "We thought it was just a drill."

"Are you kidding me?" Josie hissed, turning away from Kelsey so she couldn't hear. "You were blowing off a drill? That turned out to be real? She could have *drowned*!"

She closed her eyes and took a deep breath. Berating him wasn't going to help anything right now. They needed to worry about Kelsey. She put her hands on Kelsey's face, smoothing her hair back. "Hey, cutie. You're okay. Everything's all right. Want to go find your mommy?" Kelsey nodded eagerly through her tears.

Josie turned back to the guy. "I am in a soaking wet

Santa costume. If I come any farther out from under the
bridge, kids are going to think someone tried to drown
Santa . . . or that Santa runs around dunking kids. You
need to bring Kelsey to the Dolphin Dance. First, radio
Ethan. Immediately. What is your name?"

"Nick."

"I'll be sure to discuss this with Ethan, *Nick*." Josie
turned back toward Kelsey. "Okay, sweetie. Nick's going to bring you back to Mommy, okay? He's not going
to stop along the way, he's not going to talk to his *friend,*
and he's going to report immediately to Elf Central once
he's done so. Does he understand?" Nick nodded, color
rising in his cheeks once again. Josie handed Kelsey's wet
little hand to him. "You got her?"

He took Kelsey's hand firmly in his. "Got her."

"I'll wait here under the bridge. When you get her settled, please send your friend back here with some dry
clothes. Just have her grab something from the costume
room for now, and then she can join you in Ethan's office."
Josie grimaced as she backed under the bridge, pointing
at the sopping wet Santa suit. "If she could hurry, that'd
be great."

"Got it." Nick scrambled up the hill with Kelsey in tow
while Josie did her best to melt into the underside of the
bridge until clothing arrived. As she sat down, her body
started shaking, the adrenaline coursing through her veins.
She tried not to think about what could have happened,
but couldn't help picturing the whole situation ending a
much different way.

She'd bet money that Nick and his friend were getting
busy in the photo booth instead of searching their grid
like they were supposed to. If it were up to her, they'd be
getting busy finding new jobs later this afternoon.

Five minutes later, just as she started to think they'd

forgotten her, she heard footsteps on the gravel at the edge of the bridge, so she stood up, forgetting how close she was to the metal bracing over her head. She bonked her head on the bracing, then squeaked in pain as her back met something sharp. She tried to turn around to see what had poked her, but couldn't budge. What in the *world*? She twisted the other way, but still couldn't break free. The metal had somehow snagged the costume, and it wasn't letting go.

She pulled harder, but the motion seemed to only get her further impaled. *Great*. Just what she needed was for Nick's little girlfriend to find her under here, completely stuck. Josie could already picture the speed at which *this* story would travel the park.

At least Ethan was still in the office, not roaming around.

"Josie?"

Or not.

Ethan ducked under the edge of the bridge and paused, probably letting his eyes adjust. Of all the people in this park, he *would* be the one to find her like this. She tried to straighten up enough to pretend she wasn't stuck, but there wasn't a whole lot of space to work with.

"You okay?" he asked.

"Yup. Good. Fine." She tried not to move and risk being further impaled. "Kelsey all right now?"

"She's back with her mom."

"Did Nick tell you what happened?"

"Not yet. I'll get to him. Just wanted to be sure you were okay first."

A warm feeling tried to break through the chills enveloping her body. He had just inherited a million tasks related to this incident, but the first thing he'd done was hoof it to the pond to make sure she was all right.

"Thank you," she murmured. "I'll be fine."

Ethan looked toward the hill where Nick and Kelsey had gone. "Thank you for finding her."

"You're welcome."

"How did you know to look here?"

"I didn't, really. Her mom said she'd taken her stuffed duck, so I panicked and thought maybe she'd found the real ones. Then I didn't see anyone else when I got here, and I hadn't heard you clear the grid yet."

"Where the hell were Nick and Peyton? They've got this grid today."

Josie raised her eyebrows. "They thought it was a drill. They were in the photo studio until someone finally saw us and yelled for help."

"Maybe they were searching the studio?"

"He still had her lip gloss on his neck. Just saying."

He scrubbed his right hand through his hair. "I'll have their frigging heads."

"Maybe you should have their *frigging* shirts. And their badges."

Ethan leveled her with a look. "I'll decide what happens to them, thank you."

Josie started to retort, but realized it wouldn't do any good. She'd overstepped her bounds. It wasn't her call to make. "Fine. You're the boss. But I'd bet you money they were taking hot pics in the instant booth."

"Really. And what would make you leap to that conclusion?" He raised his eyebrows as Josie felt heat rise to her cheeks. But no. No way was she heading down memory lane and thinking of the pictures she and Ethan had taken in that very studio.

Long time ago. Long, long time ago.

"Hey! Someone under here order some clothes?" Peyton's voice startled both of them as a poofy white princess dress appeared at the edge of the bridge's underside. The dress was so huge Josie couldn't even see Peyton behind it. "It's all I could grab. Sorry. Everything else is either on the actors or at the cleaners right now."

Ethan stepped toward her and grabbed the costume. Josie could see him trying to stifle a laugh as he held the dress by the shoulders and shook it out. "Oh, I think this is just perfect. Thank you. Just perfect."

After Peyton headed back up the hill, Ethan stepped toward Josie and handed her the dress. "Couldn't have ordered a better one myself."

"Very funny," Josie muttered. Last time she'd worn this particular dress, she'd fallen off the park stage and ended up looking like a princess cupcake in a giant drum. She shook her head as she viewed the layers of tulle, still astounded by how much noise the timpani had made when she fell into it. "How is it possible you still have this ridiculous dress?"

"No idea. I'm not in charge of costumes." He stepped away like he didn't want to get any closer to her than necessary. "All right. I'm going to head back to the office. Apparently someone sent Nick there to await his doom."

"That would be me. And I'm happy to be his doom if you don't want to be."

"I'm completely capable of handling it, Josie."

She paused. "I know. Sorry."

Ethan stared at her for a moment too long. "Y'know, I'd hope that even after ten years, you know me well enough to know I'd never take a situation like this lightly. This was bad, and believe me, Nick will definitely feel the pain of it."

"But you're not going to fire him?" Josie tried to keep the incredulity out of her voice.

"He made a mistake, Jos. It's going to take him a long time and a lot of trash-hauling shifts to get back in my good graces, but no. I'm not going to fire him. He needs this job—his family needs him to *have* this job—and there is *no* way he'll ever do something stupid like this again. I guarantee it. He's a good kid, Josie."

Josie thought of Dad for a moment, wondering what he'd do in this same situation. Would he read Nick the riot act, then demand his Ho-Ho shirt and badge? Or would he, too, try to see the big picture—the long view, as he called it?

She sighed. Ethan was right. It was a mistake. A bad one, for sure. But still a mistake.

She nodded slowly, conceding. "It's your call."

His eyebrows shot upward. "Really?"

"Ethan, I'm wet, I'm freezing, and right now I have to choose between a Santa suit that's gone to wet glue, or this ridiculous excuse for a dress." She pointed to the acres of white poof. "I'm hardly in a debating mood."

"All right." He turned. "I'll be back in the office. Come file a report when you're dressed. I need to call the insurance company just in case anything more comes of this. Just leave the Santa suit here till after hours. I don't want to have you carry it across the park and have the kids think you offed Santa."

Once he'd headed back out of sight, Josie twisted, trying to figure out how to get free of whatever had snagged the Santa suit. To her chagrin, she squeaked again as something poked her from behind. Crap. She was really stuck.

Ethan's head popped back into view from the edge of the bridge archway. Yikes. He was still here. "You sure you're okay?"

"Yup. Good. I'll be right up." Josie put on her brightest fake smile, but Ethan didn't move.

"Y'know, it occurs to me that you haven't actually *moved* the entire time we've been talking."

Josie shrugged. "Wet costume."

The rest of his body appeared at the bridge opening again. "Are you . . . stuck?" He stepped closer, slowly, like she might bite if he moved too quickly. He was bent a little at the waist, since his six-foot-two frame was at least half a foot too tall for the stonework.

She closed her eyes and nodded miserably. There was no sense denying it at this point, unless she wanted to sleep under the damn bridge tonight. This costume was not breaking free without some outside help.

He took one step closer, trying to peer around her body without getting too close. He took the princess dress from her and set it on the rocks. "How in the world did you do this?"

She pointed at her back and rolled her eyes. "I'm caught on something, and this stupid costume only opens in the back."

"Can you twist it at all?"

"Tried that."

"Duck out of it maybe? If you crouch down?"

"It's too wet."

"Wow."

"If I say go ahead and laugh, would you just do so, and then get to the part about maybe helping me?"

He laughed quietly, stepping close enough for her to touch him. He reached one arm behind her, and she shivered as she caught a strong whiff of his after-shave. Then he moved closer, and she could feel the warmth of his chest as he used both of his hands to try to untangle her.

"Wow. This is . . . wow." She felt a yank and heard a ripping sound. "You are seriously hung up here." His body pressed gingerly against hers as he tried to pull the fabric free, and it was all she could do to keep her hands clenched at her sides instead of reaching out to touch him.

He pulled back and fished in his pocket for something,

coming up with the Swiss Army knife he'd probably been carrying since he was twelve. "I'm going to have to cut you out of it, I think."

"What? No! No knives!"

"You afraid I'll take out ten years of frustration on you?" His eyebrows lifted in challenge.

"Maybe? Seriously, no knives. Dad'll kill us if we ruin his Santa suit." She winced at how that sounded, given that Dad was currently in a hospital bed and could hardly care less about something as stupid as a Santa costume.

He pressed against her again to look behind. "Jos, there is no way we're getting you out of this thing without ripping it. You're snagged by a mess of nails back there, going every which way." He pressed on her back lightly. "I can't believe you're not bleeding. Shit. You probably are. Have you had your tetanus shot? These things are rusty."

"Ethan! I don't care about tetanus! I need to get out of this soaking wet costume. Can't we slither it over my head or something?"

"You'll be impaled if you try."

Josie sighed. "Could you maybe just hold it out in back and I'll try to slide out?"

He grimaced, obviously unconvinced it would work. He stepped directly in front of her, still crouched because he was too tall. "Okay, let's try it. Arms first." He held the end of the right sleeve tight as she pulled her arm toward her body. "My God, this stuff shrinks when it's wet."

After a few desperate pulls on each side, Josie's clammy arms were trapped inside the costume against her body, and Ethan stepped closer again, almost sending her to her knees with his heat. He braced himself directly in front of her and put his arms over her shoulders, trying to lift the wet fabric from her skin. "All right. Slither."

She closed her eyes and bent her knees, trying to slide out of the costume without ripping her back to shreds on the nails. After a few tugs and snags, she was finally free to stand almost upright, and it was all she could do not to hug him in thanks.

Then she caught sight of his face.

Ethan's mouth opened in an O as his eyes traveled down her top half, and too late, she remembered what she had on.

Which was not much.

Chapter 11

Josie flopped her arms across her chest, trying in vain to hide her hot-pink Victoria's Secrets from Ethan.

His mouth stayed open. "You're—what did you—you have no—huh."

Josie arched an eyebrow.

"Why—uh—why are you—" He pointed vaguely at her body.

"Naked, practically?"

He nodded, and was it her imagination, or was he having trouble keeping his eyes on hers?

"Well, here's the thing. Someone—whoever it is that does the scheduling these days—keeps putting me on the costume list. So for three—wait, is it four?—days now I've been roasted alive by noon. Today I thought I'd be smart and try fewer layers so that no one would find Santa splatted in front of Rudolph's Ridic—"

"Razzamatazz."

"Whatever." She waved a hand. "Santa. Heat stroke." She pointed her chin downward. "I obviously forgot to figure in the risk of pond-diving—or getting stuck underneath the bridge afterward. Silly me."

"Not—" He swallowed visibly, his eyes traveling over her. "Not good planning."

"Ethan, you can close your mouth. You've seen it before." Josie's cheeks felt like they were being licked by flames.

He shook his head. "I haven't seen it like *this* before."

"Princess dress. Now. Please." She held out one hand, leaving only one to guard her privacy.

His eyes darkened as they traveled her body again, this time more slowly, making her shiver in all the right places.

Dammit.

"You'll never get this thing on by yourself. Remember?" He reached behind him to grab the dress, then stepped toward her, finding the bottom hem and holding it up so she could duck her head into the opening.

He was right. She'd forgotten the damn dress needed to come with its own personal assistant.

"Can't believe we still have this ridiculous dress," she muttered as she shoved her arms through the armholes and he guided the top of it over her head. When it was in place, he slid his hands around the back of her neck to lift out her hair, just like he'd always done when he'd helped her get dressed.

Had he done it on purpose? Or was it just an old habit?

Against her will, she sighed and leaned back into his familiar hands as he smoothed her hair.

"Ethan? Ethan? You still down here?" Josie sprang backward as Nick reappeared at the edge of the bridge. "We have a little situation up here."

Ethan growled low in his throat as he stepped away from Josie, but his eyes didn't leave hers. "I'll be right there."

"It's actually an emergency. We need you, like, now."

Ethan glanced at him, then back at Josie, shaking his head slowly, like he was trying to figure out what had just happened to make his hands actually touch her. As he turned toward Nick, he shook his head quickly as if to clear it, then followed him up the bank.

As soon as he was out of sight, Josie's knees finally gave way and she sank to the pebbled ground. Oh hell. Five days back, and her ten hard years of running away had evaporated the instant his fingers had touched her skin.

This was not the plan.

"Hey, Ben." An hour later, crisis averted, Ethan strolled into Ben's cavernous maintenance garage at the edge of the park, right where the river meandered by. As usual, it smelled like metal and oil and fresh lumber, and country music was playing from the ancient radio he had dangling over his workbench.

"Ethan." Ben looked up from some piece of metal he was tinkering with. "What brings you all the way out here? Everything okay?"

"Just walking back to the office. Thought I'd take the scenic route." Ethan looked around for something to sit on.

Why *was* he here? After seeing Josie in . . . basically nothing except Santa pants, he'd barely been able to concentrate. God, for days he'd been trying *not* to think about her like that, because doing so only left him more mystified and frustrated than ever.

She'd been gone for ten years. He'd moved on. He'd learned to live without her, learned to stop hoping that someday she'd change her mind. He'd almost stopped dreaming about her.

Almost.

He wanted to hate her, damn it.

He didn't want to . . . want her.

"How's the little girl?" Ben's voice broke into his thoughts.

He shook his head, trying to clear it. "She's fine. Very glad to see her mother. I don't think she'll be chasing ducks again anytime soon."

Ben cocked his eyebrow. "Looks like you got something besides that on your mind." He went back to tinkering, but Ethan knew he was listening. "Wouldn't be Josie, would it?"

Ethan just shook his head as he sat on one of Ben's spinning stools.

"How's it going between you two?" Ben peered over his shoulder. "You putting her to work? Diana said she didn't want her to have to hang out at Mercy."

"I know." Ethan found himself torn between feeling bitterness at everyone being so concerned about Josie's comfort—and understanding exactly why she couldn't bear being anywhere near that hospital.

Right now he was leaning toward the bitterness, but that probably had more to do with the fact that he'd just survived being only inches from her luscious body, viewing all those sweet curves embraced by nothing but wet lingerie. If Josie knew exactly how *much* he'd just seen, she'd probably be appalled that he'd kept looking.

"You gonna keep sending her out in costume all day long? Or give her something worthwhile to do? Looks like she's gonna be here for a bit longer, unfortunately. Poor Andy." Ben shook his head. "Thought he'd have snapped right out of it by now, but I guess that's not how things work."

"She hasn't been here in ten years, Ben. What am I supposed to have her do? We're all staffed up, except for Andy . . . obviously."

"You and me both know it takes more than one person to run that office. Why don't you let her help you up there?"

Because she'd be way too damn close, old man. Way too damn close.

Ethan shrugged. "I don't know what I'd have her do. Everything's changed since she left. And she's not staying.

By the time I got her trained up—which would take time away from what *I'm* supposed to already be doing—she'll be gone again. It'd be a waste of time."

Ben picked up a hammer and tapped quietly on the metal, silence stretching between them. "You never know. Ever think maybe a little piece of her might want to come back someday? Might be your chance to help her decide."

"No. There's no way she'd come back here. Even before . . . everything, she couldn't wait to leave. Hell, she and Molly made up a new getaway plan every single summer, starting when they were thirteen." Ethan shook his head slowly. "They both wanted out of this town from the time they were old enough to figure out there *was* more than this town in the world."

Ben laughed his low, rumbly laugh. "Remember Broadway summer?"

Ethan felt a smile threaten to erupt. "I remember them taking serious liberties with the Christmas songs they rewrote."

"I thought Andy was going to flip his lid when he found that notebook of lyrics, but instead he just came back here and sat down and laughed till his stomach hurt."

Ethan sobered. "I bet Josie never knew he thought it was funny."

"No. I imagine she didn't." Ben's laugh rumbled into silence. "He just wanted her to love this place like he did, Ethan. He never wanted to push her away."

"I know that. I'm sure somewhere down deep she knows it, too. But it's at least ten years buried at this point. She finally followed through with her getaway strategy, and she has a new life. Molly decided to stay, but not Josie. No way she'll ever be back for good."

"Maybe she needs a good enough reason to come back. Ever thought of that?" Ben kept his eyes on his work-bench, but Ethan could tell his eyebrows were raised in that way he had.

"Well, I apparently wasn't reason enough to stay the first time. And now she's moved to Boston, started a practice, and probably has a posse of cats. Hell, she could be engaged, for all I know."

Ben shook his head. "Doubt it. No ring, and she'd have told me that. But you're right. Cats would definitely be a deal breaker."

"Shut up, old man."

"Not *that* much has changed here, Ethan. She knows the business. She knows the people in town. Having her help doesn't mean you have to give over stuff you think needs your hands on it. But there've gotta be things up in that office that are starting to pile up, with Andy in the hospital. Just give her some of that stuff."

"I don't know."

"Afraid to have her so close to you?" Ben turned his head toward Ethan, waggling his eyebrows. "Afraid old sparks will fly?"

Ethan squeezed his eyes shut and shook his head, trying to shake the image of hot-pink lingerie out of his brain. "No. We're long past sparks."

"So give the girl a purpose here. You do that, and you never know what might happen. Maybe she'd even fall in love with this place again." He turned back to the bench and started tap-tap-tapping again. "Or maybe other things."

"Mommy! It's Snow Princess!" Josie grimaced as yet another sticky three-year-old launched toward her. She'd finally emerged from under the bridge, but was already regretting it. She was decked in twenty-five pounds of tulle and sparkles that made her three people wide. Big people.

"Hi, Snow Princess!" The little girl halted just at the edge of Josie's dress, which was only about thirty feet from her body. Cripes. She could sneak ten little kids out of the park under the thing if she wanted to.

She took a deep breath. She knew the rules, and as much as she wanted to flee Snowflake Village and its CFO right now, she was on park grounds, and she was in costume. Therefore, she had to play the role.

But she could still put on that fake accent Dad and Ethan had always hated, since Dad wasn't here to shake a finger at her and remind her that Vermonters don't *have* an accent. She turned to the little girl and pasted on her best Southern-belle smile. "Well, hello, you sweet thang!"

She sighed. Somehow the little rebellion wasn't quite as rewarding at twenty-eight years old. *Never mind.*

She looked over layers of tulle to the girl's bright red hair, trying to call up her inner snow princess. "You have the prettiest hair I've ever seen. Do you think I could borrow it?"

The little girl tipped up her chin and laughed. "You have your own hair!"

"But yours is so much prettier! Look!" Josie swirled her fingers over the girl's head. "It's magical hair!"

"It is?" The girl's eyes threatened to pop their sockets.

Josie tried to lean down, but too much tulle got in the way. "Absolutely. I can just tell you're going to do magical things. What do you want to be when you grow up?"

"A vedinarian!"

"Perfect. I think that sounds just right. You should go visit the reindeer now." Josie patted her head. "Maybe I'll see you later, sweetie."

"Bye, Princess!" The little girl blew her a sticky kiss as she grabbed her mother's hand.

"Have a happy ho-ho day!" Josie called, then closed her eyes tight. Oh *God*. Had she just *said* that? Without thinking, even? She shook her head as she turned down the pathway. She needed to lose this costume before she started whistling Christmas carols.

Two hours later, she crept up the stairway in the admin house, praying Ethan had left for the night. She'd spent a full hour trying to make her way through the park in the princess costume, but after being accosted by a five-year-old's birthday-party crew, she'd snuck out behind the Snowball Chute and down to the riverbank to wait until the park closed. An hour after *that,* she'd finally dared to head to Elf Central to change out of the costume.

As she got to the top step, she couldn't hear footsteps or voices, so she breathed a sigh of relief. Finally she was alone. She'd grab her clothes, get changed, and get out of the park for the night. Ethan's desk was empty, so she scooped her bag from Dad's office chair and headed to the tiny hallway bathroom to change.

Which turned out to be a plan with only one minor flaw. The bathroom was built with one person in mind, and in the princess dress, she was three times that wide. Try as she could, she couldn't *get* the dress into the bathroom and close the door. If she knew for certain she was going to *stay* alone up here, she'd strip right here in the hallway and put on her own clothes. However, it'd be just her luck to get naked just as a security guard started his rounds, and she'd already flashed her assets at one man too many today.

Fine. She'd use the storeroom at the end of the hall. It was about five by ten feet, if she remembered right. Should be plenty big enough to lose this stupid costume and get her own clothes back on. She headed down the hallway and found the door propped open with its little kicker thingie, so she flipped it upward with her foot, then stepped into the storeroom.

Then screamed.

Chapter 12

"Ethan!" Apparently he *hadn't* left for the night yet. She closed her eyes in frustration. How had she not noticed the storeroom light was on?

Startled, he turned from the shelf, a pile of notepads in his hand. "Don't let the door clo—" He tried to leap for the door, but crashed into her wall of tulle as it clicked shut behind her. "Damn."

"I'm sorry. I didn't know you were in here. I'll go— somewhere else." *Preferably somewhere that doesn't smell like your after-shave. Somewhere less private, so I won't give in to this insane urge to run my fingers over your five o'clock shadow.*

"No you won't." He shook his head as he pointed at the door. "The lock's broken."

Josie looked back in horror. "No way." She rattled the handle, but nothing happened. It was locked fast.

She had seriously pissed off the gods today. First the pond, then the dress, and now she was locked in a storeroom with the only man she—shouldn't be locked in a storeroom with.

"You can't be serious." She jiggled the handle again.

"Dead serious."

"How long's it been broken?"

"Does it matter?"

She sighed. "Let me guess. It's been on Dad's to-do list for about five years."

"Six."

"And no one else has ever gotten trapped in here?"

"No one else has ever gotten trapped in here. Everybody *else* knows you don't close the door."

Josie looked around the small space in vain. With shelves of office supplies on three sides and one buzzing fluorescent fixture for light, it was dim and smelled like ink and copy paper. And Ethan, dammit.

He leaned back against the metal shelves, crossing his arms, as cool and calm as could be. Meanwhile, Josie could already feel her face flaming. "This place needs a window."

He smiled. "Why? So you could MacGyver your way out of it on a rope of Post-it notes?"

"Is there a letter opener or something in here? Can we jigger the lock?"

"You know how?"

She looked down. "No. Not really. Can we call somebody? Who's still here?"

"Nobody. And my phone's on my desk. Didn't imagine I'd need it in the closet. Do you have yours?"

Josie grimaced. "Mine's in my purse. In the office." She swallowed hard, bracing her throat with her hand in a vain attempt to hide her panic. Here she'd been skittering around for days trying to stay away from Ethan, and now she was trapped in a five-by-ten cell with the man . . . only hours after he'd had his hands on her, waking up a million nerve endings she'd forgotten she even had.

She turned toward the shelf on her left, trying to break his gaze. There were six sizes of lined paper pads scattered in vague piles, so she started collecting the smallest ones into a neat stack. "You're just trying to freak me out, right? We're not seriously stuck in here, are we?"

"I don't know. Do you know of a secret passageway behind the toner cartridges?"

"Can we, like, pop out a ceiling tile or something?" After the words were out, she looked up and realized the closet had a Sheetrock ceiling.

He pointed upward. "No tiles."

"Thanks, Captain Obvious."

He smiled. "What's the matter, Josie? Afraid to be trapped in here with me?"

"Nope."

He chuckled. "Right."

"Fine. Maybe. A little."

"What are you afraid *of*?"

"Nothing. I'm not—afraid." She blew out a frustrated breath. "Maybe I'm claustrophobic."

"You're not."

"I could be. You don't know . . . anymore."

He tipped his head. "True. I don't." Then he uncrossed his arms and braced his hands casually on the shelf behind him. "Want to know why *I* think you're afraid?"

"No."

"Yes you do."

Dammit. Her face was flaming and she knew it. She looked at the door again, jiggled the handle again.

"Still locked?"

She growled quietly, her heartbeat whamming double-time in her ears. "You know it is. I can't believe this."

"Tell me—are you more afraid that I'll *want* to talk? Or that I won't?"

"What? I don't know. Jeez, Ethan. Little awkward, don't you think? We've hardly spoken ten words since Friday."

"Whose fault is that?"

She turned toward him. "Yours! You keep putting me on the schedule in these stupid costumes!"

"Ah." He nodded. "But *you're* the one skulking into the office at the crack of dawn, then skipping out before I can catch you."

"I don't skulk. Or skip. I'm just being—efficient."

"Gotcha." He nodded again, taking a small step toward her, pointing at her. "Are you still stuck in that dress because you can't get it off by yourself?"

She looked down and grimaced. Excellent. She hadn't even thought of that.

"I'm—fine. I'm sure I can figure it out."

He laughed quietly. "The only reason that costume was backstage is because no one wears it anymore. They were sick of needing a two-person team to get it on and off."

"This would have been good to remind me of three hours ago when you helped me put it on."

"Maybe." He shrugged, a guilty smile playing at the corners of his mouth. "But what fun would that have been?"

Josie felt her eyes narrow. "Not funny." She turned around, jiggled the stupid handle again, because of course *this* time it'd pop open, right?

"We should yell for help, Ethan."

"No one will hear us." He took another half-step toward her. "Good news, though. If we get that dress off you, it'll make a half-decent bed for the night."

"Omigod, Ethan. We are not sleeping in here." And she would not—would *not*—let her brain remember doing just that . . . on this dress . . . a long time ago.

He shrugged, making her pretty sure his brain was heading toward the same memory. "Sleeping's overrated."

She backed up. "Aren't there tools in here? Can we drill out the lock or something?"

He gave her an amused smile. "Did you learn how to use power tools *before* you caught claustrophobia? Or after?"

"You don't *catch* claus—" She made a frustrated sound. "Never mind."

"Are you sure everyone's gone? Even Ben?"

"He won't be back till morning." He took a small step toward her. "Why so nervous, Josie?"

"Gosh, I don't know. Trapped in a deserted theme park, in a closet with a guy who hates me. No weapons besides a stapler . . ."

"You can do serious damage with a stapler. It's all in the aim."

"Good to know."

He paused, his eyes searching hers. "I don't hate you, Josie."

"That's—hard to believe."

"It's true. I've felt a lot of emotions for you over the years, but hate isn't one of them."

He reached toward her, then pulled his hand back, pointing at his own face. "Your nervous spots are out."

"What do you me—" Her hands flew to her cheeks, where she felt the heat that was probably making them flame right now. "Oh." *Dammit.*

He cracked a smile as he took another half-step toward her. "You still glow."

She backed up, but came smack up against the metal shelving behind her. Ethan's eyes were still on hers, and she did her best to avoid them by looking anywhere but at his face. Unfortunately, all that meant was getting an up-close-and-personal look at the pecs and biceps she'd run her fingers over hundreds of times.

They were currently hidden under a dark blue Snow-flake Village polo shirt, but she had no trouble at all re-membering what they looked like when he tossed a shirt like this over his head, impish grin on his face. No trou-ble remembering what they looked like, wet from the lake, as he bent over her in the back of his truck, their bodies one.

"Can't you, like, kick through the door or something?" She hated how shaky her voice sounded.

"Nope, but be my guest if you want to try." She swore he took another half-step, even though she hadn't seen him move. His after-shave was turning on a whole host of long-dead sensors in her brain.

And everywhere else, dammit.

"Fine." Josie pushed past him to the door. Anything to break the tension simmering between them. "I'll do it."

She turned and shoved as much of her dress behind her as possible, then lifted her knee and gave the door a mighty kick. It didn't budge, but she saw stars and was pretty sure she'd broken twenty-five of the twenty-six bones in her foot.

She sank against the door and slid down to the floor, too late realizing the princess dress would head upward just as fast as she slid downward. She did her best to mash it down around her, but it was a little late to worry about modesty. He'd already seen half of what she had on un-derneath, anyway.

She bit her cheek to stop from swearing as she tried to check her foot for purple bruising, but she couldn't reach it through the endless layers of tulle. "Your turn. Let's see your best cop-breaking-down-door impression."

Ethan shook his head. "Not a cop, sorry. And the hu-man foot isn't really designed to break through a two-inch slab of oak."

"It's oak? No wonder."

He chuckled. "Right. Because pine wouldn't have had a chance against your size sixes."

"It always works in the movies." She walked her hands up the door in back of her, trying to gain some control over the situation. He was taking up way too much room in here. The air was getting thinner, she swore. Her face felt flushed, and her breathing was shallow.

She rattled the doorknob one more useless time. "Is there ventilation in here? Are we going to have enough air?"

Ethan rolled his eyes. "It's not a space capsule. Yes, we'll live till morning." Then he pointed at her dress. She saw him bite his lip, but he failed miserably as a deep chuckle escaped. "I'm sorry. That dress. I just can't get one particular vision out of my mind."

"Shut up."

"That poor timpani."

Josie reached across the tiny space and poked him in the arm. "It was not funny."

He chuckled again, then caught her second poke as her finger came toward him. He didn't let go, challenge in his eyes. "Really? You're going to poke me?"

"Only if you keep laughing." Oh, for cripes sake, what was wrong with her voice? It was all husky and whispery all of a sudden. And what was with the poking? Was she *twelve*?

"If we're going to be stuck in here all night, I imagine we could think of some ways to make the time pass." His thumb edged over her wrist, exquisitely, painfully slowly.

"Stop thinking. You don't even like me anymore, remember?"

"There was a time we would have locked ourselves in here on purpose."

"We were sixteen. It was a long, long time ago."

"Not that long."

"Sixteen only comes around once, Ethan." Josie shook her head, feeling her breaths come faster. "Then we grow up. We tried. We failed. Remember? Aren't you downright scared to be caught in a closet with me after all this time?"

"I'm not scared of you. I've just seen your martial arts skills."

"Those aren't my best skills, you know." As soon as the unintentional double entendre came out, she closed her eyes, wishing she could suck the words back in.

"Oh, I *know* you have other skills, Josie." His eyes traveled over her body, then back to her face. She could swear a path of tiny flames followed.

Josie pulled her hand free, then forced it down to her side as she realized she was rubbing it. She grabbed a section of hair and twisted it nervously. "You're absolutely sure Ben's not still here? He doesn't check in before he leaves?"

"Everyone's gone, Josie." He reached one hand up to brace it on the shelf above her head, the picture of composure and relaxation. "It's just you and me."

"Long time ago," she whispered.

He stepped toward her, slowly pulled her hand away from the curl she was twisting into oblivion. "Not that long."

"Really long."

He shook his head slowly, eyes capturing hers, refusing to let go. His hand came up to her face, slid toward her ear. "Not that long, Josie. Not that long."

"No, Ethan. You're supposed to be toothless . . . and bald." She put a hand up between them, but he captured it in his own and pressed it to his chest. Her voice, barely a whisper, died in her throat.

"I'm neither." He smiled as he stroked her fingers, sending shivery tingles zinging around her entire body.

"Don't do this."

"I can't help it." He leaned in closer, touching his lips to her jaw, just shy of her earlobe. It was all she could do to remain standing.

"Ethan—"

"Shh." He kissed down her neck, still stroking her captured hand. "Stop thinking." Her head lolled back against her will, making him groan.

He lifted his head, still cradling her jaw. "God, Josie."

Josie looked into his eyes. Despite the faint lines, they were the same smoky blue they'd always been, made more intense by his lust. She'd get lost in them once again if she wasn't careful. She'd get lost in all of it if she wasn't careful.

She closed her eyes. But all she wanted to do was feel him, drink him up, melt into his body and transport back ten years when his love was almost enough to buoy her through all of the other hell. He was touching her with the same strong hands that promised heat and strength and ecstasy, all at once.

As much as she wanted to, she couldn't pull away.

He sensed her capitulation and pulled her head closer to his. Then his lips touched hers, soft and warm and sure, and Josie's breath caught in her throat. Tingles flew from her lips down her neck and straight to every nerve ending in her body. Her knees felt wobbly as his fingertips stroked her jaw, then her neck.

She knew she should stop, knew she should pull back, knew she should talk sense into her brain, but God, the kissing! It was so perfect. His lips were so sure, so familiar, so warm and comforting and so damn . . . good.

Just as she was a millisecond away from completely melting into his arms, the closet knob rattled and the door fell open, sending Josie windmilling into the hallway, poofy dress flying upward as she landed on the floor.

The last thing she saw as she grabbed her purse from the office and fled down the stairs was Ben's mouth open in a wide O.

Chapter 13

"Um—" Ben's hand was on the doorknob, head cocked to one side, looking at Ethan with a sly smile.

"Don't ask." Ethan swore under his breath as he strode out into the hallway, looking out the window to see Josie disappearing through the igloo in a cloud of poofed-up princess dress.

Ben rattled the doorknob. "This thing still broken?"

"Apparently."

"You close it on purpose?"

Ethan pushed his fingers into his hair, shaking his head. "How'd you know we were in here? Thought you were gone for the day."

"Saw your cars in the parking lot when I was heading home from the doctor's office. Figgered I'd better take a little tour and make sure you hadn't killed each other." Ben leaned down to put the door wedge back in place, shoulders shaking. "I'll put this on the maintenance list."

"I can see your stupid-ass grin even when you're look-ing the other way, you know."

"I resent that. I don't have a stupid-ass grin." Ben slapped Ethan on the shoulder as they turned to walk back toward the office. "Oh my boy. This is the best thing that's happened around here in a long, long time."

"Shut up, Ben. I can fire you, y'know."

Ben laughed out loud. "Then you'd be doing *three* jobs all by your lonesome." He stopped at Ethan's doorway and ushered him through. "Nah. If it's all the same to you, I'll stay on a while longer. It's just getting fun around here again."

Ethan sank into his desk chair and shook his head, trying to hide a smile. "Get out of here, old man. Go home to your wife."

Ben saluted as he backed into the hallway. "Yes, boss. You have a good night now. Sweet dreams!" He disappeared around the corner one second before a crumpled paper ball would have smacked him in the forehead.

"I want that lock fixed tomorrow!" Ethan called out.

"I'll put it on the list." He heard Ben cackle as he started down the stairs. "But it's an awful, awful long list."

Ethan turned to his monitor, trying to remember what he'd been doing before he'd headed to the storage closet. As he clicked aimlessly on open windows, a chime sounded and a Skype window popped up with his brother's picture in the corner. He sat up straighter and tried to put on his best game-face before he clicked on the connect button.

"Yo, big bro!" David's booming voice came across Ethan's puny computer speakers. It didn't quite match a face that seemed thinner than a month ago when they'd last talked.

"Hey! You're up a little early, aren't you?" It was five A.M. in his barracks overseas. Ethan could see a flurry of activity behind him. "Looks busy back there."

There was a pregnant pause as David looked behind him for a few seconds. "Yeah. One of those days."

"You guys on the move?"

"Looks like."

"How long?"

"Don't know."

Ethan felt his fingers tighten on the mouse. "Fear factor?"

David shrugged, but his mouth was tight. "Sixish, maybe."

"Damn." Ethan tried to swallow the golf ball in his throat. David had never rated anything above a three or four on their ten-point scare scale. "You talk to Pops lately?"

If he had, Ethan would know this mission was serious business.

"Called him last night, yeah."

Dammit.

"He sounded pretty good, though he was convinced Josie was back in town."

Ethan took a deep breath. Yeah, she was back, all right. "Andy had a stroke on Friday."

"No way. He gonna be okay?"

"Not sure yet. It's day by day right now."

"So . . . how's Josie? What's the story there?"

"No story." *Besides me going off my frigging head and kissing her ten minutes ago. If you weren't halfway across the globe, I'd have you smack me upside the head right about now.*

"Right. We'll see how long *that* lasts." A uniform appeared behind David's head, clapping him on the shoulder. He nodded, not breaking his gaze with Ethan. "That's my cue. Gotta roll."

"Be safe, buddy."

"Always. Take care of Pops, got it?"

"Got it." Ethan could see the stress in David's posture as he shifted, could see it in his eyes as he pointed at the screen.

"Take care of you, okay?"

"Shit, Dave. Don't talk like that."

David smirked. "Okay, I'm off to get a massage, then dinner at the club, then a round of eighteen holes. That better?"

"Much. Thanks." Ethan frowned. "Be careful. Don't go all hero out there, okay?"

"Gotcha." David saluted, then pasted a smile on his face as he smacked his lips on his hand and blew a kiss toward the screen. "Love to Josie!"

Ethan sat there for five minutes after the Skype window had closed. Here, the sun was just thinking about sinking over the mountains, but halfway across the world, it was just rising. For his brother, that meant another day of danger, another day of fear, another day of possible bloodshed.

For the thousandth time, he wondered what it would have been like if *he'd* been able to take that Norwich scholarship, to head overseas, to be the family hero like he'd always planned. What would life have looked like if his dreams hadn't been shattered once by a linebacker . . . and again by a runaway fiancée?

Would David be here? Would he be safe?

Would Pops have forgiven Ethan for his career-ending play sometime before the day his *own* doctor's appointment had revised all of their lives once again?

"Well, hey there, Josie! Good to see you back!" Gayle adjusted a bag of fluids hanging by Dad's head as she talked over her shoulder later that evening. "Let me just finish here and I'll get right out of your way."

"Take your time," Josie said as she perched gingerly at the edge of the chair by Dad's bed.

Gayle smiled as she closed her laptop. "All right. I'm done for now. Be back in a bit." She patted Josie's shoulder. "Your mom's down getting some coffee, I think. It's just you and your dad for a bit."

After Gayle left, Josie sat back in her chair and sighed. After she'd fled the park and headed to her parents' house, she'd finally managed to get out of the dress without a crane. Then she'd walked around the familiar rooms feeling completely unmoored.

What was she *thinking*? Getting involved with Ethan again was a one-way ticket to misery. She'd already been on that train, and she knew better.

Not that one kiss was getting involved, necessarily.

She touched her lips, which she swore were still tingling, then pulled her chair a little closer to Dad's bed. His face had more color today, but his skin was still slack, which made him appear way older than he was. It was alarming to see, and Josie found herself wondering how much of it was the stroke, and how much of it was just the aging that had happened since she'd left town.

She watched the steam droplets on his oxygen tube, struck by a memory of the time he'd taken her snorkeling at the lake when she was eight. They'd spent the entire day with the rowboat anchored in Twilight Cove, and she'd inhaled more lake water than oxygen as she'd tried to figure out how to breathe through the snorkel. On the way home, he'd bought aloe for their sunburns and a giant maple creemee for her stomach.

Josie frowned as she looked at his hand, resting on the green hospital blanket beside her. When had everything gone wrong? When had he checked out?

When had the afternoons of snorkeling and hikes up Little Arrowhead and swims in the river stopped? The chicken barbecues? The Disney movies at the drive-in that made the car reek of popcorn and bug spray for a week afterward?

Had it all stopped because Mom had started drinking?

Or had Mom started drinking because it all had stopped?

* * *

"Ethan, honey, you look like you need a Bellini Special."
Mama Bellini greeted him at the bar that same night with
a chilled beer mug foaming with the local pale ale.

"You know me well, Mama B." He slid onto a barstool
and took a grateful swallow, then lifted the mug toward
her. "Thank you."

"Was a hot day out there. Nothing tastes better than a
good cold beer at the end of it."

"Papi would be proud he's finally converted you."

"Damn right!" a voice called from the kitchen. "No
woman of mine's gonna drink that fancy-pants wine."

Mama turned toward the service window where Ethan
could see Molly's dad stirring a bubbling pot. "And you
call yourself an Italian? You're just too cheap to spring
for a glass, Papi! You want I should just drink water,
yeah?"

"Peh. Impossible woman." Papi made a dismissive
motion as he turned to the grill.

Ethan laughed. "You serving alone tonight? Where's
Molly?"

Mama raised her eyebrows up and down. "She's got a
date. Handsome one."

"You don't say." Oh, poor Molly.

"That Italian match web site's pure magic, I tell you.
She's going to need a secretary to handle all the messages
she's getting."

"I'm sure she's just thrilled you signed her up." Ethan
tried to keep the sarcasm out of his voice, but Mama
heard it.

"Well, she wasn't making too many strides finding
her*self* a husband. What's a mother to do?"

"Wait patiently?" Ethan braced for the smack he knew
was coming, and one second later, a dry bar rag hit him
in the ear. Bellinis talked with their hands, after all.

"Don't sass me, mister. I'm not going to live forever, you know. I need to see that girl married off and happy, preferably before I die."

"And preferably to an Italian."

She narrowed her eyes at him playfully. "Have you ever seen the profiles on those other sites?" She shivered dramatically. "Can't trust those men. She needs a good Italian man. Italians are good people."

Ethan decided he'd refrain from any Mafia references until after he had his dinner in hand.

She turned toward the swinging doors and poked one open enough to holler through. "How's that burger coming, Papi? You have to go kill a cow, did you?"

Ethan laughed behind his mug. "I haven't even been here five minutes, Mama."

"So why don't *you* marry my Molly?"

"*What*?" His beer went down the wrong hole, and he coughed a few times to get his breath.

"Well, think about it. How old are the two of you? Time doesn't keep waiting, you know. By the time either of you settle down, you'll be too old to even have babies."

"We're not even thirty, Mama. I think there's still time."

"I don't know. I just don't know." She wiped her rag across the already spotless bar. "I worry about you two. Just want you happy." Another swipe. "But here's good news. A date tonight, right?"

"Right. Good news."

"And here's more good news. Your burger!" A steaming plate slid through the opening to the kitchen, and she set it in front of him. The burger still sizzled, and the hand-cut fries made his stomach growl. "All right. *Mangia taj!* Shut up and eat! You're skin and bones!"

She turned to blast through the swinging doors, and Ethan gratefully focused on the television over the bar, checking out the Red Sox game. Just as he finished his third bite, though, his phone chimed with an incoming call.

He wiped his fingers on his napkin, not looking to see who was calling. "Ethan Miller."

"Hi, Ethan. It's Steph."

"Hey there. Everything okay? Emmy doing all right?"

"Not really, no. We're actually on our way to the hospital."

His stomach twisted as he pushed away his plate. "What happened?"

Steph sniffed delicately. "I'm not sure. She was talking about her head hurting, and then she started vomiting and was so dizzy she couldn't even sit up."

"What did Josh say?"

"Well, you know him. He's like Doctor Calm. He said he thinks it might just be a virus, but he'd feel better if we took her in to have the hospital docs take a look."

"Okay. Are you in your car?"

"I'm following the ambulance." Another sniff. "I'm scared, Ethan. What if it's not a virus? What if it's another tumor? What if it's in her brain this time?"

"Don't let your head go there, Steph. Josh is an excellent doctor. That's why I hired him to oversee Avery's House. I'm sure he just wants to make sure someone's covering all the angles."

"Okay. I'm going to go with that." She sniffed again. "I'll give you a call tomorrow and let you know how she is. I just wanted to let you know where we were in case you came by tonight."

Ethan pulled out his wallet and left some bills on the bar. "I'm on my way right now. I'll meet you at the hospital."

"Seriously?" He could hear the relief in her voice.

"Where else would I be?"

"Well, I imagine you have about a million other places to be."

"Maybe. But Emmy isn't at any of those others. I'll be there in about fifteen minutes."

As he clicked off the phone and headed out the door, he sent a silent prayer upward. Even though it'd been a long, long time since he'd seen the inside of a church, it couldn't hurt.

Chapter 14

"Still here?" Gayle bustled into Dad's room and hung a bag of fluids on the pole by his head.

Josie nodded from her chair. She'd been sitting there for half an hour now trying to work up the courage to talk to Dad, not sure if he could hear her if she did . . . and further unsure of whether she preferred it that way. Unfortunately, no one had enforced the five-minute rule yet and saved her from the decision.

"How are things at the park? You keeping the place running?"

Right. "That job's already well under control. I've been practicing my dress-up skills, though. I'm getting pretty good at handing out candy canes."

"Well, I imagine it's good to be back, whatever you're doing there. My grandkids just love the place." Gayle paused her hands on her little bedside laptop. "Did I say grandkids? I *meant* nieces. Definitely nieces."

"You're clearly not old enough for grandkids, Gayle. I'd have never believed you."

Gayle grinned, pointing her pen at Josie. "Good girl. I knew I was going to like you."

Josie looked at Dad's face while Gayle continued tip-tapping on her computer. He did look better—more human almost. But why hadn't he woken up? The longer he was out, the slimmer the chances of recovery, and she was frightened by all of the possible ways things could go at this point.

She was trying hard to reconcile that worry with the fact that she'd spent the past ten years gratefully *not* worrying about either of her parents.

"Gayle?"

"Hmm?" Gayle tapped, then paused her fingers.

"Why isn't he waking up?" Josie's voice came out in a whisper, and her eyes prickled, to her dismay.

"Well, he had a pretty serious stroke, hon. But he's starting to respond to stimulus, so that's an excellent sign that he's on his way back. Your daddy's strong, he's healthy, he's young. Those things are definitely working in his favor here."

"He does look better today." Josie grasped at the positive.

"He definitely does." Gayle adjusted a few tubes, then came around and patted Josie on the shoulder. "I've got a full floor of patients today, so I can't stay and chat, but I'll be back. Give his hand there a squeeze. Maybe he'll surprise you and squeeze back."

Josie took a deep breath after Gayle left, staring at Dad's slackened face. For ten years now, she'd convinced herself she didn't need him, didn't want him in her life, didn't want her trajectory to follow his. She'd chosen the path of no contact, and it had worked . . . hadn't it? She'd built a life in Boston, had a full patient load in her tiny clinic, had a social life that kept her plenty busy.

So she wasn't lonely, right? Didn't miss this town, this life, these people, right?

She glanced at his hand—the wedding ring dulled by age, the neatly trimmed fingernails, the graying hairs—and remembered darker hair, a shinier ring, a stronger hand gripping hers as she skipped through Camp Ho-Ho every summer morning checking out the rides before the igloo doors opened.

Could she let herself believe that things here had changed? That her parents were truly happy together? That maybe, just maybe, Echo Lake might really be a different place than she'd left behind?

Before she could stop herself, Josie slid her fingers toward Dad's on the bed and she placed her hand cautiously over his.

Maybe.

An hour later, Mom stepped silently into the room, startling Josie. Her eyes locked onto the bed where Josie's hand still held Dad's, but she didn't comment, just smiled. "Hey there. How's he doing?"

"Quiet."

Too quiet, obviously. He needed to wake up, dammit.

All she'd done for the past hour was try to distract herself by thinking about Ethan—about his eyes, his hands, his lips. She kept trying to counteract the confusion by listing the reasons she'd left in the first place, but right now, the hands, eyes, and lips were winning.

Mom laughed a little. "You're the master of the understatement." She put her hand on Josie's shoulder, and in a move natural to another time, another family, Josie put her free hand up to squeeze it.

"You want to go get something to eat, Jos? Are you hungry? I feel like there's probably nothing in the house for you to eat."

"Mom, you could feed a family of twelve with just the yogurt in the fridge."

"If they liked yogurt. There's hardly anything else *in* the fridge."

"That, I have to admit, is true." Josie smiled as she slid her hand away from Dad's and pushed up from her chair.

She motioned toward the door. "Should we see if we can find a seat in the cafeteria?"

Just as they reached the huge doors at the end of the hallway, one of them swished open and a young guy in scrubs pushed a stretcher through. Josie moved to the side to get out of the way, but before it passed, she could swear a knife went through her gut.

Sparks taunted her eyes and her lower body turned to pudding as she glimpsed the small lump on the stretcher. Hidden under stark white sheets and an industrial blanket was an impossibly tiny bald head, and Josie heard her own cavernous voice say "No!" before she heard nothing at all.

"You're back!" Mom's face swam before Josie's eyes. She blinked hard, trying to figure out why she was flat on her back looking up at the tiled ceiling of the hospital hallway. "Honey, you fainted."

"I fainted?" Josie started to push herself up. "I've never fainted in my life."

"Have you eaten anything today?"

"Um . . ."

"That's what I thought." Mom pulled two packages of saltines out of her purse and handed one to Josie. "Here. Nibble on these. I'll go get some ginger ale in a minute."

Josie pushed herself up to sitting, bracing her back against the wall. Mom's eyebrows were drawn together, worry lines etching her forehead as she grasped Josie's elbow lightly.

"I'm so sorry, Mom. I have no idea what happened."

"You're not . . . um . . . by any chance . . . you know, I haven't asked you if you have a boyfriend back in Boston."

Josie choked on her cracker. "Pregnant? God no.

Definitely not. No." *That would indicate actual sex at some point in the previous nine months.*

"Okay." Mom laughed quietly. "Not that you're going to be emphatic about it." She handed Josie the second package of crackers, pausing for a long, painful moment before she spoke again. "Did she . . . did that little girl remind you of Avery?"

Josie swallowed hard. "I think so."

"I imagine it's almost impossible to separate the hospital from her, isn't it?"

Josie felt her own eyebrows drawing together. What was this tender voice? This soft hand rubbing circles on her back? Who *was* this woman? Josie looked up at Mom.

"I'm sorry, sweetie. So, so sorry."

As her mother hugged her shoulders, a memory washed painfully over her.

"Josie!" Eight-year-old Avery bounced in her wheelchair as Josie came through the hospital doors.

"Hey, munchkin! Who let you escape your floor?"

Avery looked behind her at the male nurse holding the chair handles. "Jeff brought me down."

"I like your new hat." Josie tapped on the brim of the baseball cap and tried not to notice there was no espresso-colored ponytail poking out the back anymore. "Did the Red Sox guys come visit after all?"

"The whole team. It was utter chaos." Avery tried her best annoyed look, but dissolved into a proud giggle.

"So I guess this means you're famous now?"

"Nah. But I did get Ethan an autographed ball. Look!" She pulled it out from where it was tucked into the chair.

Josie picked it up and examined it carefully. "He's going to be over the moon for this. You're spoiling him rotten, munchkin. How can I compete?"

"Hmm. Get cancer, lose all your hair, and have the wish fairies bring you a baseball team?"

Josie laughed out loud. "Well, as fun as that idea sounds . . ."

"You're just jealous of my shiny head. Admit it."

"It does have a fabulous glow. And a lovely shape."

"My ears look big."

"Only when you frown like that."

"Wrong. They're even bigger when I smile."

Josie leaned down to hug her. "You have the best smile in the universe, Avery. When you smile, no one's looking at your ears, I promise." She looked up at Jeff, eyebrows raised in silent question. He nodded carefully as he pushed the wheelchair toward her so she could grab the handles and roll Avery out to the curb. "So are you ready to keep me company at Camp Ho-Ho?"

"Your dad wouldn't like it if he heard you call it that."

"That's why I do it." Josie lifted Avery into the passenger seat of Ethan's truck and buckled her in, trying not to think about how much lighter she was than the last time she'd lifted her. "It's a daughter's job to annoy her parents."

"You're seventeen. Shouldn't you be growing out of this phase?"

Josie laughed. "You're eight. Should you really be this smart?"

Twenty minutes later, Josie sat in the waiting room chair, elbows braced on her knees, while Mom went back in to see Dad, since the tiny cafeteria had closed. She couldn't believe she had fainted. She nibbled on one of the crackers Mom had pushed into her hand. When *was* the last time she'd eaten, anyway?

She looked up at the shaded windows and could see shapes bustling around. Who was that little girl in there?

She looked around the room, trying to match her with a family, but the only people in here were the teens from last time and an elderly mother and her daughter.

The poor child had looked just like Avery—her shiny head with its blue veins, her eye sockets too dark, her tiny body too small under the blanket. Josie bit her lip, too late realizing she had started rocking slightly in her chair. Suddenly the waiting room walls seemed to be caving in on her.

It felt childish to wish for shiny red shoes she could clack together and be back in her cozy apartment with her calm, predictable job and a date every few months . . . or six. Dammit, this place was cursed. Everywhere she turned was another heartbreak from the past. If Ethan wasn't looming over her, piercing her with his smoky eyes and taunting her with his bronzed skin and the aftershave she still loved, then Avery was poking her sweet little head into Josie's psyche at random moments.

She took a deep breath, trying to slow down her jiggling legs. But it was no use. She had to get out of here. She scrawled a note for Mom and took off at a fast walk down the hallway. As the elevator descended, Josie practiced the kind of breathing she taught her patients. Her heart was racing, which made the elevator seem interminably slower than it really was.

She just needed to get out of the hospital, find her Jeep, and drive. She didn't even know where she'd go. Visions of Avery kept flashing through her mind like a photo album on high speed, and as much as she wanted to, she couldn't shut it down.

Finally the automated voice said *First floor* and the elevator bumped slightly as it landed. Josie stumbled through the sliding front doors and did everything in her power not to run to her Jeep.

Maybe her parents had mended their ways, but nothing else had changed here. At least not for the better.

Echo Lake was still poison.

Ethan was still poison.

And Avery? She stifled a sob.

Avery was still . . . dead.

Chapter 15

"You'll have to talk quickly. I'm packing." Josie pulled open one of her bureau drawers as she answered Kirsten's call an hour later.

"Where are you going?"

"Boston. Home."

"What happened?"

"Nothing! Everything! I don't know!" Josie winced at the frazzled sound of her voice.

"I see."

Silence followed Kirsten's words, and Josie tried to wait her out, but failed. "Oh, stop using that therapist-silence technique on me. I know how it works."

"Why are you packing, Jos? What happened?"

"Everything! Everything's happening! Dad, Mom, Ethan. I tried, Kirsten. I came back here. I did the hospital, I did the park, I—"

"Did Ethan?"

"*What*?" Josie sputtered. "Oh my God. I'm being serious here!"

"Me, too. Did you?"

"No!"

"Did you *want to*?"

Josie looked in the mirror over her bureau, surprised at the dark pink spots of color on her cheeks, the redness of her throat and chest. Dammit, look at her. It was hopeless. If she stayed here, she'd certainly fall back under Ethan's spell, and she'd only get her heart broken.

Yes, he'd kissed her, and oh God, it had been as good as ever—better, even—but it could never work. They had separate lives. His was firmly hitched to Camp Ho-Ho's wagon, and hers never would be again. Ever. She knew the end play on that game already.

"No. Yes. No. Of course I do! It's Ethan! But it would never work. No more than it would have ten years ago."

"How can you know that for sure? You haven't been home in a long time."

"No. The situation's pretty clear. And it's no good. He has willingly signed up for my father's life. He lives and breathes this stupid park, and I've seen how that story ends. This place eats people alive. There's no room for relationships when you've got a Christmas paradise to maintain three hundred and sixty-five days a year."

No. She couldn't even fathom staying here, no matter how hot the air got when they were in the same room. No matter how looking at his sculpted body made her ache to be swatting mosquitoes in the back of a beat-up Chevy truck out by the lake. No matter how feeling his lips on her skin made her want to strip off every bit of clothing she owned and submit to his mouth and hands and . . .

She turned away from the mirror, swearing. She had to go. Now.

"How are you going to feel being that far away from your parents?"

"I've been that far away for ten years now, and it was working just fine."

"You know what I mean."

"I know. I'll only be three hours away. Dad's—stable. Mom can call if anything changes. I'll visit on weekends.

I just have to get out of here." Josie hated herself for even having these thoughts, given that in reality, Dad was far from stable. She pulled the knobs on the Venetian doors of the closet and reached up to pull her suitcase down.

Before she got it to the edge of the shelf, a big shoebox peeked over the edge of it, sliding toward her at a dangerous angle. She grabbed at the box before it could clonk her on the nose, juggling the phone clumsily.

"Josie? Jos? Hey!" Kirsten's voice squawked. "Are you okay?"

Josie fumbled the phone toward her ear as she set the Nike box on her bed. "Sorry! Almost dropped you. You are never going to believe what my mother did."

"Do tell."

"I have a feeling she knew I might try to pull a runner in the night."

"What'd she do? Lock you in your bedroom?" Kirsten laughed, but cautiously.

With her index finger, Josie traced the letters she'd taped on the box lid oh so long ago. "Worse. She put my old shoebox of Ethan's stuff on top of my suitcase."

"Wow." Molly leaned over the Bellinis counter and put her index finger under Ethan's chin. "It's ten o'clock. You look like hell, Ethan."

"Thanks. You're sweet." Ethan hauled himself onto a barstool to wait for his to-go order. He'd only managed three bites of his earlier dinner before Steph had called, and his stomach had been growling for two hours now.

"You want a drink while you wait?"

"Better not, or I'll fall asleep on your bar."

"Wouldn't be the first time." She raised her eyebrows as she poured him a Coke. "How's Emmy?"

"Josh's pretty sure it's just viral, but the poor little thing doesn't have anything extra to fight with."

"I called in extra bodies tonight to disinfect all of the common areas."

"Got masks on everyone?"

"Yup. I don't know where you found those crazy things. The purple leopard-print ones went the fastest."

"I knew the kids would love those."

Molly laughed. "Actually, the moms picked those."

"Thanks for taking care of things over there. As always."

"Well, it's my job, right?" Her smile was forced. "Always the dependable one." She pushed through the kitchen door a little harder than necessary, but he still heard the words she muttered under her breath. "The one who *didn't* leave."

Before he could decide whether to admit he'd heard her, she strode back through the swinging doors with his to-go bag. "So how's Princess Josie today?"

Soft. Sweet. Hot. "Fine." He cleared his throat unintentionally, and Molly's eyes narrowed.

"What *kind* of *fine*?"

"How many kinds of fine are there?"

Shit.

Molly paused dramatically while pretending to scrub a spot on the bar with her rag. "Don't do it, Ethan. Do *not* let her back in."

"G'nite, Mols." He grabbed the bag. "And g'nite, Mama B! Thanks for the tiramisu!" He knew Mama was hovering just inside the kitchen door, as curious for news about Josie as Molly was.

"Oh! Ethan!" Mama walked through the door like she'd been coming out anyway. *Right.* "You're still here. I put in an extra slice for your dad. On the house."

"Thanks, Mama. I'll see you two ladies tomorrow." Ethan gave a quick wave and strode out the door before either of them could fire another question his way.

As he pulled his truck door closed and put the key in the ignition, he swore silently. Molly's caution was well intentioned, he knew. She'd seen him through the months after Josie's departure, had watched him nurse more than one ginormous hangover in those early weeks, had pushed him to start living again once it became clear Josie wasn't coming back. He knew he owed her big for that.

But it really didn't matter, because he'd gone all cave man on Josie just hours ago, and there's no way she'd risk that happening again. No, she was probably well on her way back to Boston right now, so Molly could relax. No warnings needed. Josie was definitely already gone.

And he'd be damned if he could figure out how he felt about that.

Josie repositioned her pillows so she could sit comfortably against the headboard, still holding the box after she said good-bye to Kirsten. Did she really dare open it? After what had transpired earlier this evening, was it remotely wise to crack open a supersaturated container of sweetness?

Before she could talk herself out of it, she flipped off the lid and laid it on the bed. As soon as she did, a faint scent tripped her right to senior prom and special dates and nights at the lake.

And this afternoon, dammit.

Ethan's after-shave. She plucked out five little sample packets she'd scored at a Burlington mall makeup counter long ago. She couldn't believe they still held any of their scent, but as she waved one under her nose, she was eighteen again.

Of course, it had been only hours ago that she'd smelled that same after-shave, heated by Ethan's skin, desperately close to her own body. She laid the packets down and looked into the box again. On top was a pile of cards held together in a rubber band. She smiled as she remembered opening her mailbox to find the colorful envelopes.

One of the things she'd so loved about Ethan back then was his old-fashioned romanticism. He always opened doors for her, pulled out her chair when they ate at a nice restaurant, and sometimes—to her amusement at the time—sent her real letters.

Though she'd also loved his sexy e-mails and texts, there was nothing like holding a letter to her chest when the walls were crashing in around her. Nothing like putting it to her nose and letting his scent cleanse the other ones assaulting her. Nothing like running her fingertips over his words, smiling at his stick-figure drawings when there was nothing else to smile about.

Josie opened the first card and lifted it to her nose, hardly believing she was doing so. But among the sweetly sexy words, the tiniest bit of Ethan's scent remained. Or was it just her imagination? She opened each card in the pile, remembered sitting on this same bed reading them until the edges were worn.

As she read, her resolve to be on the road at first light started slipping dangerously away. With each letter, each card, her heart sped up. She put her hand to her mouth as she read words she'd seen a hundred times, words that had buoyed her through hell. Words that were so painfully beautiful, so innocent and pure, so damn sexy.

God, he'd loved her. She'd known that, right?

Under the cards was a pile of pictures she'd printed long ago. She flipped through them—she and Ethan at Homecoming, she and Ethan at Halloween, at Christmas, at New Year's, at Valentine's Day, at Spring Fling, at prom. It was like a calendar of her senior year chronicled in snapshots.

In each and every one of them, Ethan was touching

her. Sometimes his arm was slung over her shoulder, sometimes they were holding hands, sometimes he stood behind her, arms clasped around her with his chin on her shoulder and an impish grin on his face.

At the bottom of the pile was her favorite picture of the two of them. Ethan's brother David had offered to take engagement pictures for them because he was trying out a new camera, so they'd headed out to the lake to get some shots. They'd posed for what seemed like hours, until the sun went down, and a week later when David had brought a pile of prints for Josie to look over, he'd saved one till last.

In the picture, Josie and Ethan perched on a low branch facing the lake. They'd thought David was done taking his pictures, so they were relaxed, just watching the sun set over the water. In the shot, Josie was looking toward the water, but Ethan wasn't. He'd leaned back against the tree trunk and was gazing straight at Josie, his hand reaching for a wisp of her hair glistening in the shadowed sunset.

Josie felt a tear roll off the tip of her nose as she looked at the picture. She could almost feel the tree branch beneath her, hear the gentle lapping of the waves near their feet, smell the flowers that grew near the shore of the cove. When the ceiling fan above her lifted a strand of hair, she could almost swear she could feel Ethan's fingers touching her.

As she pulled a dried corsage from the box, she remembered dancing with him at prom, out on a party boat on the glistening lake. The moon had been full, the night breezy and warm.

"You look like a mermaid in this dress, Jos. It matches your eyes." Tucked against the wheelhouse up on deck, they kissed as Ethan's hands slid over the fabric, sending shivers up and down her body.

"Maybe that's why I picked it. You know what they say about mermaids."

"That they lure men to danger, only to dispose of them?"

"That's a little harsh."

He pulled her against his body, hands moving lower as he kissed her neck. *"You've got the luring part covered. No doubt about that."*

"You're not worried about the disposing part?" She smiled against his lips.

He found the bottom edge of her dress and slid his hands under it and slowly up her thighs, making her gasp in the moonlight as she pressed closer to his body.

"I'm not worried, mermaid-girl. I think you'll be with me forever."

Two hours later, her cell phone blipped on the nightstand, startling her as she paged through her senior yearbook. She picked it up to see the readout. *Mom.* She glanced at the bedside clock, which read midnight. Oh no.

"Mom? What's wrong?"

Mom paused on the other end. "Nothing, actually. I . . . I don't know what came over me. I didn't realize how late it was. I'm just leaving the hospital. Thought I'd let you know."

"Um, okay. You sure you're all right?"

"Yes. Yes, I am."

"You sound kind of weird." Josie's internal alarm bells started ringing. "Are you sure you should drive? Have you . . . had something to drink?"

"No, honey, I haven't had anything to drink in a really long time. I'm just emotional, that's all. I was sitting there alone in the waiting room, and I suddenly realized I . . . well . . . maybe I'm not actually alone. You were at home, and I could call you. So I did." She paused again. "I'm sorry. That sounds stupid. And you were probably getting ready to sleep. I'm sorry."

Josie felt the twinge of tears at the backs of her eyes. Dammit. "It's not stupid, Mom. I wasn't asleep." She traced the lines on her quilt. "Drive safely, okay? I'll have some tea ready when you get here, if you want."

"That would be just . . . perfect. I'll see you in a few minutes." Josie could hear Mom's smile.

She took a deep, shaky breath. Hours ago, she'd been convinced her only pathway was straight back to Boston. As much as she wanted to resist falling under Ethan's spell again, she'd only lasted five days before melting into his body, and that was going to get them nowhere but Heartbreak Village. Again. How could she keep her heart steeled if she stayed here any longer?

But what about Mom? How could she leave, when things were still so touch-and-go with Dad? Again, it'd only been five days, but Mom was . . . different. Real.

Sober.

And as much as she'd learned long ago not to trust that Mom would stay that way, a growing part of her wanted desperately to believe that maybe this time, maybe now, Mom wasn't going to crack the Stoli and disappear into her own hellish nightmare again.

Maybe, just maybe, they could get to know each other again.

She looked around the bed, strewn with mementos of her teenage romance, and slowly gathered each card and letter and dried flower. She put them each carefully in the box, then replaced the lid. She tried repeating a mantra of that-was-then-this-is-now, but it died on her lips.

She'd spent ten years convincing herself that she didn't belong here anymore, that her life was destined for greater things. That the people here were people she didn't need in her life.

But what if she'd been wrong?

What if they really *had* changed? What if—*God*—what if she'd been wrong to leave? What if Dad didn't make it through this, and she never got the chance to say the things she should have said long ago? Were she and Mom being given a second chance at a relationship? Did she want to erase that chance by running away?

Again?

No. She took a deep breath, blowing it out slowly as her pulse rattled in her ears. She couldn't leave right now. She had to stay, had to figure out what Echo Lake really was now. Had to be here at least until Dad was out of the woods. If he *came* out of the woods. The thought gave her shivers.

Before she could talk herself out of it, she clicked into her e-mail and tapped Kirsten's address, since it was too late to call her back. She took a deep breath before she started typing, knowing as soon as she clicked SEND, she'd have sealed at least the next few weeks of her fate.

She paused again. Good God, what was she thinking? Could she truly do it? Could she really say she was going to stay here for the next couple of weeks? Could she handle being that close to Ethan and not succumbing to rose-colored glasses about their past?

No.

But she had to.

She needed to. So she'd go back to Camp Freakin' Ho-Ho tomorrow. But she'd be damned if she was going to put on a costume and spend one more day avoiding Ethan. She was going to sit in Dad's chair and ask Ethan to give her something to do that would actually help keep the park running.

This time, she wasn't going to run.

Chapter 16

Ethan punched the calculator buttons with his middle finger the next morning. For God's sake, there were only ten receipts. How had he come up with three different totals already? He sighed and flipped the bills over, then laid his head back on the office chair. It was three hours before the park opened, so the office was deserted. Even with the window wide open, the only sounds he heard were the birds in the trees. So why couldn't he concentrate?

He glanced at the Skype window on his computer, knowing it'd be silent today. His little brother was all the way on the other side of the world doing God knows what while he sat here in his office chair.

David had turned down scholarships to Oberlin and Berklee College of Music in order to head to Norwich on an ROTC scholarship, following the footsteps laid down by Pops. He was a kick-ass drummer with a 4.0, but their years of shooting cans off the fence out back had apparently turned him into a kick-ass sniper as well.

David had never admitted he'd rather have gone the Berklee route, but Ethan always wondered if he'd be happier touring with a band or teaching music to little kids instead of risking his head and legs every day overseas. However, once Ethan had screwed up his knee in the play that'd made the ESPN high-school-hits-of-the-week show, David's path had been pretty much prescribed by Pops.

One son of his had to make the family proud, after all. And since service to Uncle Sam was the only path to that, David had packed away his drumsticks and headed to boot camp instead of a freshman dorm.

Ethan was torn between feeling guilty that his little brother had been practically forced into service . . . and jealous that Pops always met strangers with the words *My son's in the Marines.*

He checked his watch and punched the number to the critical-care floor at Mercy, getting a momentary jolt of panic when the receptionist told him Emmy was no longer with them. Then the phone was fumbled and Emmy's nurse came on.

"I am so sorry. She's subbing from orthopedics and doesn't realize what phrases like that can sound like up here. Emmy has been moved to the pediatric floor. She's up and jabbering this morning, eating up all of their lime Popsicles."

Ethan sat back in his chair and blew out a relieved breath. "So she's okay."

"Well, you and I both know that *okay* is a strong word to use right now, but she's stronger than she looks. She's fighting off a nasty bug, but it looks like this time she's winning."

"Any idea when she'll get to come back here?"

"I imagine they'll keep her for a day or so and make sure she's eating and truly on the mend. Do you want me to transfer you down there?"

"That's okay. I'll get in touch with them later. Thanks."

"She just loves that house of yours, Ethan."

"I'm glad." He craned his neck out the window, looking up the hill toward Avery's House, but it was hidden among the firs.

"Keep up the good work. I hope I won't talk to you again soon."

Ethan laughed. "I hope that's true." He hung up the phone and rubbed his eyes with the heels of his hands. Between David and Emmy and, dammit, Josie, he'd hardly slept last night.

In his heart, he knew she wouldn't be back. He couldn't believe he'd completely lost control and kissed her last night. What was wrong with him? He was old enough to know better, old enough to resist her. But the sight of her in that dress, the smell of her shampoo, the heat of her body as her cheeks practically glowed, had made him lose all sense of reason. And all he'd wanted to do was touch her, kiss her, see if she still felt as good as she always had.

He sent his hand through his hair, realizing as it stood on end that he badly needed a haircut. Like he had time to get one. He patted the hair back down as best he could, then sat back up and flipped the receipts over, forcing his attention back to them. It was beginning to look like Andy wasn't coming back anytime soon, so he needed to figure out how to run Snowflake Village without him. Starting today, starting now.

And that meant he needed to put Josie out of his brain. He needed to stop analyzing every look she'd given him, every little catchy breath she'd taken as he'd stepped closer. He needed to stop thinking about how her hair still glowed golden at the ends and how her eyelashes were still impossibly long, but not long enough to cover the green eyes that matched that damn mermaid dress she'd worn at prom.

Most of all, he needed to stop thinking about how damn kissable she looked in that stupid, ridiculous, puffed-up excuse for a princess costume, and how all he could think of when he looked at her was the night they'd

discarded that same dress on the riverbank, then made
love on top of it after skinny-dipping in the river.

No, those thoughts definitely had no place here or now.
But he hadn't been able to look at her and *not* think of
what had been . . . what could have been.

Because although he could transport himself back ten
years just by touching the curve of her jaw, the facts remained. He still couldn't give her the kind of life she
wanted, and he needed to keep that front and center in
his mind. She'd never wanted to spend her life trapped
here in Echo Lake, and even if he'd wanted to pull up
stakes and try to follow her elsewhere, he couldn't now.

Dad needed him, and Ethan'd go to his own grave before he'd move him out of his house or—God forbid—
put him in a nursing home. And though Molly and Josh
were a stellar team at Avery's House, it was still *his*
house, *his* project, *his* way of keeping Avery close to his
heart. There was no way he could leave that behind.

"Good morning, Ethan." As if he'd summoned her,
Josie's voice bounced through the doorway. She stepped
into the office looking all fresh and perky, dressed in
dark blue jeans and a red Snowflake Village polo she
must have dug out of a drawer at her mother's house.

How had he not heard her coming up the stairs? He
glanced at her feet, snugged up in sneakers today instead
of her ridiculous heels. No wonder.

"What are you doing here?" He knew his voice sounded
gruff, but for Christ's sake, he'd thought she was halfway
to Boston right now. "And why in God's name do you
have a *plant*?"

Josie placed the green ferny thing near Andy's computer, then pulled a picture frame out of her purse and
put it next to the terra-cotta pot. "It's dreary in here.
Thought I'd spruce things up a little." She hung her purse
on the back of the door and turned toward him with a

handled shopping bag on her arm. "It's gonna be another scorcher today."

She hummed as she pulled out a bright yellow happy-face cup and dumped a handful of colorful pens in it, then pulled out a teal-green mouse to replace the standard-issue black one on Andy's desk. She hung a bright pink sweater on the back of the chair, then tucked the bag under the desk and sat down.

"There. That's better."

"Josie, what the hell are you doing?"

"I'm trying to counteract the overabundance of . . . beige . . . in this office."

"Beige is a perfectly good color. We happen to like it."

"I'm sure you do, but since one half of your *we* isn't here right now, I'm taking his vote." She fiddled around with the mouse for a moment, looking adorably awkward as her bravado faded.

He shut his eyes. *Adorably* should not be part of his vocabulary right now.

She looked up. "So . . . I was thinking."

"Should I be scared?"

"No. Maybe? I don't know anymore." She looked out the window, up at the ceiling, anywhere but at his eyes, it seemed. "I, um, I sent my partner Kirsten a note last night. To let her know I'm going to take a two-week leave. And stay up here. To be with my parents. And help. Here."

Ethan raised his eyebrows. Was this the cool, calm, collected Josie? Stuttering out sentence fragments like awkward Nerf darts?

"And if it's all right with you, I think I'd like to be done with the costume gig. I'd like to be helpful in the office for the rest of my time here." She paused. "If that would be all right."

He shook his head to clear it. What in the *world*? "One kiss . . . and you're moving in a *plant*?"

"Actually, I think it's *despite* the kiss that I'm moving in a plant. Temporarily." She clicked her little happy-mouse a couple of times, then looked over the monitor at him, the nervous spots on her cheeks growing. "Listen. I know we'd both rather I was back in Boston right now. We'd both rather I had never come back. But I did, and I'm here, and until Dad's better, I can't bring myself to leave."

She clicked her mouse again, and Ethan peered at her eyes. Were those tears? "I can't pretend to have a clue how this will work, Ethan. And I'm sorry this situation ends up putting me right in your lap. Figuratively. But I need to stay. And I need to help."

She paused and looked up. "But there will be no more kissing."

Ethan swore under his breath. Here he'd thought she was on her way back to the city, was *glad* about it, and now? Now she was sitting a mere five feet from him and pretty much refusing to leave. What the hell was he supposed to do with that?

There was no way he could work with her, no way he could catch the scent of her before she entered a room, no way he could have her a desk-length away and not want her, not want things to go back to the way they'd been ten years ago. This would be utter, sheer hell.

He cleared his throat. "Josie. Seriously. We're fine here. I appreciate your willingness to help. Really do. But I don't honestly see how it could work. We—you and me as coworkers—it isn't going to happen. We're not going to be able to share an office and pretend to be friends. Not with how things were . . . or how they were left."

She opened Andy's bottom desk drawer and found a ball cap she must have remembered he kept in there, and she slid it onto her head, pulling her long curls through the opening in the back. It looked good on her, dammit.

So did the curls. He liked them a lot better than the ironed-out look she'd arrived here with.

With the cap on and ponytail sticking out the back, she looked closer to sixteen than the twenty-eight she actually was. "We don't have to pretend we're friends, if that helps. We can barely talk to each other if that's easier. If we're lucky, I'll be out of your hair in just a couple of weeks."

Ethan sighed. She wasn't kidding. She was staying. She'd brought a frigging plant, for God's sake. And she was sitting there with her arms crossed, daring him to be the bad guy and send her packing.

And seriously, a *no more kissing* rule? No worries there. He already regretted the first one. No good would *ever* come of kissing Josie Kendrew again. He hadn't been enough for her the first time around. He'd be damned if he'd let her make him feel that way ever again.

"So can I stay? Can I work in here? Please?"

He sighed. *No.* But another part of him couldn't refuse her. Still. After all this time.

He closed his eyes, shaking his head at the words that were about to come out of his mouth. "Two weeks? That's it?"

"Cross my heart." She made an *X* on her chest.

"Please don't make me regret this." Ethan opened his top drawer and pulled out a manila folder, then handed it over his computer. Fine. He'd let her try to tackle the crap he didn't have time for. First on the list, wheedling Old Man Lang for a part he'd been promising for two weeks.

"So what's the story here?" She took the folder.

"We need a part, and Lang's the only supplier in the area who can help us. The Twinkle Fairy ride's been down for two weeks while we're waiting on him, but he doesn't seem to be in any hurry to get it here."

"Ooh. Twinkle Fairy down. Critical problem." Josie adopted a firm expression, but he could see the corners of her mouth trying to sneak upward. "I'm on it, Captain." He watched her pick up the desk phone and tap in numbers, then sit back in her chair and twist her hair with her left hand. "Mr. Lang? Yes, it's Josie! Right! From Snowflake . . . Good! How are you? . . . Excellent! So listen. I think our poor Twinkle Fairy's out of commission, and I know you are just the guy to help us out . . . I know! It sure was my favorite! How did you remember? . . . Oh, you don't say . . ."

Ethan tried to block out her voice by concentrating on the spreadsheet on his screen. If she acted any sweeter, the woman would turn into maple syrup. Finally she hung up, looking at the phone almost affectionately, but also like she was a little surprised.

"So what's the story? He tell you he'll have it here as soon as he can? Which might or might not be a week from now? Or two?"

Josie closed the folder, erasing the surprised expression. "He's on his way over. Mary just baked a batch of her famous oatmeal cookies, so he's bringing us some."

Ethan sat back. Apparently he'd been lacking the right chromosome to deal with Lang. "Mary's cookies are deadly."

"Totally. But you *will* eat one."

"Oh, no I won't. Last time I tried one, I had heartburn for a week. I think she put chili powder in them that time."

"Mom and I had a long talk about the Langs last night. You will eat a cookie."

"Can't make me."

"You want Mr. Lang's parts after I leave here?" She raised her eyebrows.

"He has to know how awful they are."

"Of course he does."

"Then why does he torture others?"

"He's not torturing anyone. His wife is losing her mind, Ethan. She's been baking these cookies her entire life, and everyone has always loved them. Remember when we used to have school bake sales? Or the July Fourth auction? Her cookies were always the first to go, and got the highest bids.

"Mom said she doesn't have that recipe written down anywhere, but she's still baking them, trying to remember as she goes. She has no idea they're terrible. And if we eat them and pretend they're the same as they always were, then we give Mr. Lang a gift. For that moment, while we choke down *one* flipping cookie, his world seems normal."

She paused, drilling Ethan with her eyes. "So you think you can do that? One cookie?"

Ethan stilled his hand on the mouse. She had no idea how hard that had just hit, in all the wrong places.

"Y'know what? I think maybe we'd both be better off if you did the elf thing today."

Chapter 17

Eight hours later, Josie pushed away from her desk and rubbed her eyes with the heels of her hands. It was five o'clock, and she'd been staring at the screen all day, doing one mundane task after another. Ethan had scrammed as soon as he'd handed her a giant pile of manila folders, and he'd somehow managed to steer clear of the office for the entire day.

His phone hadn't even rung, which meant he'd forwarded it to his cell before he'd fled the office this morning. Clearly he'd had no intention of spending even one minute with her.

Sighing, she tied her hair into a loose knot with a rubber band she found in the desk. It was bleeping hot again, even in the air-conditioned office. The snack cottages had radioed in for extra ice by ten o'clock this morning, and again at three.

There was no way they had enough ice on hand to make it through another day this hot, so she figured they'd better call Ike and order an extra delivery for the morning. Since Ethan was AWOL, *they* meant *she*. He'd thank her.

Her fingers punched the numbers, still knowing them by heart, but when Ike answered, she took a quick breath, suddenly unsure of herself among old friends who had become strangers.

"Ike. Hi, it's Josie. Josie Kendrew."

"Well, well, well. How's the city girl?" Ike's booming voice hadn't changed in ten years. She could hear his gap-toothed smile right through the wire.

"Good! I'm just helping out here at the park for a little bit, and it looks like we had quite a run on ice today. Wondering if you might be able to send us a load in the morning?"

"Really?"

"Really. We went through tons of it today."

"Ethan tell you to call?"

Her cheeks burned. With that one simple question, Ike had pointed out just how much of an outsider she was now. She'd ordered ice on a weekly basis way back when, and nobody had ever asked whether she'd gotten permission to do so.

She took a breath, cringing. "Yes," she lied.

"You have someone who can help me unload it?"

Oh. Right. Ike didn't come with an assistant. Fine. She could help. How hard could it be?

"I'll help, Ike. What time can you be here?"

"Well, garage opens at seven, and I got a big engine rebuild I gotta do in the morning. How's six o'clock sound?"

"A.M.?" She winced.

Ike chuckled. "Family businesses got different hours from city-girl businesses, honey."

"Six it is. I'll bring the coffee." Josie squeezed her eyes shut as she hung up the desk phone.

"I'll take cream and sugar with mine." Ethan's voice made her jump.

"I'm not fixing your coffee." She shuffled papers into alignment, then pushed them to a different spot on the desk. Dammit. She'd been hoping to disappear before he got back to the office. Two could play this game.

"Who were you talking to?" Ethan walked past her and sat down at his desk, leaning back with his hands casually behind his head.

"Ike. He'll be here at six tomorrow morning with a load of ice."

"Really?" Ethan stayed relaxed, but the corners of his mouth were twitching. "And *you're* going to unload it?"

"Unless you want to."

"It's all yours." He shook his head. "And if it wouldn't be too much trouble, I'm down an elf tomorrow. Remember how to walk in curly shoes?"

"You don't need another elf." *You just want me out of your office.*

"Not true."

"We have plenty of elves. Speaking of which, there's one who has to be pushing a hundred and twenty. Why is Dad still making her do the elf thing?"

"That'd be Ruthie, and your dad's not making her do anything. She loves her job. Says it keeps her young."

Josie shook her head. "It's too hot out there for someone her age."

"She'll stop when she's ready. She likes it, and the kids love her." He leaned back in his chair, arms returning to their spot behind his head. "So how'd it feel to be back in the office today?"

"Cooler than walking around as Sno-Cone Sally." Josie straightened the papers on Dad's desk, then lined them up again. "It was fine." *But only because you weren't in here tormenting me with that after-shave . . . and those eyes.*

"Anything else I need to know before you go? Arrange for any other deliveries without my—"

"Permission? I was only trying to help, Ethan."

"I was going to say *advice*. But that's fine." He rocked

the front legs of his chair back down. "Have fun with that ice delivery in the morning."

Really? That was it? He was going to just sail in here, put her in her proverbial place, and dismiss her? Like he hadn't kissed her silly twenty-four hours ago?

Yes, she was the one who'd spouted the *No kissing* rule this morning, but dammit, he didn't even look like he cared. He'd avoided her all day, and now he was just itching for her to get out of the office. She gathered her purse, fumbling with the straps as she headed for the door.

Fine. Tomorrow she'd show him all of the stuff she'd done today. Tomorrow she'd play it as cool as him. Tomorrow she'd try not to give a damn if he disappeared for the whole flipping day.

She squared her shoulders. "Good night, Ethan."

He gave an absent wave. "Night, Josie."

Five minutes later, Josie sat in her Jeep, half relieved to be out of Ethan's orbit, half annoyed that she'd felt the need to escape. Her stomach growled and she realized she had forgotten to eat lunch earlier. And maybe breakfast. She needed to find some real food before she headed to the hospital, and Mom's selection of yogurt wasn't going to do the trick.

She plugged the key into the ignition and turned it, but all she heard was a click. Tried again, and *click*.

She dropped her forehead onto the steering wheel, swearing silently. The mechanic at the garage in Boston had warned her five thousand miles ago that her ignition was going, but she so seldom drove the Jeep that she'd kind of forgotten about it.

She turned the key back to the left and counted to twenty, then twisted it again.

Click.

There was only one other vehicle in the parking lot—a dark green truck that had to be Ethan's. Mom was at the hospital, Ben was . . . who knows where, and Josie felt a growing pain in her stomach that had nothing to do with hunger.

She was alone. Really alone. There was no one she could call for help in this town.

"You forget how to get home?" Ethan's voice made her jump. She turned toward him, hating the way her insides went all quivery at the sound of his voice. His eyes were crinkling in amusement as he gave her a quick once-over. "You okay?"

"My car won't start."

"Need a jump?"

Good God, why did everything the man said sound like a sexual innuendo?

Did it, actually? Or was she just superimposing innuendo on his perfectly innocent question?

"No. The battery's fine. Something's wrong with the ignition switch. I'll just call Ike." Right. Ike! He'd help her, wouldn't he?

"He won't answer after five."

Josie wracked her brain. Ike was the only mechanic she knew. "Is there any *other* garage in town that might be open?"

"Nope. Sorry."

Josie blew out a frustrated breath. Ten years later, the entire flipping town still shut down at sunset. She was stuck, and Ethan knew it.

And, by all observations, was kind of enjoying it.

"I hate to ask, but is there any chance you could give me a ride out to my parents' house? Or maybe over to the hospital?" She pointed up the mountain. "I probably shouldn't sleep here. The bears are starting to fatten up for winter."

"It's August."

"We could have some early planners." She waved

vaguely at the open sides of her Jeep. "And I have no doors."

Ethan shook his head, looking around the empty parking lot. "Have you eaten today?"

"Not really."

"Are you hungry?"

Starving. "I could eat."

"I was going to stop at Bellinis for a burger. Want to join me?"

Josie's mouth watered at the thought of Mama B's burgers, but this was obviously a pity invite.

"You know, I'm actually fine. I'll call Mom and see if she can come get me."

Ethan shook his head. "Are you that afraid to see Molly?"

"No. Don't be ridiculous. This isn't about—Molly."

Right.

"Does she still work with her parents at Bellinis?" She tried to keep the question light and breezy.

"Among . . . other things, yep. Still here."

"And you don't think it'd be awkward to show up there tonight? With me?"

"Not for me. I've got the sympathy vote, remember? You're the one who left."

He was right, of course. As far as anyone in town knew, he was the innocent groom dumped practically at the altar. It was she who'd need to brace for flying tomatoes if she walked into Echo Lake's busiest pub.

"So what'll it be?" He started to turn toward his truck. "Is a Bellini burger worth the pain of being with me for an hour?"

"It's not painful—" She growled internally. It was *totally* painful. Just not in the way he meant. But she was sort of out of options here. It wouldn't be fair to drag Mom away from the hospital.

She grabbed her purse and slid out of the Jeep, following him across the parking lot. "If you're sure . . ."

He slung his workout bag and sneakers into the truck bed, then opened the passenger door for her. "I'd hate to try to explain a bear-mauling to your father, that's all."

He closed her door and walked around the front of the truck. When he slid into the driver's seat, Josie had a flashback of the hundreds of times he'd done that when they were dating. Back then, he'd always lean toward her for a kiss before he put the key in the ignition, but tonight he just slung the seat belt across his body as he started the truck.

Did he even remember their old ritual?

Ten minutes later, they were seated on vinyl stools at the pub's counter. She plucked a menu from between the metal napkin holder and the Parmesan cheese shaker. "Please tell me the Bellini Burger hasn't changed."

"Not much has, Josie." His words fell like little shards of granite.

She looked toward the booth in the corner where the two of them had shared French fries, milkshakes, and lots of smoldering looks, and felt herself bite her lip. Ethan'd headed right for the counter stools when they came in, but maybe that's just where he liked to sit these days. Maybe he wasn't actually sending her a message with his seating choice.

He definitely was.

She looked down at the menu, and it was as if time had stood still here at Bellinis. Fish-and-chips on Tuesdays, spaghetti specials on Wednesdays, beef stew on Thursdays. Hunting season specials were still listed on the back.

"Are you trying hard not to say something about how the menu hasn't been updated since Noah built the ark?" Ethan leaned subtly her way.

Josie looked at him, feeling her cheeks color, but he kept his stare on the television. "Of course not."

"Right."

Before she could come up with a retort, the swinging door to the kitchen blasted open, and Molly came through with three towering plates. Josie had just a couple of seconds to take in her flaming red hair and green eyes before her view was blocked by the pile of plates. Apparently Molly didn't see her, either.

"Hey, Eth. I'll be right with you." Molly started toward a couple at the other end of the bar, but stutter-stepped when she spotted Josie. "Oh!" Her lips formed a startled circle, then a thin line as she delivered the steaming plates and handed ketchup and silverware over the bar. She stopped three times along the way back toward Josie and Ethan, ostensibly checking on guests, but Josie suspected she was stalling.

Finally she made her way back to their end of the bar. "Ethan. Josie. What can I get you?" Josie saw her step backward as she raised her order pad, and felt guilty for making her feel defensive. Her voice was frosty. Like, penguins-in-Antarctica frosty.

"Hi, Molly."

Molly sent her eyebrows upward, like she couldn't believe Josie had dared address her in public.

Josie looked back at the menu, trying to make her hands stop shaking. "I'll just have a burger, please. With fries. Thank you. And pickles, if it's okay." Josie knew her voice sounded stiff and formal, but she couldn't help it. She had no idea how to speak to Molly anymore.

"Same for me, Mols." Ethan smiled almost apologetically. Josie'd be willing to bet he'd get an earful from Molly once Josie was elsewhere.

"Two burgers! Fries! Side of pickles on number two!"

Molly hollered into the kitchen as she pushed through the swinging door, letting it whack the wall as she did so.

Josie propped her arms on the bar, hiding her trembling hands. "Did she say side of hemlock?" She looked around the pub, taking in the same dark-paneled walls, the red vinyl booths in the back, the bulletin board near the door, full of index cards and eight-by-ten handwritten announcements.

One of the papers advertised a benefit dance at the Grange hall this Friday night for Teddy and Grace. As she looked at the crude handwriting, it struck her that most of the people who passed through the front door of Bellinis not only knew Teddy and Grace, but knew why they needed help. Sure wouldn't see *that* in her Boston neighborhood.

She turned back toward Ethan. "So do you still *hate* pickles?"

"Still ask inane questions when you're nervous?"

"I'm not nerv—Fine. I'm nervous. Sue me."

He smiled, eyes still on the TV. "Yes, I still hate pickles."

"How about raspberries?"

"Them, too."

"Math?"

"I'm in charge of your dad's park finances. You'd better hope not."

"Good point."

Ethan turned toward her—reluctantly, it seemed. "Do I get to ask some?"

"Sure. Fire away. Just no hard ones."

"Why counseling?"

"I start with pickles and you start with my career choice?"

He nodded, eyebrows playful. "I don't want to waste my questions."

Josie looked down at the napkin she'd inadvertently started stripping into pieces. "I guess it just seemed . . . right. Given . . . everything."

"So you focus on kids?"

"More the families *of* the kids. Moms, mostly."

"Why not kids?" Ethan's eyes met hers, and for a moment Josie felt like they were orbiting in the same universe again.

Then she broke his gaze.

Because kids . . . kids kill me inside, that's why.

She shook her head. "You—um—jumped your question. It's my turn. Tell me one thing that's really changed in town."

"There's a new drugstore on the corner of Main Street where the old creamery was."

"Not buildings. Tell me something *real* that's changed."

There was a long pause as his eyes searched hers. "What answer are you hoping to hear, Josie?"

Then he sighed as he turned back toward the television over the bar.

"What if nothing really has?"

Chapter 18

At practically dawn the next morning, Ike's ice truck chugged into the parking lot and through the service gate, stopping at the shed with the big walk-in freezers. Josie had the shed doors open already, but the only reason her *eyes* were open this early was because she'd had to unearth her old bike at dawn, find a pump for the flat tires, and then pedal the five miles to Snowflake Village. After an awkward burger at Bellinis last night, Ethan had dropped her off at her parents' house with a quick wave and a *See ya tomorrow.*

She hadn't slept.

"Mornin', Sunshine!" Ike hopped down from the cab, his springy step belying his seventy-five years as he wrapped her in a bear hug that threatened to cut off an airway or two. "It is *some* good to see you, girl!"

"You too, Ike. Thanks for coming out this early."

Josie held out a coffee mug full of dark brew from Ethan's Keurig. She figured if he wasn't going to help with the ice, he could at least provide the coffee.

"Want some coffee?"

Ike took it. "You betcha." He took a swig, then set the mug on the stone wall and opened the back doors of the truck, hopping in like a much younger man. "So how's your dad doing?"

Josie set down her mug as well, then turned to catch the first bag of ice Ike threw down, stacking it on a handcart she'd dragged out from the shed. "He's—" How *was* he, really? "I don't know, Ike. He's taking his sweet time waking up. It's—scary."

"Well, these things can take time. Anybody tell you about my sister?"

"I don't think so." She pulled the ice into the shed and stacked the bags into the walk-in freezer, then came back out for more. "Is she okay?"

"Is now. Had herself a stroke, too. Took her sweet time, too, just like your dad. But one day, she opens up her eyes and says, *What's everybody fussin' about?*"

"Seriously?" Josie hauled another load into the freezer.

"Dead serious."

"And she really was okay?"

"Yep. That was six years ago. Last I talked to her, she was heading out dancing—said not to call her too early in case she had too many martinis." He shook his head. "Think we'll get this all unloaded before the park opens?"

"How much did you bring?"

"Five hundred bags."

Josie felt her eyes go wide. "Five *hundred*?" On the hottest day of the year, they probably used two hundred, absolute tops. Or at least they used to. But she couldn't very well say that, not after he'd gotten up at the crack of dawn and loaded his truck full of ice for her.

"That's what fits in the truck. And I figured if you called, you must be in pretty dire straits."

Josie wiped her sleeve across her forehead. "I'm pretty sure five hundred will get us through till at least noon, Ike."

An hour later, Josie grunted as she tossed the last bag to the top of the freezer. The temperature outside had risen at least fifteen degrees already, and alternating between the freezer and the sizzling pavement was making her dizzy. She could tell her hair was rocking some serious frizz, and her polo shirt was sticking to her in all the wrong places. She wondered if she had time to run home for a shower . . . then remembered she'd have to do it on her bike.

Never mind.

She locked the freezer door and went outside once again, only to find Ethan leaning on the ice truck talking with Ike, a funny smile on his face.

She picked up her coffee, now lukewarm. "Well, good morning, Ethan. Your timing is exquisite."

The tiny dimple in his right cheek made an appearance as he looked her up and down. *Great.* She must look even more frightful than she imagined.

"Nice work," he said.

"You're welcome. I get time and a half for this, right?"

"Absolutely. I'll pay you double what you're currently making."

Ike stepped toward Ethan, scratching his pen on a metal clipboard. He ripped off the invoice and handed it to him with a smile. "Appreciate your business. Nice to have a chance to come by."

"Thanks, Ike. Good to see you again."

Josie felt her eyebrows draw together. "Why are you two talking like you never see each other?"

"Well, we don't as much anymore." Ike cocked his head. "Not since Ethan finally convinced your dad to get one of them industrial ice-makers. Which was fine with me, because these old bones don't agree so much with crack-of-dawn deliveries anymore."

Ike looked at Ethan. "You got someone coming out to fix it?"

Ethan pressed his lips together, but Josie could see the corners creeping up. "It's not broken, actually."

Ike put his hands on his hips. "Then why in tarnation am I out here at six o'clock in the morning bringing you a load of five hundred bags of ice?"

"You brought five hundred bags?"

"That's what the truck holds." Ike looked completely mystified, but Josie felt steam building behind her eyes.

Ethan turned to her. "Wow, Jos. That's a lot of ice. And you hauled it all in there yourself?"

"We. Have. An *ice machine*?"

Ethan nodded, pointing into the shed. "It's that big black thing next to the freezers."

"And it's working just fine?"

"Mm-hm."

"And you heard me on the phone with Ike yesterday."

"Yep."

"Ordering *ice*."

"Yep."

"Which you knew we didn't need. And that I was going to be hauling at oh-dark-thirty this morning."

"That was kind of the best part."

Josie clenched her hands into fists. "You are such an—"

Ike tried to cover his mouth, but a chortle escaped before he could catch it. "Oh boy. I think I'm gonna be going now." He climbed into the cab of his truck and leaned out the window. "Now, Josie. You know my number if you need more ice. I'll be back later to tow your Jeep to the garage." He slapped the door, laughing, as he chugged back down the pathway.

Josie turned on Ethan. "I cannot believe you let me order ice, when you knew we had plenty already here."

"Well, you were all fired up playing Miss Problem Solver, so what was I to say? You're the boss's daughter, after all." He sipped his coffee, raising his eyebrows in challenge. "Who was I to question you?"

"Jerk."

"I prefer opportunist." He turned toward the administration building. "I might need you to work some overtime, though, to pay off all that ice."

At eight o'clock Ben's voice came over the handheld radio on Ethan's desk, but Josie was the only one in the office. She was still trying to cool down, both physically *and* figuratively.

She grabbed the radio and pressed the button to talk. "Hey, Ben. It's Josie."

"Well, Twinkle-toes. Ethan finally letting you in the office?"

"Not by choice, I'm afraid."

"Good for you. He'll adjust. So I need a favor, actually."

"Name it."

"I'm stuck out here trying to get that new part into the Twinkle Fairy, and I need somebody to do the upper rounds before we open. You remember how?"

Josie rolled her eyes. "Turn 'em on, make sure nothing falls apart, give the thumbs-up?"

"Yep." He chuckled. "That's about it."

"I think I can handle that."

"Good to have you back, hon. Over 'n' out."

Half an hour later, when she'd checked all the rides except the Ferris wheel, Josie took a deep breath, looking up the hill toward its gleaming red, white, and green seats. She couldn't avoid it any longer. The park couldn't open until all rides had been cleared for takeoff, and that meant she needed to walk up the hill, unlock the controls, and run the wheel around a few times to make sure all was well. There was no way around it.

She started up the hill, but didn't make it more than five steps before she had to stop, her heart racing like a hummingbird's.

Dammit, when was she going to be able to do this?

Before Avery, it had been her favorite ride. For most of her childhood, she'd been the first one on and the last one off, every single day. Ben had made sure of it.

"Ready, Twinkle-toes?" Ben clanked the bar into place across her eight-year-old body in the fading twilight.

"Ready, Captain."

"I'll need a full report this evening."

"Got it."

"Moon position, star count, number of cars at the bowling alley. It's league night."

"I'm on it." Josie saluted, then checked her pink watch. "Is the train coming through tonight?"

"Yup. Passenger one this time."

"Where's it going?" She knew, but always asked.

"Boston and New York City, m'dear." He made his voice sound like a conductor. "Boston and New York."

"Will you take me to the city someday, Ben?"

"Absolutely. We'll do a Red Sox game."

"And a duck tour!"

*"Whatever you want, honey. But y'know what? I think you'll probably take your*self *there before I'll get a chance."*

"It wouldn't be as fun without you."

"That's nice of you to say."

She frowned. "Daddy thinks I'm going to be a Snow Princess and stay here forever and ever."

"Maybe you will, maybe you won't. Time will tell." Ben stepped back and touched the lever. "Ready?"

"Ready!"

"I'll be right down here when you're ready to come down."

"I know, Ben. You're always here."

"You just remember that, young lady." Josie saw him

look away quickly before he pulled on the lever and sent her to the top of the world. "You just remember that."

Josie shook her head as she pulled her radio off her waist and called for Ben. She couldn't do it.

She wasn't sure she'd *ever* be able to do it.

"What's the emergency?" At one o'clock that afternoon, Josie peeked in the backstage door of the live theater, where five teenagers were scurrying around pulling on costumes and grabbing props. One of them had just called the admin office and asked her to come over immediately.

"Ryan's a no-show." A reindeer with a bright red clown nose turned toward Josie. "And we're on in five!"

"Who's Ryan? And why did you guys call *me*?"

"Ryan's the Table Elf. Ethan told us to call you. He said you could be our special guest substitute. And plus, we're desperate!"

Josie growled internally as she slowly pulled her body through the door. First the ice, and now she had to sub for an AWOL teenage actor? On a stage that had dumped her into a timpani twelve years ago?

"Here." Santa tossed her an elf suit. "You sit stage left on the stool."

"You have *got* to be kidding me." Josie held up the costume. "Have we not updated *any* of the costumes in the past ten years?"

"Sorry, Miss Kendrew. It's all we have that'll fit you. The Snow Princess dress is already being used."

Was it Josie's imagination, or was Santa smirking?

"I thought we never used—never mind." She dodged behind a changing screen and pulled on the costume. "It's okay. I can do this. I've done the elf thing. Do I have lines?"

"We taped them to the floor by your stool."

"Thank you. That was very thoughtful." Josie pulled the hat over her head, which sent her curls sproinging out the bottom edges like an upside-down cupcake. Her straightening iron was turning out to be little match for this week's Vermont-style humidity.

Santa grimaced and came closer, pointing at her hair. "Can you tuck in your hair? You're supposed to be a guy."

"You see that I'm trying, right?"

Dammit. For every curl she got tucked in, two more sprung out.

"But you have to flirt with the Door Elf, and she's a girl."

"Maybe you'd like to call Ethan back here and put *him* in the costume, then?"

Santa turned toward the stage. "No. We're good. It's all good."

Josie looked in the mirror mounted on the wall and made a vain attempt at tucking in her hair, but not before she heard Santa whisper, "It's gonna be a disaster."

The Snow Princess looked back. "At least there's no timpani."

Chapter 19

Forty minutes later, Josie stormed into Elf Central, determined to find Ethan and give him a piece of her mind. She flew up the stairs and banged into the office, only to find him lounged in his desk chair, feet on the desk as he talked on the phone.

She glared at him from the doorway, but he just smiled benignly and pointed at the phone. He delivered a full two-minute string of *uh-huh*s and *hm*s and *you don't say*s while Josie paced and muttered, waiting for him to finish.

Finally she stomped over to the window, and when she did, she could see the readout on Ethan's phone from behind him. There was no one *on* the damn phone.

"You miserable, conniving—" She put her finger down to hang up the phone, and he whipped around, barely containing his laughter.

"How was the show?"

Josie put her hands on her hips. "I can't believe you sent a kid on a fake hardware store errand just so I'd have to go on stage."

"I really needed those light bulbs." Ethan shrugged his shoulders playfully and put his palms up. "You said you wanted to work, right? That was work. I'm really sorry. Couldn't be helped."

"You know how much I hate that stage."

He gave her a pointed look that she read perfectly. *You hate everything here, Josie,* it said. Then he folded his hands behind his head and leaned back. "Did you survive the show?"

"I did. No thanks to you. They made me do a solo. And made timpani jokes." She spun his chair toward her. "How exactly do they know about the timpani?"

Ethan cleared his throat carefully. "There's a . . . a video."

Josie felt her eyes pop. "There's a *video*? Are you *kidding* me?"

"We use it at the beginning of the summer as an ice-breaker during training."

"You use a video of *me* falling into a big freaking *drum* as an ice—That is cold, Ethan. Cold."

"But funny."

"That was probably the most embarrassing moment of my entire teenage life."

"Which is why it makes such great viewing." Ethan smiled innocently.

"I—" Josie's phone beeped and Mom's number popped up. She pointed a warning finger at Ethan. "We are not done yet."

He did a fake shiver, then put his feet down, focusing on his computer as she took the call.

"Hi, Mom. What's up?"

"Josie! Oh thank God you're there! Your father! He's waking up!"

"He's waking up? Really?" Josie started tossing things in the backpack she'd pulled out of her bedroom closet this morning. "I'll be right there!"

She clicked the phone shut, then looked at Ethan, her mouth open in shock. "He's—awake."

"That's great!"

"I need to—I have to—"

"Go, Josie. Go see him."

She finished stuffing things in her backpack, hands shaky, then she sprinted out the door and down the stairs. Speed was key here. If she slowed down, she'd have to think about the hundred or so questions circling her brain. How would he be? What would she say to him? What if—what if he didn't want her there?

She got to the bottom of the stairs and pressed the crash bar to head outside, fumbling automatically for her keys. Then she stopped, swearing silently as she bounced her forehead softly on the door.

Dammit. She had nothing but a dead Jeep and a bicycle . . . and the hospital was ten miles away.

"Need a ride?"

Josie squeezed her eyes shut as Ethan came down the stairs, jingling his keys. She turned. "You'd let me borrow your truck?"

"Heck, no." He pushed the door open and motioned her through. "You were a terrible driver *before* you moved to the city. I can't afford to replace my truck. I'll drive you."

"You don't have to do this." She fell into step beside him as they crossed the courtyard.

"I know." He shrugged. "I want to."

Twenty minutes later, they hurried down the hospital hallway toward the waiting room, Josie struggling to keep up with his long strides.

"Ethan, seriously. You should go back to the park."

"If the park collapses because I'm gone for an hour, we have bigger problems than I want to know about right now."

He opened the waiting room door for her. "I know you're big and strong and don't need anyone . . . but maybe you will."

She looked at his eyes, and he was doing that sincere-adorable thing that used to bring her to her proverbial knees, and all she could manage was a soft *thank you*.

"Hands." Ida, the hospital-volunteer-slash-waiting-room-guard, pointed at the sink, without looking up.

"Good afternoon, Ida. It's lovely to see you, too." Josie flipped on the faucet and squirted soap into her palms, then toweled off as Ethan washed his hands. "Is my mom in with my dad right now?"

"Yes. You can't go in. One visitor at a time."

"Thank you. I know the rule. You tell me every time I come."

Josie found a seat against the wall, and Ethan settled beside her. He leaned over to whisper, "Is she always so pleasant?"

"Every single day, yes. The friendly pink smock is just a disguise."

"I can't believe they still only let in one person at a time. It's a step-down unit, isn't it?"

"It's Ida's unit."

They sat in silence for a few moments, until Ethan leaned over again. "Are you nervous?"

Josie rubbed her hands together. How had he known? "A little, yeah."

"Liar."

"Okay, a lot."

Ethan reached out a hand toward her knee, but pulled it back like he'd thought better of it.

She puffed out a couple of nervous breaths. "What if he's paralyzed? What if he can't talk?" *What if seeing me sends him straight into another stroke?*

"One step at a time. Don't worry before you have to."

"I know, I know. But I can't help it. He's been down for so long."

"You never know. Did Ike tell you the story about his sister?"

"Yeah, he did." Josie leaned forward, elbows on her knees, hands clenched under her chin. "Let's hope Dad has the same miraculous recovery."

Ethan reached his hand across the back of her chair, then touched her back tentatively. Before she could even register its warmth, though, he pulled it back into his lap.

He cleared his throat. "Do you want a coffee or something?"

"I think if I have any more today, I'm going to jump out of my own skin." Josie sat back up, but couldn't seem to figure out what to do with her hands.

"Well, if you hadn't started at six o'clock this morning . . ."

"Do not get me started, mister. I'm not going to be able to move tomorrow, after tossing all that ice around."

He laughed softly. "It's a lot of ice."

"Shut up."

Ida looked up. "Ms. Kendrew? The doctor's in the conference room with your mother. They'd like you to come in."

Josie's stomach jumped. "Doctor? Oh. Wow." She fumbled for her backpack. "Okay. This will be okay. O-kay."

She stood up, shaky on her feet, and immediately Ethan was beside her, a steadying hand on her elbow.

"You all right?" His eyes were serious now, all amusement gone.

Josie took a deep breath. "I'm fine. It's—fine. I'll be fine." She adjusted her backpack. "You should go back to the park. This could take—a while. I think. I don't know. I guess I really don't know."

God, she hated how she felt right now—like she wanted

to grab his hand and pull him down the hallway with her.

"I'll be right here, Jos."

She looked up at him, and as much as his words sent rays of warmth right through her, she also felt a keen sense of danger.

She didn't want him to wait.

No. That wasn't right.

She didn't *want* to want him to wait.

"Mrs. Kendrew, I realize this is all a little scary, but I want to assure you it's normal." The neurologist took off his glasses and set them on the tiny round table in the family conference room half an hour later. Josie had popped into Dad's room quickly on her way down the hallway, and she was still shaking. Dad wasn't . . . Dad.

"But he looks so confused. I don't think he even knew me." Mom's eyes teared up again. "He didn't know Josie, either."

Josie spun her coffee cup slowly on the table, holding it with both hands. Ethan had just brought it in and left, probably to do Ida-penance if he'd sneaked by her. He'd made it perfectly—two sugars, three creams—without even asking her. In this little universe where everything seemed topsy-turvy, the small gesture gave her a comfort she hadn't expected.

Danger.

She shook her head, focusing on the neurologist.

"Again, that's not unusual, and it's also not necessarily indicative of the way things will play out. His brain's had quite a traumatic injury, so it's going to take some time to see what his function level is."

Mom nodded, but swallowed hard. Josie stopped spinning her coffee and spoke for the first time. "Can you give us any idea at all what we might be looking at here? Just so we can try to be prepared?"

He nodded slowly. "Well, with a right cerebral hemorrhage like his, we'll generally see most of the impact happening on his left side. He may also have some trouble speaking, especially at first, and might have trouble understanding you."

He handed Mom a small pile of papers and brochures. "It's a lot to take in, I know. We've talked about it over the past couple of days, and now we'll really be able to start figuring out where he's at so we can make plans to get him better."

He tapped the brochures. "There's a lot of good information in these resources, so when you have time, take a read-through."

Josie watched Mom carefully. So far she'd been holding it together, but it looked like her string was about to snap.

Josie took a deep breath. "Dr. Edelman, what's the worst-case scenario here?"

He smiled gently. "I really hate to focus on the worst case, only because there's so much we can't tell yet about how your dad will recover."

"Well." She tapped nervously on the table. "I think we're sort of *expect-the-worst* kind of people. That way, if the worst doesn't happen, it's kind of a bonus."

Dr. Edelman looked from one of them to the other, not answering.

"We need to know. Please."

"Okay." He paused. "Well, worst-case scenario is significant paralysis, speech impairment, memory loss, incontinence, seizures . . . but again, we just don't know yet. And sometimes, many of the early impacts can be mitigated with therapies. We just don't know. Your dad could end up experiencing all of those things, or none. Only time will tell."

"So even if he's paralyzed, he could heal?"

Dr. Edelman tipped his head carefully. "To a point. Maybe."

"But we don't know what that point might be." Josie went back to spinning her cup.

"Right."

"And we have no idea *when* we'll know."

"Right again. Unfortunately, this isn't an exact science."

Josie nodded slowly. "So what's next?"

"Well, we'll keep him here overnight and assess things as best we can over the next twenty-four hours, and then we'll start looking into rehab. Once he's stabilized, he'll be better off outside the hospital, at a place where they're staffed to provide rehabilitative care. There are two excellent facilities within a half hour of here. Either would be fine, depending on whether they have space available. I'll make sure the nurse gives you pamphlets before you leave." He put on his glasses and placed both hands on the edge of the table, making it obvious he was done. "Anything else I can answer for you right now?"

Josie shook her head. "Thank you, no."

He patted her shoulder on his way out the door. "Hang in there. He's a strong, healthy guy. I have high hopes for his recovery."

After he closed the door, Josie looked at Mom, whose tears were now falling down her face faster than her tissue could capture them.

As she watched her, an old fear slammed into Josie.

If anything was going to push Mom off the wagon, it was going to be this.

Chapter 20

"Ethan! You're here!" Emmy reached out her scrawny little arms for a hug, crawling out from under the blanket on her hospital bed. Ethan knew Josie's meeting with the neurologist would take some time, so he'd come down to the pediatric floor to check on Emmy while he waited.

Ethan pulled her into a bear hug. "I missed you, squirt! How are you feeling?"

"Better much."

"You're talking backward. You *must* be feeling better."

"Yup. Might get to come back to Avery's House tomorrow!"

Ethan touched her nose with his index finger as he set her back on the bed. "Well, that's the best news I've heard all day." He tucked the blanket around her waist as she settled back on the pillows. "I can't wait to have you back."

"Who's doing my jobs while I'm here?"

Ethan sat heavily in the chair beside the bed, shaking his head. "No one's up to the task. It's a terrible state of affairs. I have *no* idea how many times that Ferris wheel's been ridden in the past few days."

"I'd better get back there, then."

"Absolutely. And Ben has a little surprise for you."

Her blue eyes widened. "What kind of surprise?"

"Can't tell you or it wouldn't be a surprise."

"Who's having a surprise?" Steph came into the room carrying a green Popsicle. "Hey, Ethan."

"Emmy was just telling me she might be back tomorrow."

"We're hoping." Steph handed the Popsicle to Emmy.

"Well, good thing. The nurses said they're running out of lime Popsicles."

Emmy giggled as she slurped the Popsicle. "I'm hungry! And supper isn't for an hour."

Steph caught Ethan's eye and gave him a tiny thumbs-up. He looked at Emmy sitting in the bed, a tinge of pink coloring her cheeks, and felt relief course through his chest.

The door swung open and a nurse bustled in with a tray on wheels. Ethan looked up. "Uh-oh. The evil nurse is here." He stood up and made his best pretend-firm face. "Now you be extra nice to my friend here. She has a very important job waiting for her and we need her back at Avery's House."

Emmy giggled from the bed. "She's always nice."

"Are you sure? She has a grumpy nose."

"Ethan Miller, you get out of here before I swat your behind and call your father." The nurse waved her pudgy hands toward the door.

"Yes'm." Ethan ducked, sending a sly smile toward Emmy. "I'm sorry, Emmy, but I know she'll do it. Celia's known my dad for a hundred years or so, so I have to listen to her."

"A hundred *years*?"

Celia wound the blood pressure cuff around Emmy's arm and pushed a button, but leveled her eyes at Ethan. "Not quite a hundred, young man. But guess what, Emmy? I used to change Ethan's diapers."

"*What*?"

"It's true."

"An-nd that would *definitely* be my cue to leave." Ethan shook his head at Celia and waved as he headed for the door. "I'll see you tomorrow, squirt!"

"I knew that would get rid of him," he heard Celia say as he rounded the corner.

"Gotta love small towns," he muttered, smiling.

"What's so funny?" Josh looked up from a chart as Ethan passed the nurses' station.

Ethan shook his hand. "Well, if it isn't Dr. Mackenzie. Celia was just threatening to tell Emmy stories from my diaper days."

"Ouch. Good thing she never babysat *me*. She keeps me in line just fine *without* blackmail at her disposal."

Ethan still hadn't figured out how Josh had time to pull long shifts at Mercy *and* oversee the medical end of things at Avery's House, but he insisted on doing both. They'd been friends since third grade, and after med school at UVM and residency at Dartmouth, Ethan had been sure Josh would head to a big hospital out west. Instead, he'd turned down six different offers and had settled right back here in Echo Lake and Mercy Hospital.

"So Molly said everybody else is fine at Avery's House this morning?"

"So far so good." Josh nodded. "I just got back from doing rounds over there. Hopefully we kept it contained to Emmy."

"Thanks for getting her here so quickly. And for helping Steph not flip out." Ethan leaned his elbows on the chest-high counter. "Feel like I haven't seen you in weeks. How are things here?"

"So busy I'm not sure I remember where I live. How come the new guy gets suckered into every committee under the sun around here?"

"Because he's the new guy."

"I think we need a *new* new guy. Hey, by the way . . ."

Josh raised his eyebrows. "You know that Hospital Hero award they give out every year?"

Ethan nodded. "Vaguely. Never paid it much attention."

"Well, you might have to pay attention this year."

"Why? Are you nominated?"

Josh shook his head. "Nope. You are."

Ethan stepped back and swallowed hard. "What are you talking about?"

"You've been nominated."

"Can't be. I don't even work here."

"You might as well work here, buddy. You're here all the time with your patients."

"Guests. Who in the world nominated me? And what do I do to politely refuse?" Ethan felt a strange sensation in his chest. He was nobody's hero, most especially this hospital's.

"Well, nominations have been coming in for the past three months. Patients, staff, docs, nurses, you name it."

"Are you going to tell me who put my name in?"

"Nope. Can't."

"Why? Is it confidential? Anonymous? Come on. We've been friends for twenty years."

"None of the above." Josh smiled, clearly enjoying Ethan's discomfort. "I just don't have *time* to tell you. You got one hundred and fifty-three nominations." Josh slapped him on the back. "It's apparently a record."

Ethan shook his head in disbelief. "Not possible."

"Every nurse and physician on this floor, the chemo bay, radiation area . . . the gift shop ladies, Marla and Julie from the front desk. Even Dottie from the kitchen. Plus every patient who's ever enjoyed your free tickets to Snowflake Village."

"It sounds like a conspiracy."

"Only the best kind." Josh stepped from behind the

desk and slapped Ethan on the back. "So congratulations, buddy. Really. You deserve it."

He shook Ethan's hand, then headed down the hall toward Emmy's room. Just as he got there, he turned to call over his shoulder. "Oh, hey. You'd better get yourself a monkey suit. There's gonna be a big shindig to celebrate the newest Hospital Hero. I'm trying to get them to spring for a red cape."

"No freaking out, Mom." Josie was trying to calm her mother down, while inside, she felt like someone was grabbing her stomach with two hands and twisting it. The neurologist had closed the conference room door behind him, and neither of them was making a move to return to the depressing waiting room. "It's good. He's waking up."

Mom dug for another tissue. "I know. I know. I do. But oh my God. What if this is—what it is?"

"It won't be. He's *just* waking up."

"I know. And hopefully things will improve."

"Of course they will."

"Of course they will." Mom's voice echoed hers, but didn't sound remotely convinced. "I'm sorry, Jos. I'm really trying not to fall apart in front of you."

"It's okay. Falling apart is a pretty standard reaction in this sort of situation."

"Well, it's not what *you* need to see right now."

"Mom, no offense, but I do see kind of a lot of this in my line of work."

Mom sniffed a short chuckle. "Good point. Sorry—I wasn't thinking. Sometimes I feel like you're still seven years old and I'm supposed to protect you from the bad stuff." She put her finger up. "And just so you don't have to choke on words you're too polite to say right now, I know I did a spectacularly lousy job of it back then."

Josie bit her lip, saying nothing. Mom was right. She

had done a spectacularly lousy job of it back then. But seeing this different mother, this woman who was sad and scared, but ultimately healthy for the first time in a long time, was sobering.

As she watched Mom dab her tears and take a deep breath as she gathered her purse, she realized she really didn't even know her.

She knew a mother who was alternately depressed or giddy, depending on the time of day and how much liquid had gone down her throat. She knew a mother who might or might not be hanging her head over the toilet by the time Josie got home from school. She knew a mother who ranted and cried and threw things when she suspected her husband was playing around because he never came home.

She knew a mother who had never seemed to know *her* at all.

So this current version of her mother, who defined *freaking out* as shedding some quiet tears in a hospital conference room, was essentially a stranger. And although a part of Josie was quietly clamoring to push the past out of the way and open her heart to this new person, a bigger part of her was still scared that once they left the confines of the hospital, her mother would use the stress as an excuse to revert to old habits . . . and seek solace in a bottle of Stoli.

"Okay." Mom tossed her tissue in the trash can and stood up. "I'm going to peek in on your dad and see if Gayle is finished with him."

"Be careful. If Ida finds out you've been in there *twice* this hour, you'll be in big trouble."

"Ida can kiss my—"

Josie laughed. "Ida can what, Mom?"

"Nothing." A tiny smile crept up the edges of Mom's

face. "What I was thinking was not at all appropriate. Want to sneak in with me?"

"Two visitors at the same time?" Josie shivered. "Going full-on rebel now?"

"If the nurse comes in, you just hide under the bed."

Josie linked her elbow with Mom's as they meandered toward Dad's room. "Thanks, but I've seen what they hang from those beds."

When they reached his room, his eyes were open, but he didn't seem to register their presence. Mom perched on the edge of the bed and motioned Josie into the chair on Dad's left. "Hi, sweetheart. Nice of you to wake up and join us."

Sweetheart? Had Mom just called him *sweetheart*?

"Andy?" Mom took his left hand in hers, but it was limp and unresponsive. Josie saw Mom's shoulders shake just a little as Dad continued to stare just to the right of her, unblinking. "Look! Josie's here. She's helping Ethan out at the park until you're better."

"Hi, Dad." Josie kept her hands clenched in her lap. His eyes didn't move, just continued to stare to the right.

Mom tipped her head to the side as she looked at him. "Do you think he's really awake?" She waved a hand gently in front of his face. He blinked, but the stare remained. "I don't like this at all."

"Time, Mom. It'll take time. It's still really early. He's been down for days."

"But this is weird, isn't it?"

"I don't know. I've never been with a stroke patient who's just waking up."

"We should Google it. Where's Gayle, anyway?" Mom kept hold of Dad's hand, not looking away from his eyes.

"Want me to go find her?"

Anything to get her out of the stifling, beeping room and a Dad-shaped man with staring eyes.

Mom nodded. "Maybe she can give us some information."

Josie pushed out of her chair. "Be right back."

As she got to the doorway, a growling noise from the bed made her spin around. When she did, she felt her eyes widen.

Dad had slumped strangely off his pillows, but looked like he was trying to point at Josie. His head leaned to the right, and though his mouth sagged to the left and his voice was raspy and rough, she distinctly heard him say, "No!"

Chapter 21

"Maybe he didn't want you to go?" A little while later, Ethan had his hands on the wheel, but they hadn't left their parking spot at the hospital. "He's not himself, Josie. You can't take this the wrong way. I'm sure he didn't mean he didn't want you there."

Josie felt tears prick the backs of her eyelids. "Why wouldn't he? In his mind, I left him, I left Mom, and I thumbed my nose at his lifelong creation. Not to mention I allegedly left his favorite guy practically at the altar."

"You're his daughter, Josie. I'm pretty sure he realizes your reasons for leaving had a lot of layers."

"That's an understatement."

"I know."

"No offense, but you don't know the half of it."

Because if you had, you would have been off like a rocket.

"Don't be so sure."

"Seriously, Ethan. And you know what? I don't even know why I'm so upset about it. I've been pissed at him since I was fifteen, and I can't say I ever made any secret about it. Why am I sitting here all upset that he didn't wake up from his stroke and reach out his arms to his long-lost daughter?"

Ethan started the truck. "Come on. Let's get out of here. You need to go for a drive."

Josie started at his words, so familiar. The slight tilt of his head made her think he was surprised at them as well. Was he remembering all of the times he'd said them way back when? All the times when he could tell she just needed to be somewhere, anywhere, but in her own life? Even though she was sure he didn't know why?

"It's already eight o'clock. Oh God, Ethan. You've been here for hours."

He steered out of the parking lot and headed west toward the lake. "Just talked to Ben. Everything's all set at the park. The guys helped him close up." He paused at a stop sign, then drove through. Only in Vermont would people stop so thoroughly at an intersection when, clearly, no one else was ever coming through.

Ethan tapped on the wheel, thoughtful. "Andy's been unconscious for days. You said yourself he was just staring into space like a zombie. I wouldn't be surprised if he wasn't really even awake, in a way."

"It was so eerie. He was just sitting there, and Mom was holding his hand, and it didn't even seem to register that we were there until he yelled at me."

"He was probably yelling at something he was seeing in his head."

Josie nodded. "I know. I know you're probably right. But it was—awful. We haven't talked in so long, and now . . . this."

"Just give it time. The neurologist said it'll take some time."

"I know. It's early." She shivered as Ethan meandered the truck around the curves that hugged the river's edge. "You know what? Let's talk about something else. Please."

"Are you sure?"

"Please. Yes. I can't process Dad right now. I just need to . . . I don't know . . . think about something else, do something else." *Because—you know—I'm a counselor, and yet my best coping strategy seems to revolve around me avoiding my own issues.*

"Anything in particular you want to do?"

"You choose."

"Um . . . have you had a maple creemee since you've been back?"

Leave it to Ethan to pick her old favorite right off the bat.

"Oh God. Maple creemees. Is the Snack Shack still open?"

"You know it." Ethan put on his blinker and headed for Back Road.

Before she could think better of it, Josie leaned over and squeezed his hand. "Thanks for coming, Ethan. You are excellent therapy."

He squeezed back. "I always was."

"I know." Josie withdrew her hand, suddenly awkward.

They were quiet for a full minute before Ethan turned to her. "Are you about to ask me another nerve-induced inane question?" She saw a smile at the corner of his mouth. "I can tell this silence is killing you."

"Nope. Not me."

"Right." He glanced over. "Tell you what. I'll save you the trouble. How about I tell you what *hasn't* changed around here? The good stuff." He paused. "Besides me, of course."

She laughed. "Okay. It's a deal. What's still good here?"

"Mama B's cooking."

"Goes without saying. Do they still yell at each other all the time?"

"Wouldn't be Bellinis without the yelling, would it? But they love each other, despite all the noise."

"Okay, so Mama and Papi haven't changed. What else?"

"Snack Shack maple creemees."

"It would be a crime if they'd changed."

"Um, Morris's French fry cart at the beach?"

"He's still *alive*?"

"Eighty-two next week."

Josie's stomach grumbled at the thought of Morris's hand-cut fries. "I'm sensing a pattern here. All the things on your list revolve around food."

"That's because I still can't cook."

"Pops never succeeded in teaching you and David? He was a great cook!"

Ethan's smile dropped off his face. "I guess I was a lousy student. And all he remem—uh, likes to make these days is goulash, so I think I missed my chance."

They crested the hill that gave the first glimpse of Twilight Cove, and Josie caught her breath. The lake glistened like a melted cherry Popsicle, lit by the setting sun. "Wow."

He slowed down. "Forget how beautiful the lake is?"

"I never thought I took it for granted. But wow."

Ethan pulled into the Snack Shack parking lot and found a space, then came around to open her door. At the little sliding-screen window, Josie watched as the server mixed real maple syrup into the vanilla creemee, then swirled it into a cone. As they walked back to the car, Josie took her first lick, and was transported back ten years. "Oh wow. These are so good." There was no way anyone outside Vermont made creemees like this.

Ethan licked his own as he opened her door. "Always were." Once he'd settled into the driver's seat and started the truck, he looked her way. "Want to head out to the cliffs?"

Josie's stomach quivered at the thought, and it was almost like he could sense it.

"Don't worry. I didn't mean it like I used to mean it when I said that. See? I'm not even winking." He smiled as he pointed toward his right eye, then headed the truck toward Twilight Cove. "It's still the most beautiful place on earth, and you should see it while you're here."

"Sure. Okay. Yes." Josie stumbled over her words. Twilight Cove would never be about the view—not to her, anyway.

Ethan parked in the grassy lot at the end of Back Road, and they headed up the pebbled trail to the cliffs overlooking the cove, as if it hadn't been ten years since the last time they'd done so. She finished her creemee in the same spot she always had, and then he grabbed her hand to help her over the same huge boulder he always had.

This time he let go once she had landed, though.

"Did this hill used to be this steep?" Josie huffed. To her consternation, she was winded before they got to the top.

"No. Definitely not."

"Good, because I'm breathing like an asthmatic poodle."

Ethan turned around, laughing. "Is that what that sound is?"

"Shut up. Bet you couldn't run this hill ten times up and down like in your football days."

"Not with a bum knee, no." She saw him wince as he hit a branch that put his leg at a funny angle.

"Does it still bother you?"

"Only when I go mountain-climbing with city girls." They clambered over the last boulders and reached the top of the hill, where Ethan caught Josie as she almost toppled forward onto the pebbles leading down to the edge. "Careful. It's a cliff, remember?"

"Holy wow." Josie scanned the horizon. Fingers of orange and purple and red splayed the sky over the lake, reflecting downward in a display that was so beautiful it almost hurt to look.

"Not too shabby, for a country view, eh?" She felt Ethan's hand lightly on her waist, and though she didn't want to like it, she also didn't want to shrug it off. "Can Boston compete with this?"

An alarm went off low in Josie's belly, but she tried to shrug it off. "No. Really aren't that many lake views in Boston. Just—you know—a big, gorgeous ocean." Josie spun around slowly, taking in the warm cliffs behind them, the grassy patch of ground where they'd spent countless hours sitting, the glistening lake below. "It's so quiet."

"Loons will be out soon."

Josie shivered, thinking of their eerie calls. The psych major in her didn't want to linger too long on why she'd chosen the sound for her ring tone. "I remember."

"Want to sit down?" He took her hand lightly and pulled her to sit beside him, with their backs against the cliff. This time he didn't let go as they sat looking at the sunset, and this time she didn't, either. The sun drifted lower and lower in the sky, and just as the last sliver was about to disappear, he whispered, "Going, going, make a wish."

She turned toward him, and before she could think about why it was a very bad idea, her lips found his, and his answered—in a kiss that was so soft, so hopeful, she didn't dare move, didn't dare break the fragile peace they'd brokered.

"What'd you wish?" he asked as he pulled slowly away.

"I—I don't know. I didn't have time to make one."

"I made one for both of us." Ethan drew her toward him again, bracing his hands softly on her jawline. His lips met hers, and this time she let herself melt into him. It was just so right, so perfect, so . . . hot. She wanted to forget everything else and just mold her body to his as he pulled her tighter. She wanted to feel more, taste more, *have* more.

But after what felt like only a few seconds, he pulled back, still holding her. "You okay?"

"A little too okay." To her consternation, her voice shook a little as she answered.

His eyes were serious and he pulled back further. Josie didn't know whether to be relieved or disappointed. The lake, the view, the scent of him, the warmth of his body all threatened to send all sense of reason right off the cliff and leave her in his arms.

"Should we stop?"

"Definitely?" She wrinkled her nose, unable to come up with any answer that made any more sense than that.

He laughed out loud, releasing his grip on her waist. In response, she slid a foot away from him, trying to put distance between them. He folded his arms over his knees as he looked out at the water, and she sucked in a shaky breath as she took in the view. The sunset bronzed his skin, caught on his eyelashes, touched his hair in a way that made her want to do it, too.

After an almost interminable silence, he finally spoke. "Do you remember the night I proposed?"

"How could I forget? I thought you were having a nervous breakdown."

"I *was* having a nervous breakdown."

* * *

After what Josie could only describe as a fairly disastrous dinner date, Ethan drove out to Twilight Cove and parked the truck so the back faced the water. Then he spread out a pile of blankets in the back, ostensibly so they could watch the stars.

After they'd settled on the blankets, she reached over to take his hand. "Ooh! First star! Make a wish."

"If I say it out loud, will it still come true?"

"Only if you say it to me."

"Being that you're my true love and all?" He rolled his eyes.

"Exactly." She turned toward him. "So let's hear it. What's your wish, Ethan?"

He didn't answer for the longest time, and Josie wondered what he could possibly be thinking. His obvious wish, being that he was male and eighteen, was pretty much a guarantee out here at the lake. She doubted he'd waste a star on it.

Finally, he squeezed her hand. "To marry you."

"No, seriously." She giggled nervously. "What's your real wish?"

"That is my real wish." He looked thoughtful, then pulled a velvet box from behind him. "Josie, I'm holding a ring that I've been trying to work up the nerve to give you all night. Will you marry me?"

She took a quick breath, seeing the intensity in his eyes. "Oh my God. You're serious, aren't you?" She sat straight up on the blankets, gripping the side of the truck.

"Diamond, Josie." He held up the box. "Yes, I'm serious. Why wouldn't I be?"

"Because we're young? And . . . young?"

"And totally in love, right?"

"Well, yes, but—"

"But what? I know that five, ten, twenty years from now, you're still going to be the only woman I've ever loved. Yeah, we're young. But I can't imagine spending my life with anyone but you, and that's not going to change, so I can't see any reason not to ask you now."

"Oh my God. I can't believe this is happening." Her face was hot, her heart threatening to whack right through a rib. Was he really, truly asking her to marry him? Right here? Right now? She'd only been dreaming of this moment her entire life, and here it was. The perfect man, hers for the taking.

"I was going to ask you in the restaurant, but it never seemed like the right moment. I finally gave it to the waiter while you were in the bathroom, and he hid it in your cake."

"Oh God." Josie clapped her hand over her mouth. *"I was too full to finish it."*

"I had this whole perfect proposal planned. Fancy restaurant, fancy clothes, fancy everything." Ethan ran his hand nervously along his five o'clock shadow. *"Are you ever going to answer?"* He pulled back. *"Do you not want to marry me?"*

"I totally want to marry you. I'm just surprised, that's all."

He laughed, relieved. *"Is that a yes?"*

"No!"

"No?"

"I mean yes! But ask me again! I want to do it right this time."

"You are completely impossible."

She laughed. *"You point that out at least once a week. And twice already tonight."*

He leaned closer, lips just a hairsbreadth away from

hers. "And I will continue to tell you that for the rest of your life." His lips touched hers. "Marry me, Josie. Be my forever."

"Okay," she whispered as he slipped the ring on her finger.

"I still can't believe I asked you in the back of a Chevy truck." Ethan's voice brought her back to reality. "What a lousy proposal."

"It was not. It was sweet."

"Seriously. Back of a Chevy truck."

"Coulda been a Nissan."

"The *one* time you didn't finish your dessert." Ethan's face grew serious and he reached a hand toward her hair. "Do you know your hair still looks the same in the sunset?" When she didn't pull away, he touched the very tips. "Your eyes, too."

Josie felt her breath quicken at his touch. Every cell of her brain wanted to run, but every cell of her *body* just wanted to collapse into his arms.

Ethan's eyes skated over her face, then slowly down her body. "And you still have ridiculously small feet. How do you *walk* on those things?"

Josie giggled. "Don't pick on my feet."

"I'll stop if you kiss me again." His voice was playful, but his eyes were anything but. And though the whole scene was loaded with ten-year-old memories and a just-right-ness she hadn't felt since she'd left Echo Lake, the saner portion of her brain was feeling for the brake pedal . . . again.

"We—we shouldn't." She backed away from him.

"But we're pretty good at it, remember?" He tried to maintain a carefree tone, but she could see the hurt in his eyes.

"I know. We are. We definitely are." She took a deep

breath and blew it out. "God, Ethan. I don't know what I'm doing. I shouldn't be up here with you, shouldn't be trying to recapture the past. It's not fair to either of us. This isn't . . . isn't real."

"I beg to differ. It feels real to me."

She sighed again, her chest hurting as she did so. *Me, too.*

"That's what I'm afraid of."

Chapter 22

"You are an idiot." Josh stirred creamer into his coffee an hour later. After a quick descent from the cliff, Ethan had dropped Josie off at the hospital. They'd barely spoken all the way back, and at this point he didn't know what to make of it.

"That an official diagnosis?" Ethan finished Mama B's spaghetti and pushed his plate toward the edge of the table. He really needed to get to the grocery store one of these days. And stop eating so late at night.

"I can't believe you kissed her."

"You're not the only one."

"I also can't believe she didn't push you off the cliff afterward."

"What can I say? It was a good kiss. And she— started it."

Josh shook his head. "You're still an idiot."

"Agreed."

"What are you going to do now?"

"I have no idea." Ethan poured creamer into his own coffee cup. "This was not the plan."

"What was not the plan?" Molly appeared at his elbow, scooping up his plate.

"Ethan kissed Josie." Josh did his best to suppress a grin, but failed miserably.

Molly set the plate back down with a clatter, motioning for Ethan to slide further into the booth so she could sit on the edge. "You kissed Josie."

"She says, in a tone reserved for kitten-torturers. Ease up, Mols." Ethan rolled his eyes.

"You kissed her? Really?"

Ethan nodded slowly, sighing as he twisted his coffee cup in slow circles, like he'd seen Josie do earlier this afternoon. Had *he* started doing that first, way back when? Or had she?

"What were you *thinking*?"

"I wasn't, obviously."

"Well, that's that, then." Molly stacked creamer cups on Ethan's plate.

He looked at her sideways. "What do you mean—that's that, then?"

"I *mean* that's that. Maybe she'll send you a postcard from Boston. Or maybe she'll never talk to you again. *Again*. We've been here before, right?"

"It's not the same, Mols."

"No, clearly it's not. By now you should be smarter. You should know better than to go around kissing girls who already broke your heart. You should *really* know better than to give them a chance to do it again."

"Yup. You're right."

"I know." Molly slid out of the booth, then reached over and cuffed Ethan on the head. "Snap out of it."

She turned to Josh. "Talk some sense into him, will you?" She grabbed the plates and headed for the kitchen, but Ethan very clearly heard her mutter *Moron!* before she got too far.

"I—um—I'm definitely not doing this because she just told me to, but seriously, what *are* you thinking?" Josh raised his eyebrows over his coffee cup.

"I really, really don't know."

"You know she's not going to stay, right?"

"Yeah, I do."

"So you know if you let yourself get wrapped up in thinking about a future again, you're just going to set yourself up for another fall, right?"

"Know that, too."

"Then now would be an excellent time to let it go no further."

"Yep."

"No offense, but you're not really convincing me you're listening."

"Yep."

"You're not listening, are you?"

"Nope."

"Nice." Josh put down his coffee cup. "I feel like a girl having this conversation over coffee, but since I happen to vividly remember the six months after the wedding-that-wasn't, and since I'd probably be the one Molly'd call to pick you up off the floor *again* this time, I'm begging you to back off and think this through."

Ethan blew out a heavy breath and slouched over his mug. "I know. I really, really, *really* know. She doesn't belong here, never wanted to be here, doesn't want to stay. And I can't leave. I don't even want to leave. I mean, maybe I *would* want to, if circumstances were different. But I can't move Dad. Not now. And there's no way I can leave Avery's House.

"And . . . hell, I have no idea what her life's like back in the city. Yeah, we kissed, and a part of me wants to think it's because after all this time there's still a flame, but the sane part of me knows it's all an illusion right now. She's vulnerable, we're both replaying memories, and it's easy to fall back into old routines. Even if that's the last thing either of us wants to do."

"That sounds very reasonable and objective. Well done."

"It's easier to be reasonable and objective when I'm not with her."

"So how are you going to handle things now?"

"One day at a time, I guess."

Josh paused, raising his eyebrows. "As a physician, I strongly advise no more kissing."

"All settled in?" Ethan tucked a quilt around Emmy Friday morning, then rolled the mini-recliner toward the window in her room at Avery's House, sitting down in the chair next to her.

She picked up a corner of the quilt and sniffed it. "Ahh. Smells like pinecones."

"Excellent. Did you order your lunch yet?"

"Peanut butter and strawberry fluff." Emmy rubbed her stomach and smiled.

"Yuck." Ethan stuck out his tongue, but was thrilled she had appetite enough to even think about eating such a combination.

"You don't know what you're missing."

"I think I'll keep it that way, if it's all the same to you."

She giggled. "I'm having a chocolate milkshake, too."

"I'm sure that will go perfectly with peanut butter and fluff."

"You can stop sticking your tongue out. What do *you* eat for lunch?"

"Fried tarantula legs."

Emmy crinkled her nose and giggled again. "That's disgusting."

"You could always dip them in strawberry fluff."

"Eww. Yuck."

"You're right. That would be a waste of perfectly good tarantula legs." Ethan pointed out the window. "So do you see Ben's surprise?"

Emmy turned to scan the park below her window. "Hm. Oh! Ethan! The Twinkle Fairy's spinning! It's fixed!"

"Just for you, squirt."

"I can't wait to go ride it! Think I can go today?"

"Maybe not today. Let's let your body get a little stronger first. When you're ready, you can ride it all day long if you want to."

Emmy looked out the window, watching the rides spin and twirl below her. Ethan could see the blue veins pulsing in her head as she sat there, and he sent a silent prayer of thanks that she was able to sit here planning a peanut butter and fluff lunch with a chocolate shake.

"Did Avery like the Twinkle Fairy?"

Ethan started. "What?"

"Did Avery like the Twinkle Fairy?" Emmy kept her eyes glued on the window. They'd never talked about Avery. Not ever. Had Steph told Emmy what he'd told her? As he composed an answer, he felt like he might just be out in the middle of a not-quite-frozen pond.

"Well, actually, she loved the Ferris wheel best."

"Hmm. I guess I can see that." She looked thoughtful. "What did you call her, Ethan?"

"I called her munchkin."

"That's good." She nodded solemnly. "I've been hoping you didn't call her squirt."

"Nope. No way. That one's all you."

"Do I remind you of her?"

Ethan paused before he answered. What did she want to hear? Of course she reminded him of Avery. Every child who came through Avery's House reminded him. But though the memories triggered by Emmy and the others ripped him apart at times, he'd made a promise ten years ago to a beautiful little girl that he would never, ever forget her.

Creating this house had been the best way he could think of to do that.

"I think . . . I think everybody reminds me of her a little bit. I loved her an awful lot, and she was a very special little girl to a lot of people."

"Does my cancer remind you of hers?"

Emmy looked suddenly smaller in the already-tiny recliner, and Ethan wished for the thousandth time that he could do more than give her a fun place to stay for a few weeks. He reached out and pulled her onto his lap, cuddling the blanket around her.

"She had a very different kind of cancer, squirt. It was one the doctors just didn't have the medicine to treat. And it was a long time ago. Things are so much better now."

She settled her little head into his chest and curled her legs up, pulling the quilt closed under her chin. Her voice was almost too soft to hear as she asked, "Am I going to get better, Ethan?"

He squeezed her gently. "You better believe it. You've got the best doctors around, all sorts of amazing medicine, and a super-strong little body. And a mom who loves you."

"And you. You love me, too, right?"

"And me. I will never, ever stop loving you."

"Even if I turn into a cranky teenager?"

Ethan laughed. "Even *when* you turn into a cranky teenager. Which, come to think of it, you better not."

"Well, I'll try. No promises." She smiled up at him, then nestled her head back down. "Why don't you have any kids, Ethan?"

He took a deep breath, staring out the window at the Snowflake Village rides twinkling through the trees. Emmy's question was a gut punch after spending a restless night thinking about Josie and the life he'd thought they'd be living by now. "I guess . . . I guess it's just not my time yet."

"You're not going to live forever, you know. Don't you think you should start looking for a wife?"

He chuckled sadly. "If you only knew, squirt."

"Will you sit with me till Mommy gets done with her shower?"

Ethan shifted in the chair, settling Emmy more comfortably and adjusting the blanket around her. "You betcha. Close your eyes and dream of the Twinkle Fairy."

"I'm going to close my eyes and make some wishes."

Ethan's eyes snapped open at words that sounded so eerily familiar. "What kinds of wishes?"

"I'm not sure yet. At the hospital I had a dream about wishes. A little girl gave me a bag of pennies and told me I could make wishes with them."

Ethan's heart raced. "What did she look like?"

"Um, I don't remember." Emmy's forehead furrowed with concentration. "Wait. She had a blue hat on. And a ponytail. She said I should use the pennies for get-better wishes."

"Wow."

Wow.

"That sounds like a—perfect—dream."

Emmy nodded. "It was. She was nice." Then she closed her eyes. "I think I need to sleep again."

"Okay, squirt." Ethan's voice was a little shaky. "Sleep tight. Happy—wishes."

Ethan closed his eyes, trying to stem the flood of memories that came with Emmy's dream. There were enough pictures of Avery around the house that Emmy could certainly have conjured her up in a feverish dream.

But the pennies and wishes? Only a select few people knew about the way Avery used to bring little baggies of pennies to the wishing well at Snowflake Village, even before she was sick.

*   *   *

"Whatcha wishing for today, munchkin?" Ethan sat down on the bench next to where Avery was pitching pennies into the wishing well.

Avery shrugged. *"I'm not sure I'm sure what to wish for."*

"That sounds complicated."

"I'm scared, Ethan."

Ethan gulped, knowing Josie had taken her to the oncologist just yesterday. *"I would be, too."*

"I don't want to be sick anymore. Who's going to take care of me?"

Ethan's gut roiled at the question, furious that an eight-year-old would even have to ask it. He put his arm around her tiny shoulders, pulling her close to him. *"We all will, Aves. Don't you worry about that at all. Josie and I will be with you through it all."*

She looked up, eyes huge and hollow. *"You promise?"*

"Pinky swear." He held up his pinky and she hooked it with her own.

"Let's call her Cruella."

"Who?"

"My tumor. She's the evil, awful Cruella de Vil and I need to crush her!"

"We will, Aves. We totally will."

Avery grabbed his hand and put her thumb on top of his, then placed a penny carefully on top. She closed her eyes tightly and said, *"Super-wish, Ethan. Double-power wish."*

"Okay, munchkin. Super double-power wish!"

"One! Two! Three! Wish!" Avery lifted both of their hands so the penny went flying into the wishing well.

"What are you two up to?" Josie walked up and sat down on the other side of Avery. *"Ethan? Are you okay? Your eyes look funny."*

Chapter 23

"You need a grape Popsicle?" Ben's quiet voice broke into Josie's thoughts as he settled beside her in the pine needles next to the river that same morning. She'd been sitting there for an hour waiting for the magic of the burbling water to take over and calm her jumbled brain. Between kissing Ethan last night and her dad's state this morning, though, it wasn't working.

"I think I need a whole box of 'em, Ben."

"How's your dad?"

"He's doing okay. Mom and I met with his physical therapist this morning. Looks like they might move him to rehab in the next couple of days."

"Well, that's good news."

Josie shrugged. "I guess. It's hard to tell. It's not like he's made much progress besides waking up. Not that that isn't huge, I mean. But wow, Ben. Wow. She spent a lot of time talking about how involved the family should be in his care, and how we're looking at months and months of rehab just to get him to a functional state. And the whole time, I just sat there feeling guilty that I need to get back to Boston in a couple of weeks."

"Maybe you will, maybe you won't." He sighed. "I went to visit him last night."

"You did? Did he recognize you?"

"No." Ben shook his head sadly. "I don't think so, anyway. Hard to tell yet." He tossed a twig into the water and watched it drift downstream.

"I don't know, Ben. My whole life is in Boston . . . and I like it that way." *Don't I?* "I took two weeks off, but I can't saddle my partner with a whole clinic for any longer than that."

She threw a twig in to chase his. "I'm worried about Mom. It sounds weird to say after . . . everything. But I am."

"Of course you are."

"This would be tough for someone who *hadn't* had her history."

"Yup."

"So what's she going to do when things get too hard to handle? That's what gives me nightmares. All the progress she's made could go up in one little slug of one little bottle."

"All true."

Josie looked up from the water. "You're not especially helping here."

"Just listening."

"I know. I appreciate it." She flung another twig, more angrily than she meant to. "Oh Ben. What am I going to do?"

He paused, studying her. "I get the feeling your dad's not the only thing on your mind."

"Ha." *You don't know the half of it, buddy.*

"Not so easy popping back into town, eh?"

She sighed. "I feel like I've been gone way longer than ten years."

"Lot of changes." He picked up a batch of pine needles and rolled them between his hands. "It's not the same place you left."

"I know. I can see that. But a lot hasn't changed. I think that's the hard part."

"Yup. S'true."

Josie watched a leaf spin in the lazy water as it headed over the shallow pebbles. "I was so sure I was so right about everything when I left."

"Part of being young, honey. We always know everything when we're eighteen."

"I just don't know what to think about anything anymore. Mom's different, Dad's . . . well, I don't even know who Dad is anymore, and Ethan's different but the same. I can't sort it all out."

"You will. You haven't been back but a week. You think you're going to figure it all out overnight?"

"Yes." Josie frowned. "But I apparently misjudged how complicated everybody got."

"It might not be my place to say it, but I think everybody got a little *less* complicated after you left."

"Thanks, Ben. That makes me feel *so* much better."

"You know that's not what I meant." He tossed more needles into the water. "I just mean no one ever expected you to up and leave. You were gonna go get your degree and come back and run the place when your dad retired. It was the plan."

"It wasn't *my* plan."

"I know. Your parents were too wrapped up in their own troubles to see that at the time. But when you left, it was like a light went off here. Your dad walked around here for weeks looking like he didn't know whether it was morning or night."

"Well, I didn't exactly make a graceful exit. I'm sure he was furious."

Ben shook his head and leaned his elbows back in the pine needles. "I don't remember him being mad. I really don't. I remember him being sad. Very, very sad. He came down to my shed about a week after you'd gone, and he could hardly string sentences together. Thought it was all his fault you'd gone sour on his dream for you. Thought you blamed him for your mom's issues. Thought he'd scared you away forever."

"Well . . ."

"He changed, honey. He knew he'd been using this park as a crutch for years. Knew he'd been avoiding your mom's problems by making sure he was never home. I just don't think he'd ever had the power to step outside himself and realize what it had all done to *you*. When he did, it knocked him for a serious loop. He never thought you'd really leave.

"So . . . he took that next week off, brought your mom to Maple Tree Farm to dry out, and he's been helping her stay sober ever since. They've been praying for years that you'd come home, but they wanted you to do it in your own time, for your own reasons."

He looked into her eyes. "Every single day they miss you, honey. Every single day."

"Ben, stop it. You're going to make me cry."

"I'm just telling you the truth. You get to decide what you do with it."

Josie threw another twig into the brook and watched it spin until it was out of sight. "Why didn't they ever tell me any of this?"

Ben took a big breath. "I don't know, honey. I think they wanted you to come home of your own accord, not because you felt guilty or coerced by them cleaning up their acts. They only wanted you to come back here if you felt the pull yourself. 'Course, no one coulda predicted *this* happening."

"Did you know Mom's been sending me letters every month for nine years now?"

"Nope." He looked at her. "You ever answer?"

Josie looked down, a new feeling coursing through her body. Was this what shame felt like?

"No. I never answered."

"Well, maybe you just weren't ready yet." Ben shrugged. "And I imagine it'd be hard to put away all those years that came before."

"I don't know. I just never—trusted them, I guess. They were all breezy and happy and—not the mom I knew. Felt like a stranger was writing to me."

"Did you ever start to believe maybe she was better? For real?" Ben raised his eyebrows.

"Well, she sounded it—obviously—but Ben. Alcoholics are the master manipulators of the universe. Even at her worst, she could have conjured up a newsy little fake letter once a month."

"*Every* month?"

"I didn't know what to think."

He nodded slowly. "Well, what do you think now?"

"I still don't know."

"She's not drinking, right?"

"I don't think so."

"So maybe you could let yourself believe it's for real? Just a little bit?"

Josie sighed. "Maybe. It's hard."

Ben took a deep breath. "I know. There's a lot else here that's for real, too, honey."

"I think I can only take in so much at one time."

He patted her knee. "When you're ready. When you're ready."

"I'm afraid, Ben." Josie wiped her hands on her jeans. A part of her felt like she was eight years old again and just wanted to be wrapped in Ben's big, comforting hug. "I don't know what I'm supposed to do."

"I'm pretty sure you'll figure it out soon enough. And

in the meantime, just keep moving, one step at a time. It's all a body can do sometimes."

"I wish I could love this place like Dad always wanted me to. I really do. It would be so much easier."

Ben fiddled with a twig, tearing off pine needles one by one. "Well, you did used to love it. But you ended up having a lot of reasons not to, in the end. Can't ignore them—they're part of you. But you also have a choice about what you do with them. They don't have to keep you away from this place forever, honey."

Josie nodded slowly. "I'm doing my best."

Then her stomach felt queasy as she remembered sitting in the Snowflake Village parking lot with a dead Jeep and no one to call.

"You know what's really depressing, Ben? I don't have even one friend left here."

"You might have more than you know."

"I appreciate your optimism, but it's a small town, and I dumped its golden boy."

He smiled. "Even small towns forgive, honey. You were young, your parents were different people then. You had an awful lot of very good reasons to go. Doesn't mean you can't come back, though. Give people a chance to welcome you back, Josie. I bet they will."

"I don't know, Ben. I just don't know. I never pictured it—not in a million years. I have a whole 'nother life in Boston."

Ben chuckled. "But you just said *a whole 'nother*."

"Did not."

"Did. And nobody outside of these parts says it that naturally—not that I've found, anyway." Josie felt herself smile. He patted her shoulder as he stood up. "Just keep your options open, honey. And maybe even your heart. You never know."

"I'll work on the options, for now, if it's all the same to you."

Ben chuckled. "The heart'll follow. The heart'll follow."

Chapter 24

When Josie pushed open the door of Bellinis on Friday night, the booths were all full, as was every stool but one at the bar. Must be Mama B's chicken and mostaccioli special was still the stuff of Friday-night legend around here. The noise level almost drowned out the corner televisions blaring the Red Sox game.

She walked slowly toward the one empty barstool, praying for courage. The main reason she was here was absolute desperation for home-cooked food. The second reason was her absolute desperation for a friend here in Echo Lake, as pathetic as that sounded. So she'd put on her brave face and was determined to make nice with Molly tonight. She'd probably end up with a plate of mostaccioli in her lap—*oops*—but she had to give it a try.

Five minutes later, Molly blasted through the kitchen doors and past Josie with six plates piled on her arms. Her bright red hair had escaped its headband and was falling in sticky wisps to her cheeks as she flew around the restaurant delivering plates and picking up empty glasses. Josie looked around, wondering where the other waitresses were, but didn't see another soul working.

Finally Molly blew back into the bar area and side-stepped down the bar, taking orders as fast as she could scribble on her little green pad. When she got to Josie, she didn't even look up. "What can I get you?"

"Peanut butter sandwich. Toasted on three sides. Chips on top. Side of pickles."

Molly started as she scribbled the first part, then looked up at Josie. "Very funny."

"Sorry."

"What do you really want?"

"Anything that's hot and doesn't taste like popcorn cakes or yogurt. That's all Mom keeps in the house, and I haven't had time to get any groceries."

"A burger fine?"

"Whatever's easiest, Mols. Really. You look like you're crazy-busy. I feel guilty even ordering."

Molly raised her eyebrows like she couldn't quite believe Josie was capable of the emotion. "Night servers both called out sick."

"Oh no."

"One Direction's at the Garden tonight. I'm sure there's absolutely no connection." Molly flipped the pad closed, then crashed through the kitchen doors and immediately flew back out with six more plates.

In the mirror, Josie had a view of most of the pub. It was a view she'd spent a lot of hours perusing, as Mama Bellini had sat her at the counter after school more times than she could count back in her junior high days. She smiled as she remembered coming through Bellinis' back door after school and smelling freshly baked rolls.

"Hey, Josie! So good you're here! I got seven pans of rolls in the oven and nobody to wrap up this silverware. Sit down, have a cookie, wrap!" Mama gathered her into a bear hug as she came through the door, then pulled off her backpack and sent her toward a barstool. "How was school? You ace the spelling test this week?"

Josie bit into a warm chocolate chip cookie as she nodded. "One hundred percent!"

"That's my girl. Knew it. Next thing you know, you're going to be in seventh grade. I swear, how the time flies!" Mama paused for a second as Josie took a long gulp of milk, then sidled through the opening in the bar, pointing at the bucket of hot, clean silverware. "See if you can get two hundred of those wrapped. I'm making my lasagna tonight. It's a-gonna be a busy one!"

"I'm on it!" Josie hiked herself up to her knees so she could reach the pile of napkins and fold them carefully around bundles of silverware.

"When you're done with that, Ike was wondering if you could come over and help him get his tools organized. How that man operates a garage in such a mess is beyond me."

Mama started to head through the kitchen doors, then paused. "And if it's all right with your momma, I could sure use an extra hand here at dinnertime if you want to come on back here."

"Can I run the register?"

"Can you do math?"

"Aced that test today, too!"

"Then you're on register tonight. Be back from Ike's by five o'clock, okay?" Mama winked, then bounced her way back into the kitchen, where Josie could hear her pulling pans from the oven. The smell of fresh, hot yeast rolls spilled into the bar area, and Josie's mouth watered.

Before she had ten sets of silverware wrapped, Mama appeared with a plate and set it down on the counter in front of her. "New recipe. Need a taste-tester. You let me know if they're okay." Then she bustled back through the door.

Josie buttered the two hot rolls on the plate, then took

a giant bite of the first. Mama always said she was try-
ing out recipes every single Friday, but Josie could never
tell the difference. The rolls were always hot, yummy,
and perfect—just like they'd been the previous week.

Josie shook her head to clear the memories. Mama hadn't
been trying out recipes. She'd just been feeding a hungry kid. She hadn't needed an eleven-year-old cashier,
either. But somehow she'd find Josie enough jobs to do
that eventually Mama would proclaim it too late to go
home, and Josie would climb the back stairs with Molly
and sleep on the trundle bed in her room.

Josie glanced in the mirror again. Although Molly was
clearly doing her best to keep up with the crowd, it was
a three-person job at least, and Josie could see irritation
rising in the crowd. Uh-oh.

"Hey, what's a guy gotta do to get a drink around here?"
A sweaty palm landed on Josie's shoulder as a chubby guy
in khakis and a polo shirt tried to create a space between
her and the next barstool.

Josie calmly pulled his paw from her shoulder and
manufactured the brightest smile she owned. "Maybe a
please would help? I'm sure you can see they're short-
staffed."

"Not my fault. Hey!" He wiggled his empty beer mug
at Molly, who was practically running down the bar with
more plates. She delivered them efficiently to a group in
the corner, and Josie watched in the mirror as she then
looked around, trying to figure out who needed what
next.

"Is there *nobody* else working in this hole?" The guy
slammed his mug on the wooden bar.

Without stopping to think through what she was doing, Josie spun around on her barstool and elbowed the
guy. "Follow me."

"Seriously?"

She cocked her head toward the door that went only to the decrepit old back porch over the riverbank, but he didn't know that. "Come on."

"That's more like it. I'll follow *you* anywhere, babe." Josie bristled as he put a hand at the small of her back while she weaved through the patrons.

When she got to the door, she undid the latch and squeaked open the door. "Come on. Right through here." Once his body cleared the threshold, she slammed the door shut and pulled the latch closed.

Then, before she could talk herself out of it, she headed back to the bar, flipped open the counter, and grabbed an apron that was hanging under the register. She tied on the apron, pulled her hair into a quick ponytail, and scooped up a pen and order pad, then went to the corner of the pub she knew Molly hadn't had time to get to in the past twenty minutes.

She'd done enough shifts here in high school to remember the drill—and, she smiled—the menu. Before Molly emerged once again from the kitchen, Josie had taken orders from three tables and delivered drinks to two others. On her way back to the bar with a stack of new drink orders, she was so busy scribbling that she barely looked up in time to avoid a pile of plates with Molly's legs. She leaped to the side as Molly flew between tables, and was drawing draft beers by the time she got back to the bar.

Molly stopped short when she saw Josie with her hands on the beer levers. "What the hell are you doing?"

"Helping." Josie shrugged her shoulders.

"Why?"

"Because you're short-staffed and I'm here and I can."

"We don't need you here, Josie." Molly practically spat.

"I know." Josie slid three beers across the bar and gave change, then put a ten-dollar bill in the tip jar as she pulled Cokes with the other hand. "You want me to go?"

"Yeah, I do."

Josie slid the Cokes down the bar to another couple as she mixed a whiskey sour. "Okay. I'm gone. I'll just finish these drink orders."

"Good." Molly slammed through the kitchen doors and Josie couldn't quite hold in a smile. She wasn't going anywhere. She would just stay behind the bar and out of Molly's way, and maybe, just maybe, she could start forging a path toward friendship and forgiveness.

A new pile of plates flew through the kitchen doors and Molly hissed, "Not done yet?" on her way by.

"Big order."

Molly delivered the meals, stopped at a couple of tables, then came back toward the bar. As she flipped the counter upward, Josie pushed a glass of seltzer into her hand. "Drink."

Molly held the drink for a moment, and Josie braced herself in case Molly decided to dump it over her head, rather than drink it. Thirst must have overpowered her, because Molly looked down, gave the lime a quick squeeze into the water, and threw a *thank you* over her shoulder as she banged back into the kitchen.

"Wowza. What are you serving with the mostaccioli in here tonight? Gold?" A guy in his mid-twenties nodded his thanks as she slid a draft beer toward his spot at the bar.

"Just Mama's magic sauce." Josie winked as she pulled two more beers and slid them toward his friends. All three wore T-shirts with the colorful logo of the local river tour company, and she assumed a trailer full of kayaks was somewhere in the parking lot. "How was the river today?"

"Might have been better without the city-slicker guests. Luckily we left them camping downstream."

"You left them alone beside a raging river? Remind me not to book a tour with you guys anytime soon."

He took a gulp of his beer, then set it down. "Last time that river raged was April. They're just fine." He winked. "Have you ever tried rafting?"

"Nope. I would be a disaster on the river."

"Can you swim?"

Josie raised her eyebrows. "I shouldn't need to, should I?"

He laughed. "No, but if you can, then there's nothing to worry about. Worst case, you get dumped. Then you swim."

"Well, as fun as that sounds . . ."

"You should try it sometime. Book a tour. Or a lesson."

Josie felt her eyebrows crinkle as she looked at him. Was he flirting with her? His open posture spoke volumes, as did the eyes that followed her every movement.

"I'm . . . just visiting, but thanks."

"How long are you here for?"

"Not sure yet, but I'm not big on being left as bear bait."

"I didn't really leave them alone down there. Promise." He brushed sandy-colored hair away from his eyes, which were a riveting blue. His face was tanned, but paler around the eyes, where his sunglasses probably sat all day long, every day. "They've got three guides with them still."

"Ah. More for the bears."

"The bears are fine if you throw them a kid every couple of weeks. You really should try it someday. It's fun."

"Maybe. You never know." Josie smiled quickly and moved down the bar to take other orders.

For the half hour that followed, as she bustled up and down the bar collecting orders and pouring drinks, she glanced his way every once in a while. Every time, he met her eyes. He was a normal, hot-ish, fit, pleasant male of a similar age who was clearly interested in getting to know her better. But as much as she wished it would do something for her, *anything* for her, it just . . . didn't.

Ethan, on the other hand . . . She just had to *think* about his lips on hers last night, and her face went all hot and bothered.

She finally stopped in front of river-guide guy again, noticing his beer was almost gone. "Can I get you anything else?"

"All set for tonight, thanks." He put a twenty on the bar and slid off his stool. "But really, if you ever want to head out to the river, give me a call." He pulled a card out of his pocket and put it over the twenty, then winked. "I'd love to take you out."

As he left, she fingered the card, smiling just a little at his efforts. Then she felt her smile turn to a frown as she realized she had no desire at all to go near the river. Not with this guy, not with anyone.

The lake, on the other hand, was a different story.

Ethan pushed his French fries around his plate as he waited for Pops to finish his lasagna. Bellinis was so busy they'd been lucky to score a booth, and even then, they were stuck in the back near the bathrooms.

"Whatsa matta? You not hungry?" Pops squirted more ketchup on his already saturated meal.

"Guess not."

"Something on your mind, son?"

Ethan looked at Pops, surprised. He sounded so lucid, so present. He was having a good day, so Ethan had decided to take advantage of it by getting him out of the house for his favorite dinner.

"Just the usual, I guess."

"Boston princess?"

Ethan laughed softly. "Yeah, Pops. Boston princess is definitely taking up some space."

"Not gone yet, huh?"

"Nope. Still here."

As if he'd conjured it, he suddenly heard what he swore was Josie's laugh coming from the bar. But it couldn't be. She wouldn't set foot in here again of her own accord, would she?

But there it was again. He slid farther out of the booth and craned his neck to see the end of the bar where the register was.

"Well, I'll be damned." There she was. In a frigging apron. *Behind* the bar. He shook his head. What the hell was going on?

"You'll be damned why?" Pops forked another mouthful in as he turned his head to see what Ethan was looking at. "Oh. Well, I'll be damned, too. We'll be damned together."

"God forbid," Ethan muttered.

"I heard that. My hearing's not going—just my mind."

"Sorry." Ethan took another drink, watching Josie over the rim of his cup. Molly had been moving so fast as she took their orders and delivered their dinners that she hadn't stopped to even say hello, let alone explain what Josie was doing here.

If he didn't know better, he'd think she'd been working *here* every night for years, not at some hoity-toity Boston office. She covered the bar like a pro, pulling beers with one hand while flipping glasses with the other. She had roped her hair into some twisty configuration that corralled her curls and left her creamy neck exposed. The apron did nothing to hide the curves beneath, damn it.

He dragged his eyes back up to her face, watching as she served draft beers to three guys from Rugged River Tours. Two of them were locked onto the game above Josie's head, but one was definitely making moves, and Ethan noticed his own hands clenching. She served them their beers, then leaned down to talk with Nathan, the owner of the company.

As she gestured and smiled, Ethan found himself increasingly irritated. She'd been kissing him breathless just last night, then practically running away—and now here she was at the bar talking with Nathan like he was the only guy in the room.

"She's not gonna stay here, y'know." Pops sopped up the last of his sauce with his bread. "You ought not get your heart all broke up again."

"I know, Pops."

"You know, but you don't *know*. Time to get over her, boy. She left you once. She'll do it again."

"I know."

"Well, maybe somebody needs to hit you over the head with a hammer. You were, what, eighteen when you got engaged? It's been ten years, son. You gonna wait forever? Or you gonna live your life?"

Ethan felt a familiar stab in his gut at Pops's words. It'd been a long time since Pops had taken him to task over his life choices, but the memories of him doing so were still crystal-clear.

"Well." Pops's jaw was tight after they came out of the doctor's office.

"I know." Ethan was barely holding it together after hearing the doc utter the words that had summarily ended his military dreams.

"I'm gonna get Coach on the phone. Gonna sue his ass."

"Pops, he had nothing to do with this."

"Bullshit. If he'd trained you better, we wouldn't be in this position."

Ethan paused. "We aren't in this position, Pops. I am."

Pops turned on him. "You were gonna be a Marine, son. A Marine. You were gonna make me proud."

Ethan felt a knife edge through his gut. He'd always known his dad believed military service was the only path to greatness, and until now, that had sat pretty well with him. He got good grades, his teachers called him a natural leader, and he'd impressed Norwich into a scholarship. He was on his dad's ideal path, and he was okay with it.

It was his dream, too.

Now it was neither of theirs, and he didn't have any idea what came next. That night he hobbled to Mom's gravestone in the family plot way out back, and he sat there for hours, until the frost chilled him numb.

Mom would have had wise words to comfort him with. She would have said something about God closing doors and opening windows, in that gentle way she had. She would have talked to him, instead of coming home, closing the bedroom door, and slamming things around until long after dinnertime had passed with nothing on the table.

Yes, with one freak play in the state finals, he'd somehow crashed and burned his entire life plan. But until it happened, he didn't realize how much it would crash and burn his own father.

Ethan shook his head. Long time ago, that play.

Long time ago, that Pops.

"So . . ." Pops looked up. "What are you gonna do about her?"

"I don't know, Pops. Maybe we just need to start over. Put the past behind us. You know, all that stuff."

"What? You gonna date her now? *After* she already did you in?"

"The thought has crossed my mind."

Pops shifted his weight, glancing over his shoulder at Josie, then back at Ethan. "Listen to me, Ethan. Listen while I make some sense. That girl? She ripped you to pieces once, and it almost killed you.

"Don't let her do it again, Ethan. Don't let her do it again."

Chapter 25

"Have a happy ho-ho day!" Josie handed candy canes to three little girls in pigtails, then straightened back up to continue down the pathway. Her calves were still screaming from last night's marathon at Bellinis, so she'd decided to don a costume this morning instead of sitting in the office.

It had nothing to do with avoiding Ethan. She was almost sure of it. Yes, she just wanted to stretch her legs, though the twenty-pound fake head she was wearing was bleeping heavy.

"Wow. You sound like you almost meant that." Ethan's voice startled her from behind.

She turned toward him, which was kind of a feat in this costume. "Hey! Don't sneak up on Sno-Cone Sally. She has no peripheral vision."

"Sorry. How *is* Sno-Cone Sally today?"

"Very blue." Josie pointed at her costume head, then at the neon pants. "And green."

"You definitely are hard to miss." Ethan paused as she handed candy canes to two more kids. "So are you trying to avoid me, or did you really think Sally needed an outing this morning?"

"I'm a counselor. I don't do avoidance."

"And yet, after you brought a plant to my office and

threatened that you weren't leaving, you're out here in the park doing candy-cane duty."

"Well, some of our college kids had to go back to school, right? So we're down a few employees. I'm just trying to be helpful."

He steered her off the pathway and behind the Dippy Doo ride, then turned her to face him. "Is it because we kissed?"

"I'm not avoiding you, Ethan."

"So you're not purposely staying away from me because you're afraid you'll be powerless against my charming wit and pecs of steel?"

Josie laughed. "Terrified, actually. You know how I love your charming wit."

"So . . . I was wondering . . . If I promise not to flex in public or display higher-than-average intelligence, would you consider maybe going out with me? Like, on a date sort of thing?"

Was it her imagination, or was he actually nervous? "A date? Seriously?"

"Yes. A date. Like, a first date, even. No pressure, no expectations. Just—a date."

"I don't know, Ethan. I don't think that's a good idea. I think we've already gotten in over our heads."

"It took me ten years and two days to work up the nerve to ask you, and you're going to turn me down?" He smiled, then tipped his head toward her. "It's just a date with an old friend. No ulterior motives. How can you say no?"

"Um, one, because we did this thing ten years ago and it ended with a sort of nuclear cloud. And two, I am adult enough and trained enough to know that I'm *really* in the wrong mind-set to start tootling down memory lane."

His face turned serious. "I'm not talking about memory lane. I'm talking about getting to know each other again, as adults. Though"—he pointed to her costume—"that sounds pretty funny to say, given your getup right now."

Josie shifted her weight on her huge neon shoes. She had to be clear that she wasn't staying. It wasn't fair to give him false hope.

Or her, if she were to be more honest.

"They're moving Dad to rehab."

"Okay?"

"So I just . . . I just don't know whether Mom will still need me here for much longer."

"I thought you took a two-week leave."

"I did, but it's my own business. If I'm not seeing patients, I'm not making any money. I have a cat to feed, after all."

"We can certainly pay you a salary while you're here, Josie. You're putting in almost as many hours as I am at this point."

"No. No salary. It'll be fine." A salary sounded *way* too permanent.

"Okay." He paused to let a group of teens pass. They were laughing and jostling each other, and you could practically smell the hormones. Had she been like that, once upon a time? Back before she'd blamed the park for all the wrongs in her world?

Ethan touched her elbow. "If I promise to acknowledge that you may disappear in the middle of the night at any point in the next two weeks, could we still maybe go out for dinner tonight? As friends?"

"Just dinner?"

"Just dinner, Jos. I just want to spend a couple of hours away from this park, away from the hospital, with you. Just you."

"Aw, dammit. Don't say—romantic stuff like that."

He looked surprised. "Was that romantic?"

"And now you'll say something inane like *Wait until I'm actually trying!*"

"Wait until—no, never mind. So tonight? I'll pick you up at six?"

"Okay." She grimaced inside the costume. What was she thinking? "Can you please wear something ugly?"

"Don't want me to look good on our non-date?"

"Exactly. And no after-shave."

"I won't even shave. And I'll wear holey jeans and a nasty old flannel shirt." He winked. "See you at six."

Josie almost choked inside her costume as he headed back down the pathway toward Elf Central. Yes, old jeans and a flannel shirt would be perfect. Because if he showed up looking any more dressed up than that, she was going to have a much harder time thinking about anything besides that damn kiss by the cliffs.

She started strolling in the other direction, alternately smiling and frowning. What was she thinking, saying yes to a date with the one man who apparently still had the power to turn her knees to Jell-O and her brain to mush?

This was destined to end badly.

"Wow, it smells good in here." Mom peeked into the open bathroom door while Josie stroked mascara over her lashes. "Does someone have a date?"

"Um, it's actually a non-date."

"That why you're shaking so hard you're about to poke out an eye?" Mom smiled. "Mind if I come in?"

"Okay. Sure?" Josie motioned her into the small bathroom, where Mom sat on the closed toilet and pulled up her knees. It struck her that normal moms probably did this with their teenaged daughters all over America, but it had sure never happened in this house.

"Is it Ethan? Or did you meet someone else?"

"It's Ethan. Thus the non-date." Josie brushed bronzer onto her cheeks, trying to tame down the nervous redness in her cheeks. She'd paired her navy blue sundress with a netted sweater and a locket Ethan had given her ages ago.

"I see. Is that why you're wearing his favorite perfume?" Mom raised her eyebrows playfully.

"I—no. Not really, no. It's just what I've always worn."

"I see."

Josie turned to face her. "You sound like me when you say *I see* like that. It's a therapist phrase, but from a mother it sounds way more loaded."

"Does it, now?" Mom smiled. "It's not loaded. I'm just listening. Happy that you're having a date." She put her finger up as Josie started to protest. "*Non*-date."

The doorbell rang, startling both of them. "Oh no! I'm not ready!" Josie scrambled to toss her makeup into her cosmetic bag.

"Don't worry. I'll stall him. I bet he can't resist my chocolate chip cookies."

Josie looked up. "Is that what I smelled last night?"

"Mm-hm. They're to die for, if I do say so myself."

"Will wonders never cease?"

"I know! I bake!" Mom flipped her hair and scooted down the hallway to open the front door while Josie shook her head. She put away her makeup, then turned left to right and back again in the mirror, hoping she looked like just the right blend of *Wow-see-what-you've-been-missing?* and *See-how-I-totally-put-no-effort-into-dressing-for-this-date-that-isn't?*

When she walked into the kitchen, Ethan was sitting at the tiny table with Mom, and his upper lip had a suspicious smudge of chocolate already. He had on dress pants and a crisp blue oxford, and his face looked freshly shaven.

Dammit.

He looked up when she walked in, and she could swear his eyes brightened. "Help me, Jos. Your mom's plying me for information."

"Using chocolate chip cookie torture?"

He scooped another one from the plate before he stood up. "I'm helpless against these cookies. Save me."

Josie laughed, but inside, she was shaking her head again. It was a scene she'd dreamed up long ago, one where her boyfriend would come to the house and be all adorable and respectful to her doting mother who'd just baked cookies in the kitchen. It had had absolutely no basis in her high school reality, of course, and seeing it play out ten years later in that same kitchen was surreal.

"Call off the cookies, Mom. He's a man. He's weak." Josie pulled Ethan's arm as he reached for another cookie.

"One for the road." He grinned as he popped it in his mouth. Oh, how she'd like to kiss that little smudge off his lip right now. "You look gorgeous, Jos. Are you ready to go?"

She pulled her purse from the chair where she'd started hanging it. "I'm ready."

"Thanks for the cookies, Mrs. Kendrew. What time shall I have her home?" Ethan's voice was playful as he guided her down the hallway with his hand at the small of her back.

"No later than Monday. Have fun, you two." Mom opened the screen door and shooed them through, waiting on the porch as Ethan opened the passenger door and waited for Josie to settle in the seat.

As they rolled backward in the driveway, Mom blew a kiss. "Drive safely! See you tomorrow!"

Out on the main road, Josie was silent, processing the scene at home.

"Well, that was . . . odd." Ethan's voice was level, his eyes on the road.

"So it wasn't just me?"

"No-o. Not just you. But it was a good odd, right?"

Josie nodded slowly. "Yeah, it was. It really was."

Ten minutes later, Ethan pulled into a curving driveway that led uphill toward a huge brick Greek Revival home at the far edge of town.

Josie peered at the sign, then at Ethan. "You didn't."

"It's your old favorite. I thought it would be nice."

"It's very date-ish, that's all."

"Well, we're kind of overdressed for McDonald's. I thought we should step it up a notch."

"About that. Weren't you supposed to wear flannel?"

He grinned. "I was fresh out. You'll have to take me in these duds."

Josie gritted her teeth. "You look very nice."

"Do I hear a *dammit* at the end of that compliment?"

"I'd still prefer toothless and bald. Just sayin'."

He parked the car and came around to open her door, reaching in for her hand as he did so. As she stepped out, she misjudged and lost her balance, tipping right against his chest. Of course.

"You really need bigger feet." He chuckled as he set her upright, looking down at her three-inch heels. "Or maybe smaller shoes? How do you wear those things?"

"Not very well, apparently."

Why had she worn heels? They totally said *date*. She adjusted her sweater and stepped away from the door, dislodging his fingers on her waist as she did so.

He stepped in close again as he shut the car door, pausing as he pushed the lock button on his key chain. "You smell nice. I still love that perfume."

"Thank you. It's revenge for you wearing my favorite after-shave all week."

"Got it." He took her hand. "Should we go see if Luciano's cooking is still the best?"

"Don't let Mama B hear you say that. Do they still have their feud?"

"Of course. They're cousins."

"Does he still make that ridiculously yummy bread?"

"I hope so."

She paused on the walkway just outside the inn. "How long has it been since you've come here?" Was it possible he'd never taken anyone else to her favorite restaurant? She hated that she loved the idea.

"Ages." Ethan looked up at the tall black doorway. "But right now it seems like just yesterday."

When they were seated at a corner table for two, Ethan proposed a toast. "To our first non-date. May there be many more."

Josie giggled as she clinked her glass to his. "Emphasis on *non*."

"Of course. As you wish. Let's pretend we don't even know each other. So Josie . . . it's Josie, right?" She giggled again. "Okay, small talk. Hm. What's your favorite zoo animal?"

"Zoo animal? Seriously? This is your first-date small talk?"

"First *non*-date. And it's been a while since I've had one. Can't get too personal, right?"

"Right. Okay. Um, giraffes. Yours?"

"Hippos."

"Hippos? Why on earth would you choose hippos?" Josie laughed. "They're huge and ugly."

"They're big and bad and they don't care what anybody thinks about it. Giraffes are smelly, by the way."

"They have cute faces."

"All right, since I already knew the answer to that one, what's your favorite kind of car?"

"Dream car or reality car?"

"Either. Both."

"Okay, reality car. I love my Jeep. I mean, if it would stop breaking I'd love it better, but I love it."

"I can't say I'd ever pictured you in a Jeep. A Prius maybe. A Camry?"

"Ugh. Old-lady car. My dream car would be a convertible Mini Cooper, I think."

"Not a Ferrari? A candy-apple-red Porsche?"

"Are you kidding? In Boston? If it didn't get swiped the first day I owned it, I'd be lucky. Plus, it would cost a mint to park it."

The waiter arrived at the table with a steaming basket of Italian bread and a shallow bowl filled with garlic dipping oil. Josie sighed with pleasure as she broke apart the bread and dipped it into the warm oil. "This is heavenly."

"Did you forget how good all the food is here in Echo Lake?" His smile was half amused, half—she wasn't sure what.

"I know you want me to say that I forgot how good a lot of things are here in Echo Lake."

"It *was* a rather brilliant lead-in."

"Then yes. I did. I have to admit I haven't had a maple creemee in ten years, or an Italian burger like Mama B makes, or God, this bread." She pulled another piece from the basket before she could calculate the calories. "I think if I hit Morris's French fry cart before I leave, I'll have recharged my culinary memory bank."

"So tell me about your patients in Boston."

Josie paused. It was such a loaded question, even if he hadn't intended it to be. "Well, I get a lot of referrals from Boston Children's. Mostly parents of the kiddos getting care there. The system takes great care of the kids, but not so much the rest of the family. I feel like it's such a gaping hole."

"Do you do grief counseling, too, then?"

"At times. But mostly I tend to get families right after diagnosis, when everybody's reeling and scared out of their wits."

"That sounds intense."

"It is. Really is." She picked at her bread. "But it's good work. Necessary work. So it feels good while it's feeling awful."

"We know all about awful." His eyes were serious, probing. "Is that why you do it?"

She paused. "Of course it is. Nothing made sense after . . . after her. But this? This makes sense. I guess."

She cringed, feeling like she'd shared too much, but sitting here with Ethan, in the warm garlic-scented restaurant where they'd spent almost every special occasion they'd ever shared, just made her feel all stupidly gooshy inside.

"I know what you mean." He nodded, then started to reach across the table for her hand. Their eyes met, and instead of touching her, he fiddled with the cloth napkin in the bread bowl, fishing out another piece. He cleared his throat. Was he nervous?

"So you do counseling all day. What do you do in your down time? How do you decompress?"

Good question. How did she? "You know, I'm not sure I really do. Between the free clinic and my practice, I probably do about sixty hours a week, and then I collapse. I taught a couple of intro-level classes at BC last spring, which was ridiculous."

"Are you scheduled to teach there again this fall?" She could tell he was forcing his voice to sound like he didn't care one way or another.

"Emphasis on *ridiculous*. No. It was too much. I like

teaching, but teaching practically for free isn't as fun as it sounds. I did enough of that as a grad student."

"Do you still bike?"

"Not on purpose. Just when I have a case of dead Jeep." Josie shook her head. "I'm a little too attached to my limbs to risk them cycling through city traffic."

She paused as the waiter delivered their food—a succulent chicken Bolognese for her and a lobster ravioli for him. Then she stared at her plate for a moment. "I sound hideously, horribly boring, don't I?"

"You sound hideously, horribly busy, actually. Do you ever go out? Have a social life?" Again she could hear the effort in his voice.

"That I *do* do. I'm a serial dater of incompatible men."

He laughed out loud. "Define *serial*."

"At least one date every three months. It's a tough schedule to keep straight."

They were both quiet for a few moments as they tasted their food. After a sip of her wine, Josie screwed up her courage. "And what about you, Ethan? How's your love life been these past ten years?"

She hated that she braced for the answer.

"Oh, you don't want to know that. Totally inappropriate question." He winked at her.

She speared a piece of chicken a little harder than she meant to. "I'll just ask Josh. I think I caught a glimpse of him at the hospital yesterday."

"The man code will require him to give an answer that best benefits me, you know."

Josie ate another bite of her chicken and washed it down with a long sip of wine. "Are you dating anybody now?"

"No." He looked at her, his face serious. "I'm finding that non-dates are more fun."

Half an hour later, after they'd dissected their favorite

movies from the past few years, Josie pushed her plate away and rubbed her stomach. "Oh wow. That was the best meal I've had in a long, long time."

"Want to go walk it off on the paths out back?" Ethan stood up and came around to pull out her chair.

"They're not still romantic, are they? Not strewn with gorgeous flowers and hidden benches?"

"Definitely not. No. It's all gone to hell back there. Full of weeds and pricker bushes." He winked as he held her sweater for her.

"Perfect. Let's go."

As they headed out the door, Josie's phone beeped with an incoming text, and she glanced at it briefly just to make sure it wasn't Kirsten trying to get hold of her about a patient. But no. It was from Mom, and oh Lord, it wasn't good.

"Oh my God, Ethan." She held up the phone, but her hand started shaking too hard for him to read it.

"What? What?" He grabbed her hand to steady it. "What's wrong?" Then he read the text and grabbed his keys, pulling her at a quick walk to his truck.

Chapter 26

"We got here as fast as we could." Josie practically ran into the waiting room, Ethan on her heels. "What's happening?"

Mom was perched on the edge of a chair, smiling and teary at the same time. "He's trying to talk, honey. He's really trying. They gave him a letter board and he's trying to point to letters."

Josie turned to Ethan, then back to Mom. "Talk? So he's not . . . dying?"

Mom's eyes widened. "No! Goodness, no! Why would you think that?"

"Your text, Mom. It says *Come to the hospital as fast as you can*." Josie held out her phone so Mom could read it. "And then you didn't answer when I called."

"Oh Lord." Mom pulled out her own phone and tapped a couple of times, then put her hand to her mouth. "Oh, Jos, I'm so sorry. The second half of the message says *Dad's talking!* I must not have clicked SEND."

Josie sank into a chair, knees suddenly jellyfish. "It's okay. It's good. I'm *glad* he's okay. But good God, maybe press SEND next time, okay?"

Ethan settled in the empty chair next to Josie. "So what did he say?"

"Nothing we can make sense of yet. He keeps pointing

at the letters, but he's so unsteady it's hard to tell what he's trying to spell so far."

"Why are you out here, Mom?"

"They had to do some . . . stuff in there. Now that he's awake, I feel like he should have some privacy, I guess?" She brushed something nonexistent off from her jeans. "That probably sounds stupid. We've been married for thirty-three years. It's not like I haven't seen all there is to see."

Ethan smiled. "Well, as a man, I can say that even after thirty-three years, I'd appreciate the privacy if some nurse was doing . . . *stuff* to me."

"Diana? Want to come back in?" Gayle stood in the doorway, rubbing sanitizer into her hands, an impish grin on her face. "Hey there, Josie. Move fast and I can sneak you in while Ida's on her break."

Ethan stood as Josie and Mom started to follow Gayle into the hallway. "I'll just wait out here for you guys."

"You don't have to, Ethan. Really. Mom can bring me home."

"I want to." He picked up an ancient, dog-eared magazine from the table beside him. "I'll be right here."

Josie tried to ignore the way his simple words made it feel like warm syrup was circling her insides, but it was a feeling so strong—so *good*—that she just wanted to wrap her arms over her stomach and hold it tight.

Gayle bustled Mom and Josie into Dad's room and pulled two chairs to his right side. "Here you go, ladies. This way he can see you better." She handed what looked like a kids' alphabet whiteboard to Mom, along with a thick black pointer. "Want to see if we can try again?"

Josie looked into Dad's eyes as she settled gingerly into her chair. They were clearer than they'd seemed last time—more focused, less vacant. He was staring right at Mom, and was she imagining it, or was his mouth trying to smile? The right side of his lips was raised just a smidge.

"Look, honey. I brought Josie along this time!" Mom pointed her way, and Dad's eyes moved slowly to lock on Josie. Josie held her breath, not knowing what his reaction might be. He looked at her face, then down at her hands, then slowly back up at her face, and again it looked like he was trying to smile. Then he lifted his right hand off the bed and reached toward Mom.

"You want to try the letters again?" Mom held the board as she curled his fingers around the pointer. "Here. Go ahead."

With what looked like almost painful effort, Dad skated the pointer over the board, struggling to stop on particular letters. When Mom had guessed three in a row, unsure of whether she was right or wrong, Dad closed his eyes, appearing frustrated.

Josie leaned toward him. "Dad, how about you blink once if we guess wrong and twice if we're right?" His eyes opened wide and he gripped the pointer again. Josie watched the board as he moved the pointer. "*O?*" One blink. "*P?*" Two blinks. "Okay, *P*! Go ahead. What's next? *I?*" One blink. "*J?*" One blink again. "Sorry. Sorry. *U?*" Two blinks. "*U! P-U!*"

Josie wrinkled her nose. "*P-U? Are you joking with us?*" One blink, then a hard tap on the board. "Okay, sorry. Keep going." He tapped and blinked as they guessed, and by the time he put down his hand, exhausted, Josie felt warm droplets of water running down her cheeks.

"*Punkin.* You spelled *punkin,* Dad." Her voice came out in a sob. "That's me."

Two blinks.

* * *

"Okay, you are banned from the dairy aisle, Mom. You have *got* to start eating something besides yogurt." Josie pushed the cart through the doors of the grocery store on Sunday morning. "Holy cow. This place is as big as a stadium!"

"Not quite the same as Gloria's Quik-Stop, hm?" Mom smiled as she looked up at the cavernous ceilings. "You should have *seen* the development board meetings before this place was approved. Half the town thought it would destroy the village character forever, and the other half couldn't wait to have a grocery store big enough to actually need wheeled carts."

"How long's it been here?"

"Just a couple of years, actually. And as much as I appreciated hearing the latest on Gloria's dermatology issues each time I shopped, I'm more than happy to not know about them anymore."

Josie smiled as she bagged up apples and plums and grapes and bananas for the cart, tossing in a melon and broccoli and green beans as they wheeled through the produce section. Mom peered in. "That's an awful lot of fruit."

"Fruit is good for you. Quite possibly better than yogurt, even."

"Sacrilege. Stop picking on my yogurt." Mom elbowed her playfully as they rounded the end of the aisle and started up the next one.

Thirty minutes later, Josie wheeled the cart toward the registers and started placing groceries onto the belt. As she pulled items from the cart, she realized Mom was biting her lip, trying not to smile too widely.

"What's so funny?"

"Nothing."

"You're going to chomp through your lip. What's funny?"

"Not funny. Just nice." Mom pointed at the brimming belt and still half-full cart. "You've got enough food here to stay for a month."

Josie paused with two jars of peanut butter in her hands and looked at the groceries. "This *is* a lot of food." How had she managed to pull so much stuff off the shelves in such a short period of time?

Moreover, *why* had she loaded so much food into their cart? Now that Dad was showing signs of improvement, she could think about heading back to Boston sooner, right? *Right?*

Mom laughed out loud. "Don't look so scared. Maybe we can learn to cook while you're here."

"That might be good." Josie exhaled slowly, loading the rest of the food on the belt. "Especially since given my dining choices thus far, I'm going to get *fat* while I'm here. I really need to get some exercise before my butt resembles Sno-Cone Sally's."

"At least your old bike works, though I really wish you'd use my car."

Josie paused to pay the cashier, then rolled the cart toward the doors. "I think Ike is holding my Jeep hostage so I won't leave town. He keeps saying the part isn't in yet."

"Well, remember, it takes longer to get stuff up here than it does in the city."

"I don't think it takes this long to get a part to Alaska, Mom."

Mom raised her eyebrows as she popped the trunk of her Camry. "You never know, I guess. Maybe someone else asked him to take his time."

"Right." Josie grinned at Mom, but felt her smile falter as she saw Mom's lips press together in what looked like anger. "What's the matter?"

Mom's eyes darted over Josie's shoulder, and then she

shook her head like she was trying to clear it. "Nothing. Nothing. Just thought I saw a ghost there for a minute."

Josie glanced over her own shoulder, then froze as she saw the woman staring their way.

"Get in the car, Jos." Mom pulled the cart away from her hands and steered it toward the corral right next to them. "Come on. You don't want to talk to her."

Josie couldn't stop staring at the woman, who also seemed frozen to the pavement. Then a loud squawk from inside the woman's tiny car startled them both, and the woman tore her eyes away and opened her car door.

The car sped out of the parking lot and before Josie realized she'd stopped breathing, Mom's arm was over her shoulder, turning her around toward the Camry. "Don't think about her. She hasn't changed. Not one bit."

Josie stumbled into the passenger seat, breathing faster than she should, but she couldn't slow down. As Mom slid into the driver's seat, Josie turned to her. "How can the state keep giving her foster kids? She doesn't deserve children."

"No." Mom shook her head emphatically as she turned the key in the ignition. "She doesn't. She didn't then, and she doesn't now. She certainly never deserved Avery."

Josie heard a sound that resembled a pathetic whimper come out of her mouth, and she pressed her hand to her lips as a memory crowded into her head.

"Are you ready, kiddo?" Josie grabbed the handles of Avery's wheelchair. Once again, Avery's foster mother had asked Josie to pick her up at the hospital after her one-week stay. Apparently her hair appointment had been more important than her child this morning.

"Super-ready, Jos! Can you do NASCAR-*style on the way out?"*

Josie laughed. "I think there's a rule in the Big Sis

handbook about wheelchair racing. If we crash, they might kick me out of the program. Then they'd give you a horrible awful new sister who'd make you eat broccoli and never take you to Snowflake Village."

"Horrors." Avery shivered dramatically, but reached up to give Josie a fierce backward hug. "Thanks for coming to get me."

"Anytime, kiddo. Anytime."

Avery waved to everyone gathered in the nurses' station as they rolled by, blowing kisses like a mini Miss America. As they rolled through the lobby a minute later, Avery was quiet. Then she put her tiny hands on the wheels to stop them. "Wait."

"What's wrong?" Josie leaned down.

"Nothing." Avery pointed toward an elderly woman sitting on a padded bench just off the lobby. "Can you roll me that way for a minute?"

"Um, sure. Do you know her?"

"Nope. Come on. Roll." Avery pushed the wheels with her hands, trying to make Josie go faster.

When they reached the bench, the woman looked up, mystified. Avery held out her hand and said, "Hi! I'm Avery!"

The woman smiled tentatively and put her hand around Avery's. "Hi, Avery. I'm Madeline."

"I really like that wrap thingie you have on your head."

In an instant, the woman's face softened as she lifted her hands to her soft turban. "Well, thank you, dear. My daughter got it for me."

"Do you think they make those in orange?"

"I bet they do, sweetheart. I bet they do." Then she put her hand on Avery's knee. "In the end, it's a small price to pay for getting better. Hair grows back, after all. You might even get curls next time around!"

"I know, but I really think I look terrible *bald."*

"I think you look beautiful, sweetheart. I bet no one even notices your hair when they see that smile of yours. Your heart shines right through it."

"Thanks, Miss Madeline." Avery squeezed her hands. "Maybe I'll see you here again."

"Maybe," Madeline replied softly. "I'd sure love that."

Avery put her hands on her wheels and pushed backward slowly, then stopped to blow her a kiss. "Flutterby kiss!"

As Josie turned the wheelchair toward the door, she leaned down to kiss Avery on the head. "Hey. I thought flutterby kisses were reserved for me and Ethan."

Avery tipped her head thoughtfully as they emerged into the bright August sunlight. "They are, but she looked like she really needed one."

Chapter 27

"So Dr. Heath called again. He's—quote—still very anxious to speak to you about the symposium in Seattle next month." It was three days later, the park had been sprouting problems like dandelions all day, and Josie had only picked up the phone because she feared Kirsten might be calling about a patient. But no.

"Does that man not understand the word *no*? I won't even agree to go to dinner with him. Why in the world does he think I'd drop everything and head off to Seattle for a conference with him?"

"You've gotta give him points for persistence. And Seattle's nice this time of year."

"Not funny, Kirsten." Josie adjusted a soda nozzle as she clamped her phone between her shoulder and her ear. "Did you tell him I've retired and moved to the Himalayas?"

"He didn't believe me. Also couldn't get him on board with your solo sail around the world. Or your midlife-crisis trip to Siberia."

"Midlife crisis? I am *not* midlife."

"I'm happy to forward him your way if you'd like to come up with better ideas."

Josie laughed. "You're doing just fine."

Kirsten sighed. "I could tell him it's really unfortunate,

but you perished in a freak moose accident. Maybe he and I could go out for drinks to mourn together."

Josie laughed out loud. "You do like Seattle."

"You're right. I *am* that shallow." Kirsten shuffled some papers on her desk and cleared her throat. "So listen. Given that it's Wednesday and you're still up there . . . what are your thoughts about next week? Still think you'll stay up there? Should I try to shuffle patients again?"

Josie clamped the front of the soda dispenser shut, then nodded to the teen manning the snack cottage as she slid out the side door. This was the third repair job she'd done already this morning, and she was only doing the easy ones since Ben already had his hands full with a couple of rides that had decided to pop screws overnight.

Ethan was—she had no idea where. He'd headed out of the office this morning with a quick wave, and she hadn't seen him since.

She put her free hand to her forehead and grimaced. "I just don't know. Dad's finding more words each day, it seems. They're still waiting for a rehab spot to open. I feel like maybe I should at least stay up here until he's settled wherever he's going to be for the short term, you know? Just to be sure Mom's okay?"

"Of course."

"But I know this is putting you in a serious lurch. I've already been gone almost two weeks, and I know you can't keep covering my patients and your own."

"Speaking of which, Britney took herself to the ER last night."

"Oh no. What happened? Did she call us first?" Britney was nineteen, with a medical file two inches thick already. Josie had talked her through a full slate of real and imagined crises over the past year, and was finally getting close to convincing her to stay on her meds regimen. Or thought she was, anyway.

"She did." Kirsten's voice was tentative. "But she wasn't crazy about talking to me."

"Ugh." Josie stopped at a green metal bench and sat down, staring into the pines. If she was a physician who dealt with people's physical issues, it'd be so much easier to leave her patient load in the care of a colleague. But emotional problems were a whole different ball game. It took forever to gain the trust of patients, to get them to open up, to get them to a space where they'd accept help.

Britney was the perfect example. She'd been working with her for months, and two weeks after she'd finally broken through the girl's ironclad shell, she'd been unreachable when Britney needed her. Dammit.

"I'm really sorry, Kirsten. *Really* sorry. Is she doing okay?"

"She's stabilized."

"Did you try to reach me?" Josie fumbled her phone while she talked, trying to see whether she'd missed Kirsten's call.

"I didn't know about her until she was admitted, and then I thought I could handle it, but she's a tough cookie to crack."

"I'm sorry."

"You can stop apologizing. It is what it is, right?" Was it Josie's imagination, or did Kirsten sound a little tense? "We'll get through this. It's part of having a partnership. If we were in a hospital, there'd be other therapists to step up and fill the gaps. But there are only two of us, so if one's down, the other's gotta make it work."

"I had no idea I'd be gone this long, though. This is too much for you."

"I'm totally taking a two-week vacation when you get back, so don't worry. I'll get my payback."

"I don't know, Kirsten. I wish I could be in both places at once. I just wish we knew someone who could—hey!" An idea flashed into her head. "Do you remember Jordan Romano? You met her at that dinner a month back?"

"The one who just moved back from Denver? Sure."

"Do you think maybe . . . could we maybe ask her to fill in for a week or two until I get back? Since she hasn't found her own setup yet?" Silence greeted her question. "I know it doesn't solve the Britney-type problems, but maybe we could have her do some of the lower-risk patients?"

"I don't know, Jos. It's a lot to ask of her."

"She might be hungry for the work. And I can't leave you alone to handle everybody. We thought I was only coming up here for the weekend, remember? And now we're going on two weeks. It's not fair to you."

"You'd do the same for me, and you know it."

"Nope. I'd have Jordan installed in your office in three minutes flat."

"Funny. It just feels . . . weird, I guess. This office is our baby. I feel strange having someone else come in."

"Just temporarily."

"You say that now."

"Oh, I *mean* that."

"You *mean* that now. I know. But you never know." Kirsten's voice trailed off.

"Just think about it, okay? We don't need to decide right this minute."

"All right. I'll think about it. I won't like it, but I'll try to come around to at least contemplating it."

Josie smiled. "Good girl."

"So I can't hang up without asking how Ethan is."

"Sure you can. He's fine."

"Any more non-dates?"

"No. The park's crazy-busy, and I've been at the hospital pretty much every other minute. We've barely seen each other."

"And you're good with that?"

Yes. No. Yes. Definitely no. "Yes. Definitely."

"Because the possibilities are frightening?"

"That's one way to put it."

Kirsten sighed. "Safe's overrated, Jos. If you're going to be up there anyway, I vote for danger."

After she hung up from Kirsten's call, Josie sat on the bench for a full five minutes. It was mid-afternoon, and stroller traffic had eased as parents headed for the water park at the eastern edge of the property. She put her head back on the bench for a moment, drinking in the quiet. As the swish of the pine boughs and twittering of the chickadees washed over her, she thought about Avery—about how much she'd loved this quieter part of the park where the wishing well stood.

Josie's head snapped up. The wishing well! Why hadn't she noticed it in the entire time she'd been back? She peered through the trees into the clearing where it should be, but instead of its simple white frame and green bucket, all she saw was a young sugar maple surrounded by a lush garden of daisies and pansies.

She jumped up from the bench and strode into the clearing. Where was the well? Had something happened to it? Would they have moved it? *How* could they have moved it?

With all the memories tied to the pennies it housed, how in the world could anyone have ever taken it out of the park?

The radio at her waist squawked, breaking into her

internal tirade. She pressed the button to answer. "Josie here. What's up?"

"Hi, Josie. It's Sarah over at the dairy bar. Two of my guys just left for home because they weren't feeling well, and it's crazy over here. Any chance you could come help out till closing?"

Josie hesitated. What she *really* wanted to do right now was go find Ethan and see what the story was with the wishing well. Sarah's voice came over the radio again. "I'm really sorry to ask, but I think something's going around. We've lost about six people this afternoon."

Josie narrowed her eyes at the radio. "Is this the week they have that Rock Fest over in Keene?" She'd seen an advertisement in the paper, and if she wasn't mistaken, there was a band playing tonight whose current song seemed to be on every radio station she'd tuned in for the last month.

"Um, yes? I think?" Sarah's voice sounded nervous. "But they really did look sick."

"Of course they did." *Right.* "I'll be right over. Hold tight."

She gave a last glance at the maple tree and shook her head, then headed for the dairy bar. Where in the world was Ethan this afternoon? Why was everyone calling her?

Didn't they know she was just temporary?

The radio squawked again and she pulled it off her waist. "Josie here."

"Uh, yeah, Josie. Nick here. Hey, we've got a kid up a tree."

She held the radio away from her like it was going to grow legs. "You've got a what up a *what*?"

"Kid. Up a tree."

"Where?"

"Over by the Penguin Plunge."

"How *far* up a tree?"

"Um, he's really up there. This is bad."

"He can't get down?" Josie started walking double time toward the Polar Plunge.

"Could, but he won't. And keeps threatening to jump if we come up."

"Oh God. Have you called the fire department?"

"They're all out on Cooley Road. Big barn fire."

"Shit."

"Excuse me?"

"Nothing." Josie shook her head. "Sorry. I'm on my way. Keep talking to the kid. Don't break contact, whatever you do."

She broke into a jog and reached the tree one minute later. She saw a couple of employees and what had to be the kid's parents, so she headed for them. "Hi, I'm Josie. I'm the . . . I work here."

Had she just almost said she was the owner? What was coming over her?

"I'm Paige. Hi. Thanks for coming." The mom's words came out in flutters.

"So tell me what happened."

"I don't know!" Paige had her hand to her throat, looking up into the tree. "Everything was fine! We were walking around, and then he just darted over to the tree and started climbing up it. But then he wouldn't stop! And now he's . . . oh God . . . look how high he is!"

Josie looked at the dad, whose hands were braced on the tree like he was ready to climb after the kid. "Sir, what's your son's name?"

"Bryce."

"How old is he?"

"Ten."

Josie backed up to a spot where she could see Bryce's

Red Sox hat through the limbs. Cripes, he really was up high. "Bryce! Hi! I'm Josie! Whatcha doing up there?"

Silence as the boy stared her down.

"You know what would be great? How about you climb back down here? These trees can really sway if the wind picks up."

More silence. Josie swore silently, wishing she'd squeezed one more pediatric counseling course into her schedule.

Josie turned toward Paige. "Does he do this often?"

"No! Never before. I don't know what came over him."

"Has he spoken since he got up there?"

"Only to tell us to stay down here or he'd jump." The last word came out like a little hiccup as her hand flew to her throat again.

Josie looked up at the boy, then back at Paige. "Is anything bothering him right now that you know of? Is he sad about something? Mad?"

"No! Nothing! Really! Everything's fine!" Paige pointed vaguely to a little boy in a wheelchair. "Brennan was having a good day, so we thought we'd come over to the park and see if we could get in a couple of hours before his next meds." She looked at her watch in the automatic gesture of parents who have to medicate their kids on a strict schedule, and Josie suddenly saw the situation more clearly.

She looked back up at Bryce, then at the people starting to wander closer, wondering what was happening. She had to act quickly if she was going to get him out of the tree before he slipped and ended up doing it himself.

She turned back to Paige. "All right. I have an idea, but you really need to trust me."

"Okay?"

"Take Brennan and Dad here out of sight. I'm going

to go up after him, and I'll do my best to talk him out of the tree."

"You're going to *what*?" A deep voice came from behind her as a strong hand circled her wrist. So Ethan actually *was* in the park today. "No. You are not climbing that tree."

Josie put her finger to her lips and motioned him away from the parents. In a low voice, she hissed, "You and I both know I've climbed this tree more times than anyone else in the known universe. And where have you been, anyway? Sarah needs help at the dairy bar. This park's falling apart today!"

"I've been busy. And no offense, Jos, but I imagine it's been a long time since you've climbed trees."

Josie leaned down to tighten her laces. "Fire guys are all out on a barn fire. We've got no ladders tall enough to get near him. Do you see another choice?"

"I'll go."

"No you won't. You're big and male and scary."

"You do know how to stroke a guy's ego."

"Seriously, Ethan. He's playing all big and brave, but he's probably scared out of his wits up there. I'm going up, and I'll bet you a maple creemee I get him down."

"You haven't bet me a maple creemee in a really long time."

"I know. So I must mean it, right?" She widened her eyes, pleading. "Get the parents out of here. He won't come down while they're watching, I guarantee."

Ethan made a growling sound in his throat. "I'm not happy about this."

"Duly noted."

"Keep your radio with you." He pulled it off her waist and fiddled with the dial. "Here. Now if you press talk it'll just go to me, not the entire park."

She took it back and shoved the clip back into her

waistband. "Got it. Okay, go. Get out of sight so I can get him out of this flipping tree."

"Do you need a boost?" He cupped his hands under the lowest branch, which was still almost over her head. As much as she didn't want to admit that she did indeed need one, she stepped into his hands and let him lift her into the tree.

"Thank you. Now go."

"Be careful."

"Always. Now shoo! Go! Seriously! Kid up a tree!"

Why was he looking at her like she was breakable? Like he wanted to stand under the tree and catch her if she slipped? He really needed to stop it.

Because she really didn't want to like it.

Chapter 28

Ethan got Bryce's parents situated with two park employees, then snuck around through the trees so he could come close to where the boy was while still staying undetected. The family had checked into Avery's House for the first time just yesterday, but he hadn't had time to talk with them yet, so he had no insider information that would help Josie talk the kid out of the tree.

As he crept through the pines, he was grateful for the needles that silenced his steps. He kept one eye on the lithe body scaling the tree branches and one ear on the radio. Unbeknownst to Josie, he'd clicked hers on so he could hear her, since he'd figured both of her hands would be busy clambering over branches.

"Oh! Ouch!" Her voice hissed through the radio. "That's gonna leave a mark." She climbed up a few more branches, but was still far below Bryce.

Ah hell. Why did his gut feel like a giant fist was stretching his innards and then snapping them back into place? The kid wasn't moving, so he was safe for now. Safe-*ish,* anyway.

But Josie probably hadn't climbed a tree in fifteen years. How safe was *she*?

"Did. Not. Sign. Up. For. This. Ow!" Ethan listened as she cursed her way up the tree. "Not trained for this!"

He crouched as he got closer to the tree, and planted himself under the low branches of the one just beside it so neither she nor Bryce could see him. At least if the kid fell, he might have time to scramble and try to catch him.

"Hey, Bryce. How's the view up here?" Josie's voice was breathless, tired. "Did you find a perfect spot?"

No answer from Bryce, and he heard Josie shuffle for a few seconds, then go silent. "Mind if I sit up here with you?"

"Don't touch me."

"I'm not going to touch you. I'm just going to sit over here, okay? We don't even have to talk if you don't want to."

"Good. Don't want to."

"I don't blame you. Sometimes you just need to sit in a tree and think."

Ethan could imagine the boy looking at her in distrust, unsure of her motives. To her credit, Josie didn't say another word, though. Not for ten whole minutes, in fact. His thighs were aching from crouching for so long, and his right knee was about to explode. How long was she going to sit up in the damn tree before she tried to get him down?

"Brennan's really sick." He started as the little boy's voice came over the radio.

"Yeah?" Josie's was soft, inviting.

"They think I don't get it, but I do."

"I'm sure."

"I didn't want to come on this stupid vacation."

"No?"

"No."

"Why not?"

Bryce was silent forever, it seemed. "Because I knew it would be like this."

"Yeah?"

"Yeah. Mom's taking a gazillion pictures of Brennan, like he's not going to be here much longer."

"Wow."

"You know what the worst part is?"

"What?"

"I know he's not."

Ethan's gut squeezed as he listened, marveling at how Josie's quiet one-word questions were cracking Bryce's shell, making him talk without him ever suspecting that's what she was doing. They sat in the tree for forty-five minutes before Josie said, "Hey, you know what? My butt is getting sore. Do you want to maybe get out of this tree and go get a Slush-Bomb?"

Bryce actually laughed. "My butt hurts, too. Let's go down."

Ethan watched carefully as the two of them climbed down the huge pine, and finally breathed a sigh of relief when he saw all four of their feet on the ground. Josie put her hand on Bryce's shoulder as they walked up the pathway toward his parents, who pulled him into an enormous hug while Josie stepped back and watched, smiling. After a few minutes and a slew of grateful hugs, the family headed toward the water park, and Josie meandered back down the hill toward Ethan.

"So. You're two for two on saving kids since you've been back."

She shrugged, but he could see the pride sneaking through her nonchalance. "I didn't save him. He could have climbed down."

"I'm pretty sure he was prepared to sleep up there, Jos. He came down because you got him down."

"Well, I just tried to help." She fussed with the pine pitch on her hands. "He's just feeling left out."

"So he climbed a tree for attention?"

"It's pretty hard to compete with a really sick little brother. And don't be under any delusion that he won't do it again. Or something like it. I didn't solve anything—just got him to safety this time."

They walked in silence for a few minutes, then Ethan stopped and put a hand on her arm. "So this is what you do."

"Well, no. I have a nice office with a couch. Tree-counseling is a new one."

"You're good under pressure."

She nodded slowly. "I guess maybe I am."

"Huh." His wheels were spinning at high speed. Avery's House was great at caring for kids' bodies, but what it hadn't yet tried was caring for their heads. Or that of their family members. He'd known it was a hole in his quest to provide the perfect getaway, but until this very moment, he hadn't seen the perfect way to plug that hole.

Would Josie ever consider . . . ? If he could show her how much Avery's House needed her, would she possibly, maybe think about . . . ?

He shook his head. He'd done a bang-up job this week of staying away from her as much as possible, determined to keep his armor intact and her at arm's length. And it was working. He got to the park at dawn, worked till he was bone-tired, then spent the evenings with Pops. In between, he did stopovers at Avery's House as often as he could, but was thankful to Molly and Josh for holding down the place so well since Andy's stroke.

He sighed. He knew better than to entertain schemes for keeping Josie here. She wasn't staying, and if he allowed himself to get his hopes up even one stupid bit, the crash would be even more painful when she left.

Josie tried in vain to scrub off the pine pitch in the little hallway bathroom, but it was stuck like Krazy Glue and she couldn't remember what in the world got the stuff off. She'd emptied a quarter of the soap dispenser, but the pitch held fast. As she walked back into Dad's office, drying her still sticky hands on a paper towel, his desk phone rang. She peered at the display and frowned when she saw that the caller was Bellinis Pub.

Had Molly misdialed trying to reach Ethan—who was apparently off somewhere else once again? Josie braced herself as she answered, but to her relief, the voice that boomed across the line was Mama B's.

"Josie! So glad I caught you!" Josie could hear pots banging in the background. "I'm thinking you're bored tonight? Nothing to do?"

"Um . . ."

"Good! You be here at five and I'll give you a free apron. It's spaghetti night and I got no help again."

"Let me guess. Your waitresses called in sick again?"

"You know it."

"Seems to be an epidemic going around."

"Only to sixteen-year-olds. Little nitwits are all heading over to Keene, thinking they're so sly. Some Rock Fest thing." Josie heard another loud clang and winced. "I'll show them sly when they show back up. You watch me."

"I'm too scared to." Josie laughed.

"So you'll help me? Even my Molly's got a date, so you can see this is dire. Otherwise I wouldn't ask."

Josie sighed quietly, rubbing her already aching feet. This day was destined never to end. "I'll be there, Mama. But I'm going to need a giant Pepsi when I arrive unless I can sleepwalk while I deliver the food. It's already been a long day."

"Eh, you get up at dawn to make the cannolis and go to sleep at midnight after the last pot's clean and you can say you've had a long day, okay? Okay. I see you at five."

Josie smiled as she hung up the phone. Yes, there sure were some things that hadn't changed around here. And the big, brusque Italian woman with the heart of gold was one of them. Her energy level could compete with an Olympian, and now Josie had to try to keep up for the night.

Two hours later, she walked into Bellinis and flipped open the counter like she'd been doing it for ten years, not just *twice* in ten years. A clean apron hung under the register, so she tied it around her waist and grabbed the suds bucket to wipe down the bar while it was still empty.

Mama blasted out from the kitchen just as she got to the end of the bar. "Oh, you're here. Thank you I love you now get those salts and peppers out would you?"

Josie smiled as Mama B punched back through the swinging doors, leaving a tray of salt and pepper shakers for Josie to deliver to the tables. Before she could grab the tray, though, Mama came back through the door with an industrial-sized jar of peanut butter and a big spoon. "Gimme those hands." She motioned toward Josie's hands, grabbing one of them and plopping a glob of peanut butter in her palm. "I don't know if I wanna know why you been climbing trees today, but you're not serving *my* food with that gook on your hands."

Josie laughed as she rubbed the peanut butter into her palms. "I couldn't remember the secret cure for pine pitch! Thank you!"

"Well, I don't imagine you've had much use for it in the city, right?" Mama's eyebrows crooked upward. "Ethan chase you up a tree today?"

"Hardly. Little kid decided to make sure mommy and daddy were paying attention, so he climbed up one of the giant pines to check."

"And you got to play monkey and get him down?"

Josie dried her hands and rubbed her biceps. "I'm pretty sure I'm going to regret it tomorrow."

Mama swished a dish towel her way. "Eh, you won't know whether it's the tree or carrying eight hundred plates of spaghetti. I'll handle the bar. You do the running around. You got the young legs."

At seven o'clock, Josie wove through the bar area to pick up an order, but it wasn't ready yet, so she took the opportunity to lean on the counter for a brief moment. Mama eyed her from the far end of the bar, then bustled her way, stopping to fill a glass with sparkling water.

"Here. Drink." Mama fanned Josie with a laminated menu. "You look like a lobster fresh from the pot. Come 'ere. Sit. Sit." Mama lifted the hinged counter and waved Josie through to the kitchen, pulling newspapers off from a chair. Josie sat down gratefully.

"What'd you do? Kill the help again?" Papi's voice bellowed from behind the grill, making Josie smile.

"Eh, she's not dead. Just forgot to drink."

"When's she supposed to drink, eh? You've had her running since she walked in. Hasn't even had time to give old Papi a kiss."

"It's good for her. City's got her all soft." Mama took her glass and spooned up a plate of spaghetti. She grabbed a bread stick and a fork and handed Josie the plate. "Here. Eat. And I don't want to hear any garbage about being a vegetarian. That sauce's got my best sirloin burger in it." She kissed her fingers and threw them in the air. "Perfection!"

Papi laughed out loud. "Mama, you'd say that even if you used horse meat." Josie choked on a mouthful of spaghetti. "Which she didn't. But you and me both know I'm right." Papi winked.

Josie smiled as she ate another bite of the spaghetti.

This was no sauce from a jar, that's for sure. And the pasta itself was perfectly al dente, just the way she liked it.

Mama nodded as she watched Josie's plate empty. "That's better. Carbohydrates are not the enemy. You stick around and I'll put some meat back on those bones."

"Her bones are just fine the way they are. Leave the girl alone." Papi ladled steaming soup into two huge bowls, then headed toward the swinging doors. "I'm gonna go eat me some soup with Mel before the next rush."

"Next rush?" Josie's voice quivered. "That wasn't the only rush?"

"Nope." Mama bustled around the huge kitchen. "That was the tourists. Locals start coming in a few minutes. Things are different than you remember, eh? Eat up! We got work to do! And you!" She pointed at Papi. "You better be back here in five!"

"Slave driver." Papi leaned toward Josie. "Hey. Why do Italian men always die before their wives?"

Josie laughed. "I don't know, Papi. Why do they?"

"Because they *want* to!" Papi quick-stepped through the door before Mama could swat him, cackling his way down the bar.

Josie stood up and brought her plate to the stainless steel dishwasher. "You two haven't changed a bit, Mama."

"Ha. And this is a good thing? I've been married to that man for forty years now. It's a wonder we're still speaking."

"Oh, you two are all bark and no bite. Can't fool me."

"Eh, we're too old to bite. Barking's all that's left. Someday you'll see. You'll be happy, too."

Josie stopped. "I'm happy."

Mama dried her hands and put them to Josie's cheeks.

"Honey, I've known you for an awful long time, and this isn't your happy."

"I'm fine. Just worried about Dad."

"Uh-huh." Mama patted her cheeks, then turned around to grab a stack of plates. "How are you and Ethan getting on?"

Oh boy. Whatever Josie said was going to go straight to Molly, so she needed to tread carefully. "We're fine. Good. It's a little awkward, of course. But it's fine. Good."

Mama turned her head toward Josie. "That was an awful lot of not-so-convincing adjectives."

"Still can't fool you, hm?"

"Italian-Mama radar is a fearful thing, for sure. I saw through you and Molly for a lot of years, so I've had practice."

"Uh-oh."

"So here's what I figure. You're single. Ethan's single. Once upon a time, you were heading for the altar, so neither of you sees any other way it could be. And that's way too scary to think about. Am I right?"

Mama raised her eyebrows. "Never mind. I'm right. So now you think—well, I can't marry him, so I'd better stay away, because God knows we can't be friends." She paused again. "Yes? I'm right?"

"Maybe?" Josie squirmed like she was thirteen again.

"So how 'bout a fling?"

Josie choked on her water. "*What*?"

"I know you, and I know you've probably psychobabbled yourself right to death about all this, but I think here's what you need to do. Stop talking yourself out of falling for him, Josie. What if a Mack truck comes along tomorrow and *poom*! That's it! Think what you would have missed."

Mama came back and put her soft hands on Josie's

cheeks again. "Every moment doesn't have to be about forever, Jos. Sometimes you just need to let a moment be a moment."

The swinging door smacked open, making Josie jump, but not Mama. Again she patted Josie's cheek. "You think about that, little one." Then they both turned around to where Molly stood just inside the kitchen.

In a flash, Molly turned back around, but not before Josie saw the bleak, hurt look in her eyes.

Chapter 29

"So how was your date?" Josie took a chance and caught Molly at the bar as they both picked up trays of drinks. Since the scene in the kitchen an hour ago, neither of them had spoken a word to each other.

"Fine." Molly turned and delivered her drinks to the corner table, then came back. "Actually, it was a certifiable disaster, but don't tell Mama."

"Oh no. What happened?" Was Molly actually going to talk?

"Two words: tractor pull."

"That was your date?"

"Don't judge. There aren't a lot of choices around here, you might remember."

"Was it . . . fun . . . at all?"

Molly leveled Josie with a frosty look, then rolled her eyes. "I cannot get the smell of manure out of my nose. Before the tractor pull we had to tour the barns and see all of the prize-winning cows."

"Um, points for being original?"

"Exactly." Molly reached for another tray of drinks Mama shoved her way. "But hey, who knew there were so many varieties of Herefords? At least I learned something new."

"Maybe you can use it to impress your next country-fair date."

Molly started to laugh, then drew her eyebrows together like she wasn't sure whether to take Josie's comment as an insult.

"I didn't mean—" Josie reached her hand toward Molly's arm.

"Whatever. You should go. I can handle things now that I'm back." Molly muttered to herself as she spun and took the drinks to another table.

Josie sighed, then jumped as Papi's voice came over her right shoulder. "It's okay. It's always two steps forward, one step back with my Molly." He put a hand on her shoulder. "You're still one step ahead."

"Thanks, Papi, but I'm pretty sure I'm still fifty or so behind."

Two hours later, Molly staggered out of the kitchen for about the ninetieth time and narrowed her eyes at Josie as she collapsed on a stool. The restaurant was finally empty and Josie was restocking bar glasses. "Still here?"

"Still want me to go?" Josie paused.

"Whatever."

Josie couldn't help but smile this time. Molly's grudging *whatever* was as close as she was going to get to an engraved thank-you card, so she'd take it. She poured a large glass of seltzer and popped two limes on the edge, then slid it toward Molly.

"Two limes? What, you think we're made of money around here?" Molly tried not to smile as she squeezed the limes into her drink and took a swallow.

"Eh, take it out of the tips." Josie pointed to the tip jar, which was just about to burst its top.

"Good God, what were we serving out here? Was it legal?" Molly scooped her hand into her server's apron and let a pile of bills fall onto the counter. "I got these, too. I'll take this pile. You take the jar."

"I was just helping out. I'm not taking your money, Molly."

"Not my money. You worked more hours than me tonight." Molly took the jar and emptied it on the counter. "Damn. Were you flirting up Nathan again?" She poked through the bills, coming up with a twenty. "Yup! You were."

"Who's Nathan?"

"Rugged River guy you were leaning over the bar talking to. Again."

"Ah, the one who leaves his guests camping down the river so he can come get a beer."

"He's a nice guy. You could do worse. Though I guess flashing your assets earned you a good tip, at least."

Josie started. "*What*? If I leaned toward him, it was because I couldn't hear over the televisions, not because I was flashing any of my nonexistent cleavage."

She looked down and pointed at her chest. "Seriously? You accuse *these*?"

Molly cracked the first smile Josie had seen all night. "You have a point."

"Thank you." Josie wiped down a section of the bar. "And thanks for letting me stay."

"You wouldn't leave."

The bell on the door jangled, and Molly swore under her breath. "Crap. I forgot to lock up. I am *not* walking across this damn floor one more time tonight. And I am fresh out of service with a smile."

"I've got it. Sit." Josie swung around to play hostess, but when she saw who'd just walked in, her feet froze.

Ethan grinned and held up two paper lunch bags stained with grease circles. "You ordered?"

Josie couldn't help but laugh at his expression, and at

what he carried. "We did not. You'd better hide those. You know what Mama will think if she sees them."

"No worries. Just saw her go upstairs. We're free to eat 'em." Ethan grabbed the barstool closest to the counter and placed the bags reverently on the counter, wafting their scent toward Josie with his hand. "Resist if you can."

"Ha." Molly grabbed one of the bags and flipped it open. "I have no pride." She pulled out two hand-cut French fries and dipped them in the ketchup she'd already poured on a napkin. "I am going to marry Morris and live in his French fry wagon."

Josie opened the other bag and peered in before she plucked a golden, hot fry out and let it slide into her mouth. "Oh God."

Ethan raised his eyebrows. "Still as good as you remember?"

"Better."

"That's because you don't actually *eat* anymore."

"I eat."

"Not nearly enough."

"Well, I'm definitely eating these." Josie popped another one in her mouth. "I can't believe Morris still does these."

"Just for another few weeks, till the tourists head back south."

"Can't your mom offer him a contract to work through the winter or something, Molly?"

Molly shook her head. "Are you kidding? If she knew we were eating these, she'd have our heads."

"Are either of you going to share?" Ethan held out a hand.

"Not me." Molly shook her head.

Ethan reached into Josie's bag and pulled out a handful of fries. "Remember you wanted to serve these at our reception?"

Josie's stomach jolted as a fry got caught in her throat. She swallowed carefully. "Well, they're good. And I was eighteen."

"Okay, you two. Enough memory lane. Tonight's already firmly in *Twilight Zone* territory." Molly shook the tip jar and wiggled her eyebrows up and down. "Speaking of which, we've got tips."

Josie paused, then laughed uncertainly. Molly couldn't possibly—"No. No way."

Years ago, they'd take their tips and go midnight bowling after a shift like this. But that was ten years ago.

"Ethan?"

"Midnight bowling? Oh, I'm definitely in." Ethan slid off his stool. "Think you can score a hundred, Jos?"

"I haven't been bowling in—"

"Ten years?" Both Molly and Ethan finished her sentence.

"Yeah. Ten years."

Ethan held out his hand. "Then it's high time you went. Come on. It's Disco Night. Lights go on at eleven."

"I can't bowl."

Molly snorted. "You never could. Never stopped you before." Her eyebrows went up in challenge.

Josie crumpled up the French fry bag, then looked down at it in surprise. She'd downed more calories in the past three days than the previous three weeks in Boston. She was going to need a new wardrobe if she wasn't careful. "You guys really still—bowl?"

A strange look passed over Molly's face before she answered. "We still do a lot of things, Josie. That's kind of how it works here." Then, in a flash, she positioned her mouth in a big grin as she swung the bar counter up and ducked under it. "Come on. Live like the simple folk. Come midnight bowling."

Molly linked elbows with Ethan and led the way out of the restaurant. As Josie followed them out the door, the irony was hardly lost on her that this time, she was the third wheel tagging along with two people who'd maybe been getting along just fine in her absence.

It made her think of another night, another world.

"What do you guys want to do?" Molly leaned on the bar at the end of the night.

Josie shrugged. "I don't know. What do you want to do?" It was early August, and if she had to spend one more Friday night at the bowling alley, she was going to scream. There was nothing to do in this town.

"Midnight bowling?"

Josie grimaced, but tried to hide it. No such luck.

"Okay, Wellesley princess, what is it that your highness would prefer to do this evening?"

"Shut up, Mols. I just wish we had choices besides midnight bowling."

"Well, in three short weeks, you can go clubbing and see artsy late-night films and take a midnight Boston Harbor cruise if you want. Meanwhile, me and Ethan will still be here . . . going midnight bowling." She linked her arm in his. "Which, I should add, you have always actually liked to do."

"I do like it. I'm just . . . I don't know. I'm just a little sick of it, maybe?"

Before the words were out of her mouth, Josie saw two different expressions of hurt. Molly didn't try all that hard to hide hers, but Ethan's disappeared behind a steely mask almost as quickly as it had appeared.

"Well." Molly pulled her tiny purse from under the register. "I'm going bowling. Ethan? You coming?"

Ethan looked from one to the other of them, sensing a female standoff but knowing instinctively that he had the wrong chromosomes to understand it. He reached out for Josie. "Come on, Jos. Let's go."

Josie sighed. "I need to use the ladies' room. I'll be out in a second." She turned to head down the back hallway, but before she got to the bathroom, she turned back to see Molly and Ethan heading toward the door, Molly's head on Ethan's shoulder.

Yup. She was leaving. They were both staying.

There were a lot of ways this could go.

Twenty minutes later, Josie felt like she'd been teleported back ten years. When they'd been teenagers—and before she'd tired of it—midnight bowling had been a highlight of the week in a town that had nothing at all going on after dusk. But she hadn't picked up a bowling ball, hadn't tied on god-awful ugly saddle shoes, hadn't washed down greasy pizza with a pitcher of Pepsi since she'd left town.

She looked around the alley as they waited for shoes, and was struck by a strange comfort. Balls bombed down the lanes and hit the pins with satisfying crashes. The smell of pepperoni hung in the air, and colorful pitchers of soda were scattered on the tables behind the lanes. Strobe lights flashed, and high-pitched laughter hit her ears every few seconds.

Ethan turned from the counter and handed her some shoes, looking down at her feet. "Can you fit into an adult shoe yet?"

Josie rolled her eyes. "I'm sure these will be fine, thanks." They made their way to the farthest lane, bypassing six empty ones on the way. "Did you request this lane on purpose?"

"Maybe."

"Afraid to have anyone see me beat you?"

Molly sat down to put on her bowling shoes. "He's probably just protecting the innocent." She pulled the laces tight. "Or maybe they still have your name on the black list up there."

Josie sat down across the table from her and pulled off her sneakers. "It wasn't my fault. The ball got stuck on my thumb."

"We know." Molly pointed up at the tiled ceiling. "You can still tell that part had to be repaired."

Ethan laughed as he tied his own shoes. "I think they were more concerned about the lane they had to repair when the ball came back *down*."

"I was still pulling ceiling chips out of my hair three days later." Josie grimaced.

"You're lucky they weren't pulling the *ball* out of your *head*."

Molly found a ball that fit her fingers and placed it on the ball return. "Well, it almost won us a trip to California for that funniest video show."

"But we were beaten out by giggling triplet babies. Go figure." Josie pulled a ball off the rack, but it almost pulled her shoulder out of its socket, so she swung it back in. Her only goal here was to not make a complete and utter fool of herself. If pins went down, that'd be a bonus.

"Okay, princess. You're up." Molly pointed her way.

"You can stop calling me princess, Molly." Josie finally found a ball she could lift, and that let her fingers slide in and out, so she pulled it off the rack.

"Sorry. Habit." Molly actually looked a little chagrined as Josie passed her on the way to the lane.

Ethan motioned toward the sides of the lane. "Need the bumpers?"

"Never mind bumpers. Alert the seagulls on the roof." Molly laughed.

Josie pushed her fingers into the slightly scratchy holes and pulled the ball to her chest, looking down the lane toward the pins. She tried to remember which foot to lead off on, when to swing the ball back, when to let go, but it had been so long that she knew it was going to be a disaster.

She took a deep breath and squared her shoulders. Then she tried to coordinate stepping and swinging and letting go and not falling, and remarkably, the ball left her hand and sailed smoothly down the lane with a deep, rolling grumble.

She backed up slowly, watching the ball, but her jaw dropped as it crashed into the pins and felled every single one of them. A strike? Her? Had that ever happened before? She turned around and laughed out loud when she saw Ethan's expression.

"Holy shit. That was a strike."

"Mm-hm." Josie blew on her fingertips, then wiped them on her shirt.

"You've never gotten a strike."

"You don't know that."

Ethan got to his feet, shaking his head, then took his time lining up his shot. Josie smiled at his concentration, knowing he'd be damned before he'd lose to her. She tried not to look too hard at his body while he stood there, but couldn't stop herself. Her eyes traveled up his jeans, focused for a moment on his perfectly tight butt, then continued up his back, where his shoulder muscles tensed.

She realized she was biting her lip just about the same time she sensed Molly's eyes on her, and she looked over, trying not to flush with guilt. To her credit, Molly kept her mouth shut, but her eyebrows went up in a knowing way, and she narrowed her eyes as she watched Ethan's ball fly down the lane.

Chapter 30

After Molly had stumbled sleepily out of the truck at Bellinis a couple of hours later, Ethan paused with his hands on the wheel. "So. Where to next?"

Josie squirmed. It was past midnight, and ten years ago, they would've sped out to the lake without a second thought, then gotten lost in the blankets in back. She was frightened by how much of her wanted to do it again, especially after Mama B's little live-for-the-moment speech earlier. "It's . . . it's late."

"Do you have a curfew?" He raised his eyebrows, the edges of his lips tilting up. God, how she wanted to take her seat belt off, slide onto his lap, and kiss those lips again.

She shook her head and swallowed hard, thankful for the darkness that was hopefully hiding the blush she could feel creeping up her cheeks. "No curfew."

He reached a hand across the cab and ever-so-gently tucked a lock of hair off her face and behind her ear. "We could just talk, you know. I know I'm a man and all, but I do have the self-control to drive us to the lake, turn off the truck, and just talk."

"Really."

"Scout's honor." He raised his right hand, then shifted

into gear. "C'mon. It's summer, it's hot, it's too early to go home. Let's go to the lake."

She grimaced as she turned to the side window. Yes, it was the hot part that was going to get them both in trouble.

When they'd both gotten out of the truck at Twilight Cove, Ethan took Josie's hand in a move so natural it transported her, like she'd time-traveled back to the days when they were still a couple. "Waterfall path?"

Josie didn't answer, just let Ethan pull her toward the path that had been one of their favorite walks back then, even in the daylight when they hadn't been trying to sneak off and be alone. The moon was full and the sky was clear, so the light among the elms and maples was a dappled grayish filter.

She swallowed hard. "This lighting is perfect for a horror film."

"Don't worry. No serial killers out here."

"They always have a first victim." Josie stumbled over a twig, but Ethan's strong hand tightened around hers, and she managed to avoid an embarrassing face plant. "Do you remember that time David snuck up on us out here?"

"Unfortunately, yes."

"We were so busted."

"He loved it. Pops gave him my truck keys for the entire next week."

"Which should have been a pretty strong reason not to let it happen again."

Ethan stopped on the path, but Josie plowed into him because her eyes were searching out rogue stones and branches. He reached out his other arm to steady her. "Apparently you were a stronger reason to risk it."

Josie swallowed hard as his eyes searched hers. If he

kissed her now, she'd be powerless to resist. The night air, the waterfall path, the sounds, the smells . . . it was just too much. His arm fell to his side, then he turned back up the path. "And even though I want to stop right here in the moonlight and kiss you silly and remind you of just *why* I was willing to risk my Chevy for a few minutes alone with you, I'll be good and keep walking because I promised we'd just talk."

Josie laughed tightly. Was she relieved? Or disappointed?

"Good boy."

A couple of minutes later, she could hear the splash of the waterfall that signaled the end of the Abenaki River and the beginning of Echo Lake. Ethan braced his arms on the huge glacial rock that had been their favorite spot years ago, and hauled himself up. Then he reached down and lifted Josie like she weighed no more than a cat.

He set her down, but didn't let go, and her eyes lifted to meet his. Long seconds passed where all she could hear was the water and her own hitched breathing, but finally Ethan slid his hands ever so slowly down her sides and back to his own. "Right. Well. Here we are. Just talking. Want to sit?"

"Sure. Yes. Okay." She floundered for words.

He spread his windbreaker on the rock and they lowered themselves to sit side by side facing the lake. "Doesn't get any prettier than this, does it?"

Josie pulled her knees up to her chest. Through a break in the trees, the lake glistened in the moonlight, the tiniest of ripples breaking its glassy surface. To their left, water cascaded down a series of boulders, pooling waist-deep in a couple of places. The rock they were on sat just five feet above the biggest pool, and unless the wind came from the north, the waterfall's spray stayed shy of their spot.

"Do you ever come out here?" Her voice was soft as she asked, somehow dying to know that he had never brought anyone else out here.

"Wouldn't have been the same."

Josie felt her shoulders relax. He may have moved on, but at least some things he'd kept sacred, like this spot. It meant something to him, too. "Remember how you were going to build a log cabin out on the island?" She pointed at a tiny spot of land in the middle of the lake. It was barely big enough to house a family of otters, let alone humans.

"I had a lot of plans for getting you alone back then." He smiled as he gazed out at the island. "Funny how reality doesn't matter all that much when you're eighteen."

"Reality's somewhat overrated."

Ethan chuckled softly. "This from a therapist."

"I know. I should know better. So do you still want to build a log cabin someday?"

"Not really. No." Ethan idly snapped a tiny twig into pieces and tossed them in the water. "So what's your apartment like in Boston?"

"Tiny. Warm. Smells like bread all day because there's a deli underneath. It's nice. Brick. Old." Josie scrambled to find words to describe it, and couldn't figure out why it was so hard. Did she not want him to find fault with it, even from afar, even without ever seeing it? Didn't she love it there?

"It's—charming, I guess. But mostly tiny."

"Must be nice to have everything so convenient."

"Dangerous sometimes. Lou's pastrami on rye is going to be the reason I die of an early heart attack."

Ethan leaned back on his hands, casual, like he had all night. "So are you getting rich and famous now?"

"Sickeningly so, yes. I might be able to move to a full eight-hundred-square-foot apartment in a few years."

Ethan shook his head. "Jos, did you ever, even once in the past ten years, consider coming back here?"

"That depends."

"On what?"

"Whether you mean back here . . . or back to you."

"Either. Both. I don't know."

She picked up a piece of shale and started doodling on the rock under her legs. "Of course I did. This place is all I knew. Boston was big and scary. The first year was a little hellish."

"But you never?"

"I never. I couldn't. I was trying so hard to make my own way, do my own thing, be my own person."

"Without me."

She paused, thoughtful. "No. Not really. It wasn't nearly as much about that as it was about figuring out who I was, Eth. I knew nothing but this town and Camp Ho-Ho. We never even took a vacation anywhere else. I'd never crossed the state border till the time you and I snuck up to Montreal, and the second time was when I left for college. I just needed to . . . I don't know . . . it sounds so stupid and clichéd, but I needed to find out who I was."

"So you got your degree, you started a counseling practice, you got a cat. Does that mean you've figured it out?"

Josie doodled faster. "I thought I had."

"Until?" Ethan's eyes probed hers.

"Until now, I guess."

"Now, as in this moment? Or as in this year? This month? This week?"

"Until I came back."

Ethan nodded slowly and looked out toward the lake. The haunting call of a loon made Josie jump, losing her grip on the rock she'd been doodling with. Ethan looked at her scratches in the rock, then chuckled.

"What's funny?"

"You are."

"Why?"

He looked back out at the lake. "Did you even realize what you were drawing there?"

Josie's eyes widened as she shifted her legs to the side and saw the elaborate heart she'd scratched into the rock, along with the initials *JK +EM*. How in the world had she done that without even noticing she was doing so?

Ethan laughed. "Force of habit? I drag you out to one of our favorite make-out spots and suddenly you're doodling hearts?"

Josie smiled. "I only drew about seven million of these hearts in this rock back then."

"We'll have to find our tree sometime when it's light out. Wonder if our initials are still there?"

"We really were a cliché, weren't we? Small-town high school sweethearts and all."

"I don't know, Jos. It didn't feel clichéd at the time."

"Clichés never do when you're the one doing them."

"That's just psychobabble."

"I do not traffic in psychobabble." She popped a pebble at his knee, but he grabbed her wrist before she could launch another one.

He held it for an interminable minute, searching her eyes in silence. Finally, he spoke. "What are you feeling right now, Josie?"

God, if she only knew. Scared, hot, bothered, terrified. Sitting here on this rock, in the spot where they'd spent half of two summers exploring each other's bodies by moonlight, it was impossible to erase those memories and pretend the sound of the waterfall and call of the loons didn't bring her right back.

It was impossible to pretend she didn't want to pull Ethan back right now and feel his arms gather her tight, feel his lips on hers, feel his hands roam to places he hadn't touched for so damn long. It was, in fact, all she could do to stop herself from abandoning all reason and letting it happen.

But suddenly his lips were on hers, and he braced himself at her side as he buried a hand in her hair to pull her closer. Instead of resisting, all she could do was moan as she felt her every nerve ending spring to life.

Forget scared, forget terrified. As she opened her mouth under his and heard his answering groan, all she felt was pure, unadulterated lust.

Chapter 31

As Josie's lips parted, Ethan pulled her body closer to his. God, he'd waited so long to feel her like this again. She'd never believe he hadn't had ulterior motives bringing her out here, but damn. He'd do everything in his power to make sure she wouldn't regret it in the end.

The skin of her neck was silky soft under his hand, and as he lowered his lips, he could feel her pulse flipping like a baby bird's. He put his left arm around her and felt her relax as she sank backward.

Ah hell. If she did that little moaning sound one more time, he couldn't be held responsible for his actions.

Pebbles bit into his forearm as he supported Josie's back, but he barely registered the discomfort. Just as he felt her bones turn to mush, though, she pushed back upward.

"Ooh. Ow." She reached back to find whatever had jabbed her. She closed her hand around a big pebble and tossed it into the waterfall. "I don't think I remember this rock being so . . . rocky."

"We used to bring a sleeping bag." He kept his hand tangled in her curls, his lips on her neck, praying for the spell not to be broken.

"We used to get eaten alive by the mosquitoes."

"There you go again, ruining a perfectly good memory."

Stop talking, Josie. Stop thinking.

"Sorry. Do you remember, though—"

"Shut up, Jos. You're babbling. You're nervous. I get it. But it's me." He slid his hands up her jawline and into her hair, forcing her to meet his eyes. "It's me." He lowered his lips again, tentatively, then more insistently as she didn't pull back.

Oh holy heaven. It was all the same as he remembered, only better. Her lips tasted of strawberry and mint, and her hair was still as soft as that ridiculous sweater she'd knit him for Christmas when they were seventeen. It was a little more salon-perfect than he preferred, but at least she'd been letting it go curly again.

She pulled back and braced her hands on his chest.

Ah hell.

He sighed and pulled his hands away from her body, but to his surprise, she grabbed them tightly. "I'm going to regret this. I *know* I'm going to regret this. I'm going to hate you tomorrow for driving me out here. Hate you for bringing me Morris's French fries. Hate you for letting me win at midnight bowling."

She let go of one of his hands and brought hers to his face. "Dammit, Ethan. I can't do this. I can't sit here on this damn rock—which is really hard, by the way—listening to the waterfall, getting spooked by the loons, smelling your after-shave . . . *feeling* your hands on me. I can't."

"Why the hell *not*?" Even he could hear the raw pain in his voice.

"Because, moron, if you touch me one more time, I'm sixteen again, losing myself to you on the riverbank."

"And what is wrong with that?"

"We're not sixteen anymore. We're not. We can't pretend we are."

"Nobody's pretending, Jos." His hand encircled her wrist and he brought her palm to his lips, planting small kisses as he talked. "Everything I've said, everything I've done, I've meant. I was sixteen when I fell in love with you, I grant you that. And I remember every minute of it. I'm not trying to recapture being sixteen. I'm way more aware of reality than I really want to be. But Jesus, Josie, how can you not feel this? How can you not—want this?"

Her breath trembled as she spoke. "I do."

He paused. "What did you say?"

"I do. I do want this. God, Ethan, I've been trying so hard not to want this. But I do." She slid both hands around his head and pulled him toward her lips, sliding onto his lap at the same time.

"Touch me, Ethan. Please just touch me. Make me forget about everything but you."

Josie winced as she dabbed Neosporin on her knee, then covered it with a new Band-Aid. She turned to the desk and slugged down another gulp of Pepsi before turning to the other knee. "Ow. Ow, ow, ow." It was eight o'clock the next morning and Ethan had dropped her off at her parents' house a mere four hours ago. He'd said he had stuff to do this morning, so she was alone in the office, having ridden her bike once again.

She pulled her cotton skirt back down over her knees and sat back in her chair, stretching her arms over her head. She might have banged-up knees and razor burn in places a proper lady wouldn't talk about, but it was a delicious sort of pain. She closed her eyes and tried to wipe the silly grin off her face as she relived last night.

God, it had been good. So *damn* good. Everything she

remembered, only better. Back when they'd been teen-agers, their intimate moments had been stolen, enhanced by the danger of being discovered. Last night had held that same sort of secret-lover energy, only this time they were older and wiser enough to know better.

But that waterfall. That rock. Those tumbling, chaotic, beautiful memories crowding through her mind as Ethan had touched her, kissed her, murmured in her ear. There was no way she'd have been able to resist him. And she hadn't wanted to. She'd wanted every kiss, every touch, every lingering, blazing look from his smoky eyes.

She touched her lips, still tender, and she knew her cheeks were still flushed. It was a good thing she'd escaped the house before Mom woke up, or she'd have been totally busted. It was also a good thing Ethan wasn't here yet. He'd dropped her off with a kiss that could've led to much, much more . . . again. As his headlights swept across the lawn as he backed out of the driveway, she'd almost run back to the car. But she'd closed the door softly and crept to her bedroom, knowing that sleep was futile.

And it had been. She'd lain there for three hours, alternately glowing and scared. They'd been magic together, just like they'd always been. Even at twenty-eight years old, on a rock by a waterfall at the end of a dirt road . . . it had all been as perfect as it was ten years ago. Ethan was still the same generous, teasing, un-godly hot man he'd been then, but the years had been oh, so kind to his body.

And, by extension, to hers.

But what would today bring? In the harsh light of day, what conclusions would each of them come to about what had happened? About what was going to happen now?

The radio on the counter squawked, startling Josie. *Ethan? Are you there?*

Josie picked it up and pressed the button. "Ethan's out. This is Josie. What's up?"

"Oh. Hi, Josie. This is Nick. Listen, we have an early visitor. I think you might want to come over to the duck pond and check him out."

"The human kind of visitor? Or the bear kind?"

"Old guy. Says he knows Ethan. Looks like he came through one of the fences."

"You've never seen him before?"

"Nope. He says his dad dropped him off for the day. But seriously, he's old. Too old to still have a dad alive."

"I'll be right there." Josie clipped the radio to her belt and headed down the stairs and out the front door of the office, walking quickly toward the duck pond. Great. There was a poor, senile old man wandering the park. As she walked, she tried to figure out who she'd call to help figure out who he was and where he belonged.

Echo Lake still had only one part-time police officer, and his hours were apparently saved for nights and weekends. The man knew Ethan, though, so maybe she'd recognize him from the past? Or maybe Ethan would, when he got here?

When she rounded the corner by the stone bridge, she saw Nick leaning casually against the stone side, looking down the bank. She signaled to him, and he pointed toward the spot where she'd found Kelsey.

Josie could only see a glimpse of gray hair when she peered over the bridge. Dammit. She was going to have to go under there again. "Keep your radio on, okay? Hopefully he's just pleasantly confused, not dangerous."

She tiptoed back down the bridge, then hopped over the low fence and headed slowly down the bank. Funny how much easier it was in her own clothes. The man had his back to her, but she could hear him muttering about goulash or something. Goulash?

She crept closer, and when she was still a safe enough distance away to run back up the hill, she spoke. "Sir?" No response, but his body stilled. "Mister? Are you all right?" She took one step closer, putting a hand out toward him in case he turned around. "Sir? I'm Josie. Are you okay? Can I help you with anything?"

The man stopped muttering, and his head tilted like he'd registered her voice but wasn't sure where it was coming from.

"Boston princess?" he asked, then turned quickly toward her.

What?

"Sir, what's your na—" Josie stopped as he raised his eyes to hers.

She knew those eyes. Oh God. She knew those eyes.

Chapter 32

"How could you not *tell* me?" Josie paced the office again as Ethan sighed.

"No offense, Jos, but when exactly might it have come up?"

"Ethan! He's—omigod—it's Pops! How could you not tell me he was sick?"

"Are you serious right now? Really? You're serious?" Josie saw color rise in Ethan's cheeks.

"Why would I not be serious?"

Ethan stood up, and Josie instinctively backed up when she saw the anger in his eyes. "You're acting like I held out on you . . . like you've got some right to be pissed that I haven't caught you up on ten years of Echo Lake history."

"But it's—Pops." Her voice was pained. Had she even *asked* about him since she'd been here? Of course she had.

Hadn't she?

"It's early-onset dementia. That's the clinical term you'd give it, right? His phrase for it is a lot less polite. He was diagnosed three years ago, and we're figuring it out as we go."

"He's so young, though." Josie shivered. "I can't believe it."

"He took some pretty serious blows to the head during his service overseas. That might have kicked it off. We don't know. Nobody ever knows with these things."

"Do you—have help with him? Are you doing this all alone?"

"I've got a part-time nurse who keeps an eye on him most days. Not this morning, obviously." He ran his hand through his hair. "On the positive side, he seems to have forgotten that he hates me for not becoming a Marine like him, so that's good, right?"

"Oh God. What?"

Ethan shrugged. "Seriously, the more his mind goes, the—the more he's let go of all that energy he spent resenting Mom for dying, me for screwing up my knee, David for liking his drums better than his gun . . . I don't know, Jos. It's been a trip, okay? I don't know how to explain it. And I don't have time right now."

"I just—wow. I can't believe I didn't know." Her stomach actually hurt as she said the words.

"Josie, you left. You left without a backward glance, and never gave one indication that you gave a damn about anything here. So really? You making like the victim of nondisclosure here? It doesn't fly."

"Ethan—"

Oh God, he was angry, and oh, she deserved it. Like she'd uncorked a mad genie, he continued.

"Ten years ago, you made a *huge* decision that affected both of us, only you forgot to bring me into it. So you know what? You can get off your high horse, sit your perfect little butt down, and run the damn park until I get back. Pops isn't your problem."

Josie bit her lip and sat down slowly in her chair. He was right. So, so right. She had no place berating him like this. What was she thinking? When she'd seen Pops by the pond, she'd frozen. His eyes were a mirror image of Ethan's, but the blankness in them had scared her silly.

Clinically, she'd known what she was looking at. But it was Pops, not a sterile case in a textbook. It was Ethan's dad, the guy who'd claimed to use the iron fist of doom with his boys, but snuck them out of school to go fishing every spring. It was the guy who'd grounded Ethan soundly for a missed curfew, but made him chocolate chip pancakes on Sunday mornings. It was the man who'd taught Josie to drive because her parents . . . couldn't.

And now? Dementia? She had a hundred questions for Ethan, but he was right. First, it was none of her business. And second—well—it was just none of her damn business.

"I'm sorry, Ethan. It just surprised me. But you're right. I'm sorry."

"You should be." His shoulders relaxed just the slightest fraction. "You should be, dammit."

Then he reached down and hauled her into his arms, capturing her squeak with his mouth as he lifted her off the ground. "Goddammit, this would be a hell of a lot easier if I didn't want you every time I look at you. A hell of a lot easier if I hadn't been an idiot and driven us out to the lake last night."

He kissed her hard then, possessive and angry and lusting and so damn hot. "Why the hell did you come back, Josie? You're sending me to a fresh hell here." He set her down and backed up.

"Christ." He put both hands through his hair. "I don't even know if I'm coming or going." He looked around the office, then grabbed his keys. "I have to go. Need to see if Pops is settled in back at home. Call his doc."

Josie nodded as he spat out sentence fragments. "Okay." Her voice was almost a whisper.

He turned to go, then swung back. "I know you're sorry. I do know it."

Then he shook his head. "I just don't know if you know yet what you're sorry *for*."

"Get your monkey suit dry-cleaned yet?" Josh slid into the booth across from Ethan at lunchtime, startling him. The barstools at Bellinis had already been occupied when he came in, which was fine. He didn't feel like making small talk anyway. He needed to figure out what to do about Pops. He'd never wandered before, and this morning's incident was scaring the hell out of Ethan.

He'd gotten him settled at home, and the part-time nurse had agreed to stay for the afternoon so Ethan could leave. Good God. Between Josie and Pops, he could barely think straight, and now Josh was talking about tuxes for that damn Hospital Hero thing.

Ethan shook his head. "I'm not going. No way, no how."

"It's bad form to skip an event held in your honor."

"Who in the world invented this award, anyway?"

"Probably someone who was hoping to receive it. Get a date yet?" Josh bounced his eyebrows up and down.

Ethan set down his menu and pinned Josh with a glare. "No, I do not have a date yet. Nor will I have a date."

"What about Josie? She's still here, isn't she?"

"Thought you recommended I stay away from her."

"I just told you not to kiss her again." Josh raised his eyebrows. "Which you haven't. Right?"

"Pleading the fifth."

Just then, Molly arrived at the table with coffees. "Gentlemen. I assumed the usual?"

Josh nodded. "Thanks, Molly."

"Who's pleading the fifth? About what?" She perched on the edge of Ethan's seat, as per usual.

He looked sidelong at her. "You have bat ears."

"I know. So handy in this business!" Molly grinned. "So what's the story?"

Josh pointed at Ethan. "He's not talking, but I'm guessing he and Josie are driving each other crazy."

"Again?" Molly cuffed Ethan lightly on the head as she slid back out. "You're an idiot."

"Certifiable, yes."

Molly stopped halfway off the bench, her face suddenly serious. "Jesus holy Mary and Joseph. What. Have. You. Done?"

If Molly knew how much she resembled her mother at this moment, she'd be furious. "Ethan Thomas Miller, where did you go last night after you dropped me off?"

"Home."

"Which *road* did you take home?"

"Molly, seriously. I don't need the third degree."

"Oh. My. God." She sat back down. "You went to the lake, didn't you?" Ethan didn't answer. "You drove out to the lake, didn't you? Tell me you didn't walk up to the waterfall."

"Stop it. Seriously, Molly."

"You did." When Ethan looked up in consternation, he saw two distinct emotions at war in her eyes. One was the anger he expected, but the other . . . was that fear? He took a long, defensive draw on his coffee as Molly moved to the other side of the booth and pointed her finger at him. "What are you thinking, Ethan? You have been here before. You have seen the end play already. How can you do this again?"

Josh cleared his throat, lifting his chin toward the next table. "I think you've got some parched people over there, Molly. Maybe you'd better take their order?"

Molly growled in frustration, still pointing at Ethan. "We're not done yet."

As she headed toward the new group of diners, Josh raised his eyebrows. "Seriously? The lake? The waterfall?"

Ethan sighed as he nodded miserably.

"Did you guys . . . y'know . . ."

Silence.

"You totally did." Josh's face cracked into a smile. "Jesus, buddy. What were you thinking?"

"I think we've already covered that I wasn't."

"How are things today with her?"

"Fine. Terrible. Great. Awful."

Josh chuckled. "Sounds like true love."

"Shit, Josh. What am I doing? I know better. I'm older, wiser, all that shit. I *know* better."

"I dunno. Maybe you should start thinking with the big head instead of the little one?"

"Shut up."

"Seriously, buddy. She's not staying, so whatever's going on here . . . it's just temporary, right? Are you okay with that? You going to be able to come back from that when she goes back to Boston?"

"Boston's not that far away, really." As the words came out of his mouth, Ethan wished he could shove them back in. Idiot. What was he thinking? This wasn't college, where a few texts and steamy phone calls could keep a relationship alive. They were both grown adults, with adult responsibilities, and neither of them could just pull up stakes.

"You didn't just say that."

Ethan winced. "I know."

Molly came back with steaming burgers and fries, clattering them on the table and pointing at Ethan. "Not done yet." Then she whirled around and checked on the other tables around them.

"She's gonna have your head on a platter before we leave, you know." Josh squirted ketchup on his burger.

He raised it to take a bite, but paused. "Does Josie know about Avery's House yet?"

"As far as I know, no."

Josh cringed. "I know we all promised a long time ago not to tell her—to let *you* do it when you thought it was time, but buddy, she's here. Only reason she hasn't seen it herself is because she's racing from the park straight to the hospital every day. Aren't you worried she's going to drive by it one of these days?"

Ethan sighed. Yeah, he was worried she'd see it. Of course he was. And if it weren't tucked up at the cul-de-sac end of Sugar Maple Drive, she definitely *would* have seen it by now.

"I know it's not my place to tell you what to do, but I think you'd better tell her before she finds out some other way."

"I know. You're right."

Josh stirred his coffee. "Nervous about how she'll react?"

"What do *you* think?"

"Terrified."

"Pretty much." Ethan nodded, putting his bun back on his burger and spinning it to spread out the ketchup. "It's—too soon."

"There might never be a perfect time, you know. Maybe you just need to brace yourself and take her over there."

"Not yet."

"When?"

"I don't know, okay? Maybe—maybe I don't even *want* her to see it."

Was that true? Was he purposely playing Avery's House close to his chest? Why? What did he think would happen when Josie did find out about it?

"Ethan, seriously. That house is as much a part of you

as—I don't know—anything. If you don't show her that part of you, how can she really know who you are now?"

"That's a little deep for this hour, isn't it? The house doesn't define me."

"You sure?"

Ethan sighed. "I'm not sure of anything right now, no."

Josh set down his coffee and leaned forward. "Here's a crazy thought. Have you ever considered that seeing Avery's House might actually make her think about coming back?"

Ethan paused, silent.

"Honestly, I'm more afraid the house might convince her to go."

Chapter 33

"How is your dad today?" Molly sat down in the waiting room next to Josie late Thursday afternoon, startling her.

What was *she* doing here?

"Um, okay." Josie put down the magazine she'd been pretending to read while her thoughts skittered around in her head. It hadn't even been eight hours since she'd seen Ethan, and one part of her was dying to see him. The other part was pulling hard on the reins, trying to knock some sense into her idiot brain.

"Have you been in to see him?"

"Yeah. But they're doing stuff right now. I'm just—I don't know—waiting, I guess?" For what, she didn't really know. Dad's condition was improving bit by bit, but no miraculous leaps or bounds yet. "I think they're going to move him tomorrow. A bed finally opened up over at Fairview."

"That's kind of depressing."

"I know. There aren't too many ways beds open up at these places."

"I bet if you studied the names of all of the rehab facilities in the United States, over half of them have *view* in the name. Why is that, do you think?"

Josie glanced sidelong at Molly. "I have no idea. Sounds peaceful, maybe?"

"I'm sure Fairview will be nice, though. It looks nice from the outside. They'll take good care of him."

"I hope so." Josie nodded. "We were lucky to get him so close."

"Josh said they're really family-oriented."

Josie nodded again. They sure were. She and Mom had met with the social worker for an hour yesterday trying to figure out what that all meant and how they were going to possibly accomplish it.

"So what does that mean for you?"

Josie could tell Molly was trying to compose her features into a nonchalant expression, but she'd known her too long to buy it, even if it *had* been ten years. She slid further down into the uncomfortable chair, bracing her neck on the padded back. "God, Molly. I have no idea."

"You think your mom can handle this on her own?"

"I don't know. I've only been here two weeks. I have no idea what she can handle these days."

"Is she doing okay?"

"As far as I can tell."

"Not drinking?"

Josie spun her head toward Molly, narrowing her eyes.

"What?" Molly raised her hands. "Did you really think I never knew?"

Josie shook her head, sighing. "I don't know what to think anymore. As far as I can tell, she's handling things."

"That's great. Really great. Because if she can handle this without backsliding, that's a huge test, right?"

"Yes, it is."

"You worried about what she'll do if you leave?"

"Of course I am."

"What about Ethan?"

Josie paused. Uh-oh. "What *about* Ethan?"

"Seriously, Jos. What do you *think* I mean? Last night

was like a ten-years-ago flashback. The only thing I don't know for sure is whether it *ended* like it used to." Molly searched her face, then her mouth opened. "It did, didn't it?"

"You don't know that. You have no idea." Josie pushed herself back up in the chair.

"I do, too. Feel your cheeks."

"I will not."

"They're as red as cherries. You totally went to the lake, didn't you?"

"Molly, stop."

"You really let him take you out there, let him believe there was hope, let him think maybe you returned his feelings?" Molly pushed herself up from her chair. "Y'know what? He's a man. He's ruled by testosterone. But you? You should know better. I can't believe you threw him a bone, only to yank it back when you leave."

"Maybe I won't lea—"

"Yes you will. You know you will. *I* know you will. This is why I'm not entertaining any stupid fantasies about us being best friends again. You never wanted to live here, and that hasn't changed. You're only here because of your father, and once you can figure out how to handle it, off you'll go."

"Molly—"

"Don't *Molly* me." She stopped at the doorway, scrunching her nose like she was weighing options. "You know what? You need to see something. Come with me."

Ten minutes later, Josie grabbed for the door handle as Molly took a corner way too fast. "No offense, but you still drive like a maniac."

Why had she agreed to get in Molly's car, anyway? The woman was acting like she'd like to dump Josie in the lake with a cement block tied to each foot.

"Yup." Her eyes were locked on the road.

"Where are we going?"

"It's a surprise."

"Is it scheduled for takeoff in three point two seconds? Why the rush?" Josie grabbed the dashboard as Molly screeched to a stop at the Back Road intersection. "Just tell me now, are you trying to kill me?"

"Nope. Just trying to show you something important." Molly sped through the center of town toward Snowflake Village, but banked a hard left a quarter mile before the park and slowed to a crawl as she headed up Sugar Maple Drive.

Josie peered out the windows at the Victorians lining the street, which had earned a record seventeen appearances in *Vermont Life* magazine over the years. "Okay? Why are we here?"

"Just look around. See what you see."

"It's still gorgeous."

"Historical Society got some grant a few years ago and got all the houses repainted in original colors."

"They're beautiful." Josie stared at the wide front porches, the turrets, the acres of windows and shutters, the sugar maples that lined the street, forming a canopy over their heads. She and Ethan had always dreamed of living on this very street, way at the end.

She crossed her arms across her stomach.

Long time ago.

Molly continued to crawl slowly up the half-mile-long street, finally pulling to a stop just shy of the last house. *House* was a funny word to use for it, she guessed. The thing was huge—an old 1900-something hotel that had been converted to a B and B somewhere along in time.

Way back when, she and Ethan had always called it their someday-house. It sat back from the street, its sunny yellow paint and dark blue shutters making it look quaint and welcoming despite its size. The wide front porch was lined with Adirondack chairs and wicker rockers with bright cushions, and hanging flowers dotted the entire length of it.

"Remember this house?" Molly raised her eyebrows as she finally spoke.

"Of course I do. You know I do." Josie's voice softened. "Ethan and I were totally going to live here." She twisted to look out the back window of the car. "And you were going to buy that one, remember?" She pointed to a dark green Victorian with a matching porch.

"And our kids were going to play in the sandbox and ride bikes together. Yadda yadda." Molly's voice was sharp as she shook her head, and Josie couldn't help but think of the last time she'd been on this street.

"Someday I'm gonna buy you this house, Jos." Ethan's face was serious as they sat in his truck, parked just shy of the yellow B and B at the end of Sugar Maple Drive. "Someday."

"Right after you win the lottery?" Josie smiled as she looked at him, but inside she was quivering. There was no way she'd ever own this house, or one anything like it, if she ever came back to Echo Lake after college. Neither would Ethan—not if he kept his rope firmly tied to Camp Ho-Ho.

"You never know."

"Are you hoping for a big raise from Dad?" She grimaced. Ethan had started working at the park in December, and Josie still hadn't gotten used to the sight of him in a Snowflake Village polo shirt. "I hope you're not thinking you'll eventually get a daughter's-boyfriend rate or something, cuz that'll never happen."

"You never know. He and I have had some talks lately."

This was news to Josie. "About?"

"About whatever." *Ethan shrugged.* "About the future. You know, things I could do here. That sort of thing."

"Here as in Echo Lake? Or here as in Camp Ho-Ho?"

"Snowflake Village."

Josie closed her eyes tightly, then turned to look out the side window. "You . . . you want to stay working at the park?"

"It's good work, Jos. Your dad's a good boss. The money's okay. I could do worse."

"You. Ho-ho. Like, permanently?"

"Well, I don't know about permanently. Who knows what'll happen ten years down the road? But I guess for the next few years it could be just what I need, right?"

Josie turned toward him, searching his eyes, then finally daring to ask the question that had been banging around her ribs for months. "What happened to all of your plans, Eth? You were going to get a degree! Get out of Echo Lake! Live somewhere besides this go-nowhere little town! What happened?"

"You know very well what happened." *He pointed to his knee.* "So now I need a new plan, and your dad's offering one. I'd be stupid to pass it up."

"No. No, no, no, Ethan. You'd be **smart** to pass it up. You're so much better than this stupid park. Better than this stupid town. You can't give up just because you damaged your knee and lost one scholarship."

"Right. Because there are ten other ones waiting in the wings? Be realistic. I can't afford to go to school—not now, not anytime in the near future. So I've got to figure out how to make a life, and right now the options are a little narrow."

"Not true." *She hated how pitiful her voice sounded.*

Ethan put his fingers under her chin. "True."

"So this is it? You're happy with this plan? You're going to settle in at Ho-Ho and live your life in Christmas la-la land? Seriously?"

"I wish you didn't hate the idea so much, but yeah. Maybe I am."

Josie stared out at her someday-house, sadness actually causing her chest to hurt. She couldn't believe he'd willingly sign up for this life. He knew very well how the job consumed her father. Was that what he envisioned for his own life? For his own someday-marriage?

If so, she'd be wise to get off this train right now, before it went any further into heartbreak territory.

She spun the ring on her left hand, the tiny diamond feeling suddenly . . . heavy.

Josie shook her head to return to the present, sitting here on that same street, but this time with Molly. She turned forward again, looking at the house. There was a small, tasteful sign on the lawn, but she couldn't read it. "Is it still a B and B?"

"Sort of. It's kind of a . . . care facility."

"A retirement home?"

"No-o. More for kids, really."

"Oh. I interned at a place like that in Roxbury. I didn't know Echo Lake was big enough to need transitional housing." She felt her eyebrows scrunch together. "Especially this much. I forgot how huge this house was."

"It's not transitional housing, Josie. It's a medical facility. It's for kids with life-threatening illnesses. They can come stay here with their families for a couple of weeks. For free."

"No kidding? Disney World has something like that. Wow. That's—incredible."

"It's gotten a lot of attention. National, even."

"I can imagine. Who runs it? The hospital?"

Silence greeted her question, and for a reason she couldn't quite put her finger on, Josie's internal alarms started pinging. Molly stared out the front window, looking like she was sorting through possible answers. "It's . . . it's kind of a team effort, I guess you'd say."

"I see." Molly was definitely holding back for some reason, which made Josie only want to push harder. "Who owns it?"

Molly pulled her eyes away from the windshield and shifted her gaze to Josie.

"I know you think nothing's really changed here since you left, but a lot has."

"I know. I do."

Molly shook her head. "You think you do, but you don't. And there's no way that in two weeks, you've had time to figure it out." Molly's voice had a definite bite, making Josie realize she'd better tread lightly.

"What are you trying to tell me?"

Molly took a deep breath. "Ethan owns it."

"*What*?" Josie's eyes snapped back to the house. *Ethan* owned their someday-house?

"He sold his house when this one came up for sale." She laughed bitterly. "Actually I think he sold everything he owned, then wrote a bunch of grant proposals in order to finance the renovations. Now it's a state-of-the-art medical facility posing as a getaway house."

"Oh my God."

"Last year more than a hundred kids came through here."

Josie stared, her heart thudding against her ribs. He had bought this house. *Their* house. And turned it into a getaway for sick kids? She reached for her throat, trying hard to swallow, but failing. "I don't understand." Her voice came out in a whisper. "He hasn't said anything about it."

"I know."

"Why didn't he tell me?" The question was out before Josie could suck it back in. Did she really want Molly to know Ethan had kept something this huge from her?

Again Molly was silent except for her fingers tapping nervously on the steering wheel. Finally she said, "I don't know. I imagine maybe he wasn't ready for you to know about it."

"Oh," Josie whispered as she held her stomach. After what they'd shared in the past few days, this seemed like a rather glaring omission.

"You left, Josie. Life went on here."

"As you're very fond of reminding me."

"It took Ethan a long time to pick up the pieces, but he did. He's made a life here, and it doesn't include . . . you. The park, this house . . ." She swept her hand at the windshield. "It's all awesome. It's working. It's amazing."

"I can see that." She paused. "And you're worried I'm going to mess that up? I'm just visiting, Molly."

Aren't I?

"Then don't screw with his head, Jos." Molly spat out the words like bullets. "Don't kiss him and . . . and take him to the waterfall and then dump him again."

"I'm not—" Josie paused again to gather herself. "He's a big boy. I'm not making him do anything he doesn't want to do."

Molly turned. "Don't you get it? Are you still so selfish you don't see what you're doing?"

Selfish? What did she mean, *still*?

Josie shook her head slowly. "I didn't mean to cause problems. I really didn't. I'm *not* trying to. I just—"

Oh, how was everything suddenly going horribly wrong?

"I know. And that's the biggest problem. You have no idea what you're doing. You need to go back to Boston,

Josie. You're playing with fire here, and Ethan doesn't deserve it. If you have any heart at all, you'll leave him alone and go back home."

Josie squeezed her eyes shut at Molly's harsh words.

"How long has he owned the house?" Her voice was smaller than she wished.

"Five years. Took him a year to do the renovations, so he's had patients coming for four years now."

"Does he have a medical staff?"

Molly nodded. "Of course. Josh is the medical director, and we—he's got six nurses working different shifts."

"We? Do you work here, too?"

"Yeah. I do." Molly straightened her shoulders. "I'm not just a waitress, Josie. I got my business degree, and Ethan hired me to oversee things here."

"You're the—" Josie couldn't keep the incredulity out of her voice.

"Director."

"Wow." Josie put her hand to her chest, which was hurting as her breaths shortened. She couldn't believe this. Ten years ago she'd thought Ethan's plan was to park his butt in Dad's office and live out his life at Camp Ho-Ho, and instead, he'd created a little getaway paradise for sick kids and their families. Apparently in *addition* to keeping the park running in the black.

And he'd installed their best friends from high school in the two most prominent positions. They were a team, the three of them.

She rubbed her chest, trying to ease the shame . . . and the loneliness. She hadn't believed in him back then, and he'd known it.

And look what he'd done.

"You want to see the inside?"

Yes. No. Yes.

Josie shook her head. "I don't want to just walk in. I'm

sure it's—busy. They're busy." Her hand fluttered in her lap.

"Rather have Ethan show you?"

"Yeah. I would."

Molly stared out the windshield. "Well, newsflash. He asked us years ago *not* to tell you about this place, so I don't think he has a tour planned anytime soon."

"He asked—" Josie felt tears prick the backs of her eyes.

Molly sighed. "Look. I'm sorry. I never should have brought you here. Ethan's going to kill me if he finds out I did." She shifted the car into gear. "I just thought you should see it. Maybe it'll give you some—I don't know—closure."

"In the sense of *he's fine without you, all is well in Echo Lake, and please go home before you screw up our lives? Again?*"

"You said it, not me."

Josie unclipped her seat belt just as Molly stepped on the gas. "Stop the car, Molly."

Molly's eyes widened as she braked. "Why?"

"Because I'm going into that house."

Chapter 34

When Molly dropped her off in the driveway, Josie walked up the curving stone pathway to the front porch. Up close, she could see that the shutters had little cutout hearts, and that the flowers dripping from porch pots were vivid pink and purple pansies. The railing was painted bright white, and the cushions decorating every chair made for a rainbow of color.

She tried to imagine walking up this pathway as a patient . . . or a parent. Despite the riot of emotions crowding her brain right now, she felt a sense of peace as she stepped up the wide stairway. It was welcoming, homey . . . happy.

She rang the doorbell, and a chipper male voice from somewhere inside called, "Come on in!"

When she opened the door, she found herself in a wide foyer with polished wood floors and a curving staircase. Hallways stretched to the left and right, as well as directly in front of her, where quick footsteps were coming from the back of the house.

"Hannah? That you?" Josie's head snapped up at the familiar voice just in time to see Ethan's old friend Josh stutter-step as he entered the foyer. "Josie?"

"Josh?" She stopped as he walked forward, trying to

reconcile the gawky teen he'd been with the confident—um, gorgeous—man he now was. Kirsten would totally swoon.

He held out his hand, smiling widely. "Did Ethan finally invite you over here for a tour?"

"Not . . . exactly." She shook his hand carefully. "Molly brought me."

"Well, come on in! Ethan's busy with one of the guests, but I can tell him you're here." He looked at her face, doubt crowding his features. "Or maybe not tell him quite yet?"

She grimaced. "I'm not exactly sure how he'll feel about me surprising him here."

"Got it. Well, I give a better tour anyway." He motioned her down the hallway. "He's too modest. Come on back here. I'll tell you about the place. It's so good to see you!"

An hour later, Josie sat in Josh's office sipping lemonade. Situated in the back of the house just off the kitchen, it had floor-to-ceiling windows and gleaming wood floors. The scent of freshly mowed grass wafted through the lacy curtains and she took deep breaths, letting them out slowly.

She scanned the walls of the office, full of framed black-and-whites. All children, all here, all smiling. She stood up and walked to one wall, looking at each picture in turn. Many of the children were bald, many were in wheelchairs, and still others had metal crutches. Josh had spent the entire last hour filling her in on what Ethan had done here, and she still couldn't wrap her head around it.

She couldn't believe he'd created a foundation, then talked the Spencers into selling him their B and B way below market value when they'd retired to Arizona.

According to Josh, Ethan had spent the last five years pounding the pavement all over New England trying to fund a house where sick kids could stay for free.

And running Snowflake Village.

Her breath hitched as she looked again at the sign in a picture of three kids on the lawn. Avery's House. Ethan had named this little slice of paradise after Avery.

She rubbed her stomach as a sourness threatened to rise to her throat. How could she have thought *she* was the one serving Avery's memory best?

Josh leaned his hip on his desk. "So."

"So." She turned from the wall. "I don't even know what to say. Or think."

"I know."

"I can't believe you guys have been doing this for five years already. *And* you work at the hospital?"

Josh nodded ruefully. "This is why I have no life, yes." He pointed at the pictures. "Ethan wouldn't even think about opening the house without a physician on board, though. And I just look at that wall and think about all these kids, and how can I not be happy?"

Josie studied his face for a long moment. "Is *he* happy, Josh?"

He stared back. "In a lot of ways, yeah. He is. He loves this place, loves the kids, spends pretty much every moment here when he's not at the park or with his dad."

Josie thought back to how he'd cared for Avery when he was way too young to have a clue *how* to, and her chest hurt as she pictured him hauling the little girl around Snowflake Village on piggyback, or sitting with her at the wishing well while she plonked in her pennies. Or in those last weeks at the hospital.

"Are you going to try to get some sleep?" Josie slumped in the uncomfortable chair next to Avery's hospital

bed, watching Ethan pace the floor slowly, Avery in his eighteen-year-old arms.

He shook his head. "She wakes up if I stop moving. And then she hurts."

"Ethan, you're going to fall over from exhaustion. Let me take a turn." She pushed herself up from the chair and reached out for Avery.

"I'm fine. She's too heavy for you to carry."

"She's not that heavy, Eth." Josie's whisper of a voice got stuck in her throat. "Not anymore. I can hold her."

"I've got her. I'll let you know if I need you to spell me. It's three o'clock in the morning. You should close your eyes and get some sleep."

"I can't sleep." She felt tears threatening to break free. "I'm too scared."

"So am I, Jos. So am I. I wish this didn't have to happen . . . here. In this dismal, stupid little room. There has to be a better way."

Josie sank back into the chair, but her eyes wouldn't close. Instead, she watched Ethan as he walked back and forth across the tiny room, blanket wrapped around Avery's scrawny shoulders, her knobby little knees folded over his forearm. In sleep, she looked peaceful for the first time all day.

Ever since Ethan had accepted the job at Camp Ho-Ho, Josie had been struggling to figure out what that meant for her, for him, for their future, and her conclusions had ranged from dire to miserable. The man she'd fallen in love with had been full of dreams, full of hope, full of mischief.

Now, though? Now he seemed content to watch everyone go off to college while he stayed behind and learned the ropes at the park. Seemed content to kiss his old dreams good-bye, nurse his knee injury, and probably go fat and bald in Dad's office.

Here they were, scheduled to get married in less than a month, and she was frightened they'd rushed into the wedding because of Avery, rushed because they were scared to be separated by her enrollment at Wellesley, rushed because they were so, so stupidly young.

The flowers were ordered, the hotel booked, the dress hanging in her closet, but every day her doubts loomed bigger. For six weeks now she'd been one breath away from asking if they should put the brakes on, postpone the wedding, take a break and figure out if they were really doing the whole wedding thing for the right reasons.

And then Avery had taken a turn for the worse, and here they were. Josie had brought her to the ER, and her foster mom had been too busy with the other kids at her house to even come visit since she'd been admitted. Ethan and Josie hadn't left the hospital for three days, and Josie's hope was fading that Avery's chemo was going to win this time.

She sighed. The two of them hadn't managed more than a couple of hours of sleep each night. It was hardly the time to bring up any sort of deep discussion on the topic of their future. And honestly, if Avery wasn't destined to be part *of their future, she didn't want to think about it anyway.*

Avery whimpered softly, and Ethan tucked the blanket around her. "Shh, munchkin. It's okay. I'm right here. Josie and I are right here with you."

No. It definitely wasn't the time.

Josie shook her head, knocking the memory loose as she glanced again at the pictures on Josh's office wall. Look at what Ethan had built here. Then one picture caught her eye, and she leaned closer to the wall to see it clearly. It had been taken at the base of the Ferris wheel, and she put her hand to her throat as she realized it was Avery. Avery, healthy and full of spunk. Avery, hands up in the air, face practically cracking from her supersized grin. Avery, holding up a Slush-Bomb and pointing to her Official Slush-Bomb Tester T-shirt—the green one this time.

"Do you still miss her, Jos?" Josh's voice was gentle at her shoulder.

She took a deep, shaky breath. "I'll never stop missing her."

"I can't imagine how hard it is coming back here."

"*Hard* would be a bit of an understatement." She sat down on the love seat that faced his desk, and he perched on its arm. "I just—God, Josh, I feel like I've spun myself into another universe here. Parts of it have stood still for ten years, and others?" She waved vaguely around her. "Others are so different I don't even know how to take it all in."

"And Avery's everywhere."

"She is. And here I am a counselor, and ten years out from . . . everything. But I come back here and feel like I'm eighteen again, all discombobulated and anxious and unable to figure any of it out."

"Maybe you never really gave yourself enough time to—quote—figure it out then. Have you considered that?"

"Because I hightailed it out of town with the cans practically still clanking on the bumper?"

Josie took a deep breath, looked at Josh sitting so comfortably in this space, this space that was Ethan's answer to Avery's death. What had *hers* been, really? "I just—just can't believe I never knew about this place. Can't believe my mother never said anything."

Josh shifted awkwardly. "It's probably not my place to say it, but I have a feeling . . . maybe Ethan asked her not to."

"Wow." She forced the word over her swollen throat. "Molly said . . . Wow. Mom, even?"

"In his defense, I'm pretty sure he didn't think you were ever going to come back. Or care *what* he was doing."

"I know," she whispered, then cleared her throat. "It's just so . . . so *huge* what he's done here. And Avery's such a big part of why. And Avery was such a big part of . . . well . . . *us,* I guess. It just feels so strange not to have known."

Josh pointed at the pictures again. "The hospital's giving him a huge award Sunday night. Did he tell you about it?" He shuffled some papers into a folder on his desk, then stuck the folder in a wire rack beside his computer. "We both know he had other plans for his life, Jos. We both know it didn't work out that way, for a lot of reasons. But look at this place."

Josie felt tears gathering behind her eyes, but resisted swiping them and making it obvious to Josh that she was an emotional grenade right now. She blinked quickly, willing them back, and when they wouldn't quite cooperate, she turned toward the French door that led off from his office. She really needed to get a grip.

"What's through that door?" It had a lacy, opaque curtain over it, but behind the lace she could see sunlight streaming into a big, bright room.

Josh turned toward it. "Owners' quarters."

"Ethan lives here now?" How had she not figured that out in the time she'd been here?

"No. Not yet. No." Josh shuffled more folders, not meeting her eyes. "He's living back at his parents' house for the time being. Helping his dad."

"Of course." She peeked through the door, but couldn't see much beyond the curtain. Just glowing wood floors and buttery yellow walls. "Is he ever going to move in, do you think?"

"Maybe someday." Josh looked directly at her now. "I'm not sure it's even a conscious plan, but I think maybe he's been saving it."

"For what?" She felt her eyebrows draw together.

He was silent for a full five seconds. "What do you think, Josie?"

"And this is the dinosaur room." Josh motioned her inside the second-story room ten minutes later, giving her a tour of the upstairs. "No one's in here right now. Go ahead in and check it out."

"I'm still trying to get over the creemee machines on every floor."

"Well, what could be more fun than creemees any time of the day or night, right? Of course, we had to change it to *soft serve* on the website so anyone outside of Vermont would know what it even is."

"Ethan always did like his creemees." Josie felt a smile steal up her cheeks, the first one since she'd entered the house.

"So." Josh adopted his tour-guide voice. "Kid rooms all adjoin adult rooms so families can spread out a little bit. He had someone come in and paint all the kid rooms, but he didn't touch the décor of the old B and B rooms."

Josie peeked through the open door into a lovely, plush room with a fireplace and canopy bed. "I bet they never want to leave."

"That's the goal."

Josh pulled back a bright curtain near the bed. Mounted on the wall were the very same sorts of emergency equipment she'd seen at the head of Dad's bed in the hospital. And Avery's. Then Josh lifted the bedspread to show her the bed. "See? Everything's all hospital-grade equipment. We just hide the fact that it's . . . hospital-grade equipment."

Josie sat gingerly in the rocking chair by the window, feeling the warm breeze lift the hair on her forehead. "It's beautiful, Josh. I can't believe you guys have done this with this house."

"I didn't do it. Ethan did."

"It must have cost an absolute fortune."

"He's an incredible grant-writer. And it's an incredible place—the kind people want to get behind."

Josie heard the unmistakable giggle of a young girl. "Is that one of the patients?" Her stomach flipped.

Josh nodded. "But we call them guests, not patients. That'd be Emmy. She just got out of the hospital and is back for a bit with her mom." He paused at the doorway. "Want to meet her?"

Josie followed him around the huge staircase at the center of the hallway, going by three sets of guest rooms as they made their way to Emmy's room. At the doorway, he put his hand out to stop her, but what she saw inside the room would have glued her feet to the floor anyway.

Chapter 35

Ethan sat in a rocker by the window with a tiny girl on his lap. Their heads were bent toward each other, his dark hair almost touching her shiny little head as they pointed at pictures in an I Spy book. His arm was around her waist and she leaned into him comfortably, swinging her little legs as he rocked slowly.

Josie put her hand to her chest as she watched, and this time there was no way to stop the tears. Emmy looked just like Avery, only smaller. She had the same tiny body in a too-big princess robe—the same tiny feet, the same tiny, bald head.

The same future?

She must have made a sound, because as one, Ethan and Emmy turned toward her. She ducked to the side of the doorway and scraped her sleeve over her eyes, then pasted on her best fake smile as she took a step into the room.

Ethan's eyes were wide as she paused just inside the doorway. "Josie!"

She took a deep breath. "Molly surprised me. Brought me here. I'm sorry to intrude."

"No! It's fine! Come on in. This isn't exactly how I would have introduced you to the house, but you're here!" If she hadn't been so shocked by finding out about the house, Josie would have been almost tempted to laugh at his obvious distress. She could totally picture Josh making *I'm sorry* gestures behind her back.

"Um, okay. This is great. I'm so glad you're here." The little girl raised her eyebrows, seemingly sensing his discomfort. "Josie, this is my friend Emmy. Emmy, this is Josie."

Emmy turned fully toward her, and in the first moment Josie saw her eyes, a profound relief melted over her body. Where Avery had had eyes the color of chestnuts, Emmy's were bright, heavenly blue. Where Avery's smile had been huge, gap-toothed, contagious . . . Emmy's was tentative and sweet.

"Hi, Josie." Emmy smiled up at her as she snuggled closer to Ethan.

"Hi, Emmy." Josie crouched down so her head was at Emmy's level. "It's lovely to meet you." Josie looked around at the fluffy, very pink space. "You have an excellent room here."

"Best view in the whole place!" Emmy pointed out the window.

"I see that! Have you been to Snowflake Village yet?"

"Not yet this week. Dr. Mackenzie says I have to wait two more days. It's okay, though. Ben's saving me the pink-princess car on the Twinkle Fairy for when I come. He said I can ride it all day if I want to."

"Lucky you!"

Ethan chuckled. "Josie loves the Twinkle Fairy, too. Don't you, Jos?"

"You said she threw up on the Twinkle Fairy." Emmy poked Ethan in the chest.

Josie stood back up. "Never eat three hot dogs, a box of popcorn, and two Slush-Bombs before a ride that spins."

"Yuck. You should have stuck to ice cream." Emmy tipped her face up to Ethan's. "Speaking of ice cream . . ."

"I'm gonna run *out* of ice cream if you stay much longer, squirt. I'll have to get a cow to keep up with the demand."

"Me eating too much ice cream is a *good* problem."

"That's true. What'll it be? Dr. Mackenzie? Can the lady have chocolate today?"

Josh smiled. "Does the lady's tummy think chocolate will work?"

"The lady's tummy *definitely* thinks it'll work!" Emmy jumped off Ethan's lap and grabbed Josie's hand, surprising her. "Come on, Josie. Have you *seen* the ice cream machine? Let's go make creemees!"

With a bewildered look over her shoulder at Ethan and Josh, Josie followed her down the hallway into a sunny kitchenette and watched as she used a stepstool to pick out a cone and pull the chocolate lever to deliver a perfectly sculpted creemee into it.

"Wow. You've had a lot of practice at this." Josie reached out to take the cone Emmy handed her. "Thank you."

"Ethan says he's going to give me a job at the park when I'm older." Emmy spun her cone around and made another perfect creemee, then hopped off the stool. "Let's go eat on the porch!"

As they settled into two Adirondack chairs, Emmy said, "Are you Ethan's girlfriend?"

Josie swallowed, the ice cream growing spikes. "No. Just a friend."

"Are you sure?"

"Pretty sure, yes." Josie laughed as she licked her ice cream. Subject change time. "So how old are you, Emmy?"

"I'm eight. But Ethan says I'm terribly mature for my age."

"Oh, he does, does he?"

"Yes. I have to agree with him. But cancer does that."

Josie looked sideways at her, but she was just spinning her ice cream cone around, licking the drips. She had the same matter-of-fact demeanor Avery had always had. "That it does, sweetie."

"Ethan was talking about you. He says you help people? Talk to them to help them feel better?"

He'd said that?

"I try to, yes. It's really hard work to have things like cancer. Especially when you're a kid. So I try to help."

"Do you have kids, Josie?"

"No . . ." Josie bit her own cone. "No, I don't." *Because I don't ever, ever want to be attached to another child who could rip out my heart, sweet Emmy.*

"Do you have a husband?"

"Nope. No husband, either."

"Why not?" Emmy asked the question like she couldn't imagine anyone choosing not to get married and have children.

"I think maybe it's just not my time yet."

Emmy shook her head. "I think Ethan would be the perfect dad."

"Think so?" Josie's cone got stuck in her throat as it tightened.

"Oh, definitely. If I didn't have one already, I might ask him to be mine."

"Well, I'm sure he would be very honored to be asked."

"Hey! I have an idea." She pushed the final bite of her cone into her mouth and chewed thoughtfully. "Ethan needs a wife. You need a husband. Why don't the two of *you* get married?"

Josie laughed tightly. "That is quite an idea, young lady."

The screen door swung open and a young woman peered out. "Emmy, are you talking someone's ear off out here?" She leaned toward Josie with her right hand outstretched. "Hi, there. I'm Steph, this little imp's mom."

"She's good company." Josie smiled. "I'm Josie, Ethan's . . . friend from way back."

Emmy hopped off her chair. "I'm going to go tell him."

"Don't you dare!" Josie warned, but with a delighted squeak, Emmy banged through the screen door and headed up the stairs.

"Uh-oh. What's she telling who?" Steph propped her hip against the railing.

"I'm pretty sure she's telling Ethan I'm about to wither into spinsterhood and he'd better save me."

Steph laughed. "Oh boy. Is she planning your wedding already?"

"Quite possibly." Josie's gut quivered as she said so.

"So how do you know Ethan?"

"We went to high school together, actually."

"Lucky girl." Steph winked. "Did you ever date him?"

Josie paused for a long moment. "Yeah, we dated."

And almost got married, but we'll leave that part out for now.

Steph sat down in the wicker chair next to Josie, pulling up her knees like a schoolgirl waiting for a juicy story. "How long were you guys a couple?" When Josie paused again, Steph shook her head. "Oh, wow. Listen to me. I'm obviously desperate for girl talk, aren't I? I'm so sorry to pry! It's none of my business at all! I just adore Ethan, and I've never figured out why he's still single after all this time."

"Long story, Steph. But it's probably his to tell, not mine."

"Still love him?"

Josie felt her eyes widen, even as she smiled at Steph's directness. "Is this you not prying?"

"Sorry. Again. I think I've spent a little too long with only Emmy for company. My self-censor button seems to be broken."

"We were together a long time ago. A lot's happened since then."

"Ever wish you could go back to when it was all so much simpler?"

Josie paused. Yes. No. Maybe.

"Sometimes, I guess. I'm not sure it was that much simpler back then for us, unfortunately."

"The angst of first love." Steph smiled wistfully. "You never really get over it, do you?"

Josie shook her head slowly. "I'm starting to think you don't."

"Hey!" Steph pushed herself up from her chair. "Did Ethan show you the back part of the house? The owners' quarters?"

"Not yet."

"Come on. You have to see this. If I was a lesser woman, I'd pretend to fall in love with him just so I could live here full-time." She opened the screen door and held it while Josie stood up and walked through. "You might rethink your stance on rekindling things with Ethan once you see it. Just warning you!"

When they reached the kitchen, Steph pointed toward the breakfast nook, where a French door with lacy curtains was tucked up against the bay window that looked into the backyard. "Oh shoot." She looked up at the kitchen clock, then her watch. "I need to go give Emmy her meds, but you should go explore. Right through that door."

Josie shook her head. "I shouldn't go in there. It's not my place."

"It could be your place if you play your cards right!" Steph grinned. "I'll keep Ethan busy upstairs while you go explore. Seriously, you're going to fall in love with this house, if you haven't already."

Steph winked again as she turned to head back down the hallway. "Then you can work on falling for Ethan again."

Chapter 36

Josie cracked open the French door, unable to resist the golden sunlight peeking through the lacy curtains. She'd just take a quick look—just open the door a smidge and poke her head in, then close it before anyone was the wiser.

The door slid easily, and as she looked into what must be a living room, her breath caught in her throat. Sunlight slanted through a bank of windows to her right, sending warm beams onto a buttery wood floor and soft yellow walls with wide white trim.

She stepped into the room and closed the door softly behind her, despite her quick-peek-only stance. Two couches with big cushions angled toward a warm brick fireplace, and soft folk-art rugs decorated the floor. In one corner, two floor-to-ceiling bookcases snugged against each other, barely holding games and puzzles and what had to be three hundred or more books.

Josie spun in a slow circle. No television, no radio, no computer. Just a bright, cozy space to pluck a book off the shelf and curl up on a gooshy couch for hours. Or play a game at the low, square table in the corner that had huge cushions on four sides instead of chairs.

She stepped hesitantly toward an arched doorway, then felt her mouth open in awe as she came through it to the huge kitchen. Glass-front cabinets with antique white trim lined the upper walls, and a dark granite countertop sat atop beadboard cabinets. The appliances were stainless steel, and the oven was a chef's dream, complete with six burners and a warming drawer. An oblong island in the middle of the room had a prep sink and three green-shaded lights hanging from the ceiling, along with five wrought-iron barstools brightened with pale green checkered cushions.

She pictured the galley kitchen in her Boston apartment for a moment. It would almost fit on top of just the island here, she mused. On one hand, it was awfully convenient to have everything within reach. On the other, she'd never fit another human in there with her.

Josie walked by a sunny breakfast nook complete with a vase of daisies, a cozy den, and a huge dining room with a long maple table and matching hutch and sideboard before she came to a wide stairway with curving balustrade. It sure looked like someone lived here, or at least took really, really good care of the place. How did Ethan possibly find the time to keep a house he didn't even live in dust-free?

She peered up the stairs, still feeling like a trespasser in Ethan's home, but after seeing the . . . well, perfection of the first floor, she couldn't resist heading up to get a peek at the bedrooms. All those years of dreaming about what the inside of this old hotel looked like had never prepared her for the reality of it.

Thick folk-patterned carpet cushioned her steps as she climbed the stairs, and when she reached the top, a wide hallway stretched both left and right. She headed to the left, catching her breath as she poked her head into each doorway. Every single bedroom was decorated like the B and B rooms at the front of the house, with a casual elegance and thick, soft duvets on the beds.

After she'd seen the four bedrooms to the left of the stairway, she turned to check out the other end of the hallway. The first bedroom looked like a nanny's room, and the next one was decorated like a nursery, with bright blue walls and white furniture.

At the end of the hallway was a double door, and Josie gasped as she opened it and got a look at the master suite. A king-sized four-poster bed sat between two huge windows, a lacy canopy softening its lines. Acres of pillows and a downy comforter made her wonder how anyone could leave that bed in the morning.

Especially if a man like Ethan was still in it.

She shook her head, walking slowly across the plush carpet to three doors on the same wall. The one on the right held a walk-in closet bigger than her apartment's bathroom. The door on the left opened into a huge dressing room decorated in deep rose, teal, and gold tones. A huge beveled mirror sat in one corner, and there were built-in drawers and cubbies covering one full wall.

Oh Lord. Steph was right. Who would *not* want to live here?

A cushioned window seat with colorful pillows made Josie sigh, just aching to curl up with a cup of cocoa and a novel. She looked back through the door toward the bed. *After* curling up with Ethan in that big, lovely bed, that is.

She pulled the lacy curtain aside and had a clear view of the back patio, the flower gardens, the . . . wishing well? Avery's wishing well?

Her knees buckled, sending her pitching forward toward the window seat.

"Whatcha doing, munchkin?"

Avery looked up, fuzzy brown hairs peeking from be-

neath her Red Sox hat. "Making wishes." She closed her eyes and flicked a penny into the water.

"What are you wishing for?"

"Can't tell or it won't come true." Plonk.

"You sure have a lot of pennies there."

"I've got a lot of wishes to take care of today."

"Why today?"

"It's time."

Josie's heart lurched. "What do you mean?"

Avery looked up, eyes wiser than they should have been at her age. "You know what I mean, Jos."

Josie sat down on the bench, elbows on her eighteen-year-old knees. All she wanted to do was gather Avery in her lap and infuse her strength into her frail little body, but she'd tried that before. Tried it for two years now. It hadn't worked.

"Sure you don't want to tell me your wishes? Promise I won't spill your secrets."

She tossed another penny into the well, murmuring under her breath. "You'll tell Ethan."

"Not if you don't want me to."

"Baloney. You two are glued together, practically. I bet you tell each other everything."

"Maybe almost everything. But not special secrets we're keeping for other people."

Plonk. "You promise you won't tell?"

Josie made an X on her chest with her index finger. "Cross my heart, munchkin."

"Okay." She lifted up the bag, which had to have at least three hundred pennies in it. "I tried to find enough pennies for everybody I know." She set the bag on one of Josie's knees, then climbed into her lap and held her face in her tiny hands. "I'm wishing . . . wishing for everybody to be okay when I'm gone."

Josie felt her eyes water, so she gathered Avery close so she wouldn't see. "That's a very generous wish, Avery."

"I've been saving up these pennies for a long time so I could be ready, but I still don't have enough for everybody."

"You sure know a lot of people."

"I got lucky, didn't I?"

Josie squeezed her softly. Avery was ten years old, facing her own death, and talking about being lucky?

"We're the ones who are lucky, munchkin. We're the ones who got lucky."

Avery put her tiny arms around her neck and squeezed her hardest, then climbed down from her lap. "Come on, Josie. I have a lot of wishes left to do. Help me?"

For the next two hours, Josie held her baggie while she plucked one penny at a time out, murmured her wish, and tossed it into the well. As it started to get dark, Avery sat back on her lap and tossed from there, exhausted.

Ethan found them a few minutes after the park had closed, and leaned over to kiss first Avery, then Josie. "Whatcha doing, Aves?"

"Making wishes."

"Good ones?"

Avery nodded. "The best kind."

"Are you ready for us to bring you home yet?"

"Almost." She looked at the sky, where the first stars were starting to twinkle. "Do you think Ben would give us one last ride on the Ferris wheel?"

Ethan stood up, pulling her onto his back. "You better believe it. Let's go find him."

Minutes later, the three of them sat at the top of the Ferris wheel, swinging slowly in the soft twilight breeze. Avery leaned toward Ethan and pulled his head down, then blinked her eyes rapidly against his cheek. "Flutterby kisses, Ethan." Her voice was so soft Josie could barely hear her. Ethan leaned down and tickled Avery's cheek with his own lashes, making her giggle softly. "Flutterby kisses, Aves."

Avery turned to Josie and did the same, then leaned her head on Josie's shoulder and took Ethan's hand in hers as she sighed and closed her eyes. "Guess what I wished last?"

"What, sweetie?"

"I wished that every time you see a butterfly, you'll think of me."

The next morning, when they arrived at Avery's house together, an ambulance was parked in the driveway, along with a long black car from Freeman's Funeral Home. Josie clapped her hand to her mouth and screamed silently, then louder. No! No, no, no, no, NO!

Ethan slammed the truck into park, and she felt his fingertips reach for her across the cab as she leaped out of the truck and sprinted up the driveway toward the stretcher just emerging from the house.

They were too late.

Josie knew Ethan had never cried before, at least not since his mom had died. It just wasn't done in the Miller house. But as he pulled Josie away from the stretcher, as he rocked her on their knees in the middle of the gravel driveway, she felt his tears falling on her neck for a long, long time.

"You okay?"

Josie jumped as she heard Molly's voice behind her. She swiped at her eyes, grabbing for a tissue on the vanity.

"I'm fine."

"You're not fine."

Josie turned to her, and suddenly, a hot fury enveloped her. Yes, she'd fled Echo Lake ten years ago. Yes, she'd done it badly. Yes, she'd left both Ethan and Molly in her wake.

But she hadn't meant to hurt them. She really hadn't. And dammit, it was just about time for Molly to stop punishing her for it.

"You're right, Molly. I'm not fine. How fine did you *expect* I might be, coming here?"

Molly shrugged, but her glance didn't waver.

"It wasn't your place to do this, Mol. This is Ethan's home, and you should have let *him* show it to me, when he was ready. *If* he was ready. The only reason you brought me here was to hurt me."

Josie blotted her eyes with the tissue. "Well, congratulations. You did. Does it make you feel better?"

Molly still didn't answer—just stood in the doorway.

"I'm sorry, Molly. I'm sorry for how things happened, I'm sorry you got caught up in it, I'm sorry I couldn't see how to stay friends with you without—without dying of heartbreak, dammit. Forever, it was the three of us, and I didn't want you to have to choose between us." She put up a finger when Molly opened her mouth. "We were eighteen. You would have had to choose, and you know it. I tried to make it easy, so you didn't have to."

"We were best friends, Josie." Molly's voice was soft.

"I know."

"You killed him, Josie. And you left me to pick up the pieces."

"I never meant to. Either of those things." Josie took a shaky breath. "Everything was falling apart. Mom was—a mess, Dad had abandoned her for the stupid park, and Ethan . . . as far as I could see, Ethan was setting out to become a cookie-cutter version of my dad.

"And me?" She shivered, remembering her last night

in Echo Lake. "I don't know what I was headed for, but it scared the hell out of me."

"Why didn't you ever talk to me? Why'd you just take off in the middle of the night? You just—left."

Josie took a deep breath. "That night . . . it was bad, Molly. I just—had to go. I can't explain it. I don't know *how* to explain it."

Molly stepped slowly into the room and sat on the bed. "Okay, fine. I get that. But Jesus, Jos. It's been ten years. No way to explain it *since* then?"

"I don't know. Explaining it meant . . . reliving it. I buried it, Mols. I tried to bury it in work and exercise and . . . God, anything I could."

"Did it work?"

"I don't think so." Josie shook her head as she sat gingerly on the edge of the bed. "I'm sorry I hurt you, Mols."

"Are you?"

"Yes. I never meant to. Really."

"You're not just saying that because you're desperate and have no friends here anymore?"

Josie looked sidelong at her, relieved to see a tiny smile. Ah, now that sounded like the old Molly.

"Not just saying it. I've missed you like crazy."

Molly sighed, shaking her head. "Ditto."

"Any chance we could be friends again?"

"Maybe." Molly shrugged uncomfortably. "This isn't third grade, though. It's not that easy."

"I know."

"What about Ethan, Jos?"

Josie traced the seams of the quilt with her finger. "I don't know. I really, really don't know, and that's the honest truth."

"Well, friends or not, if you hurt that man again, I will hunt you down. I mean it."

"I know."

"I mean it, Josie. You need to decide, before things go any further, just what you're after here. Because this little jaunt down memory lane might be easy for *you* to leave behind, but it won't be for Ethan."

"Wouldn't be easy for me, either." Josie's voice was a whisper, and she could almost hear the alarms ringing inside Molly as her old friend's expression hardened.

"Do you—still love him?"

Josie looked at her, feeling tears threaten again.

"Oh, Mols. I wish I didn't."

Chapter 37

"No." An hour later, Molly crossed her arms like a four-year-old. "No freaking way."

Ethan sighed as he took a seat across from her desk. "How do you *really* feel, Mols?"

"Ethan, are you seriously this dense? Are you seriously under some delusion you can convince Josie to come back here by offering her a job? You think she's going to *take* a job from you? Seriously?"

"Could you please use the word *seriously* at least one more time so I know you're serious?"

"This is insanity."

"It's not." He pushed his hands through his hair, then braced his elbows on his knees. "It's not, dammit. You know she'd be perfect for this place. You know we need this sort of care available. Think about how it would round out what we've currently got."

He hadn't been able to stop thinking about it since he'd seen her work her magic on Bryce-the-tree-climber. Hadn't practically *slept,* thinking about it. And then she'd appeared here, thanks to Molly, before he'd quite figured out how to approach her gracefully about the whole thing.

And then she'd walked around the house like she was going to break it if she stepped too hard, spent twenty minutes exploring the living quarters, came out looking like a deer caught in the headlights, Molly close on her tail.

When he'd come toward her, she'd put up a hand, halting him. "No. I need to process this. I need to . . . to . . . just go. For a while. I don't know. Avery. Everything. The well!" She'd made a motion toward the back windows, where the wishing well was.

Dammit. Showing her the well's new home was just one more thing he had been hoping to do more gracefully, but he'd waited too long.

And then she'd left.

Bad. It had all been wrong. And he was furious at Molly for bringing Josie here without even asking him first. It hadn't been her place.

Had it?

Molly sat back in her chair, lips tight. "I have a date. I do not have time for this discussion. Were you planning to advertise an opening for a counselor anytime in the next six months?"

"That's not my point."

"Were you?"

"You know I wasn't."

"Then you are making up a need here, in a desperate attempt to convince your ex-girlfriend there's something still here for her. Which there isn't."

"Not true."

"Ethan, be serious. She lives in Boston, for God's sake. She has a practice that does business with Boston Children's Hospital. She's got patients coming out the wazoo. You really think she's going to be satisfied sitting in this house seeing maybe two or three patients a *day*?"

"Maybe? Or maybe Mercy is looking as well? Why not? It's good work, Molly. You know it is."

"Yes, *I* know it is. And *you* know it is. But I have absolutely zero confidence that *she* will agree. She moves at a different pace now, has different expectations. She didn't want this life, remember? Have a few grown-up make-out sessions completely clouded all reason? One trip to the waterfall?"

Ethan felt bile rising in his stomach. She was one step away from being out of line, but if he was honest, it was partly his fault. He'd laid this conversation on her without any warning, and Molly was not one to mince words on the best of days.

"Mols, she didn't want the life she thought she was going to have. She was eighteen. She could barely see past the end of her nose, let alone what her life might look like in ten years. Her parents were a disaster wrapped in a holiday package, and I was one big old barrel of laughs back then, with my scholarship down the drain and a future at the park she hated staring me in the face. Of course she wanted to leave."

"Shouldn't have mattered that you were going to be an elf. Not if she really loved you."

He leveled Molly with a look. "Be serious. She wanted more than this town had to offer, and she went and found it. She had a whole lot of really good reasons to take off for greener pastures, and at the time, I was one of them."

"And you think that's changed now, just because she's been back for two weeks and you've seared her with your golden lips?"

Ethan coughed. "Golden lips?"

He was surprised to see color rise in her cheeks. "Be realistic, Ethan. So the two of you still have chemistry. Great. You're still sitting in her father's office at her father's precious park, and you show no signs of leaving. You'd be offering her exactly the life she didn't want."

Ouch.

"It's not that simple."

Molly looked down at the papers on her desk, silent for so long that Ethan shifted uncomfortably. Molly never held her tongue. Finally, she looked up and took a deep breath, then blew it out slowly between her lips. "Ethan, if you offer Josie a job here at Avery's House, I will resign."

"Don't be dramatic."

"Don't be patronizing."

"How am I being patronizing? Why would you need to quit your job if I'm lucky enough to convince Josie to be a part of this house?"

"There wouldn't be room for anyone else here, Ethan. This is her house, remember? The one she used to dream about living in . . . with you. It's a house built on the memories of *her* Avery. Not mine. You and Josie loved Avery. I was on the periphery.

"I spent way too many years playing the third wheel, Ethan. I won't do it again. If Josie comes back, then *she* needs to sit in the director's chair, not me. She needs to come back, heart and soul, not just dabble in some part-time counseling. And if she can't, then she really doesn't belong here."

He sat back, scrubbing his fingers through his hair. Shit. This is not how this was supposed to go. "You're serious, aren't you?"

"Dead."

Ethan winced. "Wow. I don't even know what to say."

"Say *Go back to Boston, Josie.* Easy-peasy."

Ethan smiled tightly, but couldn't miss the fear in Molly's eyes. Time to tread lightly. Very, very lightly.

"I don't know, Mols. I have no idea what's going to happen. She could show up here tomorrow with her suitcase packed, saying her good-byes."

"Exactly my point, Ethan. She could do that *any* day, job offer or not. Or not show up at all and just be AWOL some morning. I think that's the part you have to re-member. She's pretty good at the running-when-things-get-sucky thing."

He nodded slowly. "I know."

"Well, then?"

"Well, then?" He sighed. "I guess I just want to believe that maybe we're worth *not* running from this time."

Three days after her mind-altering trip to Avery's House, Josie drove gingerly into her parents' driveway. She felt like she was in a daze, suffering from three sleepless nights in a row. Coming to terms with Ethan buying their someday-house and naming it after Avery was big enough. Realizing he'd done it all with Molly and Josh was a whole different level of shock she hadn't quite fig-ured out how to process yet.

On one hand, she felt a sense of awe so huge it made her chest hurt. What he'd done was incredible. It was amazing. It was—*God*—inspiring, and it humbled her in a way she hadn't yet come to terms with.

She'd been so afraid of him following in her dad's footsteps that she'd forgotten to figure in that this was . . . Ethan. She should have known better. Way bet-ter. And she was ashamed of herself for not believing in him ten years ago. Ashamed that she hadn't believed he could be the kind of man she'd want to spend forever with.

She'd been dead wrong.

She'd texted him the day after she'd seen the house, asking for time and space, and he—so far—was abiding by her request. She'd spent the days sitting with Dad, al-ternately relieved Ethan was doing as she'd asked—and wishing he'd ignore her and come charging in on a white steed, scooping her up and promising to make everything all right again.

A tinny version of "Jingle Bells" assaulted Josie's ears as she unlocked the front door of her parents' house and stepped inside, making her stop warily. What in the world? Christmas carols played twenty-four-seven at Snowflake Village, but Josie couldn't remember a time when she'd ever heard one playing at home.

Even when it was really the holiday season, Mom had never allowed carols in the house. Said they drove her crazy as a loon. *Right,* Josie had always thought. *Because that'd be such a long trip.*

"Mom? Mom?" She stood rooted in the doorway, instinctively ready to flee. A lump of fear settled deep in her stomach. Mom had been doing so well. Had something finally made her snap? Was Josie about to walk around the corner and see her sprawled half-cocked on the couch, a wine bottle in her hand, even though it was only one o'clock on a Sunday afternoon?

Her breath came faster as she peered around the corner, but instead of the scene she feared, she saw Mom standing on tiptoes to put a little glass angel at the top of a freshly cut Christmas tree.

Um . . .

"Mom?" Josie padded softly into the living room, trying not to startle her, trying not to admit to herself that she was walking like she might approach a fragile patient. Mom was humming—humming!—a sound Josie hadn't heard since she was really little.

Three steps more, and she'd be close enough to get a look in her eyes. Then she'd know whether she needed to play the let's-go-to-the-hospital game so Mom could get dried out before she did more damage.

Mom finally turned toward her, bright smile and clear-as-glass eyes flashing her way. "Josie! You startled me! I didn't expect you yet! Shoot! I'm not quite finished!" She crossed the room and grabbed Josie into a fierce hug. "Come on in! Want to help me do the last decorations?"

"Mom?" Josie tipped her head. Was she witnessing a woman about to step over the proverbial edge?

"Don't worry. I'm not going nuts. I just needed a pick-me-up, so I had Ike cut me a little tree and bring it over this morning. Thought we could decorate it and have our own little mini-Christmas in August."

"Do you . . . do this often?"

"Nope! First time!"

Suddenly a scent hit Josie's nose, and she looked toward the kitchen in alarm. "What's that smell?"

Mom tried to mute her smile, but only lasted a second before she broke. "That, my dear, is called roast chicken."

"From the actual oven?"

"Yes, with mashed potatoes, crisp green beans, and fresh, hot yeast rolls with butter."

Josie stared at Mom. "Are you an alien posing as my mother?" She sniffed again. "What else do I smell out there?"

"You wouldn't believe it if I told you." Mom motioned her into the kitchen, and Josie followed, madly trying to reconcile new-Mom with old-Mom. Apparently she wasn't done being startled by the differences.

As they came into the kitchen, Josie spotted gingerbread men on a cooling rack and little bowls of pastel frosting at the ready. She looked at the cookies, then at Mom, then at the cookies again. "You made gingerbread cookies?"

Mom nodded. "They used to be your favorite, remember?" She winked, then opened the fridge.

Josie nodded warily, checking out Mom's pupils as she did so. Had she given up drinking only to move on to something more serious?

In the midst of taking cranberry sauce out of the fridge, Mom stopped mid-turn, then set the bowl carefully on the counter and put both hands on Josie's shoulders. "Honey, you look like you're seeing a ghost." Then she put one hand to her mouth. "Oh God. You kind of are, aren't you?"

Josie nodded carefully, not trusting herself to speak.

"I promise you I'm fine right now. I'm not on any sort of manic high, or any sort of mood enhancer, or any sort of . . . anything. I'm just starting to feel optimistic about the strides your dad is making, and feeling incredibly grateful that you're here." She paused for a long breath. "And I got to thinking about all the terrible, lousy Christmases we had over the years, and I thought it'd be nice to have a normal one."

"In August."

"Well, yes. In August. But in my defense, I don't know that you'll be here in December, so I had to catch you while I could." Mom tweaked her cheek like Josie was five. "I'm good, honey. Good. Happy. Things are going to be very different around here, but for today, for right now, I've got my daughter here and y'know what? We're going to have Christmas!"

As she finished, the doorbell rang, and Mom got a cat-ate-the-canary look on her face. "Want to get the door?"

"Who's here, Mom?"

She shrugged her shoulders. "Go see!"

Josie walked to the door, shaking her head. Fresh tree in the living room, fresh chicken in the oven, fresh cookies on the counter. She'd definitely been away a long, long time. She opened the door and swallowed hard as she caught sight of the person on the other side.

Chapter 38

Ethan grinned as he held up a bottle of sparkling grape juice and a Santa bag full of packages. "Ho-ho-ho! Merry Christmas!"

"Are you kidding me?" Josie couldn't help but laugh as she opened the door to let him in. "You're in on this craziness?" She almost looked behind him for the white steed.

"Better believe it." He planted a kiss on her nose as he came in, like they'd just seen each other last night, not days ago. Like they'd left things all cozy and warm, not fragmented and strange. "It's only the best kind of crazy, though."

She stepped back and got a better look at him. "Omigod. What are you *wearing*?"

"A Christmas sweater, of course!"

A laugh burst from Josie's very stomach as she looked at his impish eyes. "I cannot believe you still have that ugly thing!"

"Are you insulting my sweater? That you *made*?"

"It's awful, Ethan." She turned him around. "It's got dropped stitches and holes all over the place. And—omigod—the left sleeve is about three inches longer than the right one."

"It's perfect." He pulled her close and she couldn't help

but melt into him, scratchy wool sweater and all. "I loved it then and I love it now." He leaned down and kissed her softly. "Are you okay?"

She nodded carefully. "I think so? I don't quite know how to process this scene." She waved vaguely toward the kitchen. "That's not my mother in there."

He laughed, running his index finger playfully down her nose. In an automatic gesture that surprised her, she grabbed it as she swatted it away. He looked into her eyes for a long moment, then squeezed her fingers. "I've missed you at the park."

"Well, there's something I bet you never thought you'd say."

"True enough." He caressed her palm slowly, carefully, making her knees go squishy. "I'm hoping maybe you'll be done avoiding me soon so we can talk."

"I think I already told you that I don't do avoidance."

Dammit, why was her voice doing that shaky thing again?

"Of course you don't." He rolled his eyes. "You've just been very, very busy the last three days."

"I have!"

"Okay." He used his chin to indicate the kitchen. "Do I smell chicken?"

Josie nodded, still a little mystified. "I think she actually cooked it."

"This I gotta see." He gave her fingers another squeeze, then motioned for her to precede him down the hallway.

As they walked into the kitchen, Mom was putting mashed potatoes into a bowl. The roast chicken was on a platter surrounded by greens, and a basket of perfectly browned rolls rounded out the picture. Josie stopped fast, causing Ethan to bump into her from behind. She looked over her shoulder at him, and he nodded encouragingly, then squeezed her waist as he sidled past.

"Diana! It smells delicious in here!" He walked over and kissed her on the cheek, pulling a bunch of flowers out of his Santa bag. "For you, madame."

Mom grinned, taking the flowers and giving Ethan a hug. "Thank you! They're lovely! I hope you're hungry!"

"Dad sends his regrets, but he was bound and determined not to miss his poker game. Even for Christmas."

"That's fine. It'll be just the three of us." She motioned them toward the dining room. "Come! Let's eat!"

When Josie walked through the archway into the dining room, she stopped again. What in the *world*? Candles were on the table, china was set, and the tiny chandelier over the table was decorated with swags of gold ribbon. She couldn't even remember the last time they'd used this room, let alone had an actual dinner in here.

Mom's face was glowing as she watched Josie take in the scene. She bustled back and forth from kitchen to table, bringing in the food, then sat down, motioning Ethan and Josie to join her. "Sit! Sit!"

They sat. And ate. And ate some more. The food was delicious, better than anything Josie remembered Mom ever cooking. Ever. Josie couldn't stop watching her the entire time they sat at the table. This mom was the one she remembered from way back in elementary school, the one who'd spin funny stories at dinnertime, the one who'd ask just the right questions and listen intently to the answers, the one who drew you into her light and made you never want to leave.

After an hour, Ethan pushed his chair back with a contented sigh. "Diana, I would never say this in front of Mama Bellini, but that meal rivaled anything I've ever had at the restaurant."

"High praise indeed, coming from someone who eats there as often as you do." Diana winked, and Josie was struck once again by the thought that this was one of those scenes she'd dreamed up long ago, where she'd bring home a boyfriend for dinner, and Mom would cook a chicken and joke around with him while Josie made plans to get him alone later.

"Should we do presents?" Ethan's eyes were playful as he grabbed a couple of serving dishes and headed to the kitchen. Diana followed him, but Josie was momentarily too stunned to even stand up. Is this what Christmas was supposed to be like? Warm and soft and delicious-tasting? Cinnamon candles, laughter, and horribly adorable wool sweaters?

She thought back to Christmas of her senior year, when Christmas had been anything *but* those things.

Josie stared at the last embers of the fire Dad had started hours ago in a delusional fit. Because, of course, a fire in the fireplace would make it feel like Christmas even if Mom was already half in the bag and he was already half out the door. She drained her glass of eggnog and picked up the Malibu Barbie Mom had ordered from the Internet. It was exactly what she'd wanted . . . eight years ago. Same with the stuffed puppy and Easy-Bake oven on the coffee table.

She leaned over to look down the hall, but there wasn't a sound. Dad had left for the park two hours ago, and Mom had responded by finishing her bottle of Stoli and dragging her muttering self to bed. At least there hadn't been screaming this year.

Josie reached under the couch and brought out three gaily wrapped packages with bows and ribbons and shiny tags, all addressed to her. She opened the first one and gasped dramatically. It was the book she'd

*been eyeing at Turn-the-Page for weeks. Four hundred
pages of pure, unadulterated escapism, and she couldn't
wait to sink into the recliner and start it. The next package was a CD of the group Ethan had taken her to see
in Boston. Just listening to it would bring her back to that
long car ride together, the energy of the concert . . . the
whole weekend away from Camp Ho-Ho.*

*The last present was soft, and at first she grimaced.
"Clothes." Then she smiled and ripped open the paper,
pulling out a brand-new Wellesley College sweatshirt.
She put it to her cheek, grinning like an idiot. Her early
acceptance had come last week, but she hadn't told anyone yet.*

*She gathered up the paper, folding it carefully, then
the ribbon. Lastly, she grabbed the tags so she could
make sure they hit the trash before anyone saw them.*

*After all, seeing three tags marked "To Josie, From
Josie" would pretty much peg the pathetic scale, and she
didn't need anybody to know she'd bought her own damn
Christmas presents this year.*

"Jos? You still awake?" Ethan leaned down and whispered
in her ear, making her shiver deliciously. Damn him.

She shook her head, knocking the memory out as she
pushed back her chair to help clear the rest of the table.
"Yup. Sorry. Just a little discombobulated."

"That a therapist word?" His eyes looked too knowing, like he could see right through her.

"Nope. I'm just trying to process . . . everything.
Avery's House, you . . ." She motioned to the table, the
candles. "This."

He picked up a bowl of pickles. "I'm really sorry you
had to find out about it the way you did. Molly had no
right to do that. I really am sorry."

"You're not responsible for Molly's actions, Ethan."

"No, but if I'd told you about Avery's House myself, I wouldn't have given her the opening to do it like she did."

"True. But what's done is done, Ethan. Molly's—she's just trying to protect you."

"From?"

"Me."

"I hardly need protecting, especially from—you."

"Well, she doesn't agree." Josie picked up the salt and pepper shakers. "And I understand. I do."

She did. Of all the thoughts flipping through her mind the past three days, this was the part that surprised her the most—this sympathy for Molly's actions. And though she wished Ethan *had* been the one to show her Avery's House, and do it his own way, at least now she knew.

Diana came back through the doorway. "You know what? I think I might head back to the rehab hospital and check on your dad for a bit. I trust you can find something to do to entertain yourselves?"

"Diana, I think you just made your daughter blush." Ethan winked at Josie as he gathered their plates.

"I'm too old to blush." Josie grabbed two serving bowls and headed into the kitchen.

Mom joined her at the sink, brushing shoulders conspiratorially. "Never get too old to blush, sweetie." She washed her hands, then turned to grab her purse off the barstool at the counter. "Leave the dishes. I'll get them later."

As she headed down the hallway, she blew a kiss. "Be good!"

After they'd done the dishes, Ethan pointed to the gingerbread cookies. "Was she hoping we would decorate these?"

"I have no idea. This is not a scene I've ever been part of before."

He picked up a cookie and a knife. "I bet I can frost more than you."

"Oh really? Now you're a pastry chef, too?"

"Nope. Just love cookies. Mom used to let David and me race."

"That sounds messy. Two boys, frosting, and a race?"

"Yeah. She loved it."

Josie smiled, picking up a knife and a cookie. "Ready?"

"Set, go!"

He started slathering green frosting on gingerbread men as fast as he could pick them up, but Josie matched his pace for the first few cookies. Then she laughed as she noticed frosting all over his fingers. "You are making a serious mess, Ethan."

"We're not going for style—just speed."

"Who's making up these rules?"

"Me, of course."

"Well, new rule." She started to reach across the shelf for a new bowl of frosting, but inadvertently caught his spoon with hers on the way, and a glob of frosting smacked into his nose.

His eyes widened so far that she leaped backward off her stool, laughing, almost upending it. He picked up a spoon. "You did not just do that."

"I didn't mean to!"

"Not sure I believe you."

He reached toward the counter and pulled a bowl of orange frosting to him, reaching in with his index finger. "Come here, sweet Josie." His voice was silky, deep, and it was all she could do *not* to walk toward him.

"Nope. Don't *sweet Josie* me."

He stepped toward her, wiping frosting from his nose. She backed up, but the kitchen was tiny, and she found herself up against the wall in two seconds flat. "Uh-oh. Nowhere to run?" His smile was mischievous.

Josie felt her breath catch as he got closer and closer, and though she knew she should duck and put some space between them, she felt like invisible magnets were holding her in place, waiting for him to close the distance.

And then he was almost touching her. His eyes were suddenly serious as he looked into hers, then looked at her lips, then back at her eyes. "New rule. Winner gets to kiss the loser."

"You keep making up new rules." Her voice was doing that breathy, catchy thing again, dammit. "And you're not the winner."

He leaned closer. "I am, too, the winner. You cheated."

He reached his hand up to stroke her jaw. Instead of the slightly callused pads of his fingers, though, she felt a creamy paste hit her skin. Before she could react, he nuzzled her neck, planting soft kisses along the trail of frosting. "Mmm. You taste even better than usual."

She fought to stay standing while he turned her lower half to jelly just by kissing her. Then he pulled away and reached back into the bowl, pupils dark and hungry. She felt her heart pick up speed as she watched him, but couldn't force her voice above a whisper. "What are you doing?"

"I'm thinking of other places I might like to put this."

"Oh." *Oh.*

He chuckled, then ran his finger along the V-neck of her sweater, leaving a trail of frosting in its wake. He bent down and placed a gentle kiss on her collarbone. "Like here." Another kiss, one millimeter lower. "And here. And here." He moved with exquisite tenderness, making her ache with anticipation.

As he slid his hands under her sweater, she moaned involuntarily, and he reached down to pick her up, carrying her into the living room, where Mom had already pulled the curtains. The colored lights of the tree gave a warm glow to the room as he laid her down on the plush carpeting.

He propped himself up on his elbow beside her, and she ran her fingers over the strong lines of his jaw. She could see the tree lights reflected in his eyes, and a Christmas carol played softly from the stereo. For the first time in ten years, the sound of it didn't make her twitch.

"Y'know, I think I could learn to love Christmas again."

"I'm glad to hear that." He kissed her nose. "Do you think you could ever learn to love Snowflake Village again?"

"Ooh, now that's more of a stretch." She smiled. "I don't think I've called it Camp Ho-Ho in at least a day or two, though. Progress, right?"

"How about Avery's House?"

She propped herself up on her elbows. "What do you mean?"

"Well, I've been thinking . . . kind of a lot, actually, since you haven't spoken to me in three days. I know you said you don't really counsel kids all that much . . ."

"I don't."

"But I've seen you over the past two weeks. You're not half bad with them."

"Ethan, please don't extrapolate two emergency situations into me being qualified to counsel kids."

"I think you're more qualified than you're willing to admit, Josie. Emmy doesn't warm up to just anyone, you know. And yet she glommed right onto you the moment you walked in. Just like Avery did."

Josie sighed. "That's exactly the problem. I can't do it, Ethan. I can't let myself get attached to another child like that. It's too dangerous. It's too hard."

"I thought so, too." Ethan nodded thoughtfully. "For a long time, I couldn't imagine getting close to another kid. But then I started doing stuff on the pediatric floor at Mercy and I realized I *could* heal. Most kids get better, and the ones that don't? We can make their time here better. We can be a special oasis on a mountain, with great care and fun rooms and creemees on demand."

"Can you imagine if we'd been able to give Avery that?" Josie felt tears threatening.

"Exactly. And that's why I bought the house. That's why I applied for the grants. That's why I named it after her. We did our best for her, and I have to believe we made her life better. I couldn't imagine going through the rest of my days steeling myself against that sort of connection. I had to take a risk that it could happen again . . . but that in the meantime, I could do a lot of good."

He paused, running his fingertips down her jawline. "We were a good team, Jos. We could be again."

"At Avery's House?"

He nodded slowly, kissing her nose softly. "Maybe not just there. Maybe . . . maybe you could stay? Maybe we could give this a second chance? Us?"

In his eyes, she could see the reflection of the Christmas lights, could see the flames from the fireplace behind her. Could see what she'd seen ten years ago, and never since. This man loved her. With his heart and soul, he still loved her, despite everything that had happened, and as she fairly melted into him, she knew she loved him, too. Always had, always would.

"So what do you think? Am I worth taking another chance on?" His words were playful, but his posture was anything but.

She slid her fingers around his neck to pull him closer. "It's possible. You're kind of growing on me."

He gathered her into a tender hug, then laid her softly back and kissed her neck. "Have you ever made love under a Christmas tree?" He kissed her lips tenderly, slowly, as he traced the neckline of her sweater with his fingertips.

As his head dipped toward her neck, a loon call sounded from the vicinity of the coffee table where he'd set his phone earlier. Josie jumped, thinking it was her phone, but she'd left hers in the kitchen. The loon sounded again.

Wait. It was *his* ring tone, too? How had she never heard it since she'd been home?

He growled and reached for the phone, hitting the decline call button before he even saw who was calling. "Sorry about that." He kissed her again, but ten seconds later, they heard the loon again.

"Are you kidding me?" He rolled away from Josie and pulled the phone off the table, checking the readout this time. "It's Ben. I'm sorry, Jos. I should probably take this. He wouldn't keep trying unless it was important."

"Of course," she said, but her voice was pathetically small as she sat up and crossed her arms across her chest. Her stomach actually hurt as she realized what was about to happen.

He answered the call, speaking in monosyllables in response to whatever Ben was saying, and then hung up, sighing. "I can't believe this, but I have to head over to the park."

"Oh."

And there it was. One minute ago she'd been clouded by dreamy kisses and hot promises, but this was the reality of Ethan, the reality of Camp Freaking Ho-Ho. It always won.

"I know. I'm sorry. The timing—" He brushed his hands through his hair as he reached for her, but she pulled back. "I wouldn't go if I didn't have to. I *really* don't want to, Jos."

"Of course."

Of course. I know how this works, Ethan. Camp Ho-Ho is wife and mistress, and I'll get the leftovers. Oh yes. I definitely know how this goes.

He stood up, reaching down to help her up as well, but she waved him off. "Go ahead. They need you at the park."

"Aw, dammit, Jos. You look—ah hell—I feel terrible."

"It is what it is, Ethan. This is how it works."

He turned toward the door, then stopped and turned back. "I really am sorry."

"I know."

"I'll pick you up later for the dinner, okay?"

Josie took a deep breath. "I think I'll actually ride with Mom, if that's all right."

"Okay? Sure?" He looked mystified. "I'll see you there, then?"

She worked up a smile. It wasn't his fault. He didn't know any different, right? This was his life. He just hadn't yet figured out that it was going to make having any *other* life virtually impossible. "Okay."

With a quick kiss, he was out the door and off to the park, and she was left sitting on the living room floor, staring at a Christmas tree alone. Again.

Chapter 39

"Diana, I think we need to talk about hiring someone else to work in the office." Ethan paced his office at the park, practicing his speech, the latest crisis handled and averted. He'd tried to reach Josie, but her phone was turned off. "Diana, I know this isn't really the time to talk about this, but I'm wondering what you might think of me hiring an assistant."

He ran his hands through his hair. Christ, the woman's husband was still in the hospital. How could he ask a question that would make her think he was convinced Andy wasn't ever coming back?

But he had to. He *never* wanted to leave Josie like that again—never wanted to see that bleak look on her face as he'd put on his coat. He might be CFO of the park, but he was determined not to let Snowflake Village own him.

Josie'd spent her life coming in second place to this damn park. He squeezed his eyes shut. And he'd just demonstrated, in crystal-clear fashion, that she still did.

He tried her phone again. Straight to voice mail. Again.

The office phone rang, startling him. He picked it up without looking at the readout, and was surprised to hear Diana's voice on the other end of the line.

"Ethan? I was just calling to leave you a message. What are you doing there at the park? I thought you were with Josie."

"I was. Something came up here, and I had to come back."

"I see." The silence hung in the air, making him think again of Josie's face as he'd left her sitting by the Christmas tree.

"I've actually been meaning to talk to you about something," he started.

"That's good, because I've been meaning to talk to you as well."

"Do you want to go first?"

"I think we need to hire you an assistant."

"Wha—"

Diana bulldozed forward. "I do. I've been thinking about it for days. Andy's getting better, but this isn't going to be a short journey, and we can't have you collapsing from exhaustion while we wait. And maybe . . . maybe he'll never come back to the park. We don't know yet.

"Ethan, you've been burning both ends of the candle for so long I don't even think you realize you're doing it anymore, but as the de facto boss of Camp Ho-Ho, I'm officially telling you to cut your hours. Starting next week."

Ethan chuckled. "De facto boss of Camp Ho-Ho? Has Josie heard you call it that?"

"Sounds rather pompous, doesn't it? I'm serious, though. I've been giving it a lot of thought, and if Andy isn't going to be back to one hundred percent, then I need to learn this business so we can keep the park running. I'm going to start coming in next week, and you can show me the ropes."

"*You're* going to be the assistant?"

"No. We're *also* going to hire an assistant. But I'm going to try to learn as much of Andy's job as possible so you can go back to owning just the financials instead of the entire operation. Then you can concentrate on where your heart is . . . at Avery's House."

She paused. "And if I can be bold, maybe with Josie."

"Wow."

"How was Josie when you left?"

"Fine. Good." He winced, picturing her face. "Quiet."

"Ethan, I am definitely not the person to give *anybody* advice, and we both know it, but I'm going to, anyway."

"Should I sit down?"

"No. You should listen to me while you're getting in your truck and driving back to see my daughter."

He sat.

"You know what'll send Josie straight back to Boston?"

"Honestly? A lot of things."

"True. And you can't control some of them. But you *can* control others. Do you still love her, Ethan?"

He spun to look out the window at a park that hadn't been the same since she'd left ten years ago. Then he looked at the lacy sweater she'd started hanging on her dad's chair for when the AC went wonky. He looked at the happy-face mug and the bright pens and the sparkly mouse on Andy's desk, and he liked it.

He liked it a lot.

He braced himself. "Yeah. I do, Diana. I didn't think I would, didn't think I *could* . . . but I do."

"Then you need to show her that a life with you isn't going to mirror the life she saw Andy and I have back then. We made terrible choices, and we paid the biggest price—losing our daughter."

Diana paused. "Don't let her go back to Boston. Don't lose her again, Ethan."

* * *

"Hey, Ike! How's my Jeep?" Josie stepped into the open garage bay, finding Ike's legs sticking out from under a late-model Lexus, even though it was Sunday afternoon.

He rolled the rest of his body out from under the car and peered up at her. "Why? You going somewhere?"

Yeah. Boston, as a matter of fact. "Maybe. Is it done yet?"

Ike nodded, groaning as he pushed himself awkwardly off the rolling cart and stood upright. "Damn old bones." He wiped his hands on a red rag and motioned toward her Jeep out in the back parking lot. "She's done. I put in the new ignition switch yesterday and got her all shined up today for you. New oil, new washer fluid, pumped up your tires."

"I really appreciate it. What do I owe you?" Josie took her wallet out of her purse, anxious to get out of town.

Ike stood there silent for so long she thought he might have fallen asleep on his feet. Finally, he waved away her wallet and turned toward his little office. "I'm not taking your money, Josie."

"Ike, I fully expect to pay you. You spent hours working on the car, ordered parts . . ." She glanced back at the Jeep. "It's shinier now than when I bought it. Did you *wax* it?"

He shrugged as he turned back toward her. "Maybe."

Josie opened her wallet. "I insist on paying you. How much did the switch cost?"

"Eh, I had one lying around."

"You've been telling me for a week that you were waiting for it to arrive."

"Dunno. Memory's not so good these days."

"Liar."

His mouth crept up at the corners. "Tell ya what. Give

me five bucks I can pass on to my grandson. He helped with the waxing."

"Ike, listen—"

Ike put his hands on his hips. "Y'know what? I think you're maybe the one that needs to listen right now, missy. Your cheeks are flaming like they used to when you were good 'n' mad, and I can see you're itching to get on the road. I don't know what happened just now, but whatever it was, stop and think before you take off again."

"No offense, but honestly, Ike. You have no idea."

"Maybe. But I know some things."

Oh, for God's sake.

"What are you talking about?" She looked at her watch pointedly. She had to be gone before Ethan realized she wasn't coming to the Hospital Hero dinner. Gone before Mom realized she'd finally packed her suitcase and had it ready to go.

"Jos, I know you think that this whole damn town is stuck in time—that nothing ever changes here, but it's not true."

"I know that."

"I know you *think* you know that, but I'm not convinced you *really* know that. I also don't think you have any idea how many people in this town loved you then, and would love you now if you'd let them get attached to the woman you've become. Especially one particular man who's never forgotten you—or loved anyone else."

"Ike, seriously."

"Oh, I'm being dead serious. You spent a lot of hellish years trying to pretend everything was fine, trying to convince us all you were just fine, but honey, we knew."

"No. Stop it." Josie put up her hand, backing away.

"Think about it, Josie. Why do you think Mama Bellini had you at the restaurant so much?"

"She needed help!" Even as she said the words, Josie knew it wasn't true. Had known it in her heart all along.

"She didn't need help any more than I needed somebody to organize my wrenches on Friday nights, Josie."

"But they were always a mess . . ." Josie heard her voice fade as she spoke.

Ike sighed. "Honey, I messed them up at three o'clock every Friday so you'd have something to do besides go home."

"No."

"Yeah, I did." He stepped toward her, putting an arm gingerly around her shoulders. "We all knew what you were living, Josie. And we all did what we could, but obviously it wasn't enough, because you still had to go. But we got it. Even Ethan, though it took him an awful lot longer to be able to admit it."

"Stop." Josie put her hand up slowly, trying to stem his words.

"I don't think I will. I don't know what happened to put you in this state, but somebody needs to say this, and since you've got two wheels on the road already, I guess I'm elected. I know you came back two weeks ago thinking you'd just put in your time till your daddy's better. Well, that's gonna be a long road, and that means you've got some deciding to do. Are you going back to Boston and leave your mom here alone? Leave Ethan and Molly and Josh to do the good work they're doing, without you? Is that what you really, truly want?"

He threw his rag into a pile by the door. "You going to ditch the love of your life and try to forget him . . . again?"

"You have no idea what you're talking about, Ike."

"Wrong. I know exactly what I'm talking about, because I had a chance forty years ago to make the same choice, and my grandpa took me by the collar and asked me the one question that made it all clear. He said, 'Son, where does your *heart* live?' "

Ike let his arm drop from her shoulders as he backed up three steps. "I'll get your keys, but you think about this, Josie, and you think hard.

"Where does *your* heart live?"

Chapter 40

"Ethan! Check security camera nine! Quick!" Molly blew into his office, face flaming. He only had an hour until he needed to leave for the hospital dinner, and still hadn't been able to get hold of Josie. Yes, she'd said she'd see him there, but his gut clenched when he remembered how she'd looked, sitting there on the living room floor.

And now Molly was here with another emergency. Yeah, he definitely needed an assistant.

He spun in his chair, clicking the Polar Plunge camera to life. "What's the matter? What happened?"

Molly leaned over his shoulder. "Right there! Look!" She pointed at a strikingly Italian-looking guy lounging against the ride, guzzling a bottled water.

"What am I looking at, Mols? Did he do something?"

She spun his chair around, then grabbed her chest dramatically. "I think I found true love."

He spun back to take another look at the guy, then faced Molly again. "True love? What?"

"Isn't he gorgeous?" She looked over his shoulder, practically drooling.

"I'm not the right gender to appreciate his assets, sorry. Where did you meet this guy? Oh God, Mols. Tell me he's not from that Italian dating site."

She laughed. "Funny story, actually. No, he's not. But

I was out on another disastrous Italian Match date the other night with some guy who called himself Mario, and when the slime ball went to the bathroom, I spotted this guy at a table by himself."

"So . . . you're on a date with . . . Mario . . . and he goes to the bathroom, so you make the moves on a single guy at a different table? Do we need to talk about dating etiquette, Mols?"

Molly leveled an annoyed look his way. "No. We don't. *Mario* never came back. And Michael here—" She pointed at the computer. "Michael came over and asked if he could sit down, and we got to talking, and, well, wow!"

"Molly."

"Oh, Ethan, don't go all dad-ish on me. It's fine. I'm a big girl. He's a really, really nice guy."

"And you know this after one evening together? Any guy can be *really, really nice* for one night."

"I'm twenty-eight years old. I've figured that one out, thank you."

"I—I don't even know what to say."

"Say you're happy for me."

"I am, but you have to admit. It's a little out of the blue."

"Sometimes that's how it happens." She fanned her face. "I just never thought it would happen to *me*."

"One date, Mols. Or—half a date, I guess."

"I like him, Ethan."

"I can see that."

"Don't be a killjoy. Josie's back. You should be all—I don't know—hopped up on love again, shouldn't you?"

He looked at her. "You've been calling me a moron for two weeks now."

"I know." She looked at the camera again. "Maybe I needed a perspective adjustment."

"I see. So now that you're madly in lust, the rest of the world has permission to be happy?"

"Something like that." She smiled. "Plus, Josie and I talked the other day when she was at Avery's House. She said some things, I said some things . . . and I'm finding it harder to hate her now."

"That's . . . good."

"I know. Weird, though. I was seriously good at—the hating."

Ethan sobered. *Weren't we both . . .*

"So, speaking of Josie . . ."

"Were we?"

His gut tightened. She still hadn't turned on her phone. Should he go back over to her house? He should, right? Yes. But first, flowers. A big bouquet of daisies. Where could you get flowers on a Sunday, anyway?

"Focus, Ethan." Molly spun his chair to face her. "Here's the thing. I know I pulled a hissy fit when you suggested that Josie work at Avery's House, but . . . you're right. She does belong there. It's her someday-house, for God's sake. She always dreamed of living there, and you bought her that house."

He put his hand up, but she waved it off. "Don't even try to argue with me. Can you honestly tell me, in your heart of hearts, that you never wanted Josie to know about this house? Can you honestly say you haven't spent the last five years building this legacy in hopes that she would come home and fall in love with it—and you—again?"

He stayed silent. An Italian woman on a rant was a force to be reckoned with.

"So I have a plan, and you can't comment on it until you have time to think about it and realize I'm right."

"I'm scared."

She sighed. "I'm going to resign from Avery's House,

but I'll do it in a way that's respectful and graceful, and allows time for my replacement to get trained up. I think it should be Josie who takes the job, but I guess that'll be up to her. So I'm not leaving you in a lurch, but I am clearing out, and I hope the space I leave there is one she can feel comfortable filling."

"Molly, have you been drinking?"

"I know I'm acting completely bipolar here. Believe me, I know it. I have been on a Josie bender for two weeks, trying to think of a way to get her back out of town. But maybe it's good she came back."

Ethan narrowed his eyes at her. "Do you have a fever?"

"Shut up. I'm serious. And as embarrassing as it is to admit, Mama sat me down for one of her famous come-to-Jesus meetings last night. I barely survived, thank you very much. But she was right about a lot of things. Everything, really. But I can't admit that openly."

"Molly, this is huge. Don't you think you should think about it a little longer?"

"I've been thinking about it for years, Ethan. This isn't about some gorgeous Italian who just walked into my life two days ago and swept me off my feet. Ever since Josie came back, I've known this was coming. When you two are together, the heat's so intense I have to back up so I don't burst into flames. You belong together, Ethan. She belongs . . . here. I just hope to hell she figures that out sooner than later."

He sighed, picturing her driving south. "I'm more afraid she's already figured out the opposite."

Molly sat down in Andy's chair. "I have a question for you."

"Great."

"Nice tone." She fiddled with one of Josie's pens. "I asked you this a long time ago, but you wouldn't talk. Did you—did you ever go after her?"

Yeah, he'd gone after her. After a month of unreturned calls and e-mails, he'd headed to Boston one weekend, determined to sit down face-to-face with Josie.

"I went down there once. It didn't go well—obviously."

"What happened?"

Ethan shook his head. "She wasn't there."

"Did you wait?"

"No." He frowned, feeling the same stab to his gut that he'd felt when Josie's roommate told him she'd gone off for a weekend at the ocean . . . with her new boyfriend.

"I don't get it. She could have been at class . . . or dinner . . . or the library."

"It was a Friday night, Mols. And according to her roommate, her new boyfriend had just picked her up for a weekend in Maine."

"Oh." Molly put down the pen. "Oh ouch. God, Ethan. No wonder you never wanted to talk about it."

"Yeah."

"Wait. Oh no. Was that the weekend—"

"That you and Josh had to babysit me after I decided to raid Pops's liquor cabinet? Yeah, that's the one."

Molly winced. "I think the only reason Pops didn't kill you was because you'd already inflicted so much pain on yourself that he couldn't think of anything worse to do to you."

"Death would have been preferable, yes."

Molly was silent for a long moment, and then she stood up. "Okay, here's the plan. We go to the hospital dinner, because you have to. But then? Whatever it takes, and wherever she is, you go find Josie."

"Again, I have to ask if you're drunk or feverish."

"No, Ethan." Molly shook her head, sighing. "I've just finally realized I'm never going to get to put that damn dating profile live, because your heart's been glued to Josie since eleventh grade, and that's never going to change."

* * *

Josie pulled into the rest area just north of Concord, feeling like the car roof was closing in on her. She just needed to get out, walk, get some air. Something. The rest area had walking paths out behind the building, picnic tables scattered beside a little brook, peace and quiet. That would help, right?

Fifteen minutes later, it hadn't. She couldn't stop thinking about what Ike had said, couldn't stop picturing Ethan at the waterfall, under the Christmas tree, with Emmy at Avery's House. Though he had aged ten gorgeous years since she'd first loved him, in some ways he was still the same boy she'd had her first crush on.

Those eyes still undid her without even trying. His voice had grown only deeper with age. His hands. God, his hands had only gotten better. But just like ten years ago, all that was good about him was shadowed by the fact that he'd hitched his wagon to Ho-Ho, and that was a twenty-four-seven commitment he'd have until he retired . . . or worse.

What had happened at her parents' house earlier had been a perfect example. On the verge of a beautiful moment, he'd taken that call, had left her alone. That's how it would be. And no, she wasn't her mother. She at least was confident now that she would never turn into the quivering, alcoholic mess that had been Diana ten years ago. But still. He was destined to turn into Andy, and he was actively choosing that life.

It's exactly what she'd feared so long ago. It's exactly what had made her say good-bye.

"Josie, what are you saying?" Ethan's eyes probed hers as they sat in his truck at Twilight Cove, her head pounding like never before.

"I'm saying . . ." She drew a shaky breath. "I'm saying

I think we need to take a break, figure things out, have some space."

He looked out the front window, face stricken. "I can't believe this. Where is this coming from? We're supposed to get married! In two weeks!"

"We're not ready, Ethan. You know it, I know it. We rushed into it for all the wrong reasons. Because of Avery. We wanted her to be part of the wedding, wanted to—I don't know—give her some stability. But now . . ." Her voice caught on a sob. *"Now, she's not . . . she won't . . . it's just not right anymore."*

"Us breaking up isn't going to make anything more right, Jos."

"It's not breaking up. Not really. Just taking some time, some space."

"Breaking up."

"God, Ethan, I can't even think straight right now. I can hardly get dressed in the morning. I don't even know what to do. But I don't think I can stay here. I can't be where Avery was. I can't see her little face everywhere I turn, hear her little voice, see her . . . at the end."

"We can help each other through this. We can!"

"Ethan, we both know it's not going to be that simple. We'd be married, but I'll be at school, and you'll be . . . here." Even she heard the disgust in her voice, the disappointment that he was willing to accept that life began and ended here in Echo Lake.

"And here isn't good enough for you anymore. I see." His voice had a dead quality that scared her.

"It's not that. I don't know. It's just . . . Oh God, Ethan. I don't know! I'm not sure this plan ever *made sense. I just think I need to leave. And I don't want you to be here waiting. It's not fair to you."*

"Josie, up until five minutes ago, I was pretty much thinking I'd be perfectly content waiting for you while

you went to school. Perfectly content working at the park and seeing you on weekends and vacations. Perfectly content planning a life with the woman I love."

And that, she realized, was exactly the problem. He would be *perfectly content, sitting here in a go-nowhere town with a go-nowhere job in a go-nowhere stupid Christmas park that would own his every minute. Forever.*

And that wasn't going to work for her. She was not going to grow up to be her parents.

"I'm sorry, Ethan. I have to go. And I need to do it alone."

He looked at her, hard, furious. "So you've decided."

"I have." She wished her voice sounded stronger.

He nodded slowly, and she could feel his anger coming off him in waves. Then he looked out the windshield and started the truck. "Then I guess there's nothing more to talk about."

Chapter 41

"I think the whole town's here, Ethan." Molly glanced around the ballroom.

"Looks like it." Ethan's voice was tight as he glanced at the empty chair beside him. As he looked around the room full of people, he realized he'd never felt more alone.

Pops was on the other side of Molly, fussing with his apple crisp. "Where's the Boston princess? She coming?"

Ethan shook his head. "Guess not, Pops. Not tonight."

"How come? She on her way back to the city?"

Molly looked at Ethan, cringing. She put her hand on Pops's knee. "We don't know for sure."

Pops pulled his napkin from where it was tucked into his collar. "So you gonna let her go this time?"

"Says the man who warned me not to get involved with her again?"

"Did I say that? I don't remember saying that." Pops pointed to his head. "Memory, you know. It's a funny thing. And besides, you didn't listen, anyway. You've been in love with that girl since you got facial hair. I don't think it's gonna change even if I think it's a bad idea."

"Um—"

"I'm just sayin'. You go up and do your speech and

everything, but if I was you, soon as you're done, you get your butt on the road and get that girl." He spooned a bite of apple crisp. "You've been impossible since she got here. I know what I'm talkin' about and you know it."

Before Ethan could respond, Josh's voice came over the microphone. "Good evening, everyone. Thank you all for joining us this evening, and for your donations to the hospital's pediatric fund. I—and the kids who will pass through Mercy's doors this coming year—thank you from the bottoms of our hearts."

Molly leaned over to whisper in Ethan's ear. "Can you believe he was once the guy who was so shy he could barely say his own name out loud?"

"So, we all know why we're here—to hand out this year's Hospital Hero award." Hoots and claps greeted Josh's words as he adjusted the microphone. "And I'm pretty sure no one in town would argue that we've got the perfect candidate. Well, one person might, but that would be the guy himself."

As Josh started giving the history of Ethan's volunteer efforts at Mercy Hospital, starting way back in high school, Ethan surreptitiously glanced around at the people gathered in the ballroom. He recognized almost every single one of them, and for a brief second, wondered if anyone was actually left in Echo Lake tonight, as it appeared the entire village was here in this function hall two towns away.

"But enough from me." The lights dimmed as a huge screen lowered from the ceiling. "We have someone here who knows Ethan better than anyone in the world—someone who couldn't be here tonight, but wanted to make sure he could express his congratulations."

Who was he talking about? Ethan tried not to let his smile waver, but it was an effort. He couldn't imagine whose face was about to appear on that screen, and when the picture finally emerged, he almost fell off his chair.

"Hey, Ethan. It's me, your pain-in-the-ass younger brother." David's grin filled the screen, and there was a collective gasp from the audience, then a round of applause. "I'm taping this from the wilds of—well, I can't tell you where, but it's really far away." Titters of laughter filtered to Ethan from around the room.

"I know a lot of you in the room have known Ethan since he was—well, probably since he was a baby. Others of you met him in school. And I'm sure there's a whole herd of you there who've met him through his work at Avery's House. I know you all have a million stories to share, but I'm the only one who's known Ethan since the first day I was alive, and that makes me the luckiest guy *in* this room." He looked at the empty space behind him. "Well, figuratively."

Ethan clasped his hands together tightly as David described their early years of playing army-guy, to their junior high years in rec basketball, all laced with humor that had the audience laughing right along with him.

Then he got to Ethan's senior-year football season, and the room hushed.

"That night, probably most of you were there. That night, Ethan was scheduled to go out in a blaze of glory, not an ambulance. And the next morning, with his leg hanging from the ceiling and a stupid johnny on, we still thought it was all temporary. A little cast time, a little PT, and by spring, he'd be training up for Norwich.

"We all know that's not how it went, but maybe not all of you know just how difficult it was for Ethan to kiss his dream good-bye, to watch his idiot little brother head off to boot camp the next year, to completely readjust his future because of one torturous second on a muddy playing field.

"He had two choices: wither up and regret the cards he'd been dealt, or head over to a different table and play a new game. We all know which choice he made, and the hundreds of lives he's touched because of it.

"So Ethan . . ." There was a long pause as David looked down and pulled in a long breath, his voice cracking only enough for Ethan to hear.

"I couldn't be prouder of the job you've done there. I know your dreams crashed and burned that night, but you came back stronger and you fought harder because of it. What you've done for that hospital, what you've done for the town, what you've done for the kids? In my book, there is nothing more heroic than that. The fact that we're all celebrating you tonight is testament to the fact that I'm not the only one who thinks so."

David turned and nodded to someone offscreen. Suddenly, what looked like an entire platoon of soldiers filtered in behind him. "This is for you, big brother. You are *my* hero."

As one, the soldiers saluted, then shouted a loud "Hooah!"

The audience sat in silence for a moment, and then a roar of applause started at the back and rippled toward the front. Before Ethan could take a deep breath and gather himself, the crowd was on its feet, clapping and whistling. He looked around in awe, then at Molly, whose eyes were glistening.

Josh's voice came back over the microphone. "We chose someone very special to present this award tonight— someone who's known Ethan forever, someone who grew up with him, loves him, and has threatened to marry him if he doesn't settle down one of these days." The audience tittered again as Ethan leveled a glance at Molly.

"She claims she's got secrets that could tarnish his

heroic reputation, but she promises not to reveal them . . . for the right price." Josh cocked his head and his eyebrows furrowed. "Sorry, Ethan. I'm not sure I want to know what that means." More laughter. "But without further ado, to present this year's Hospital Hero award, Miss Molly Bellini."

Ethan glanced toward the doorway one more time, but his heart already knew he'd find it empty. Josie wasn't coming. In fact, Josie was probably already halfway back to Boston. His feet were cement blocks as he pasted on a smile and took Molly's arm to walk toward the podium.

"Josie? Where are you? Are you all right?" Kirsten's worried voice came across the line as Josie sat at a picnic table, idly scratching at the wooden surface with a twig.

"I'm fine. Good." She took a deep breath. "Well, actually, I'm kind of a disaster, but I'm a disaster with a semblance of a plan."

"Which is?"

Josie closed her eyes tightly. "I need to go back, Kirsten. I thought I could leave, but I only got to Concord before I had to stop. I'm sorry. I know this isn't okay. We have a practice together. I need to be in Boston."

"Josie—"

"I'm so sorry. I hate that I'm doing this to you, but omigod, I love that damn man. I love him even though he's destined to spend half his life in a stupid Santa costume. I love him even though he needs to learn that there are things more important than the damn park. I just . . ." She rubbed her forehead. "I can't leave. I just can't leave."

Kirsten laughed, just a tiny one at first, but then it grew. And grew. Josie could picture her rocking back in her lawn chair grabbing her stomach and wiping tears from her eyes, and for a moment, the image choked a surprised laugh out of her own throat.

"Why is this so funny?"

"Because, Jos, you are the most controlled human being I've ever met. I've never once seen you cry, never seen you frazzled, never seen you out of control of your own emotions. And right now, you're a certifiable disaster!"

"And this is *funny*? What kind of a friend are you?"

"It's beautiful. It's gorgeous. It's . . . it's love, honey. And you are in it up to your eyeballs and I couldn't be happier for you. So get in your car, find the next U-turn, and get your butt back to Echo Lake. Everything else will figure itself out, but you need to find Ethan and tell him what you just told me."

"Oh boy."

"Second chances are a gift, Jos. Grab this one with all you've got."

Josie nodded slowly, but her gut was still roiling with another emotion. "Okay. You're right. I know you're right." She tossed the twig, getting up from the picnic table. She stared down at the heart she'd drawn without even thinking, stared at the initials she'd scratched inside it.

As she looked around, trying to gather her courage, a butterfly landed on the heart, fluttering its wings in the low evening sunlight. Her breath caught as she stared at the butterfly, reached her fingers toward it.

Her voice was shaky as she steadied the phone. "I'm going back. I'm going to find him. But there's something I have to do first."

"Dad?" Josie knocked on her father's door. He looked up, and Josie smiled as she saw the right side of his mouth lift in the motion that passed for his smile right now. She sat down next to his bed, checking out the view outside his window.

"Wow, this is quite an upgrade from Mercy. Look at the flowers!"

Carefully manicured gardens decorated the outside lawns of Fairview, and colorful butterfly houses were scattered among the blooms.

Dad motioned with his chin, pointing at his bedside table.

Josie looked over. "Are you thirsty? Need a drink?"

He shook his head.

The only other thing on the table was his letter board. "Want to talk, Dad?"

He nodded, and Josie grabbed the board and set it on his lap, helping his fingers close around the pointer . . . then stilling them.

"Can I go first?"

He looked at her, nodding imperceptibly.

"I . . . I just headed back to Boston. Just now. I packed up my suitcase and I left."

His eyebrows furrowed as he tapped slowly. "Why?"

She took a deep breath. "I don't know. I thought I did, but I don't."

He tapped again. "Ethan?"

"Yes. No. Yes. Of course. But also Molly, you, Mom . . . I don't know what to think anymore. I don't know what I want anymore."

Tap. Tap. Tap. "Love him?"

She smiled sadly. "Yeah, Dad. I do love him. It'd be a lot easier if I didn't."

She paused, and then she reached over and took his hand, squeezing it gently. "I think I want to stay, Dad." She took a shaky breath. "Echo Lake has changed . . . a lot."

Dad nodded and squeezed back.

"I think Avery's House is amazing, and I think—I think maybe I'd like to see if maybe there's a place for me there. I'm sure there's way more to do than there are people to do it. I could maybe do some counseling, and maybe—I don't know."

She thought back to her visit to the house—how the entire place had seemed so warm and inviting and . . . hopeful. She could see herself there. She could see herself and Ethan there together.

She took another shaky breath. "I wish I'd believed Mom was better. I wish . . . I wish I hadn't waited so long to come home. Maybe then . . ." Tears prickled, and she closed her eyes. "Maybe we would have had more time, you and me."

Dad tapped on the board again. "Stay now?" His eyes were hopeful, and Josie smiled.

"Yeah," she whispered. "I want to stay."

He pushed aside the letter board, and for a moment, she was unsure of what he was doing as he struggled to reposition his upper body. Then he slowly, slowly put his right hand over his heart.

"Love you," he said.

Chapter 42

An hour later, Josie sat in a green Ferris wheel chair, pushing softly with her toes to make it swing. The tree frogs were trying to outdo the crickets, and a breeze carried the scent of pine to her nose. She closed her eyes, drinking it in, wondering why it had taken her so long to figure everything out.

She'd gone to Avery's House, had made herself walk across the lawn to the wishing well, had made herself sit there and remember a little girl with a Red Sox hat and long brown ponytail plonking in pennies and making wishes.

And it had been okay. Well, actually, it had hurt like hell, and she was pretty sure her eyes were still red. But it was a healthy hurt. The kind of hurt she'd been running from for ten years, but the kind of hurt maybe she was ready to finally face.

Sitting at the well had given her a sense of clarity she hadn't even known she was missing, and though she knew it would be painful to be back where Avery's sweet face lurked at every turn, she would be okay. With Ethan at her side, everything would be okay.

"Going for a ride, Jos?"

Josie jumped at Ethan's soft words. "How'd you know I was here?"

"Security camera." He pointed at a black box mounted in the fir tree. "Ben saw you sneak in."

"Damn technology. And shouldn't he be at home watching a game or something?"

He started up the metal stairs. "Can I sit with you?"

"Sure. We're not going very far, though. I don't have the keys."

"But you're here. You're on the Ferris wheel."

"I know." Josie nodded and took a long, cleansing breath as he settled beside her, keeping his hands clasped in his lap. "I am. It's progress. I'm sorry I missed the dinner."

"You look like you're thinking deep thoughts."

"Something like that."

"Anything you want to share?"

She sighed. "I don't know. I really don't know. I just came from Avery's well. I saw a butterfly . . . earlier . . . and I had to make myself go to the well."

"How was it?"

"Awful. Sad." Her breath hitched a little. "But just a little bit okay, too. If that makes any sense."

"Makes perfect sense. It took a long time for me to get to *little bit okay*."

"I don't know how you did it. I don't know how you stayed here afterward without losing your mind."

He shook his head. "Some days I did. Some days I sat by that well and cursed cancer, cursed the doctors, cursed God . . ."

"Cursed me?"

His smile was rueful. "At times."

"How did you finally get over her?"

He slid his arm behind her shoulders, gathering her closer. "God, Jos, I don't know. Some days I don't think I ever got over her at all. Other days, I look around Avery's House and just hope she'd be proud of what we've done. Some days I see kids like Emmy and feel like there's hope. On others, I just pray I can get through."

He sighed, long and hard. "Jos, when you left that summer, I knew it was because you couldn't handle being here where Avery's memories were bound to strangle you at every turn. I got that. I really did. I was pissed at first—royally pissed, as Molly will gladly attest. But after some time went by and I no longer wanted to kill you for ruining my life, I tried to understand it.

"And some part of me did. I knew you had to get out of here. Knew your parents were a disaster tangled up in Christmas lights, knew your mother was sloshing her way to an early death, knew the park was your father's first wife. So I got it. I did."

"But?"

"But nothing. Or but everything, maybe. I don't know. I just—I just thought you'd eventually come back. I thought you'd take the summer, get some space, do some healing, and then you'd come back. To this day, I still don't always think I really understand why you never did. Why I was never worth coming back *for*."

Oh boy. Was she really ready to have this conversation? She'd thought she'd hidden her home life from Ethan for so long that it had become second nature to lie to him. She'd thought he had no idea Mom started the day with a Bloody Mary and often ended it with a bloody lip as she conked her head on the toilet. No idea Dad stopped in for a change of clothes at best. But apparently she'd been wrong on all of those counts.

Apparently the whole damn *town* had known.

However, she did know something he didn't.

She knew he had no idea that after Avery's funeral, she'd driven home in a freakishly calm fog, opened the linen closet and reached behind the washcloths to pull out a vodka bottle. No idea she'd driven to Camp Ho-Ho, hiked the dark pathways to the Ferris wheel, climbed up its metal framework like a possessed monkey, and sat at the top, downing shots until Ben found her and took her back home.

And *that* was the final straw that had sent her running. On top of everything else, *that* was the night that had convinced her that if she stayed in Echo Lake, she was destined for the same messed-up life her parents were already living. Because when push came to shove, she was her mother's daughter, no better.

When the going got tough, she'd reached for the same damn bottle that had consoled her mother.

"It wasn't nearly as much about you as it was about . . . everything else."

"Avery?"

"Of course, but . . . other things, too."

He didn't answer, just looked at her intently, leaving space for her words.

She blew out a breath. "I drank, Ethan. After the funeral, I got rip-roaring drunk. I got so drunk that I climbed this damn Ferris wheel in the middle of the night—*with* a bottle of Stoli—and Ben had to bring me home when he found me. I'm lucky I didn't fall off and die."

Ethan's eyes widened, but instead of pulling away as she half expected, he only gripped her shoulder tighter, squeezed her closer to his body. "That must have been terrifying."

"What?" She shook her head, confused at his reaction. "I mean, yes. I mean, God. I don't know what I mean."

"Let me see if I can summarize. Six months before that summer, your fiancé was looking forward to a scholarship at Norwich and a medal-strewn military career, but by June he was hitching himself onto the Ho-Ho wagon for what looked like eternity, and you were looking at the possibility of a marriage as miserable as your parents'. And then something really, really awful happened, and you hit the bottle."

"That summary doesn't paint me in a very good light, I'm afraid."

"Wrong. That summary paints you in a very *human* light. How could you not be scared out of your wits?" He put his finger under her chin, lifting it so she was forced to look into his eyes. "You were eighteen years old, Josie. You *should* have wanted more than that. You had the right to *expect* more than that."

"But I shouldn't have hurt you to get it."

"No. You should have believed in me. But luckily for you, I can heal from the jagged wounds you left. If you stay this time."

She smiled sadly. "That's all it would take?"

"Stay, Josie." His voice was gruff, emotional. "Stay here. I can help you."

"I don't—I don't need help."

"Everybody needs help sometimes. Even big, strong oxes like you."

She pulled her head away from his chest. "Oxes?"

"See? You're already smiling. I'm helpful!" He ran his fingers down her jaw, stopping at her chin as his eyes searched hers.

Josie blew out a careful breath. "I don't know. I just don't know. My head is spinning. I've spent so long running without even knowing that's what I was doing. I'm not sure how to turn that part of me off. I'm really not."

"Y'know what, Jos? We could just take it one day at a time and see what happens."

"That's a great strategy when you're sixteen, Ethan. But we're not."

"I don't personally think it's a bad strategy even at twenty-eight. Certainly helps me sometimes." Ethan looked up at the stars. "Hey . . . since we're on here . . . want to go up?"

Her stomach fluttered. It was one thing to sit here practically on the ground. Quite another to sail two stories up, where she and Ethan had sat with Avery on her last night. "Do you have the key?"

"I do." Ben emerged from the pathway, jingling a huge ring of keys.

Josie glanced from one to the other. "Is this a setup?"

"Nope." Ben grinned. "Just doing my rounds. Just happened by. Ethan definitely didn't call me in to check the security cameras. Nope." He inserted the key, then leaned over to give Josie a kiss on the top of her head. "I'll be right here when you're ready to come down, Twinkle-toes."

His words were like a warm blanket over her shivering shoulders. "You always used to say that to me."

"I know it. Every night." He saluted as he pushed the lever forward. "Count the cars at the bowling alley, would ya?"

"Is it league night?" Josie let out a shaky laugh.

The wheel rose slowly, and as it cleared the ground, Josie reached for Ethan's hand. "I can't believe we're doing this."

Ethan held on to her hand as he pulled her close. "I'm here, Jos. I'm here."

When the wheel reached the top, it slowed to a stop, leaving the car swinging softly in the night air. "Oh no, you didn't. You did *not* tell him to strand us up here."

Ethan looked over the edge of the car, making it tip forward. "Ben? Ben!"

"Sorry, boss. That switch has been sticky all day. Looks like I need to go get my tools. Might take me a while, though."

"Ben, this is not funny." Josie gripped the bar.

"Sorry, you two. Do your best to entertain yourselves till I get back." They both watched as he headed down the pathway, chuckling.

"You totally paid him to do this, didn't you?"

Josie expected to feel panicked, but as she tucked back up against Ethan, all she felt was the rightness of being here, in this moment, with this man.

"I wish I'd thought to, but no." Ethan stretched his arm around her shoulders and pulled her close. "Come here. Want to count the cars?"

A distant train whistle broke through the crickets and tree frogs. "Here comes the train." Josie pointed toward the tracks as she leaned her head tentatively on his shoulder. "I spent so many years wishing I could hop that train to somewhere more exciting than here."

"Well, you did. Figuratively, anyway."

"It seemed like the best plan, at the time."

Ethan was silent for a long moment. "How about now? Do you have a plan for now?"

Josie's silence matched his. Then she pulled her head upright and moved her body away from his. "I think I do."

"Do tell."

"Would you believe it was Ike who finally helped clear my head today? I went into his garage all fired up to head out of town, and after telling me a whole lot of stuff I still can't digest, he asked me one stupid, simple question. He said, 'Where does your heart live, Josie?' "

"That sounds awfully wise for Ike."

"So I blasted out of the parking lot and headed for home, packed up my stuff and made for the interstate. I was so out of here."

"But?"

Josie turned toward him. "I hate that this is true, Ethan. I hate it with all my might because I can't control it, I can't fight it, I can't talk any sense into my own head. But dammit, as much as I've tried to tell myself for the past ten years that I don't love you . . . that I don't miss you . . . I've been lying."

Ethan's eyebrows went sky high as his mouth started to curve into a smile. "Are you just saying that so I'll call Ben back here to get us down?"

"Absolutely."

"Well, I'll take it." He pulled her close again, tucking her head under his chin. "Josie, are you serious? Are you thinking about staying?"

She nodded slowly, hardly still believing it herself.

He gripped both of her arms and pushed her away so he could look into her eyes. "Seriously?"

"Seriously."

"Staying?"

"Staying, Ethan. With you, if you'll still have me."

He gathered her in a crushing hug. "Are you kidding? I'll have you, Jos. I'll have you till we're both doddering around with our canes and walkers." He pulled away enough to tip her head up and kiss her. "I'll never let you go again, Josie Kendrew. Never again."

"I'll hold you to that."

"In that spirit . . ." He pulled away for a moment and dug for something in his pocket. "I was hoping to do this later, at the lake, but I can't wait." He fumbled for a moment, then took her hand in his. "It would be a little awkward to try to get down on one knee up here, but at least it's not the back of my old truck."

Her heart jumped as she caught a glimpse of sparkle and gold in his hand. "I know we tried this once before, and maybe we really *were* too young at the time. But Jos, I have never, *ever* stopped loving you. Never stopped hoping you'd come back to me someday. And here you are."

He pressed his lips together, smoky eyes blazing into hers. "I've been holding on to this ring for ten years, but if it's all right with you, I'd really like to put it on your finger and spend eternity with you, riding on Ferris wheels and making your dreams come true."

His fingers traced her jaw, his lips breathlessly close. "Josie, will you marry me?"

Josie's eyes threatened to spill over as he cupped her face carefully in his hands. "I never dared give up hope, Jos. So? Will you say yes again? Will you mean it this time?"

Josie threw her arms around his neck and hugged him with all the strength she could muster. "Yes, Ethan. I'll say yes. I'll mean it this time."

An hour later, they sat snuggled together watching the stars, still waiting for Ben to return. "Remember the last time we were on this Ferris wheel, Ethan?"

"I won't ever forget." His voice rumbled against her cheek as she nestled into his chest.

"Do you still think of her every time you see a butterfly?" He nodded. "How does it not crack your heart into pieces?"

"It does, but I just try to focus on the last thing she said. That's what gets me through."

"Flutterby kisses, Josie."

Josie took Avery's hand tightly as they sat at the top of the Ferris wheel the last night of her life. "Flutterby kisses, Aves."

Avery tipped her chin up and brushed her eyelashes over Josie's cheek, blinking rapidly. "Guess what I wished last?"

"What, sweetie?"

"*I wished that every time you see a butterfly, you'll think of me.*"

"*We will, munchkin.*" Ethan squeezed her gently. "*But we'll think of you every day whether we see a butterfly or not.*"

"*Know what else I wished?*"

"*What else?*"

"*I wished that someday you and Josie will get married. And live happily ever after.*"

"*That sounds perfect,*" Josie murmured, eyes glistening as she looked over Avery's head at Ethan.

"*Promise?*" Avery put out her pinky, and Josie and Ethan both hooked theirs onto her tiny one.

"*Promise.*"

Epilogue

"Who gives this woman to be wed?" The minister looked out over two hundred white chairs decked in tulle, placed in rows facing Avery's wishing well.

"Her father and I do." Mom's voice was strong from the front row, where she sat hand in hand with Dad, who smiled his crooked smile from his wheelchair.

Josie broke her gaze from Ethan's so she could look out over the crowd. Even though they'd capped the guest list at two hundred, she could swear twice that many people were here. Beside her at the altar were Kirsten and Molly, decked out in bridesmaid dresses the pale purple color of Avery's favorite butterfly. Behind Ethan, David and Josh looked stiff but proud in their tuxes.

Holding Josie's hand in her own little one was Emmy, who'd spread daisy petals all the way up the aisle, skipping in her buttercup-yellow dress, hair grown out to her shoulders.

"I do, too," Emmy said, eliciting a quiet roll of laughter through the crowd.

As the minister spoke the words they'd chosen, Josie felt a warm glow encasing her entire body. Her smile felt like it might actually crack her face, but she couldn't stop. She looked over the crowd, saw the smiling faces, felt the happy energy, and knew she'd made the right choice at that Concord rest area last summer.

Yes, it had been a long, curving road back here to Echo Lake, but as Ethan's eyes caught hers, she knew she was right where she belonged.

After the reception tent had been taken down and the guests had left, Ethan and Josie sat in the Adirondack chairs beside the wishing well.

Ethan took her left hand and kissed it. "I really like this ring on you."

She smiled. "Turns out I'm better at this whole wedding thing the second time around."

"Are you excited for the honeymoon?"

"A week in Barbados? With you? Swimming, snorkeling, reading the ten novels I packed while I drink fresh margaritas?" Josie shook her head. "Nah."

He laughed. "And you thought I'd never take a vacation."

"I appreciate you proving me wrong."

Ethan squeezed her fingers. "You're the one who's going to have trouble finding time off soon."

"I know." Josie smiled. "It's perfect, though. I'll work with the guests here in the mornings, and then work at Mercy in the afternoons. Might even put in some weekend hours at Ho-Ho, if the boss lets me."

"The boss will definitely let you. You're sure Kirsten's okay with all of this?"

"Ha. Kirsten had moved her desk to my office before I'd even moved out." Josie smiled. "She'll be fine. It was tough to transition my patients, but you know what? She's good. Her new partner will be good. It'll all be . . . good."

"And you can be here, making a different kind of difference."

"Yeah." She nodded thoughtfully. "I really can."

"You're a new woman, Mrs. Miller."

"Nah." She shook her head, looking at the wishing well. "Not new. Just had to figure out the old one."

"I'm glad you did." He tugged her hand, pulling her gently onto his lap. "Come here."

When she was snuggled with her back against his chest, he pointed at the wishing well.

"Look, Josie."

Dusk softened the lines of the well, and Josie squinted to see what he was pointing at. Then something fluttered, and her hands flew to her mouth.

"Oh, Ethan. It's a butterfly."

They held perfectly still for long minutes as the tiny purple butterfly opened and closed its wings, poised on Avery's wishing well. Finally, it lifted off, swooping in circles around them before it headed for the trees.

Josie watched it until it disappeared, and until Ethan ran his fingers down her cheek, she didn't realize a tear had escaped her eye.

"Flutterby kisses, Jos," Ethan whispered in her ear.

Josie reached her arms up around his neck, sighing happily as she closed her eyes.

"Flutterby kisses, Ethan."

Look for the next novel in the heartwarming
Echo Lake series
by **Maggie McGinnis**

HEART LIKE MINE

Coming in April 2016 from St. Martin's Paperbacks

And don't miss **Maggie McGinnis's** e-original story

"Snowflake Wishes"

Available now from St. Martin's Press!